Seducing the Princess

MARY HART PERRY

ALSO BY MARY HART PERRY

The Wild Princess: A Novel of Queen Victoria's Defiant Daughter

WRITTEN AS KATHRYN JOHNSON

The Gentleman Poet

Diversion Books
A Division of Diversion Publishing Corp.
443 Park Avenue South, Suite 1004
New York, NY 10016
www.DiversionBooks.com

For more information, email info@diversionbooks.com.
First Diversion Books edition March 2013

eISBN: 978-1-626810-01-3
print ISBN: 978-1-62681-051-8

Seducing
THE
Princess

MARY HART PERRY

DIVERSIONBOOKS

1

Hesse-Darmstadt, Germany—April, 1884

Cold, as cold as death itself. I might as well be in my tomb.

Beatrice inched closer to the fire crackling in the castle's immense black-granite fireplace. She extended icy fingertips toward the leaping flames and felt grateful for the precious warmth rising up through her frigid hands, along the velvet sleeves of her gown and into her shoulders. *How glorious it must be to live in the tropics, where it never gets cold!*

She smiled at the mere thought of spending lazy afternoons basking under a Grecian sun or sailing aquamarine waters on the royal yacht between Caribbean islands. Instead of shut away in a drafty German castle that set her bones to aching.

Beatrice sighed. Little chance of that for a daughter of Queen Victoria. Their mother rarely had granted any of them permission to travel, except with her. After the older girls married that had changed, of course. Her four sisters had found husbands to escort them on their travels. Unfortunately, marriage no longer seemed likely for her, at the advanced age of twenty-seven.

Some days—like this one, caught up in the middle of a giggling, shrieking bridal party of younger, prettier girls—she felt utterly ancient. Most women her age were popping out babies, managing their own homes and servants. In this progressive age of modern medicine, steam engines, factory-made lace, and (the latest miracle of the age) electricity—she should be enjoying the productive prime of her life.

Stop it! she scolded herself, feeling selfish for thinking of her own welfare on the eve of her dear niece's wedding. Weddings were meant to be cheerful times, and Vicky was a delightful girl, really more like a sister to her they were so close in age. The bride deserved her affection and full attention.

"Auntie! Oh, Auntie Bea, do you really think this gown will do?" her niece's voice cut through the female chatter around Beatrice. "It isn't too prissy with all these ruffles and flounces, is it?" Vicky spun on the tips of her toes, setting full skirts of petal-pink tulle and lush satin shimmering in a wide pool around her. Diamond clips pinched her earlobes. A stunning ruby-and-enamel locket hung about her neck. "I don't want to look like a child on the night before my wedding."

Beatrice smiled, shaking her head as the ladies-in-waiting who had been attending the bride flew like a noisy flock of bright-winged birds from the room, gowns rustling. The wedding ball was less than an hour away. It was time they joined the rest of the Court.

"My dear, you needn't worry. So very grown up you look with that daring décolletage. Your gown is perfection, and you are truly a lovely sight."

Tomorrow Princess Victoria of Hesse, granddaughter to the queen of England, would marry Prince Louis of Battenberg. Beatrice was happy for her...for *them*. Really, she was. Although she had more than enough justification for the nugget of regret lodged in her throat, and perhaps even for a lingering bitterness. Secretly. Guiltily. Tucked away in her heart.

Beatrice gave the girl her best smile, ignoring the twinge of envy that came with her words. "Louis is so very lucky to have you as his bride. Tomorrow when you marry, I shall look on with such pride."

Vicky beamed, holding out her tiny gloved hands. "You are an old sweetie to say such lovely things. And to think the first time I ever heard of Louis, his name was mentioned with—" The girl suddenly blushed, her blond eyelashes fluttering in agitation. "Oh, dear, perhaps I shouldn't have said." She squeezed her aunt's hands.

Beatrice pulled stiff fingers free from her niece's warm little paws. "Ah well, that was nonsense, yes? Court gossip. You know how they exaggerate." Her smile, she feared, was a bit watery as she turned away and back toward the fire. She welcomed the blaze that heated her cheeks. The raised color would cover for her discomfort at Vicky's mention of the stories about her and Louis.

"Louis's heart is all yours, my dear," Beatrice murmured. "Anyone can see that by the way his eyes light up whenever you walk into a room." It was true. And the two were a fine match both in humor and appearance, although he was a good deal older than she.

Before Beatrice had a chance to fully recover her composure, the massive oak door to the bride's bedchamber creaked open. Vicky's gasp and squeal, "*Grand-mere!*" announced the arrival of Queen Victoria.

Beatrice drew a breath to calm herself. The queen would no doubt insist Beatrice accompany her to the Grand Salon where the family gathered in preparation for the Lord Chamberlain announcing them to the bejeweled guests, already waiting in the ballroom. Louis would be in the salon too, with his family. *How awkward.* But she resolved to confront the evening with equanimity, if not with enthusiasm. Balls were pleasant enough when a few of the more attractive gentlemen approached her for a dance. Then she could at least pretend to be admired and happy.

Just the hope of whirling across the ballroom floor cheered her considerably. She loved to dance. Adored it, though she didn't have much chance to practice these days.

Family legend had it that, at a mere three years old—golden ringlets agleam beneath the crystal chandeliers, wearing tiny satin slippers to match her first ball gown—Beatrice had performed a perfect waltz across Buckingham Palace's ballroom, partnered by her beaming father, Prince Albert. The entire Court had gazed on, enraptured. It was nearly the Prince's last public appearance before his sudden and shocking death from typhoid fever. A loss from which the family had never truly recovered.

Yes, dancing seemed almost enough to make the night bearable. Unfortunately, she knew not to expect her partners (at least the young, good looking ones) to return for a second waltz or polka or anything else. Beatrice suspected her mother was right—she wasn't the type to entice men romantically, not pretty enough to encourage them to stay for more than one dance, and certainly not intelligent or witty or special enough to prompt a man to ask for her hand in marriage.

Anxious at the thought of having to pretend she was enjoying herself in front of the critical gaze of Europe's nobility, Beatrice smoothed her ebony taffeta skirts while the bride-to-be curtsied and kissed the queen's hand, then rose to touch her lips to the plump older woman's proffered cheek.

"Oh my child, you do look precious," Victoria cooed. "How pretty in this delicate pink you look. Thank goodness it's not that unfortunate bold rose some girls are choosing this season. Your dear mama in heaven, my Alice, will be so proud of you tonight, and tomorrow of course in church."

Beatrice observed her mother from a distance. Victoria wore no color at all on her barely five-foot-tall figure, a choice of wardrobe that had become a habit over the past two decades. Not since the death of the Prince Consort could Beatrice remember her mother wearing anything but black-black-black. Although she now allowed members of her court a reprieve from deep mourning, she still insisted that her youngest daughter share her grim obsession with death. The queen preferred seeing her in true mourning garb but, on occasion, allowed the very deepest shades of blue or gray, almost indiscernible from black, relieved only by a narrow collar of white linen about the throat.

Even their everyday jewelry had to be subdued—only jet stones allowed, all gold settings dulled with coal dust. No sparkle. No joy. Beatrice recalled her younger years—when her sisters or governess sometimes implored the queen to "permit Baby a bit of color." She'd been granted a pretty dress for a few special occasions. But now, as Beatrice crept toward the disturbingly advanced age of 30, her mother flew into a rage if she saw even a scrap of brightness in her daughter's wardrobe.

Beatrice shrugged in surrender. God forbid there appear a glimmer of cheer in their lives. "You, my most precious and faithful child," the queen was fond of saying to her, "shall be my constant and loyal companion until I am lowered into my grave and join your dear Papa."

Which apparently meant Beatrice must mirror her mother's choice to remain unmarried.

"Beatrice." Her mother held out a gloved hand to her, startling Beatrice out of her grim musing. "Come, give me your arm. I'm having a terrible time with my limbs tonight. The pain is unbearable. A return of the cursed gout, I expect."

"Perhaps if you sit before the fire, Mama, you'll be comforted by the warmth." Lord knows *she* could use a little more time out of the castle's damp drafts.

"Nonsense. Cold air is bracing, healthy. They keep this place far too hot." The queen cast a grave eye about the room and latched onto the roaring fire with a disapproving grimace. "Mr. Brown always said fresh air is good for me." Even after the burly Scot's death, her self-proclaimed body guard, John Brown, seemed to hold a mysterious power over his sovereign. Some said he had been more to the queen than a loyal gillie and escort. A few even suggested he'd taken over Albert's most intimate duties to Victoria, in the bedchamber. But Beatrice believed their relationship had never gone that far.

She herself had been very fond of the man and missed his powerful masculine presence at Court, and his calming effect on her mother. In many ways, he had made her life easier.

Beatrice left the fire with reluctance and obediently crossed the room. She offered her arm to her mother, lowering her gaze in submission to the parquet floor. Slowly, they paraded with the rest of the party out the door and down the long hallway lined with the Grand Duke of Hesse-Darmstadt's ancestral portraits. The paintings' arrogant countenances seemed to glower down at her, challenging her right to be in their home.

Beatrice took a deep breath, raised her chin and gazed straight ahead. *I am the daughter of a queen,* she thought. *Don't dismiss me yet.*

2

Henry of Battenberg, third of four brothers known across the continent for their striking good looks and fine physique, stepped back a pace to inspect his brother Louis. "I don't know," he said. "Somehow you look far too cheerful to be the condemned man. Can't you adopt a more serious and resigned attitude?"

Louis laughed. "But I'm delighted to be marrying, and Vicky is a delightful girl."

"All of this delight has nothing to do, I suppose, with your bride being a granddaughter to the Queen of England?" Henry teased. He knew his brother better than anyone. Just like their father, Louis didn't give up easily once he had a goal in mind. Even if fate initially seemed pitted against him.

Hadn't he, Henry, sat at the same table that infamous night, years ago at Buckingham Palace, when his older brother had been so cruelly snubbed by one of the queen's daughters? Hadn't he seen the stricken look on his brother's face? Princess Beatrice might just as well have slapped his cheek in front of the entire assemblage.

"If you're implying that I've been trying to worm my way into that family all these years, I am highly insulted."

"Did I say that?" Henry put on an innocent face as he held out lavender gloves to Louis. "I just wonder what others may think. You have to admit, it's a bit curious you've chosen a wife from that odd family, after—"

"After that appalling scene six years ago?"

"Exactly."

Louis grinned. "I am nothing if not persistent, brother. And I tell you, I don't give a damn what others think. There was never really anything started with Beatrice. That was Father's idea. My word, I'd barely spoken to the woman before she cut me off at the knees."

"What did she say to you that night at dinner? You never told me." Henry frowned at the tilt of his brother's tie and stepped forward to straighten it. Their footmen and dressers had left moments earlier, having been recruited for service in the dining room and ballroom. Now it was just the two of them alone in the suite.

Louis shrugged. "That's just it. She wouldn't speak to me, not a word."

"You must have said something to offend."

"I swear I did not!" Louis laughed. "Pleasant, harmless conversation. That's all I offered. The woman looked straight on, avoiding my eye, and refused to respond to anything I said."

"Weird old bird."

"Not so old. She's your age, sir." Henry was ready to argue the point but his brother continued. "Though I have to say in that drab mourning garb and a coiffure appropriate to a dowager twice her age, she certainly looks the part of an old maid."

Henry thought about the younger Princess Beatrice he'd known only through short visits his family had made to the English royal properties—Osborne House on the Isle of Wight, Windsor Castle, and Balmoral in Scotland...and, of course, Buckingham Palace. "Come to think of it, I don't believe she and I have exchanged a single word in years."

"I'm not surprised. She's either dull-witted, a shrew, or just painfully shy. And—" Louis held up a finger to make another point. "—awkward as hell in good company, I dare say."

Henry shook his head, puzzled. He was accustomed to the young daughters of nobility being sheltered and unaccustomed to the company of men other than those in their own family. But he remembered a yellow-haired sprite, the Prince Consort's joy and youngest of his nine children. Henry had actually played with Beatrice in Buckingham's gardens one afternoon when a flock of royal cousins, and children of the queen's ladies and gentlemen, had been invited by Victoria to a children's tea party. It was a distant memory though. Perhaps he was confusing her with another little girl?

He'd seen Beatrice again when he was around twelve years old, and she would have been about the same age, if his brother was right. She was still pretty but sadness shadowed her eyes. While around him, though, her bounce returned. Her teasing sense of humor and the way she took his hand to make him run with her made him feel bashful and excited all at once.

And then, years later, when he'd seen her at that disaster of a banquet at Buckingham, he'd been shocked by the change in the young woman. She never left her mother's side, wore unrelieved black and no jewelry, and seemed unable to meet anyone's eyes when they tried to converse with her. He'd spent as little time around her as possible, and he noticed others seemed to avoid her, finding her poor company.

Thinking about this now, he puzzled over what mysterious happenings might have changed the exuberant imp he'd once known into this somber, prematurely aging woman.

"My Albert's death has struck Baby the cruelest blow of all," he seemed to recall the queen explaining her daughter's lack of social graces to his own mother. "She has never been the same, poor child."

Henry wondered: Had Beatrice's grief so affected her she'd succumbed to a forever-sadness, taken up the role of a prudish old maid and shut herself away from the pleasures of society? Or had her spirit been broken? Ruthlessly crushed by her mother's obsession with death.

Louis brushed Henry's hands away. "Leave me be, brother. You're fussing over me like an old nursemaid. Waistcoat, collar and tie are all perfectly fine."

"Sorry." Henry lowered his arms and stepped away, unaware within his dark thoughts that he'd annoyed his brother with his attentions.

Louis took out his pocket watch and winced. "We're late. I'll blame you if my bride complains. I shall tell her my little brother can't get himself dressed without my supervision."

Henry chuckled wickedly. "You do and I'll tell her about that girl in Rotterdam."

"At risk to your life, Liko!" Louis cuffed him on the back of his head. Henry suspected his punishment would have been far worse if the occasion hadn't demanded they appear in spotless, un-bruised condition.

Henry Battenberg followed his elder brother out of the room. A lone footman waited outside in the hall, ostensibly to guide them. The halls of the bride's family residence were familiar enough for Henry to have found his way on his own, but many tiresome rituals had to be honored this day and the next. The Battenbergs were sealing a dream alliance. The match would bring the family much-needed wealth and property, not to mention priceless esteem.

Henry was glad to see his brother so happy. That was a bonus. He'd like to find a girl for himself as sweet and lively as Vicky. Though one with a bit more of a head on her shoulders would suit him better. Still, as long as she was compliant in bed, gave him children, and let him run his life as he liked, he wouldn't complain.

3

The orchestra that night leaned heavily toward waltzes by Strauss, Lanner, and von Weber. But the queen's favorite mazurka—she always pointed out with a girlish giggle, she'd been taught it by the Grand Duke himself before she married her Albert—was not played at all, which put her into a sulk. Other than that mistake, the dance master kept the mix of music fresh and lively by ordering the occasional polka, one Schottische, two Polonaises, a quadrille, and a gavotte for variety.

Beatrice had sat out the Grand March at the ball's opening, as this was reserved for couples who came together. Likewise, a gentleman always danced the first waltz with his lady. It was considered bad form to do otherwise. Since Beatrice's first responsibility was to attend to her mother, she had come, as she almost always did, without a gentleman-escort.

In theory, though, she could fill her dance card with promised dances for the remainder of the evening.

She tapped her finger on the creamy vellum card, embossed in gold and vermillion with the duke's family crest, and stared at the blank spaces. She'd been asked to reserve one dance for her brother Bertie, the Prince of Wales. Another dance belonged to the Grand Duke, and a third to the Earl of Kent. (If he survived that late into the evening. He seemed so frail these days.) But that was all she had to show for a very long night. It seemed word had got round that she carried some sort of deathly plague.

Beatrice sighed and looked around the room, ablaze with

11

the light of crystal chandeliers. Her bored gaze slid from the gleam of jewels at pale throats to starched white cuffs secured with gold or diamond studs. Perhaps, if she danced well with Bertie, other gentlemen would see she was harmless and a pleasant enough partner. Unfortunately, her brother's dance was halfway down her card. *Pooh!*

Beatrice had learned patience at her mother's side. But sometimes it was hard to just sit while the music beckoned to her, setting her heart singing and feet itching for a spin across the vast floor.

She turned her attention to her right and the far end of the table. Just past her mother was her sister Alice's widower, the Grand Duke, father of the bride. Next to him was an empty chair, where her sister-in-law Princess Alexandra had been sitting earlier in the evening, beside her husband Bertie. Alix, a Danish beauty, was in constant demand on the dance floor. Despite being the mother of three children, and unlike either the queen or her eldest daughters, Alix had kept her slim figure. Maybe it was all that dancing?

Beatrice looked down at her own still-trim waistline with concern; she feared it was just a matter of time before the family curse of fleshiness caught up with her. She wished she could dance more often, like Alix. The daringly swift Viennese waltzes and energetic polkas would offset the rich food to be served later in the evening. But if no one asked her to dance, what could she do but sit here like a lump?

Her mother seemed absorbed in watching the dancers. Beatrice turned over her card so she wouldn't have to look at it. She flipped open her lace fan and pretended to cool her face as if from the exertion of a turn around the floor. She smiled pleasantly at couples whirling past. After another moment she snapped her fan closed then draped her shawl over the back of her chair and tried more earnestly to look available as a partner.

It was then that Beatrice became aware of the conversation at the far end of the table. The Grand Duke had moved into Alix's empty seat and, head lowered close to Bertie's, was speaking to him in an urgent whisper. She was unable to catch any of their words, but it seemed to her, from the tension in their voices and their sharp gestures, that they were arguing.

What might they be quarrelling about tonight, of all nights?

Bertie's face flushed as he gripped the duke's arm. He looked so agitated, she was tempted to leave her seat and go to stand beside her brother to calm him, or ask if she might help in any way. But before she could move, a hand lightly touched her shoulder. She looked up and behind her, into startlingly blue eyes and a smooth-shaven, smiling face that looked only vaguely but agreeably familiar.

"May I have the honor of your next available dance, Your Royal Highness?" the young man asked.

She swallowed, looked away quickly then reached for a water glass, forgetting that all refreshments were kept out of the ballroom, in the adjoining salon. The man was waiting for her response. Her throat felt horribly parched. She tried to think what to say. Yes? No? A no would require an excuse of the vapors. But she didn't want to lie. Didn't even want to say no, did she? She wished she could remember his name. Of course they must have been formally introduced at some time. Otherwise he would never have dared approach her.

How embarrassing.

She sensed him straightening up, taking a step back from her chair. "If you'd rather not," he said softly.

"No, no! I mean—" What was the matter with her? Why did she always feel so inept in society? "I'd love to dance. Yes, of course."

She gathered her skirts, dismayed by how odd she'd look on the dance floor, like a widow in her weeds among all the pretty young things in their floaty white and pastel tulle. A raven among peacocks. A toad among flitting rainbow damsel flies.

He drew back her chair for her as she stood, giving her room to step away from the table and ease her full skirts clear of the furniture, and offered his arm. She took it, her mind whirring with a long list of names, none of them fitting the tall, elegant, beautiful young man beside her.

Oh, God…oh, God, who are *you?*

His hair was dark, his eyes mesmerizing when he looked down at her. They seemed bright with curiosity, or amusement. What did he see when he observed her with such intensity? She feared it was unpleasant. She hoped she wasn't repulsive to him.

The music had faded from the previous gavotte by the time they reached the edge of the dance floor. Ladies were being escorted back to their seats, new partners located, couples sorted out. The orchestra tuned up again, and lively chatter filled the ballroom.

"I believe it's to be a Viennese," her partner said. "Does an aggressive waltz please you, Princess?"

She was momentarily terrified that she'd lost her voice but, miraculously, sounds crackled out. "Oh…why yes. Viennese. Lovely."

"Battenberg! Liko, how goes it, old man?" A man in a black swallow-tail coat passed by, clapping Beatrice's dance partner on the back.

Ah. Now she had it. One of bridegroom's brothers. The youngest? No, there were four, she recalled, and she'd never met the youngest. But she had met the eldest, Alexander—Sandro to his friends and family. And the second son was Louis. Then came Henry, who also had a quirky family nickname, Liko. *Henry. Henry. Henry.* Yes, now she remembered. She recalled having played with him when they were very young. She should say something to show she was pleased to see him again.

Beatrice cleared her throat and straightened up as tall and slim as she could. "Henry," she said, to let him know she really did recognize him.

"Yes?" He was still smiling but with a touch of restraint, perhaps even concern that he was now obliged to a dance with a woman incapable of expressing her simplest thoughts.

"It's been a very long time," the words burst from her lips all at once, "since you were last in England."

"Yes, it has, Princess. I should like to visit again, soon."

Violins broke into the opening strains of *The Blue Danube*, one of her favorites by Strauss. Beatrice felt her partner's palm settle gently yet firmly at her waist. His other hand opened, palm up, inviting her fingertips. She timidly rested her gloved hand in his. As soon as they were in proper position, he stepped bravely into the whirl of dancers. Off they flew, as if on a hawk's wings. Beatrice tensed, suddenly aware of the speed at which her feet must continue moving to avoid tripping herself up.

"It's all right," Henry whispered, his breath warm against her ear. "Relax, let me guide you."

It was the strangest thing. Just his saying those words made every taut muscle in her spine and shoulders loosen a notch. It hadn't sounded like an order, the way her mother would have made it seem, but her body obeyed instantly.

Beatrice tilted her head and gave him a shy smile. "You dance very well, Henry." She meant it. Her partner wasn't a hobbling octogenarian or, just as bad, a brother or cousin with a stiff gait and sweaty shirt front.

"Thank you. As do you." He executed a clever heel turn at the end of the room and brought them back into the swirling crowd with a roguish twinkle in his eyes. "I ought to, after all the damned lessons Mother and Father forced upon the lot of us."

"I love to dance," she said a little breathlessly.

"Do you? I'll have to ask you more often. If you like, that is."

"Oh yes," Beatrice said, "this is ever so much fun." Then she laughed because she sounded like a child, pleased to be taken out to play on the swings. *Push me higher…higher!*

He chuckled. "What's so funny?"

"Just that, I don't know, I feel years younger when dancing, don't you? Sitting all night and making polite conversation becomes so very dull."

His eyes fixed on her face, and she thought she saw his mind working. "It does, doesn't it?" he agreed. "All the silly gossip, the forced chit-chat. I'd rather be doing something too. I guess tonight we'll have to settle for dancing. Though a carriage ride would be brilliant, on a full-moon night like this."

She gasped in delight at the thought. "Oh, it would—wouldn't it just be too perfect?" The music swelled, the tempo raced, pulling her pulse along with it. She tried not to think about her feet, letting them do the work for her. It was better that way. If she thought too hard about the intricate steps, she'd flub it up and they'd end in a sprawl on the floor.

"Do you ride?" he asked. "Horseback, that is."

She gave him a sideways look that said, *Are you joking?* "Remember who my mother is?"

He blushed. "Of course. The queen is a dedicated horsewoman so certainly her daughter must be too. I understand you're inseparable, the two of you. Mother and daughter. " Was there a question behind his words? Or teasing? She wasn't sure.

"I love to ride," was all she could think to say at first but then plunged on. "Riding fast is the best. Faster than *she* ever does. At a canter at the least, better at a gallop. Mother says running a horse is far too dangerous, but I think racing across a field is rather like dancing the Viennese."

"Exactly." He grinned. "Funny. I wouldn't have thought you'd be so keen on speed."

No, of course not, she brooded. *You'd think me dull and clumsy and uninteresting, like the rest of them do.* She ducked her head and lowered her eyes, feeling chastened and reminded of her many inadequacies.

Too late, Beatrice realized her mistake.

How many times had she been scolded by her dance master for peeking at her feet while dancing? It threw off the body's posture, disturbed the fragile balance between partners, and courted disaster.

Then, she missed a step. And another.

Before she could recover she felt herself falling forward, out of control, the toe of her slipper catching the hem of her gown, making everything impossibly worse. She imagined herself dragging Henry Battenberg down with her to the floor, other couples coming upon them at speed, so suddenly they would be unable to avoid the fallen pair beneath their feet. Dozens of dancers would plummet to the floor, creating a messy, embarrassing pileup.

All because of her clumsiness.

Before she could cry out in alarm, Henry's arm at her waist hauled her firmly upright and into his hard chest. The soles of her slippers lifted ever so slightly off the treacherous floor. Then, magically, they were all right again—an elegant couple skimming down the length of the ballroom as if nothing at all had happened.

Henry adjusted the distance between their bodies to a more decorous space and smiled down at her. "That was a close one, yes?"

She laughed. Laughed out loud for the sheer relief she felt. "Oh, yes. Very close, I'm sure. I'm sorry. I can be such a clumsy ninny."

"Don't apologize. It happens. I doubt anyone even noticed."

"You think not?"

He shrugged. "And what if they did? It's not the end of the world. Now is it, Princess?"

He's right, she thought. *It's not.*

And suddenly her world seemed a happier place. Except… now the dance was over, couples bowing and taking leave of each other, and Henry was walking her back toward the long table from which her mother's narrowed eyes were following her with somber concentration. And the last thing in the world Beatrice wanted to do was to sit at that damn table for the rest of the night.

"Thank you," Henry said, pulling out her chair for her and helping her sit. "May I ask that you reserve another waltz for me, later in the evening?"

Her heart sang. "Oh, yes, Henry. Of course."

"Call me Liko. All my friends and family do."

"Liko." How strange but sweet. "Yes, I'd love another waltz." She checked her card; six more dances before the next waltz. "Number fourteen then, if you're free?"

"Until then." He gave her a parting bow.

She closed her eyes for a moment to hold the shimmering image in her mind of his eyes—his startlingly azure eyes—lingering on hers as he backed away. He was so perfect, so kind and intelligent. And didn't he dance like a dream? Oh, how he made her feel as they flew, light as air, down the polished floor with—

"Did you have a good time, Baby?" Victoria's voice intruded on her dream.

Beatrice opened her eyes and took a steadying breath. Back to reality. "Yes, it was a delightful waltz." She flipped over her card and moved the tiny pencil attached with a gold silk cord down to line 14 and wrote: Prince Henry Battenberg.

"I'm so glad," her mother said. "I asked the boy at luncheon if he wouldn't give up just one dance for my Baby. You always look so lonely sitting through the evening. I'm glad he didn't mind."

"Oh." Beatrice sank in her chair, her insides twisting in agony though she tried to show no outward reaction. She turned over her dance card, took a deep breath and looked straight ahead. A pity dance. That's what it had been.

Beatrice pressed a palm to her side, where *his* hand had been.

4

Prince Wilhelm II of Germany did not attend his cousin Vicky's wedding. He'd been invited, of course. Wasn't he next in line after his father to become king of Germany and emperor of Prussia? Hadn't his mother been the Crown Princess of England? No royal bride on the Continent with any sense would dare snub him, with such a lineage.

In point of fact, he recalled with a smug smile, getting out of traveling to Darmstadt hadn't been all that easy. His parents had nearly insisted he accompany them. But, supported by his mentor Otto von Bismarck, Wilhelm had wriggled out of the annoying obligation at the last moment on the excuse of not wishing to interrupt his studies.

In truth, he had more important trout to fry, here at home in Bonn. And they involved neither weddings nor books.

"Enough of this!" Wilhelm snapped the textbook closed and shoved it away across the table. It slid off the edge and fell to the floor with a dull thump. "I hate *das Englische*. Let the Brits learn German if they wish to communicate with me when I am emperor."

Bismarck eyed Wilhelm over steepled fingertips. The steely glower that had terrified the prince as a child, these days provided a strong role model for Wilhelm's own temperament. The old man had taught him *alles*. Everything. Even ways he could rise above his deformity—the birth gift of his incompetent English mother.

Wilhelm stared down at his left arm, withered, ugly, and nearly useless. It was *her* fault of course. His mother's. If she hadn't got him somehow turned around inside her, he'd not have been born in breech, his infant arm crushed, paralyzed for years, stunted forever. He'd have been normal.

Bismarck had shown him ways to camouflage the disgusting thing, to make the shortened arm barely discernible when he was clothed. A military jacket, expertly tailored so as not to hang long over his gloved left hand. The clever tactic of holding an object in the crippled hand—a pair of gloves or walking stick or even a pup from the royal kennel—distracted the viewer's eye, making his arm appear longer. While meeting a person of importance he always kept the bad arm and hand tucked close to his body or clasped in a seemingly casual pose by the good one. The artists of his portraits understood that they too must use illusion to save the prince from ridicule—and protect themselves from his wrath.

Yes, Bismarck had taught him many things. But these days Wilhelm grew impatient with the old man.

"You must master the tools you need to rule your empire," Bismarck now insisted, still speaking in that weak-sounding English tongue. "Great Britain may become an ally or an enemy to *das Reich*. And what of the Americans? If you know their language, you will understand the way they think, how they will react to your politics." Bismarck's gaze drilled into him as if hoping to turn his mind by the sheer force of his dominant will.

Wilhelm looked away. "I know enough of their ridiculous language. More than enough. I'm no longer a child. And haven't I spoken it with my grandmother whenever we've visited London?"

"I've seen how you are with Queen Victoria. You mix a few German words into the conversation, then a few more, and soon she shifts to your mother tongue to appease you. After all, you were her first grandchild, her little 'Willy'." His tutor grimaced. "Clever of you to manipulate her. But avoiding knowledge of the finer points of her language will not serve our purposes."

"*Our?*" Wilhelm's eyes snapped back to the old man's face.

"Your Highness." Bismarck twisted his lips into a strained smile. "It is only a manner of speech."

"In English perhaps, but not in German or to *my* ears." Wilhelm flung himself against the back of his chair and slid down, kicking his boots up onto the table as if he were in a café with his school friends. How he longed for his college days. At university he'd enjoyed as much freedom as any young prince might hope for. "But tell me more about this *Allianz* you propose. Much as I detest the English people, if they prove useful…" He waved a careless hand.

"*Gut.*" Bismarck's eyes brightened. "And so I will. Consider your future. Your grandfather, though we might wish him to live forever, will not. He is feeble and ill. On his death, your father will take up the double crown, King and Emperor of the German-Prussian states."

"As will I on his death. We needn't review the rules of accession. Go on." Speaking of the men in his family dying never saddened Wilhelm. What did trouble him was that they might live too long for him to fully enjoy the benefits of ruling over a vast and (if he had anything to say about it) growing empire.

"The English people," Bismarck was saying, "including their Parliament, grow nervous of German power and the links through marriage between Prussian princes and English princesses. The marriage of their Princess Louise to a commoner was greeted with enthusiasm because he was a Scot and a subject of the queen. But more importantly, because he was *not* a foreigner, *not* German. It is a message that Your Highness can't afford to ignore. They don't want a German king."

Wilhelm rolled his eyes. "As if I would want their ridiculous island. So what if I hate the English and they hate me." He slammed the heel of his boot on the table top, making it shiver. "Why should I care?"

His mentor glared at him, but Wilhelm was no longer a boy to be so easily intimidated. He was twenty-five years old and, unless his grandfather somehow clung to life far longer than anyone expected—and someone discovered a way to cure his father's recently diagnosed throat cancer—he, Wilhelm, would have his accession day within a few short years. Maybe even sooner, God willing.

"You should care because," Bismarck's voice lowered, his tone grave, "you may grow your empire by bullying, thereby having to fight for land, inch by bloody inch. But, if you are clever, you'll form beneficial alliances with the English and your Continental cousins. Then, assured they will do nothing to stop you, your army can march in and take over the territory you covet with only the weakest of excuses."

Wilhelm brooded over the old man's words. Perhaps he was right. But this waiting was intolerable.

Bismarck leaned across the table and stabbed a finger at its surface for emphasis. "If the English are not on your side, and they step in to stop you the moment you cross a border—you have a very big problem, Your Highness. You don't want a war with the British Empire. Believe me, you do not."

Wilhelm tossed his head and laughed. "Why the hell not? We are strong and a far larger nation than their little island. There is no better army in all of—"

"*Dummkopf!*"

Wilhelm stared at the man, lowered his boots to the floor and sat up, his spine rigid. "Watch it, *mein Freund*. No one calls me a fool." He reduced his voice to a warning growl. "Certainly not a glorified tutor."

He had never spoken to Bismarck in such a way before. Never would he have dreamed of doing so in years past. But he felt his own strength emerging, his impatience surging even as he watched the generations before him weakening, withering like his arm. His father's aging cronies had become a handicap to be overcome. He must seize his destiny.

For the first time, Wilhelm saw something in the old man's eyes he'd never believed possible. It wasn't fear. Not yet. It was doubt, an indecisiveness as to his protégé's next move and his own countermove. As in a chess match, hesitation revealed an opponent's weakness.

Wilhelm took a deep breath and boldly continued. "You say I must be aware of what my enemy thinks of me. I must learn their politics to protect my interests."

"Precisely."

"I can't do that without spending time in cursed England, hanging about in the queen's Court, pretending friendship with her ministers."

"I'm sure your grandmother would welcome you." Bismarck's voice dripped with sarcasm.

They both knew Victoria disliked her eldest grandson because of his temper tantrums and his daring to stand up to her. As a child, he'd developed a mean temper. The queen never forgot the day he'd snatched one of his aunt's muffs and threw it out the carriage window. Worse yet, while attending a family wedding, and blocked into the pew by two of his older uncles with the hope of containing his restlessness until the end of the service, he'd bitten one of the young men on the ankle. The queen was not amused.

"She might tolerate my company," Wilhelm admitted, chuckling at the memory, "but I'm not sure how long I could tolerate hers."

Besides, he hated the way she always stared at his arm, as if he were carrying a snake. Even in recent years, she'd persisted in embarrassing him, calling him "Willy" in public, scolding him for his temper as if he were still a child. "Your arrogance and willfulness will be your ruin!" she'd snapped at him in front of his parents on their last visit.

"Better that I send eyes and ears on my behalf, I think," Wilhelm said.

"A spy?" The old man's heavy brow smoothed—a sign of interest if not approval. Spies were one of his favorite tools. "Yes, a man in her court. That might work."

"*Nein*," Wilhelm said, "not just in her Court. In her *family*."

Bismarck shook his head, his eyes darkening. "I doubt you'll find any of her sons or daughters, even those related through marriage, willing to be disloyal to the queen."

Wilhelm laughed out loud. "Have you no imagination, sir?" For the first time he was enjoying this conversation. "There is another princess to be married off. Another husband to be found."

Bismarck frowned. "Beatrice? The old maid?"

"Only a few years my senior. Victoria was popping them out even as she was being given grandchildren by my parents." Wilhelm scooped his English language text off the floor and dropped it on the table with a satisfying whack. "If living with my grandmother, day after grim day, is anything like I imagine— Auntie Beatrice will be ripe for a mate to free her from the old witch."

"So you will turn matchmaker, Your Highness?" The idea appeared to amuse Bismarck. His eyes twinkled, a rare and remarkable thing to witness. "I'm not sure it's a practical solution, but maybe…maybe… How do you imagine you'll pull it off? Where would you find this man to sweep a mother-shackled princess off of her feet? He'll also have to charm the queen, you know."

Wilhelm rubbed his withered arm in thought. A moment later he smiled at his teacher. "I believe I already know the ideal suitor for my dear aunt."

5

Beatrice expected to spend the morning helping her niece prepare for the wedding ceremony later that day. She and Vicky had grown close, even though most of their lives they'd lived in two different countries, hundreds of miles apart. Their correspondence started in childhood, playfully, and became intimate and warm over the years, their visits pleasurably anticipated. Beatrice had to admit, she often felt closer to her niece than to her real sisters, with the possible exception of Louise, since the others were separated from her by so many years.

And so, Beatrice thought nothing of it when Vicky asked her to come with her back to her bedchamber after the wedding breakfast.

As soon as they were in her room, the bride shooed off her attendants and ladies, and turned to Beatrice with an anguished expression. Tears glittering in her eyes, she flung herself into her aunt's arms. "I'm so very afraid. What shall I do?"

"Afraid of what, my dear?" Beatrice asked, shocked at this unexpected outburst of emotion. She tried to disengage herself from the girl's arms, but Vicky held firm.

"You always have calming words and intelligent advice for me, dear Auntie. I'm so very nervous." Vicky's voice lowered to a whisper as she looked up into Beatrice's face, "About *tonight*."

Beatrice felt her cheeks go hot. "Oh, well, yes, after the ceremony and reception, your wedding night." She gripped

Vicky by the shoulders and set the girl away from her a few paces to enable them both to breathe. "I'm told that Louis is a kind man. I'm sure he'll be...gentle."

Why did the girl assume she knew anything at all about the physical relations between a husband and wife? She wasn't like her sister Louise, who had sought—well, *experiences*, as a very young woman. Beatrice had never been allowed alone in a room with a male, other than her father. Even in the company of her own brothers she'd been chaperoned by Nurse, or a trusted female tutor or servant.

As to the sexual education of any young woman of a socially elevated family, convention declared that the bride depend solely upon an elder female's discreet instruction before her wedding day. What the details of that instruction might be, Beatrice didn't have a clue. She'd heard, though, that some new brides learned absolutely nothing of what was expected of them, of their wifely duties in the marital bed that is, until their husband took them to said bed.

And if there was to be no marriage at all, ever? No wedding night?

Then there was no need for a woman to ever know of such things. At least, that was what her mother, the queen, had told her. Several times.

For desperate minutes Beatrice tried to calm her niece with vague reassurances that physical intimacy between husband and wife was completely natural. She dredged up every slyly murmured phrase she'd overheard between her sisters Louise and Helen, closest to her in age, both of whom were now married. She called up the whispered words of ladies of the court. Anything that had to do with the sexual union of a man and a woman.

She heard herself mumble frantically, "And I'm told that there is sometimes pleasure for the woman during the act of procreation. In addition to a sense of fulfillment of one's wifely duties—" And at that fortuitous moment, the queen stepped through the door and into the bridal chamber.

Never had Beatrice been so glad to see her mother.

Her gratitude, however, was short lived.

Victoria, apparently having overheard enough of the conversation to ascertain its topic, and Beatrice's hopelessness, dismissed her daughter with a peremptory, "I have everything in hand, Baby. You'll only confuse the poor child." The queen turned to Vicky, snapping open her black lace fan in front of her face, as if to hide her words from all but her granddaughter. "Your poor aunt knows nothing of these things. Come, dear little one, we'll have a chat." And she took the bride's hand and tugged her across the room to the window seat, where they sat together whispering while Vicky stared wide-eyed at her grandmother.

Feeling pathetic, useless, and ignored, Beatrice stood in the middle of the room, looking around her as servants burst into the room bringing articles of clothing, dishes of dried fruits and nuts, scented linens to place on the bed. The bride's little sister Elle appeared and curled up in a blue slipper chair on the opposite side of the room from the queen, chattering at anyone who would listen. Vicky's tutor and old nurse arrived, and suddenly the room was awash in crinolined skirts and happy female activity, none of it involving Beatrice.

She sidled meekly toward her mother when she sensed, from Vicky's quivering smile and her mother's reassuring pats on the girl's cheek, that the critical information had been delivered. "How may I help, Mama?"

Victoria wrinkled her nose at her and huffed through her nose. "You will get out from under foot, Baby."

Beatrice swallowed her disappointment. "But everyone else has something special to—"

"Fine then. Why do you not take a few of your rambunctious younger nieces and nephews for a ride? The stable master will provide mounts and escort. You'll be doing the dear duke a favor by keeping the children occupied."

"Yes, well, if you think… " Beatrice stared longingly at Vicky as more and more of her attendants arrived to fuss over her. *To be pretty like her. To be loved…*

At one time she would have given almost anything for a serious suitor. But she was past her prime now. She was *Auntie*. And it seemed she wasn't any good at being even that.

"Go, go," Victoria urged. "Stop dithering, Baby. You're just getting in the way." She stood up from the window seat and all but pushed her out the door.

Beatrice found herself standing in the empty hallway of the duke's palace. She took three deep breaths, closed her eyes for a moment, soaked up the comparative silence. Such peacefulness, this rare moment of privacy, almost made rejection pleasant.

Beatrice stood for a few more minutes, listening to the muffled voices behind the heavy oak door. It was unlike her mother to let her out of her sight. Beatrice wondered if something more than the wedding was on the queen's mind, distracting her.

No matter. She walked slowly down the long corridor with its vaulted ceiling, ivory walls and gilded cornices, then through a great crystal chandelier-draped foyer where two footmen in smart livery stood at attention. She strolled outside through glazed doors and into the sunshine.

Alone. Blessedly alone. An oh-so-rare treat.

So rare, in fact, that by the time she'd taken a short stroll around the grounds then returned to her room and changed into riding dress and, finally, reached the stables, she still hadn't been able to locate the gaggle of nieces and nephews she'd intended to take for a ride. Not that she tried so very hard. Surrendering this golden personal time to play nursemaid to a rowdy crew of little royals appealed less and less with every passing minute.

Impulsively, she changed her plans.

I shall ignore Mama's suggestion. No, not suggestion— command. Every request from a queen was without doubt a command. But Beatrice chose today to be just a teeny bit reckless, daring, adventuresome. She'd ride out alone. Totally alone. *Delicious!*

And why not? She was an experienced horsewoman.

Everyone else on the estate was busy with preparations for the wedding, although it was still hours away. She had nothing better to do. And anyway, she always felt physically stronger, less achy in the joints when she moved about. A touch of rheumatism, her mother's doctors had said, and prescribed soothing heat and rest for the pain, laudanum if that didn't work. But she knew her own body. A good, brisk ride without anyone telling her what to do—that seemed a far better cure.

She marched toward the duke's stables, already looking forward to her adventure.

Her favorite mounts had always been her two ponies from the royal mews. Tarff and Wave, which had been bred at Hampton Court for riding. She also had Noon and Dawn both gentle, well-mannered bays that she drove as a pair. But she was unfamiliar with the temperaments of the duke's horses. A few stalls were empty, so maybe someone else had already headed out, but she saw no sign of other riders as she scanned the meadows that stretched out and away from the castle.

She sent a stable boy to fetch the chief groom, who appeared quickly and recommended a beautiful mare with gentle eyes. "Genevieve's got a bit of spirit in her though, so you watch she don't take you for a ride, Your Highness. Let her know who's boss."

"I will," Beatrice assured him then told him a mount for an escort wouldn't be required.

He blinked at her, as if such a thing simply wasn't done. She ignored his nervous suggestion that she ought not ride alone.

"I'll be fine," she assured him.

Minutes later, Beatrice rode out through the paddock at a leisurely pace, seated side saddle as all Victoria's girls had been taught. "The only lady-like way to ride," the queen stated. After ten minutes or so Beatrice felt as though she and the horse had become sufficiently accustomed to each other. She cropped the horse into a comfortable canter and enjoyed the familiar rhythm and bounce of the horse's stride. The air smelled sweetly of spring flowers and new grass. She followed a dirt path into woods lush with new growth. The perfume of damp moss, pungent pine needles, and feathery ferns pleased and soothed her, dissolving the tension she always felt when forced to converse with strangers or appear before a large group of people. *Lovely, this is absolutely perfect!*

"Hello, hold up there!" a shout came from behind her.

Beatrice tensed at the sound of another set of horse's hooves. Her first thought was that she had strayed off the duke's land and offended a neighbor by trespassing. But was that really possible? She'd ridden less than a mile; the estate covered hundreds of acres. She turned her mount to face the oncoming rider.

With a jolt she saw it was a lone man. He rode a gleaming black Arabian that seemed as spirited as her mare was calm. The approach of the other horse made her own mount anxious. Genevieve danced in place apprehensively. Beatrice checked her with the reins.

"Sssshhh, it's all right, my pretty," Beatrice soothed, stroking the horse's silky neck. "It's one of your pals." She recognized the Arabian as a horse the groom had passed over when choosing hers, no doubt having assumed the powerful animal would be too much for her to handle.

The rider came closer and, at last, she recognized him. "Liko! Henry, hello."

"Are you escaping the madness too?" he asked cheerfully, stopping close to her. "Wise woman. The palace is crammed to the gills with guests. Louis is a mad man he's so nervous. And Sandro claims he's in love with a girl whose Russian mother despises Germans. I told them both they'd be better off not falling in love at all. Find a girl with money who offends no one. Marry her, if you must marry at all."

"Oh, do you really believ—" she started to object, but then saw he was laughing at her. "You're trying to get a rise out of old Auntie, aren't you?"

He looked perplexed. "Old—? Who is that?" He turned in his saddle to look around the woods. "Oh, you mean *you*? How can you think of yourself as old? You are no more aged than I?"

It was true, she now remembered. They were the same age. And yet he seemed so very young to her—utterly dashing in his military uniform and on that magnificent steed that looked as though it wanted to bolt down a hill in a cavalry charge.

"Why are you out here on your own?" he asked. "You could have sent someone for me. I'd have been happy to accompany you."

"*You* rode out alone. Why did you not send for *me*?" She swallowed, shocked by her boldness.

"You're right, Your Highness." He laughed and turned his horse as if to go. "There's no reason you can't seek solitude. If that was your intent, then I'm intruding." Smiling, he gave her a jaunty salute. "I shall leave you in peace." "No!" she cried out, but immediately controlled her impulse to plead with him to stay. More calmly she said, "It was nice for a bit, riding alone, but I'd enjoy your company. That is, if you're not wanting solitude."

"The company of a lovely lady suits me just fine." He flashed her another smile, and this one melted her down to her toes. He's teasing me, she thought, but decided she didn't mind. Perhaps she'd just pretend right along with him. Pretend that he meant what he said. Play the part of a worldly, attractive woman. Flirt!

They rode further into the woods, side by side for as long as the path accommodated two horses. When it narrowed, he let her take the lead while they chatted about their families and swapped Court gossip until they emerged into an open field dotted with red and white poppies.

"Do you have any idea how much you surprise me?" Henry said as they cut through tall grasses whose feathery tips brushed her stirrups.

"Surprise you. How?"

"Louis told me you were quite the cold fish."

She cringed. It wasn't the first time she'd overheard such comments. "I don't see how he'd know," she said with a brusqueness she hadn't intended. "We've barely ever spoken."

Henry brought his horse up alongside hers. The animals seemed to have calmed down in each other's presence and walked along amicably. "I think that's the point." He gave her a sidelong look. "Louis tried to start a conversation with you, once, a long time ago."

Oh, *that*, she thought and grimaced. "If you're referring to that awful dinner several years ago."

"He was very upset, you know, that you wouldn't speak to him."

She closed her eyes for a moment, as if to shut out the memory. "I *couldn't* speak to him."

"Why on Earth not?"

"Because my mother forbade it."

She sensed his horse coming to a stop; she reined in her mount as well. When she turned to look at him, his long face was no longer smooth. His dazzling eyes had darkened to a stormy gray-blue, and his smile seemed to have never been. "On what grounds did she swear you to silence?"

Beatrice pursed her lips. Was it disloyal to question the queen's decisions? Hadn't her rules been made with her daughter's safety and happiness in mind?

She sighed. "At the time, it seemed to make sense, what she told me to do. Mama was concerned that Louis was showing interest in me; she said it was of an unhealthy sort." Beatrice dared not look Henry in the eye as she spoke. This was, after all, his beloved brother they were talking about. "And anyway, he was older than I and intent on a career in the Royal navy. Mama said I was not to encourage him in any way. If Louis was sincere, it wouldn't matter that I was cool toward him. She told me he would make his true intentions known, and then we would see that it was not simply a flirtation."

"But you didn't just behave coolly." Henry caught her eyes with his own. "You were silent the entire dinner. You refused to join his polite conversation."

She shook her head, suddenly feeling sick to her stomach. "I can't imagine what he thought of me. I know now he's a good man. He didn't deserve to be mistreated. But I–" She shuddered and turned her face away so Henry wouldn't see her self-loathing.

"But you did as the queen demanded."

"Yes. It was horrid of me. I see that now. But you don't know what it's like, living with her. I love her. She is my mother. But you cannot reason with the queen when she has her mind set on something…or against someone." Near tears, Beatrice let her gaze fall to her hands on the reins. "You just can't know—"

"But I can damn well guess."

"I don't blame you for hating me," she whispered.

"Hate you?" He coughed out a laugh. "Dear girl, I don't hate you. You puzzle me, that's true. But hate? How could I hate such a lovely, intelligent woman? You have done me no harm."

"But your brother—I spurned him."

"And look at what happiness he has found with your niece. It was meant to be, you see." He grinned, a bit naughtily she thought. "Besides, if he had married you, we wouldn't have been able to meet like this. Now would we?"

"No, I guess not," she said, her heart shimmying in her breast. *Like this?* What did he mean? "I would be your sister-in law."

"And the thoughts I had last night while we danced—they would have been highly improper."

"Oh?" A rush of heat filled her. She had to look away from him. Again. The effect he was having on her was most… disturbing.

He laughed. "I'm sorry, Beatrice. I'm shocking you. Is it wrong to admit that I find you attractive? It just comes out when I'm near you."

She was so flustered now she could hardly speak. She didn't need a mirror to see that her face was afire. "I am flattered, Liko. But I know what I am, and I know men—not even kind men like you—see anything pleasing in me."

An expression of pure astonishment flashed across his face. "Oh, come now, Princess. What game are you playing?"

"No game."

He leaned out of his saddle, toward her, and the aroma of leather, musky shaving lather, and pipe smoke came at her, a wall of masculinity. "I'm not blind, Princess. Let me tell you a secret. Come a bit closer."

She leaned forward, holding on to her saddle for fear of falling out of it, curious at his tone but also wary. Before she could turn her head to hold her ear toward his lips, he kissed her full on the mouth.

"There!" he cried triumphantly. "I've wanted to do that since we were twelve years old."

"Henry!" She was sure now he was toying with her. "You shouldn't."

"Why not? This isn't the dark ages. People can say what they feel. I like you, Beatrice. My brother thinks you're a strange little fish, and I'm glad he does because you're still swimming free in the stream for me to catch."

"To—" she swallowed, widening her eyes at him "—catch? Me?"

"Yes!" He laughed and made a grab for her that she wasn't entirely sure was sham.

And then...*then*, it was as if she remembered what it was like to play with little Henry Battenberg as they chased through the gardens at Buckingham and along powdery sand at Osborne by the sea.

She tossed her head at him. "I dare you, Liko," she challenged, feeling the corners of her lips turn up in a mischievous grin that hadn't been there for ages. "You just try and catch me."

And she dug her heels into the muscled belly of her mount and shot across poppy-strewn fields with a laughing prince in pursuit.

6

That evening, it was with considerable surprise that Beatrice found herself feeling genuinely and whole-heartedly happy as she watched Vicky walk down the cathedral's aisle on the arm of her father to join Louis Battenberg before the altar.

How fast life changes, she thought.

Here she stood in church, observing the very event she absolutely had known would break her heart, because she'd honestly had such a terrible crush on Louis all those years back…but she was feeling elated. As the pretty blonde bride took her place at her fiancé's side, Beatrice's gaze drifted toward the younger Battenberg brother. Henry, in his striking regimental colors. Henry, with his long, lean body and strength of shoulders, and eyes that—was she imagining this?—crackled with blue fire whenever they drifted, ever so cautiously, in her direction.

She smiled, and he returned her silent greeting for the briefest moment before rearranging his features in a solemn, soldierly expression more suited to the occasion.

For the next several minutes she watched him, unable to tear her eyes away, her heart thrumming in her ears. He stood with his left hand resting on the ornate hilt of his sword, polished Hessian boots planted solidly on the marble floor as if he were claiming possession of the very ground beneath him. Chin high. Braided collar emphasizing his long neck. Eyes reflecting hundreds of candles lighting the grand cathedral. Her pulse raced as if she were back on Genevieve, galloping across the open field with Henry giving chase.

Had she, dull Auntie Bea, really found the nerve to do that?

And when he had caught her—even though she'd made him work to do it—he'd claimed another kiss. This one she'd seen coming but didn't try to escape. She'd melted at the softness of his lips touching hers. When his hand reached out to lightly hold her fingertips, she'd turned to molten silver.

Now the organ sang out, its lush chords reverberating low in her stomach and waking her from her daydream, announcing the end of the ceremony. She was startled to have missed so much of it. She'd been far away, imagining sun-stroked days when she might ride again with Henry. They would talk of intelligent matters, compare preferences of foods, music, opinions of a political nature. He would describe his travels with the royal navy to places she'd never seen. She'd respond by expressing an interest in seeing foreign lands. He might catch her subtle message (*Take me with you. Oh, please!*). He'd understand, where others had not, that she was more exciting, more daring than she appeared.

It was such a pleasant fantasy, still spinning through her mind, her mother had to grasp her arm and give it a shake to rouse her.

"What is wrong with you, Baby? People are waiting for us."

Beatrice wanted to scream, *I am not your baby! I am a grown woman with a name and a life of my own.*

But was that really true? A name, yes, she had that—but not a life. She was chained by duty to her mother. She whispered, "Sorry."

Victoria folded her own arm around her daughter's as they moved in slow motion up the aisle, out of the incense-perfumed church and into the sunlit courtyard. The queen leaned toward her to murmur, "There is trouble brewing. I feel it."

Beatrice felt a momentary jolt of panic. Had her mother found out about her unsupervised adventure with Henry?

Then she followed Victoria's gaze toward the wedding party. "Surely not. Vicky and Louis look in perfect bliss."

"Not the bride and groom." Her mother's voice sounded pinched, testy. "Vicky's papa."

Beatrice studied the Grand Duke, standing proudly beside the bride and groom with his younger daughter Elle on his arm. A shadow of sorrow grayed the happy family portrait. *Alice should be here*, she thought.

Her sister Alice, the duke's wife, had died not long before their brother Leo passed, due to complications of his hemophilia. Both her siblings had left her at relatively young ages. But whereas Leo had been a fragile child from birth, cursed by the bleeding disease that haunted European royalty, always needing to be protected and worried over, Alice had been the very picture of health until diphtheria struck the Grand Duke's court. Then, despite doctors' warnings, she had insisted upon personally nursing her family and eventually perished from the disease herself.

"What is wrong with the Duke?" Beatrice hoped her brother-in-law wasn't sick. She found him a delightful man— generous, handsome in a fatherly way, always ready with his charming sense of humor to lighten family gatherings haunted by the specter of Prince Albert and, now by Victoria's renewed grieving over her son and daughter.

"He invited *that* woman to the wedding," Victoria snapped, her tiny eyes sharp as flint and throwing off sparks. "Can you imagine?"

Beatrice followed her mother's glare as it shifted toward a cluster of guests standing in the courtyard, beneath an early-blooming rose arbor. She didn't have to guess which woman had annoyed the queen. She stood out, a strikingly sensual figure, outshining every other woman in view. She looked to be only a few years older than Beatrice, wore a daring crimson gown that contrasted dramatically with her dark hair. Rubies the size of song-bird eggs glittered at her throat. Her pretty eyes rested on Beatrice's brother-in-law, across the garden, with obvious adoration.

"She's beautiful," Beatrice whispered. "Who is she?"

"No one, dear child. No one you will ever need to meet. I shall tell the duke she must be made to leave. She is not welcome at dinner."

"But if she is his guest—"

Her mother's stony glare cut off her objection. The queen raised her right hand a few inches, and one of the duke's attentive footmen immediately stepped forward. He leaned down when the queen motioned him closer. She whispered a few words to him, and he left, his expression neutral.

Once the wedding party had moved back inside the palace and were seated at their assigned places along the single, long banquet table set—Beatrice had heard—for 340 guests, the rest of the guests moved toward their chairs. Beatrice looked around for the woman she'd seen earlier. She'd seemed exotic, interesting. Beatrice was dying to talk with her and find out where she'd come from. She'd have to do it soon if her mother was intent on making her leave.

But the grand duke was standing alone behind the chair at the head of the table, and the lady in red was nowhere in sight. Apparently, the queen's message already had been delivered. Beatrice felt sorry for the man. Was it fair that her mother's whims should deny him a companion on his daughter's wedding day?

Beatrice excused herself and stood up from the table. Any other day, Victoria certainly would have noticed and stopped her. But the queen was busy talking with Sandro, and the second of the Battenberg sons had her so enthralled that Beatrice was able to slip away.

She approached her brother-in-law and rested a hand tentatively on his arm. The duke turned with a subdued smile. "Ah, Your Royal Highness," he murmured, "you are looking well. Thank you for doing so much for Vicky. She values your love and advice even more in the years since she's lost her mother."

"It's my pleasure. She's a charming girl. I adore her."

He nodded. "Thank you."

Beatrice bent down closer to him. "The dark-haired lady in

church, I understand she was your guest. She could not join us for the banquet?"

His face reddened. "The queen suggested it was inappropriate for her to be here."

"Why shouldn't she be?" If Beatrice had inherited anything from her mother it was her preference for speaking plainly and openly, to get to the root of the matter.

"She is a dear friend. Her name is Alexandrine von Kolemine. She is from Poland originally, the daughter of the count of Hutten-Czapsy. A widow, as I am a widower, and we are close friends." He sighed. "I believe it offends your mother that I keep company with her."

Beatrice considered his choice of words. The queen never allowed her brothers to speak in front of their sisters about their private social lives. But over the years she'd overheard snatches of conversation. "Keeping company" seemed, to her, code words for something more intimate than tea shared before the fire.

If Alice had been alive, Beatrice would most definitely have been offended on her behalf. But her sister had been gone six years, and the duke had seemed so very sad and inconsolable that Beatrice was happy he'd found someone to comfort him and share his days. And perhaps his nights?

"She is your mistress?"

The duke tensed and avoided her eyes. "Princess, I shouldn't be discussing such things with you."

"Because my mother would be furious."

"She would likely banish me from ever again setting foot in London." His eyes flashed, but his dry laugh held no humor.

Beatrice shook her head. "Alice wouldn't have wanted you to be alone forever."

Her own words struck home. Wasn't she alone too? And likely to remain so for the rest of her life. A mother, siblings, nephews and nieces were no substitute for a beloved spouse. The only difference between her situation and the duke's was— she'd never been married and likely never would be.

She couldn't recall much about her parents' marital relations. She'd been so very young when Albert died—just four years old. But she had a hazy memory of warm exchanges between her parents, of standing between them as a toddler—the sandwich filling to their sturdy, loving bread slices—feeling the vibrancy of their affection pass through her. And she'd heard courtiers say that the queen and her prince consort had been totally devoted to each other.

"I'm sorry if my mother has spoiled the day for you," Beatrice murmured.

The duke took her hands between his and patted them. "She hasn't, Princess. I have seen my daughter married to a good man. And my mistress, she will forgive me when I make everything right very soon."

"How will you do that?" She really was curious. "Mama seems so set against her."

"In good time. In good time, you will see." He smiled. "Now off you go to enjoy the banquet, Beatrice. And later, your mother will be distracted by all of the family happenings. Perhaps this will buy you a little time to spend on your own, in your own way." He winked at her. "Maybe another ride through the woods?"

Her eyes widened. He knew? Did they all know she'd been riding with Henry?

No, not all of them. If her mother were aware she'd been alone with a man she would have burst her corset stays.

That vivid image brought a sudden smile to her lips.

7

This is impossible! Henry Battenberg stared the length of the banquet table that stretched from one end to the other of the ornate dining salon. He'd hoped the seating arrangements would put him close to Beatrice, but as luck would have it there must have been fifty chairs between them. She might as well have been on another continent.

Now he had no hope of conversing with her, or even swapping flirtatious glances, until after the meal. But by then her mother might well whisk her away to their chambers. The little queen was known to dislike lingering at table after a meal.

He couldn't say what it was about Beatrice that so fascinated him. When he told Louis he'd gone riding with the princess, his brother laughed and shook his head. "Surely you can do better than that dry old stick. There are plenty of pretty young things in Darmstadt."

Henry had shrugged and let it go. Maybe Louis was right on at least one point. Bea was a bit of an odd duck. But he sensed there was more to her than most people realized. He welcomed the challenge of discovering what lay beneath all of that dreadful black bombazine, forced upon Beatrice by the queen's endless grief.

Not *physically* beneath her gown, of course. One didn't set out to deflower a princess. He'd have to be mad to even consider such a thing. No, he told himself, Beatrice was just interesting and surprisingly fun to be around.

Added to that, something about her made him break out in a compassionate smile. She was like an orphaned kitten in need of protection. A charming stray he'd treat to a dish of cream, for the sheer pleasure of watching her lap it up. She'd laughed a few times in his presence, and he'd basked in the music of her joy. He wanted to hear more of her laughter. It made him feel good inside, as if he'd given her a precious gift.

At the end of the meal, after the many toasts to the bride and groom, the queen stood. So did everyone else, producing a colorful wave of formal frock coats and gowns all the way down the long table. Henry stood with them and watched for his chance. As if fate had intervened on his behalf, the queen didn't wave her daughter to her side. Instead, she accepted the arm of the Grand Duke and let him escort her from the room. Henry imagined himself bolting the length of the room and intercepting Beatrice before anyone else could take her away from him.

He hastily excused himself from his dinner neighbors and worked his way up the room through the crowd, intent on the young woman in black who followed meekly behind the queen. Still at a distance, he lifted a hand and tried to signal Beatrice to wait for him, but she seemed unaware of anything in the room around her. His breath came quicker, his pulse sped up. He jostled aside two footmen blocking his way, frantic to reach her. He had no idea what to say to keep Beatrice in conversation but he felt compelled to talk with her again.

At last, Henry pressed between glittering couples immediately following behind the royal party. Some were heading out to their carriages, others upstairs to suites reserved for guests who had traveled great distances. He was nearly on top of the royal family, Beatrice just an arm's reach away. If she turned her head to the right she would see him. He stretched out his hand to tap her on the shoulder, his body electric with anticipation. But, at the very last moment, someone grabbed his arm and yanked him roughly to a stop.

"I say—" Henry protested, furious at the rude interruption.

But when he turned to confront his attacker, he found himself facing the Prince of Wales. "Your Royal Highness!" Henry swallowed back harsher words. This was Albert Edward, the queen's eldest son and the man who would become the king of England the day Victoria drew her last breath. All he had to do was outlive her.

"Spare me a moment, will you, Liko?"

Henry smiled at the Prince's use of his nickname, which set them on casually friendly terms. But then, a terrible thought rushed through his mind: What if the heir to the English throne had read his mind and was about to publicly chastise him for chasing after his baby sister?

"Of course, Bertie. What is it?" Out of the corner of his eye, he saw Beatrice moving farther away. Soon she would reach the staircase to the rooms above. He ached to break away, but the prince still held his sleeve in an urgent grip.

"I need your advice. I'm afraid I'm in a terrible fix." The prince's eyes darkened and flashed nervously around the room, as if he feared someone overhearing them.

Henry let go of the breath he'd been holding. Sadly, there would be no chance of speaking with Beatrice tonight. He glanced her way, one last time. She and the queen were already ascending the elegant curving staircase with funereal pomp.

Resigned to the change in plans, Henry gestured toward a door. "Let's step into the duke's study for privacy. I'm sure he won't mind."

Rather than reassure Bertie, this suggestion seemed to rattle him all the more. "No, no. Good lord, no, not in there." The Prince looked around them, eyes tight with panic, then keeping his voice low said, "The terrace."

They slipped through a short passageway lined with statuary, armor, and ancestral coats-of-arms, then back into the dining salon, now deserted except for staff—rushing about, clearing the table of silver, pewter and crystal, rolling up miles of damask tablecloth. No one spared Henry a glance when he snatched a brandy decanter and two glasses off a tray. Out through glass doors and onto the dark terrace he rushed in the wake of the Prince of Wales.

As soon as Henry had nudged shut the doors behind them, he turned to find Bertie lighting a cigar while pacing the stone pavers.

"What is it, Your Highness? Not more trouble from the Fenians, I hope, or another workers' revolt back home." So far, England had avoided the violent political uprisings that had plagued France, Germany, and many other European countries in recent years. But Henry knew the queen feared a revolution of the poor in her own country. And the Fenians, Irish separatists with a penchant for dynamiting London to make their point, hadn't given up their fight.

"No, no, thank God. Not any of *that* at least." The prince puffed on his cigar and strode up and down in front of Henry in agitation. "Listen, I would have gone to Louis for advice, but it's his wedding day and he likely has no mind for anything other than his bride."

"Of course." Henry despaired of having lost his chance to speak to Beatrice, but he felt flattered the prince had come to him for help. He set the two glasses on the stone wall, poured a brandy for himself and one for his royal companion. "Tell me what troubles you, my friend."

The Prince of Wales stood still long enough to accept a crystal snifter with a generous portion of the amber liquor. He took three fast swallows and rolled his eyes. "Vicky's father, the Grand Duke, is about to instigate a monumental social disaster."

Henry shook his head, at a loss. "He's not going to withdraw his blessing is he?"

"No, of course nothing like that. But in many ways, it's worse."

"I can't imagine—"

"He intends to announce his engagement to his Polish mistress tomorrow."

"Oh Lord." Now it was Henry's turn to take a fortifying gulp. He let the warmth of the brandy flow through him and settle low in his stomach before he spoke again. "The man must be mad."

"My mother didn't even know that he had a mistress until we came here. At least, I don't think she knew." Bertie chewed his bottom lip and turned abruptly to start pacing again, alternating worried cigar puffs with sips of his brandy. "The queen has this notion that my sister's widower should never again marry. After all, wasn't Alice the perfect mate? Isn't she irreplaceable? Why should her husband ever want another woman in his life after having had a royal princess and fathered seven children with her?" Bertie laughed. "Mother!"

"Oh dear." Henry took another, longer swallow of his brandy. Victoria terrified him even on her mildest days. And he wasn't alone. He'd come upon her own family members literally tiptoeing away through the garden at Windsor or hastily ducking out back doors when the queen was in a temper. Often, her most vile moods had been brought on by nothing more than a casual remark. The current situation was far more serious.

"I take it your mother will be furious at the very idea of the duke's involvement with the lady?"

"Mother will explode. She will take his behavior as a personal affront and betrayal of the family." Bertie knocked back the rest of his brandy and reached out a hand toward the decanter. Henry gave it to him. "The problem is this engagement. Alexandrine has been his mistress, I suspect, for many years, and she's here in Darmstadt now. The duke's besotted with her. He invited the woman to his daughter's wedding and intends, foolish man, to use the occasion to announce his betrothal to her."

Henry found it imperative to sit on the stone wall for support. He stared up at the full moon in the chill, black April sky. Anyone who had ever witnessed Victoria's ire or, worse yet, been the object of her temper, would know that tomorrow was bound to be a nightmare if the duke persisted in his plans.

"Have you spoken to the duke? Have you told him how poor his timing is?"

"I have, last night at the ball. And he won't listen to me. I told him, best to wait until the English contingent has returned to London. He says he is not ashamed to choose another wife and will do so despite anyone's disapproval—even the queen's."

"Then tomorrow will be a bloody awful day." Henry shook his head in despair. He had hoped for a peaceful few days following the wedding, when he could seek out Beatrice and spend more time with her.

"What do I do?" the Prince pleaded. "Can you think of anything at all I might do or say to lessen the scandal? You're such a sensible fellow, Liko."

Though flattered, Henry felt ill-suited to the job. "I don't know." He thought for a moment. "Perhaps all you can do is try to reduce the impact of the announcement."

"But how?"

Henry thought for a moment. "You must go to the queen tonight and tell her what the duke intends to do."

"Good God, no!" The prince leaned heavily on the wall, as if he'd collapse to the ground without its support. "Please, anything but that."

"All right then…what can you say about the woman, his mistress, to make her seem worthy of taking Alice's place?"

The prince laughed. "Liko, you must be kidding. She was married to a Russian before she took up with the duke. And you know how suspicious my mother is of *them*. On top of that, she's not royalty, and she's a divorced woman, and her reputation is, to say the least, highly questionable. It appears she's had a string of lovers." He shook his head. "I'll admit that Alexandrine is exquisite and charming, but that's likely to be held against her by my mother. In Victoria's mind, no one can ever replace Alice as the mother of her grandchildren."

"Then there's nothing more you can do other than warn your mother of what's to come, with the hope that foreknowledge will reduce the fireworks."

Bertie groaned.

"Listen, Your Highness, my brother's wedding, indeed the entire town of Darmstadt will be left in shambles if you allow events take their own course. If you can't stop the duke from publicly announcing his engagement and marrying the woman, all we can hope is to either postpone the announcement, at least until the queen has returned home, or prepare her for the inevitable. Those, as I see it, are your only two options."

Bertie tossed down his cigar and crushed its glowing end with the heel of his boot. "You honestly think that will do any good?"

"It must. Coming from you, her eldest son and heir to the throne, it will cushion the blow for her."

"But who will protect me from *her* blows? As the messenger, I'll be in direct line of fire." The prince's face turned an even lighter shade of pale. "You have no idea of the power of my mother's fury. No bloody idea!"

Another possibility suddenly struck Henry. Before he'd thought it through, he blurted out, "Enlist the aid of your sister, Beatrice."

Bertie choked on a laugh. "How is Baby going to help? My sister is the most helpless little soul. She does and says only what our mother commands."

"I expect she has more influence over the queen than you think." Henry remembered Beatrice's intelligent eyes and the spirit she'd revealed to him as they rode. "Let me go to your sister tonight. I will enlist Beatrice's help in this matter."

"Better I go, given the late hour." The prince lifted a heavy brow, meaningfully. "I doubt she'll even see you. I know her women would never let you in."

"No, no. You must return to the duke and try one more time to dissuade him from this madness. I will find a way to get word to Beatrice. Besides, coming from outside of the family, the news may be taken more seriously." He gripped the prince's arm in what he hoped was an encouraging way. "Between the three of us—you, me, and Beatrice—we may yet prevent disaster."

Bertie took another splash of brandy in his glass and raised it to his friend. "May God grant us the strength to endure this trial."

"Here, here." Henry drank with him, feeling an optimism their mission didn't merit. But all that really mattered to him was one jewel-bright thing—the Prince of Wales had given him an excuse and permission to see Beatrice.

8

Lady Marie Devereaux, Beatrice's lady-in-waiting, loosened the laces at the back of the princess's gown as they chatted about the day's exciting events. Beatrice had shared news of her secret ride with Henry, and Marie gasped at her daring, properly shocked and concerned for her safety. Which pleased Beatrice all the more. The idea of shocking anyone by her behavior was delicious.

At the unexpected knock on the door of her room, they looked at each other.

"Oh this is just too much." Beatrice sighed. "What can it be now?" It had taken her nearly an hour to settle her mother in her own bedchamber. Victoria had been so overexcited and stressed by the events of the day that her attending ladies—exhausted from dealing with her—had begged Beatrice to remain at her bedside and read the queen into a less agitated, drowsy state.

Marie frowned. "If it is your mother's lady-of-the-bedchamber come to fetch you, shall I tell her you are already asleep?"

It was a tempting lie. Just make herself not available to her mother's whims. But years of serving as the dutiful daughter proved a hard habit to break.

"No, it's all right. Get me out of this corset and into my dressing gown then see what she needs. At least I will be more comfortable for as long as the queen requires me."

Minutes later, a hushed conversation transpired between

her lady and whoever was on the other side of the door. Beatrice sensed something out of the ordinary. Instead of allowing her mother's lady to step inside, Marie physically blocked the doorway with her body. Beatrice caught a smattering of increasingly urgent and breathy words: "Quite inappropriate... no, surely another time...but Her Highness, *elle est déshabillée*!"

Beatrice scowled at the door. Why was the girl making such a fuss about her not being fully dressed?

Her lady firmly closed the door, leaned her back to it and turned to face the middle of the room. "*C'est un monsieur*, Your Highness. I have told him it is *non possible* for you to see him at this late hour as you have retired for the night."

"A gentleman?" If it had been one of her brothers Marie still might not have let him in, but her response certainly wouldn't have been as staunchly protective. And she would have mentioned his name. "Who was it?"

"One of the groom's brothers, I believe. The strangely named one: Liko. At least that is what I thought he said." The French woman's lips pinched in disapproval.

"Oh!" Beatrice's hand flew to her mouth to cover a wide smile. "But I wonder what he wants. It must be terribly important for him to come here at this hour, don't you think?"

Marie looked skeptical. "*C'est très mauvais pour votre réputation.*"

"Yes, very bad for my reputation, coming at night to my private chamber. You're absolutely right. But I'm sure Henry would never have come if it weren't an emergency." Beatrice slipped her arms into a silk dressing gown and hastily tied the satin ribbon around her waist. "However, I'm sure you'll agree that I can't greet him in the salon where anyone might wander through. Not at this hour. Do let him in."

"Mon dieu!" The young woman rolled her eyes. She turned and opened the door a crack, peering out as if she hoped the groom's brother had tired of waiting and left. Apparently he had not.

Henry Battenberg pushed wide the door, closing it quickly after himself, as if afraid someone might see him entering.

Beatrice took in his worried expression and the mysterious dark glint in his eyes, and immediately wanted to send Marie away to leave them in privacy. But staying alone in any room with a man, even had it been one of her brothers, even had they been in a much more public space than her privy chamber, invited scandal. Her lady was at least right on that count.

"Marie, *s'il vous plaît*, help me off with my jewels. Then see they are packed away safely for the night, while I have a few words with Herr Battenberg."

Marie gave her a side-long look that said she knew exactly what the princess was doing—keeping her busy and at a distance. The heavy, brass-strapped trunk where her jewels were kept had been pushed into a niche on the far side of the room, almost a tiny room of its own. Marie unclasped the pearl necklace at Beatrice's throat, slipped off her bracelets and rings, and disappeared to carry out her task.

Satisfied, Beatrice turned to her caller. "I hope nothing sad or terribly upsetting has brought you here, Henry."

"My news may not be bad from the perspective of some individuals, but it is certain to prove unsettling to the queen." Henry's manner, though strong and outwardly calm, still hinted at urgency.

"Oh dear." Beatrice's hands fluttered toward her chest and gripped the closure of her robe.

"I'm so sorry. I don't wish to distress you, Princess." He stepped forward, reaching out for her but stopping short of touching her arm. As if he, too, were aware of their delicate circumstances. "But I could think of no other way of handling the pandemonium that will almost surely occur tomorrow."

"You needn't apologize for coming to me. Please, go on," she said. Despite his alarming words, all she could think was how terribly, heart-breakingly handsome he looked, standing here facing her, not more than six feet from her bed. A naughty thrill rushed through her.

Henry looked away from her for a moment before turning back to meet her eyes. "Your brother came to me a short while ago. Bertie is most concerned, as he has learned that the Grand Duke intends to remarry."

Beatrice smiled. "Oh, but that's wonderful. My brother-in-law is such a good man and deserves to be happy. He has suffered so from the loss of my dear sister."

Henry visibly winced. "I don't think you understand, Your Highness." He took a deep breath and stepped closer to her, as if to insure she would be the only one to hear his words. "The duke seems to have had a mistress for some time now. It is *she* that he intends to marry. Moreover, he plans to publicly announce their engagement tomorrow at family breakfast."

She still couldn't quite understand why he looked so troubled, although this was more than a little irregular. "Is it that beautiful lady I saw in the church?"

"Yes. Her name is Alexandrine. She is Polish, and yes, very beautiful, but not…of…royal…blood."

Beatrice frowned at the seriousness of his expression. Clearly, joy wasn't the reaction he had expected from her. And now, slowly, she began to understand. Her mother, who cherished the memory of her daughter Alice, would never accept this woman. "I see. So you've come to warn me that tomorrow may be a time to steer clear of the queen?"

"On the contrary. I've come to beg you to intercede on your brother-in-law's behalf."

Beatrice bit down on her lower lip. "I'm confused. Henry, intercede in what way?"

"Bertie is even now trying to dissuade the duke from his folly. If he will only agree to keep the lady as his mistress and handle their affair discretely, then we shall all survive the next few days. But if the duke refuses to be sensible and insists upon marrying the woman—"

"You need say no more," Beatrice said. "I understand. At first I was thinking only of the duke's happiness. You're right. Mama will make a most terrible scene." Whatever joy these days of wedding celebration had brought to them all, it would surely be stifled under the virulent cloud of Victoria's fury. Heads might not literally roll. But lives would be changed. And likely, not for the better.

"But there is one thing I still don't understand," she whispered. "You say you've come to beg my help, but why? How can I do anything?" Standing so close to the young man, she became aware of his breathing, felt her own breath mystically alter to match his. She imagined their heartbeats taking up the same rhythm. Their thoughts running in parallel lines as they together took up the challenge of dealing with a family emergency. Her skin tingled in recognition of what Henry was telling her—he *needed* her. Perhaps not in a romantic way but as a co-conspirator of sorts, which seemed nearly as exciting and the most she could ever hope for.

"I believe with all my heart," Henry said, taking up her hands in his, "that you are the only person alive who can soften the blow for the queen. It is her feelings that Bertie is thinking of, I'm sure. Your brother believes this will be a terrible shock to Her Majesty. She may assume the duke has forgotten about her Alice. She must be convinced that the duke's wish to remarry *does not* dishonor her deceased daughter or the family."

"But what can *I* possibly –"

Henry leaned down over her, so near his warm breath swept across her cheek, so near the ribboned medals on his chest brushed the swell of her breast as he whispered in her ear. "Beatrice, no one is closer to the Queen than you. She will listen to you. You're the duke's only hope, even if he doesn't know it. He refuses to listen to reason, and so he will proceed with his foolish plan. All we can do to save his skin and my brother's wedding celebration is to soften the blow for Victoria."

Even as he continued speaking her head started involuntary shaking movements of denial. She'd spent all of her childhood, and her adult life to this very day, trying to avoid confrontations with her mother. He might as well ask her to step into a lioness's den without a weapon. He must be mad if he thought anything she could ever say or do would change her mother's mind. About anything!

Good lord, this wasn't as simple as the choice of a meal or deciding whether or not they should ride out across the Scottish moors in a chill rain. And she'd never once won either of those arguments.

Beatrice stared at the floor, working up the courage to tell Henry this was just not possible. He *must* seek help elsewhere. But then she felt him squeeze her hands and draw them up between them in a gesture of supplication. Startled she looked up into his kind eyes, as blue as Crown Jewel's star sapphire, as pleading as the gaze of a child.

"Please, dear Beatrice, do this for all of us. Not just for your brother-in-law. We had such a happy time today, didn't we? Riding together. And last night, dancing. I can't bear to see it spoiled."

His eyes, his touch and sincerity mesmerized her. "Oh yes. It was lovely. All of it." *Particularly, the kisses.*

"Nothing would make me happier than to ride with you again. But I fear if your mother is taken by surprise tomorrow at the duke's announcement of his engagement, she will order her party immediately back to London. And I will be robbed of the pleasure of spending more time with you."

Her knees suddenly felt spongy, her head floaty. He *liked* her. He wanted to be with her. She smiled at the thought. But how could he expect so much of her?

And yet it was obvious, from his earnest expression and the honesty of his words, that he actually believed she could influence her mother. He was betting on *her*, in a battle of wits and will with the Queen of England. He thought she, Beatrice, actually had a chance of prevailing.

How wonderfully sweet.

"Henry?"

"Yes?"

"I'll try. That's all I can promise."

He squeezed her hands again, and she felt the warmth of her blood traveling through her body. Giving her strength.

"She's asleep now," she said. "If I wake her, she will be up all night fretting, and we will all be the worse for it. I promise to go to her, first thing in the morning, and tell her of the duke's intentions. In the meantime, you must go to Bertie and have him impress upon my brother-in-law that he needs to delay his announcement for as long as possible. The more time she has to get used to this idea of his remarrying the better. If you can do that much, I will try to find distractions to keep her from dwelling on his plans."

Henry beamed at her. "Oh, you are a brave and clever girl." He shot a quick glance toward the alcove where Marie could be heard latching the trunk lid. He planted a chaste kiss on Beatrice's cheek then released her hands. "I go now to find Bertie and the duke. Send for me if you need me in the morning. And good luck."

He was across the room and out the door before she realized she probably should take a breath. Beatrice collapsed onto the tufted satin stool beside the four-poster bed. The room spun around her. She wasn't sure whether she was more terrified of confronting her mother with the shocking news, or of the feelings she was beginning to have when she thought of Henry Battenberg touching her. Kissing her.

9

Beatrice slept barely an hour the entire night. Tossing and turning, she imagined the various ways she might break the news to her mother that Alice's widower intended to remarry. She knew the way her mother's mind worked, and apparently so did Henry. The queen would take the duke's engagement as a sign of disrespect for her precious daughter's memory, a personal attack on her family.

Beatrice wished she might have an opportunity to speak with her brother-in-law before approaching her mother. But if Bertie had already failed at convincing the duke to wait for a less public moment to make his announcement then what were her chances of having any effect on the man?

"Your Highness, do you wish anything to eat now, or will you wait for family breakfast?"

Beatrice opened her eyes to find Marie standing over her bed, wearing a compassionate gaze. No doubt the woman had overheard most of her conversation with Henry the night before. Marie probably dreaded the day as much as she did.

"I certainly can't eat now. As to family breakfast, we shall see if I am able to choke down a bite or two."

Marie pursed her lips and lifted aside the coverlets for Beatrice to rise from bed. "Just because *un monsieur* asks the favor does not mean Her Highness must agree," she said.

Beatrice gave her lady-in-waiting a sideways glance. "I shall remember your advice. But now, you'd best get me dressed. I'll go straight to my mother and, hopefully, reach her with the news before anyone else does."

"*Oui*, Princess."

Beatrice accomplished her toilette in record time. She let Marie choose a day dress for her. As if reading her mind and hoping to lighten her mood, the young woman selected the least severe of her dark-colored dresses with a pretty ecru lace collar.

"I heard the queen's lady moving about next door moments ago," Marie said.

"Then we'd best hurry."

"I will accompany you of course."

"No," Beatrice said, "that isn't necessary. Better you stay behind in the room and wait for me to return. I expect I shall need your soothing words when this is all over."

Stepping up to the door that separated the two chambers, Beatrice drew a breath for courage and knocked lightly. The vibration of the wood against her knuckles felt almost painful. She swallowed, closed her eyes briefly, knocked again. Her mother's lady-of-the-bedchamber opened the door with a smile.

"Good morning, Your Highness. I hope you have slept... um, well?" The look she gave Beatrice said she had only then noticed the circles beneath her eyes.

"Not very well, but that's beside the point. Will you and the queen's other attendants leave my mother and me alone for just a few minutes?" The woman blinked at her, uncomprehending. "Please."

"Of course." The woman curtsied then efficiently cleared the room.

Beatrice stepped inside the queen's bedroom as gingerly as if the floor had been made of tissue paper, and she might fall through it at any moment. Her gaze turned to Victoria, seated at a dressing table. She was consulting a silver-backed hand-mirror, touching the string of pearls at her throat as if trying to decide whether they were too pretty for a still-mourning widow to wear.

She shifted her gaze upward to consult Beatrice's reflection in the mirror. "Is something wrong, my dear?"

"Not wrong, exactly." The words barely escaped her tight throat. "Some information has come to my attention. Happy news, actually." She might as well try to introduce the duke's plans in as positive a light as possible. "I thought you might want to hear about it before word got around to the Court."

"What news is this?" Victoria turned to fully face her but did not rise from her seat.

Beatrice took a hesitant step forward. "Mama, you know how very much I loved my sister Alice."

"Of course you did, my dear. We still do—as if she were here with us at this joyful time for her precious daughter." Already her mother's eyes glistened with emotion. Not a good sign.

Beatrice swallowed. Twice. "And I've come to love my brother-in-law, as I do my own dear brothers," she added. "The Duke is such a wonderful, deserving man. Is he not?"

Victoria's plump face wrinkled in puzzlement. "Yes, he is a good man, though not an angel. It troubles me, some of the things he does in his private life. But we will give him a good talking to, and I'm sure he'll come around." *The royal we, that is. Oh, dear, another bad sign.*

Beatrice pictured Henry's trusting gaze, drew a breath for strength, and took a leap of faith. "The thing of it is, Mama—as you yourself have so often stated—men are very different from women. Men think of love and romance in a less…" She paced the carpet, wishing the perfect word would come to her. "In a less *enduring* way. But that doesn't mean they are disrespectful of the memory of a beloved wife."

"What in heaven's name are you babbling on about, child?" Victoria's face flushed with irritation.

"I'm just trying to say that, often, when a gentleman is widowed, he chooses to remarry.

This happens all the time." She forced out the words, rushing for fear her mother would cut her off again. "And is it not better that a man remarry and be public about his affections than take as his company various ladies of poor reputation, thus invoking scandal, gossip, and ruin to his reputation, not to mention his family's—"

The queen rose to her feet, peering at Beatrice through narrowed eyes. Her regal chins trembled. "You are hiding something from me, child," Victoria accused. "Say what you mean and stop this stuttering and stalling."

"Of course, Mama," Beatrice murmured. "I was just trying to say—"

"Speak up, Baby! No wonder everyone thinks you clumsy and poor social company. Nobody can understand a word you say when you mumble so."

Beatrice lifted her chin and forced herself to meet her mother's turbulent glare. How her sisters had ever made a place for themselves in this world, despite the queen's attempts to control every aspect of their lives, she'd never know. Now that she was the only daughter still at home with their mother, every ounce of the queen's obsessive need to control her family had focused on her, the youngest child. The last princess.

Beatrice very nearly gave up delivering the news of the duke's intentions. But she'd promised Henry. She couldn't let him down. She just couldn't.

With an effort, she kept her voice calm. "What I'm trying to say to you, Mama, is meant to save you from grief. If you'll just give me a chance to shape the news in my own words, I believe you will be grateful to me."

Victoria raised an imperial brow. "I shall be the judge of whether or not to feel gratitude. Now out with it, girl."

Oh Lord, Beatrice thought, there's no hope now. But she plunged on.

"It has come to my attention that the grand duke intends to announce his engagement to the woman he invited to the wedding yesterday." She rushed to keep her mother from interrupting again. "Mama, the duke was a fine husband to my sister and has been a loving father to their children. He has deeply mourned Alice's passing for almost six years. Now he deserves some happiness. If he is in love with this woman and truly cares for her, isn't it a crime that they should be kept apart?"

There. She'd finished. Beatrice stood gasping for breath, her hands trembling while she clutched the folds of her skirt, her stomach cramping.

The queen stared at her, mouth agape, eyes as black as cinders.

Say something, Beatrice thought. *Please*. Silence as a response was worse than a wail of sorrow, cursing, or even a thrown vase.

Beatrice slid her tongue between dry lips. "Mama, I am sure he will ask for your blessing. As you so love your grandchildren, his and Alice's sweet children, it would be a kindness to him and to the children to accept this woman into the family. I am told she is gracious, and one only has to look at her to see her beauty. What a lovely addition to your Court in London she would make, and—"

"Enough!" The queen held up a hand, glowering at her. "We don't know where you heard such vicious, evil gossip. But we do not want it repeated in our hearing. The grand duke would never be so foolish as to think he could marry that whore. And he certainly can't expect me to ever speak to the woman, let alone accept her in my Court. She will never take my dear Alice's place. *Never* be allowed anywhere near Alice's children."

Beatrice clenched her hands until they ached. She must make her mother understand that she simply couldn't dominate and control everything and everyone in her life. "But, Mama, if it is already a *fait accompli*? If the duke is determined to proceed and announces their engagement this very day—"

"No!" Victoria roared, her face a mask of rage. "It is unthinkable. I said to leave it, Baby." She turned back to face the dressing table's mirror. "Prepare for family breakfast. I will hear nothing more of this matter. *Ever*."

10

Henry paced the corridor outside the breakfast room. This was to be a much more intimate meal than the wedding banquet—fewer than twenty-five at a cluster of round tables. Had Bertie not come begging him to intercede on behalf of the grand duke, he would have been looking forward to this meal as the perfect opportunity to spend time with Beatrice. Instead, all night long he'd worried about her.

Was he asking too much of the princess? He should have insisted on accompanying her to speak with the queen. How could he have thought to send the poor young woman in to that dragon, alone? Although he'd expressed great confidence in Bea's ability to help Victoria face the Duke's announcement with equanimity, he'd begun to have second thoughts the moment he left her room. Didn't foreign ministers tremble before the woman? Didn't courtiers blanch at the prospect of delivering bad news?

He turned and paced back the way he'd come and saw the Grand Duke of Hesse-Darmstadt approaching. Henry's heart very nearly stopped. The man's lovely mistress walked at his side, smiling, her hand resting on his arm. Apparently, they intended to make their announcement together. *Oh God!* This was far, far worse than he ever could have imagined.

Not waiting for the couple to reach him, Henry darted inside the breakfast room and straight to Bertie. The Duke of Wales was seated beside his wife Alix, at one of four tables meant to cozily accommodate the royal clan.

"He's here," Henry whispered, his voice hoarse. "And with the lady in question."

Bertie dropped his head into his hands. "Bollocks."

"What do we do?" Henry asked. "I see no sign yet of the queen or Beatrice. We don't even know if she's told her yet."

Bertie looked up at him. "My poor, poor little sister. She's eaten Bea alive."

Henry studied the prince for any signs of humor but saw none. "I should have offered to go with her. Maybe—" Dare he hope? "—maybe the Queen will be so angry she simply will not come down to breakfast."

The prince's eyes brightened. "That's possible. Yes. It's the best we can hope for. When my mother's upset she cloisters herself and refuses to speak to anyone. She might choose to simply ignore the duke's personal life, pretend he and it doesn't exist." Bertie took up his wife's hand between his two and kissed her fingertips lightly when she smiled questioningly at him. "It wouldn't be the first time she simply pretended whatever she found unpleasant didn't exist."

But it was not to be. Just then, the duke and his mistress entered through the same door Henry had rushed through moments earlier. At the same time, through another door at the opposite end of the room, Victoria arrived with her small retinue.

"Lord, help us," Bertie breathed, coming to his feet and holding out a hand to help his wife rise to greet the queen.

Henry gripped the back of the prince's chair and tried to appear poised and assertive. He looked around for Beatrice. To his surprise, she followed far behind her mother, head meekly lowered, lips set in a firm line, sad eyes trailing the floor. When no acceptable gentleman was at hand to escort the queen, Victoria nearly always rested a hand for support on her youngest daughter's arm as they walked companionably together. But this morning she had chosen one of her ladies as an escort, placing the princess in her wake as if to punish her.

Henry caught Beatrice's eyes for a brief moment and

tried to silently convey his apologies for subjecting her to such humiliation. Beatrice blinked once then looked away again. She seemed so sad he wanted to rush up to her, throw his arms around her and comfort her. She must be thinking that she'd let him down. But he'd never have blamed her, of course.

"Bloody hell," Bertie cursed under his breath. "There's nothing for it now but to wait for the fireworks, Liko. You, at least, are lucky. You've got the entire continent of Europe to hide in. I'm the one who must return to London with Mother."

The queen stopped at the largest table. On the far side of the room, the duke hesitated at the first table he reached, the one Henry would have chosen had he been in the queen's disfavor—closest to the door for an easy escape and farthest from Victoria. But after a moment the man straightened his shoulders, walked on and indicated a chair to his mistress at the queen's table.

Everyone remained standing at their seats, waiting for the Queen to give her permission for them to sit. After another minute, it became clear to Henry that Victoria had no intention of sitting while the duke's mistress remained in the room. The air vibrated with the electric tension that warns of a storm. As if the footmen spaced around the perimeter of the room sensed this too, they remained at attention, unmoving. No staff entered with food. Henry felt as if everyone in the room was posing in a formal tableau, waiting for an invisible painter to record the moment.

Sweat trickled down his back beneath his shirt. Henry tried to unlatch his clenched teeth, but the muscles in his jaw refused to release. Pain shot up through his jaw.

He was a military man. He'd experienced war. But facing an opponent on the field of battle had never torn at his nerves this fiercely.

Then, as though Victoria had summoned them by a silent act of will, two guardsmen entered the dining room.

"That woman," she said, "is unwelcome in our company. Remove her."

The duke pounded his fists down on the table, shot to his

feet and glowered at her. "Your Majesty!"

Victoria held up a hand. "This is a *family* breakfast. That woman is not now, nor ever will be, part of my family. Guard, escort her out of the castle."

A rustle of silk and choking sobs accompanied the duke's mistress from the room. The duke started to follow them, but then turned back again as if to say something more. After opening and closing his mouth twice, he seemed to think better of it and rushed after his mistress.

The queen took her seat with a satisfied sigh and lifted her hand to signal others that they might also sit. The rest of the company took to their chairs as if climbing out of icy water onto life-saving rafts.

Order restored, thought Henry.

Very little conversation accompanied the meal. Henry kept darting looks at Beatrice. She pushed food around on her plate, but he saw her eat very little. He glanced at Bertie, beside him; resignation darkened the prince's face.

"We tried," Henry whispered. "I really thought Beatrice had a chance."

"Poor Bea," Bertie murmured. "I fear we've made life even less pleasant for her. I should have known. If Mother wouldn't listen to me, the Crown Prince, who would she listen to?"

Henry shook his head. "I feel badly for having put Beatrice in this position."

Alix gave both men a reassuring smile, and he realized she must have picked up on most of the conversation. Maybe her husband had even informed her of what was going on. "It's nothing new to Bea, dealing with her mother's moods. Besides, the Queen will eventually forget that her daughter was in any way involved." The Danish princess spread clotted cream on her scone. "Her Majesty will take the Duke to task and demand that he put aside any relationship with the woman. Once that's done, Beatrice will be off the hook."

"But, Alix, what if the duke refuses to give up the woman?" Henry asked.

"He might, I suppose," Bertie said, eyeing the eggs and sausage a footman had brought him. "He claims he is in love with her. It may be she was his mistress even before Alice died. But of course no one would dare suggest such a thing to my mother."

Henry stared at his hands in his lap. There was nothing more he could do to aid Bertie or the duke. His only concern now was for Beatrice. "I must apologize to your sister. It's my fault for suggesting she play a role in this madness." He waited for a reaction from Bertie, but the prince seemed intent upon restoring his own frayed nerves with a hot meal; he began eating ravenously. "Is there anything you can suggest that I might do to cheer Beatrice?"

"Cheer up Baby?" Half a smile tweaked the prince's lips. "Don't bother yourself. It's her nature to be grim. A reflection of my mother's personality, I fear." He shrugged. "But, if you are determined to try, she loves nothing better than red flowers of any kind, and she does have a passion for riding."

Henry nodded his head. He'd already discovered the second of the two. *Then I will feed her passions*, he thought but didn't dare say.

As soon as the queen stood to leave, Henry timed his own exit from the breakfast room to reach Beatrice before she could follow her mother's entourage out the door. He offered her his arm, as if merely to escort her from the room. She barely glanced at him as she laid her hand on his arm. But when they came to the first crossing hallway he slipped his arm low around her waist, turned and guided her down the other corridor and away from the rest of the company.

Beatrice startled and stared up at him. "I'm expected to retire to my room, Henry."

"And if you do not?" He observed her solemnly.

"My mother will be all the angrier with me." She gave a deep sigh then laughed, but her eyes did not light up as they had when they'd been riding. "Although I'm not sure she could ever be any angrier than she is at this moment."

"Precisely," he said.

"So maybe it doesn't matter. Is that what you mean?"

"Yes. I just hate seeing you look so distressed. And I'm sorry that I put you in such a thorny position. I shouldn't have asked you to intervene."

"No, it's all right. I'm glad you did. I would have wanted to help." She lifted one shoulder in a half-shrug. "But I've let you down. I let the duke down. The right words just wouldn't come to me when I went to her this morning. She hardly let me say anything at all before she shut me out." She shook her head, and the gesture of helplessness tore at his heart. "I'm the one who should be apologizing to you, Henry. And to Alexandrine. All my words did was prepare Mama to *exert* herself at breakfast. How humiliating it must have been for that poor woman."

"You can't blame yourself for your mother's behavior." Henry patted Beatrice's hand, still resting on his coat sleeve. "I think you are incredibly brave, my dear princess. And caring. To stand by the queen so steadfastly...even though she doesn't value your loyalty."

"You don't understand her," Beatrice said, lowering her eyes to stare at her own hand, curled on his arm. "She's been so very lonely since Papa died. Her grief has been made all the worse by losing other people close to her. John Brown, such a brave companion and protector. Then Alice, and my brother Leopold, who was always so sickly. She has taken their deaths so very hard. Everything she does, these days, seems to be to protect herself and the family from further hurt. She must think the duke's mistress is an evil, designing woman, or she would never have treated her that way."

Henry studied her for a moment but kept them moving forward. "You give your mother a great deal of credit. I hope you're right and it's deserved."

"I've never believed it wasn't," Beatrice murmured, her voice so soft he barely made out the words. Maybe she hadn't intended him to hear her?

They walked in silence the length of the mirrored corridor.

He felt infinitely happier than he had a right to be. Just because she was beside him, her little hand resting on his sleeve. When they came to the end of the hall, Henry didn't know what to do. He didn't want to return Beatrice to her chamber, to be alone or, worse yet, to face another cruel scolding from her mother. He longed to protect her, yearned to find a way to make her smile again.

"The garden is lovely for so early in the spring," he said. "Will you stroll with me? And then, perhaps later in the day, we might venture out for another ride?"

"Just the two of us again?" Her pretty eyes widened in surprise.

"We did so before and no harm came to you." He grinned. "Of course if you'd rather have a chaperone, or bring others along, that's fine with me. Don't you trust me?"

"Oh, of course I trust you. It's just that—well, Mama doesn't approve of us girls being alone with a man. She says it's proper only for married couples to have that kind of privacy. Even a man and woman engaged, a chaperone is still correct."

"Then who shall be our chaperone?"

"I don't know." She let out a soft groan of frustration and pouted in a way he found sweetly appealing. "It's such a bother, isn't it? Always having to be around people one doesn't really enjoy being around."

"And am I a person you don't enjoy being around? Were you only being polite when we rode together yesterday?"

She blushed. "Oh no, Liko, I truly enjoyed being with you. Even now, I feel ever so much calmer than a few moments ago in that awful breakfast room. And I would love a walk in the gardens." She paused in thought. "Mama's so distracted by family events at the moment—first the wedding and now this business with the duke. And I believe she's received a few dispatches from the prime minister about troubling foreign affairs. I'm sure she wouldn't even notice if I were to disappear for a few hours."

"Then come with me and I'll show you the most beautiful early blooming red roses I have ever seen. I will cut an armful of them for you to take back to your room. To perfume your bedchamber and make you forget about this morning's unpleasantness."

"And will we ride later this afternoon too?" *There* was that sparkle in her eyes he'd wished for! And a rosy glow suffusing her cheeks.

"Only if you like, Princess. Shall I have the chief groom tack up the same mount you rode yesterday? We could ride directly after lunch."

"Oh, yes, please," she cried. "Red roses and a jolly canter across the heather and poppy fields. I can think of no more perfect day."

Henry grinned. Of all the women he'd ever known, none had been so easy to please. And, come to think of it, none so delightful to make the effort for.

11

Aberdeenshire, Scotland

"Release the dogs," Wilhelm ordered.

Gregory MacAlister gave a nod to his father's game warden who let loose the pack of gundogs for the fifth time that day. In an explosion of barking and snuffling the Springers took to the brush.

"You've already bagged eight stags and a brace of pheasants," Gregory reminded the Prussian prince. "It will be dark soon. Aren't you tired, Your Highness?"

"As long as there's game, I'm for the hunt." Wilhelm trod onward through the tall grass, intent on the kill.

Gregory shook his head, tucked his rifle under his arm, muzzle angled toward the ground, and followed along. "You might want to leave a few birds for another day."

If the prince heard him at all, he didn't show it. Gregory sighed in resignation. Wilhelm had arrived in Scotland three days earlier, and he still didn't know what had prompted the visit from his old school chum. He felt itchy with anticipation but knew from experience not to rush Wilhelm.

The dogs didn't take long to flush a dozen bronze-feathered grouse into the air with a frenzied clatter of wings. This time Gregory didn't bother to raise his rifle. He let the prince take down all but three of the birds and watched the survivors flutter free. *You're the clever ones,* he thought. They'd lain low a few extra seconds, taking to air only after the first shots were fired and the hunter was occupied with the first targets. He felt an affinity for them. *Cleverness, waiting your best chance, kept you alive.*

Wilhelm turned and scowled at him. "Why didn't you fire?"

"I'm all for a good hunt, but my father won't be pleased with our greed, depleting his stock as we've done today."

The prince shrugged. "I don't believe in doing anything by half measure. The laird should keep a better supply."

"If you find our Scottish game thin, why don't you just hunt in Germany?"

Wilhelm shrugged, flashed him a Cheshire-cat smile. "I wanted to visit my old friend."

"And I'm honored." Even without that telltale smile that had so often presaged mischief in their younger years, Gregory wouldn't have believed the young royal's trip was based on sentiment. Wilhelm was not the sentimental sort.

They'd reconnected just twice since their university days. The first time, the prince had offered Gregory asylum when the laird's son found it prudent to hide out after getting himself into legal hot water. Gregory had lost a game of cards to the son of his father's stable master but refused to honor his debt. The lad threatened him with a hay rake, forcing Gregory to pay up, embarrassing him in front of his gambling friends. Later that night, Gregory and two of his mates from the village jumped the boy. They might have killed him had the stable master himself not shown up and stopped them.

The other time, Wilhelm was the one who sought help. He had come with his parents to visit his grandmother Victoria, aunts, uncles and cousins at Balmoral, the British royal family's estate in Scotland. The young prince invited Gregory to come as his guest to the castle, and the two of them eavesdropped on the queen, spread rumors through the court, and generally amused themselves by making trouble. At first Gregory believed it was all purely for the sport. Only later did he recognize their pranks as a childish form of revenge against the queen for a remark she'd made about Wilhelm's withered arm.

So now, Gregory assumed his talent for clandestine pranks had brought Wilhelm back. The crown prince needed a favor—though what that might be Gregory had, as yet, no clue. Something done on the sly, possibly violent, most likely illegal. Fine by him. He owed Wilhelm for keeping him out of prison.

Finally, the servants carted the slaughtered game back to the MacAlister estate. The carcasses were turned over to the gamekeeper and kitchen staff. During the course of the day the two of them had killed more than the family and guests could possibly eat. But Gregory knew it wouldn't go to waste. His father was generous. He would see that the staff enjoyed a feast of their own. Any remainders would go to lucky villagers.

It wasn't until later that night, after Wilhelm had been entertained lavishly by Gregory's parents at a dinner in his honor, that the prince indicated he wished to speak to Gregory in private. They retreated to the old library, sat smoking and sipping a fine Monnot cognac. Although Wilhelm appeared relaxed, boot heels crossed carelessly upon the ebony table top, Gregory sensed something disturbing in the prince's attitude. His friend's sly, sinuous attitude suited the salamander printed on the vintage bottle.

Still, Gregory didn't press. At last his patience was rewarded.

"I have a job for you, *mein Freund*," Wilhelm said.

Gregory merely nodded. "I'm at your service as always, Your Highness."

"One of my English aunts is at risk of becoming an old maid."

Gregory burst out laughing. "Those are perhaps the last words I'd ever have predicted coming from your lips. How does this present a job for me? Am I to become matchmaker for the old biddy?"

"Not at all." Wilhelm studied the glowing ash at the end of his cigar. "I would like to see her with a man who has not only her best interests in mind but mine as well."

"And you think I might be able to find a suitable mate for her?"

"I think you might *be* a suitable mate for her."

Gregory choked on his shock, his eyes tearing up as coughing spasms turned to laughter. "You must be joking. I have no doubt who you're talking about. She's the only princess still available, is she not? Beatrice."

Wilhelm nodded his head gravely. "Yes, Beatrice. You know her then."

"I've seen her a few times with her mother, coming and going from Balmoral. Even from a distance she seems quite plain and...unappealing."

"If she were *appealing*," Wilhelm snapped, "don't you think she'd be wed by now? She's the daughter of the Queen of England, for God's sake! Anyone who weds and beds her, in either order, will be set for life." He seemed to realize he'd been shouting and quieted his voice though his face remained flushed. "I wouldn't have come all this way to ask you this favor if it were so easy anyone could do it. I'm here because I believe you are uniquely qualified."

Gregory stared at Wilhelm in astonished disbelief. "I'm the third son of a minor baron. I have no money of my own. And not even my own mother would recommend me as husband to a princess. How does this qualify me?"

"Stand up," Wilhelm demanded.

Gregory rolled his eyes, ground out his cigar in the crystal ashtray on the butler table beside his chair, and rose to his feet. He felt like a schoolboy called to task by his headmaster. Propping fists on his hips he stared down at his royal friend. "Well?"

"When I look at you, do you know what I see?"

Gregory laughed. "A penniless nobleman?" Having to humor Wilhelm was beginning to irritate him.

"Not at all. I see a young Scot who looks remarkably like the old Queen's dear, dead companion, John Brown. You could be his son, you know. The features are all there. Similar height. If your hair were a little redder in color, the resemblance would be startlingly obvious to anyone."

Now he was just confused. "And how does this make me of

value to you, Your Highness?"

Wilhelm pulled so hard on his cigar, its tip glowed like a fire opal. He rested his head back, eyes closed, savoring the pungent smoke—the picture of contentment. "I need a man inside the queen's palace. Someone loyal to me, but also someone who can win the queen's trust."

"And I'm supposed to be…what? The reincarnation of Brown?" Gregory shook his head. "You're out of your mind." It was only after the too-casual words had passed his lips that he realized the thinness of the ice upon which he was skating.

Wilhelm's eyes flared with dark fury and kicked out viciously with one boot, barely missing Gregory's knee. "Our friendship will buy you only so much. Do not presume that my patience is unlimited."

Gregory fell back a step as if he'd actually been struck. He had forgotten how volatile the prince could be; his rage was legend. "I meant nothing by it, Your Highness. I spoke without thinking. You know you can count on me. Please, just tell me what you would have me do."

Wilhelm settled back into the soft leather of his chair. "It seems to me, with the smallest effort, you might win over the trust, perhaps even the heart of my dear Aunt Beatrice. Emphasize your brogue. Take to wearing your clan tartans. Use a little of that charm I recall you so easily employing on the *frauleins*."

Gregory returned to his chair. "But such a prank if discovered—"

The prince put up his hand before he could say another word. "You think wooing the princess is treasonous? No, that's too strong a word. Neither is it a childish prank. This is a serious strategy to improve my dear aunt's life and, by the by, mine as well. There is a purpose to my request, if you will permit me to explain."

Gregory didn't like the spark of excitement in those pale eyes. But he kept his expression neutral, leaned forward, forearms braced on his thighs in a posture of rapt attention.

"Bismarck," the prince began, "believes I should do more to understand my grandmother's political philosophy, as well as gain early knowledge of any decisions she may make that will impact upon Germany and Prussia. My time as monarch is fast approaching. The emperor, my grandfather, might as well be in his grave. My father is ill and unlikely to remain on the throne for more than a year before the cancer takes him."

"My sympathies, Your Highness."

Wilhelm waved him off. "Let us not be maudlin. Their departure is all to the good, as far as I'm concerned. The sooner they leave this world, the quicker I take my rightful place as emperor. And I have plans, Gregory. Grand and glorious plans for my empire."

Gregory felt a chill descend his spine, a slow trickle of ice water, and yet he was beginning to catch the prince's enthusiasm. "Go on, Your Highness."

"Bismarck believes that Britain will stand in the way of my plans, if I do not bring her to heel. I must have England as my ally."

"Then why do you not simply ask your grandmother to stand by you in return for your promise to do the same for her? A simple alliance within the family." It seemed reasonable to him.

"If only it were that easy. Victoria hates me, but no more than I despise her. Even if I could force myself to grovel to the old woman, I doubt she ever will take my side in a serious dispute over borders or sovereignty. Unless I somehow get the upper hand over her."

"But you're her grandson, her *first* grandson, and surely all the more precious to her. Are you sure you aren't imagining—"

The prince cut him off with a furious slash of his withered arm. "The queen has said to my face that she doesn't trust me. So I must either change her mind—difficult if not impossible—or I must *know* her mind before she makes a move against me. That means I need someone inside Buckingham Palace who is physically close to her but loyal only to me."

"A spy."

"Exactly. Ideally, my man should be someone inside the family—all the better to learn her mind. And that is why I need to find a husband for the last princess."

The idea intrigued Gregory. He wasn't convinced it was possible, but he was growing excited at the challenge. "And if I were to succeed in wooing the old maid?"

"It doesn't take a genius to foresee the vast rewards," Wilhelm said. "Victoria may be as cold as a Siberian winter, and dangerous, to me and those who cross her. But for the most part, she looks after her own. Any man who marries her youngest daughter will have land, a title, and need not lift a finger to support himself for the rest of his life. Added to that, he will have my gratitude and generous financial compensation."

Gregory tipped his head to one side, considering. "You make it sound easy. As if you really believe it could be done."

The prince studied the ash about to drop from his cigar. A smile edged up the corners of his lips beneath his trim mustache. "How many young girls did you seduce when we were at university? I expect you lost count. I never saw you fail."

"Ah, but—a young virgin is eager to be plucked. An *old* virgin is resigned to her status." Gregory sighed and sat back in his seat, drumming his fingers on his crooked knee. It was admittedly a pretty daydream. He, the wastrel third son everyone said would never make good, moving into the queen's palace in London. But there were so many ways the prince's plot could go wrong. "Have you ever thought, Your Highness, that Princess Beatrice might not *want* to marry?"

"Then it will be your task to change her mind. Convince her she's desirable. Whisper sweet words in her ear. If my aunt wants to escape her life as Victoria's enslaved companion badly enough, and if you charm the old Queen by reminding her of her precious John Brown, you cannot fail."

"Seduce the princess and make my fortune," Gregory mused.

"Are you game?"

Gregory tapped the rim of his cognac glass. The fine crystal rang. "Why the hell not?" His prospects, it seemed, were looking up.

12

Buckingham Palace, London

"They're *both* coming for a visit? Oh, Marie, I can't wait!" Beatrice thrilled to the news of her sisters' visit. It had been too long. Miserable weeks of rain and gray skies. Boring weeks since the excitement of the wedding. "Mama says Louise and Helena should arrive sometime this afternoon. Isn't it wonderful?"

"A family is to be cherished," Lady Devereaux murmured. She brought Beatrice her sensible black leather shoes to go with her dour might-as-well-be-black dress. "Sisters are the most precious of all. I'm so glad you have them in your life, Your Highness."

Beatrice thought she caught a wistful tone in the woman's voice, but before she could ask if anything was wrong, she became swept up in making plans for Louise and Helena's stay. Maybe they would go shopping together—a rare treat—or spend a few blissful hours browsing through the newest selections at her favorite bookstore in Kensington? Louise's American friend Stephen Byrne had mentioned a new book he'd enjoyed by a Mr. Mark Twain, *The Prince and the Pauper*. He'd called it "most entertaining." And hadn't that other young writer, Robert Louis Stevenson, recently published a new adventure? She'd adored his exotic adventure, *Treasure Island*. If she couldn't have her own adventures, at least, through books, she might imagine daring escapades in distant lands.

No matter what she and her sisters did together, it would be a marvelous relief from the routine of Court. These days, she saw too little of any of her sisters. One by one, they had escaped the Court and their mother's iron-willed dominance over their lives. Each of the elder daughters had found her own path toward making a life for herself. Baby being the sole exception. And yet Beatrice held neither their freedom, nor her own captivity, against them.

Crown Princess Vicky, the eldest English royal daughter—incurably bossy but dear to her nonetheless—had wed Fritz, the Prussian crown prince. He would likely become the Emperor of the vast German-Prussian empire any day now, as his father was frail and sickly, making Vicky an empress. They had eight children, and their first son, Wilhelm (Willy to the family) was now in his twenties. Although a troubled child, Beatrice had hopes he would outgrow his temper and obstinate nature. He would naturally be the next one to follow in his father's footsteps and wear the crown. She hoped for his mother's sake, and his country's, that he would have matured, and his temper mellowed, before he came to real power. She remembered him torturing insects, plucking off their wings and laughing as they crawled helplessly about, before he gleefully squashed them. She suspected his cruelty had found other victims in the higher life forms.

Alice, mother to the recent bride, came next of the five girls in the English royal family. Beatrice had adored and looked up to her second eldest sister, who had gently mothered her when their own mother was too busy with affairs of state. Married to the Grand Duke Louis IV of Hesse-Darmstadt, Alice had given birth to seven children. She still missed Alice with an aching sorrow, but tried to fill the void by corresponding regularly with her sister's children.

Then there was Helena, nicknamed Lenchen, married to His Serene Highness Christian of Schleswig-Holstein-Sonderberg-Augustenburg, with five children and possibly more to come. Helena spoke little, and only in serious tones, of her marriage. Which made Beatrice wonder if she was truly happy. Nevertheless, the match was considered a success by their mother, who seemed to have her own gauge for measuring marital harmony.

Finally, closest to her own age, came her sister Louise, wife to John Campbell, 9th Duke of Argyll, called Lorne by those close to him. How she would have loved to travel with Louise to see the wilds of the vast North American continent while Lorne was the Governor General of Canada. But of course, her mother wouldn't hear of it. Too dangerous, she said. Too distant for Baby. For years she'd believed that her mother's extreme measures to protect her meant she was specially loved. Now she wondered just how much of the queen's mother-bear tactics were self-serving.

But Beatrice refused to think ugly thoughts of any kind today. She loved her mother, and she cherished each and every one of her sisters. If she occasionally envied them their independent lives, she quickly reminded herself to be thankful for the little treasures in her own existence.

Red roses. A reckless horseback ride across a field of blooming wildflowers. A stolen kiss by a prince. She tingled, fingertips to toes, at the memory.

As Marie helped her dress for her sisters' arrival, Beatrice let her gaze wander to the small stack of letters bound with a thin blue ribbon, lying on her dressing table. Henry's letters. Another treasure. She let out a little whimper of pleasure.

"Sorry. Have I laced your corset too tight?" Marie asked.

"No, it's fine. Mama thinks I should wear it as constricted as possible." She gave a dry laugh. "She likes her girls slim, even if she is not."

Marie clucked her tongue in mild disapproval. "Now, now. The queen is a matron in years and allowed a bit more padding, as they say. You are too young for the matronly figure, Your Highness."

"Am I?" *Does it matter?*

"Of course. Your young prince from Darmstadt, I think he

will come for you and be pleased with your *belle figure.*"

Beatrice felt a flutter in her heart. Again the letters called to her. "Do you know, until my niece's wedding, I thought it the most natural thing in the world to spend the rest of my life as my mother's companion and secretary. To never marry."

"You had no curiosity for boys as the *jeune fille?*"

"As a young girl or even as I grew older. No, not really." She sucked in her breath to let Marie cinch her waist in another inch. "I was terrified of the mustachioed, gruff old men who came to my mother's office to discuss politics. Marry one of them? Never. And whenever I brought up questions about married life or having babies, the queen complained about the pain and humiliation of giving birth and how much trouble children were." Beatrice gasped. "There, that's tight enough, or I shan't be able to eat a bite."

Marie spared her a fraction of an inch then tied off the laces. "*Meilleur?*"

"Yes, much better. Thank you. Anyway, Mama once told me she sometimes wished she'd had no children at all, as hers no longer appreciated her. Can you imagine, telling your own daughter that you wished her and her brothers and sisters never born?"

"I'm certain Her Majesty was not serious."

"Well, I'm sure she *was* serious." In fact, rather than being offended, Beatrice had felt so sorry for her mother she'd tried to make up for the lack of attention her siblings paid their mother by being all the more attentive herself.

The trouble was, tied to her mother as she was, even the company of the ladies and gentlemen of the Court did little to cure her loneliness. In fact, watching the ways they complimented, flirted, and competed with each other made her feel all the more left out. She became even more aware of the special courtesies and the looks men gave attractive women. But never, ever gave her.

"Do you know, Marie," she said, lifting her arms to slip into her daydress, "just once in my life I wish someone would say of me: 'That Beatrice, she is *the belle of the ball…a prima donna…* or, *the toast of the town.*'" She sighed. "I wonder what it's like to be beautiful, or just to be thought of as beautiful by just one person. I would surrender ten years of my life to feel that special."

Marie was clucking again. "*Mais non*, Princess, you *are* a beautiful person. In your heart, in your soul…and when you smile, I see a—"

"Stop, Marie." Beatrice spun around to face her lady-in-waiting. Marie with her heart-shaped face and delicate dark curls and lush French accent that attracted men as honeycombs lure bears up the tallest trees. "You're just being kind. I know what I am." There was no escaping what she saw in the mirror each and every day. She looked old for her years. Drab. And her conversation was awkward and mundane. To deny these things was to deceive herself.

And yet, there had been Henry—a true cavalier, who had seemed to honestly enjoy her company. When she had been with him—on the ballroom floor or riding out across the fields—she at least *felt* beautiful, even if no one else saw her that way.

In the days following the wedding, before her mother ordered her reduced retinue away from Darmstadt and back to London, Beatrice and Henry had found opportunities to leave the crowd and go off by themselves. He had behaved as the perfect gentleman—except for those times when he stole another kiss or two, which had thoroughly delighted her. He dressed smartly, rode as though the devil was at his back, asked her opinion on all manner of things, and admired her sketches of the castle. His blue eyes snatched at her heart every time he looked her way. She wanted to be near him more than she'd ever wanted anything in her whole life. And yet she dared not hope that he would feel the same about her.

Until his letters started coming.

And then…and *then*, she'd discovered a breathtakingly beautiful lacework of hope stitched around and through his penned words.

She intended to show the letters, particularly his most recent one, to Helena and Louise when they arrived at Buckingham. She must ask them, as women who had actual experience with men, what she should think of them. Would they hear in Henry's words what Beatrice believed she heard? Was he telling her in his own quiet way that he cared for her? Was it possible he wanted her in his life the same way she wanted him?

Or…was she being naïve and foolish?

A knock sounded at her door. Marie answered it, whispered a few words then returned just as Beatrice finished clasping her favorite gold charm bracelet around her wrist.

"They have arrived early," Marie said. "Your mother is napping but the princesses wait for you in the Blue Salon."

"Wonderful!" Beatrice cried, leaping up from her dressing stool.

~

The happy chatter of voices greeted Beatrice as she approached the doorway to the room that had long been one of her favorites in the entire palace. Helena sat on a gilded divan with the second youngest of her children. Louise walked up and down in front of the expansive windows overlooking the sunny park, cuddling and cooing to the baby in her arms.

Of the four married sisters, only Louise had produced no children. It wasn't clear to Beatrice why this was. Perhaps, as their mother had once vaguely suggested, some physical complication, resulting from Louise's high-strung nature, kept her from conceiving. But whatever the reason, it was clear that Louise loved children, and she thoroughly enjoyed spoiling her nieces and nephews.

"Oh, there she is!" Helena cried. "And not in the same room with Mama. What a shock!"

Louise cast Beatrice an apologetic look. "Don't be cruel, Lenchen. Poor Bea so rarely enjoys time on her own." She tipped her head toward the letters in Beatrice's hand. "Has she got you

81

answering her correspondence even while she's off napping?"

It was the perfect introduction to the conversation she'd hoped for. "No, these are my letters, actually. I'm not exactly sure how to respond to the writer and thought you and Lenchen might help me out."

"Help in what way?" Helena asked, sounding impatient with her already. "If it's an invitation to a social occasion, you always turn them down anyway—no matter what we advise." She looked up at Louise "I don't know why Baby doesn't just hang a sign around her neck: *Go away, don't bother me!*" She laughed, but looked mildly contrite at Louise's glare. "I'm sorry, Baby, but no matter what I do, or who I've tried to introduce you to, you always crawl into your little shell and insist upon playing the wallflower."

Not always, Beatrice thought to herself.

She rather enjoyed recalling her secret assignations with Henry, and keeping them to herself. Cherished moments, unblemished by others' criticism. But sooner or later, if she wanted to do anything more than flirt with the handsome young prince, she'd have to tell someone. It might as well be Helena and Louise. And now.

"Please sit down, Louise. I want to read this letter to the two of you and see what you think." When neither of her sisters said anything, and Helena only let out a bored sigh, Beatrice looked pleadingly at Louise. "I'm serious. This is important to me. Something very special happened to me in Germany. I believe it may have changed my life."

Helena hooted with laughter. "Oh, my! That does sound dramatic, doesn't it, Loosie?" She set her toddler on the carpet in front of her to play, and rubbed her hands together as if eager for a tasty meal. "By all means, let's hear this most extraordinary letter."

Louise propped the baby on her hip and sat on the far end of the divan, allowing her little niece to teethe on her finger. Louise lifted her chin in an encouraging gesture to Beatrice. "Go on then, dear. Read."

Beatrice sat in an upholstered chair opposite her sisters, cleared her throat, and tenderly unfolded Henry's most recent letter in her lap. "Just so you'll know, this comes from a gentleman." She thrilled at the very words. Before either of her listeners could comment on that shocking bit, she started reading:

"'Dearest Beatrice...'"

Helena let out a soft sound of surprise at the implied intimacy.

Louise's eyes widened. Just a little—but then, it took a lot to shock Louise.

Beatrice tried to ignore them and keep her gaze fixed on the masculine spikes of black ink across the page, feeling the strength of Henry's presence in his words.

"'I believe,'" she read, "'you know how much I enjoyed the time we spent together during my brother's recent wedding celebration in Darmstadt. When I told you that I'd rarely felt so deeply moved by a young woman's company, that wasn't the entire truth. In fact, I've *never* felt so close to anyone of the opposite sex. There always has seemed a barrier or a competitive aspect in my relationships with females, which stood in the way of true friendship. And friends are what we have become—you and I. I hope you will agree with at least that much.'"

Beatrice felt the beginnings of happy tears tickle the outer corners of her eyes. How many times had she reread these delicious words? And yet they moved her on every visit.

"He goes on to say this: 'Now I dare to suggest making of our friendship something more permanent and precious. I could not speak from my heart while you were in Germany with your mother, because of the Grand Duke's announcement, which had been so stressful for her. I knew that I needed to hold back, to wait until she returned to London and recovered from the shock. To add to her concerns would have been selfish on my part. Aside from that, I feared her response to my proposal might be too hastily made and not in my favor. These weeks while we have been apart have served not only to strengthen my resolve to have you in my life but also, I hope, to soothe your mother so that she might wisely and impartially consider my proposition.'"

Beatrice sneaked a quick peek at Louise, needing to see her reaction. But her sister's expression remained closed, revealing nothing. Beatrice felt as if she might burst with excitement, but reminded herself that she was inexperienced in the ways of men, and words like *proposal* and *proposition* might have meanings beyond her understanding. It sometimes seemed to her that her mother's courtiers spoke in riddles when flirting with her ladies. Was that what Henry was doing here? Playing word games?

"Baby," Helena said, with a nervous laugh. "This can't possibly be—"

"Hush," Louise said. "Let her finish."

Beatrice read on. "Then he says, 'You see, even now, I have trouble coming to the point, my darling.'" *He'd called her darling!* "'I would make a pretty speech on bended knee before you, but because you are who you are—daughter to the Queen of England—I know I must first ask your mother's permission to even hope. Then all must be arranged through her. But I will not appear before her until I have your permission to do so.'" Beatrice took a deep breath, not daring to look at either of her sisters now.

"But this is—" Helena began again.

"Shut up, Lenchen!" Louise snapped. "She obviously has more."

Beatrice took a shaky breath. She wondered if her heart had ever beat faster than it did now. "Yes, and he goes on to say... 'I ask these questions of you, dearest girl. First, do you feel as I do? Secondly if so, do you believe the time is right for me to come to London and ask the queen for her blessing?

"'All depends upon you, my darling Beatrice. Please tell me I have not given my heart in vain. Please tell me I may come and make my intentions... *our* intentions known to your mother. The moment I hear from you I will begin my journey. I wait for your response, my dove.

All my love, Henry Battenberg.'"

Beatrice held her breath, eyes brimming with tears of joy but still afraid to believe. Was this a proposal of marriage, or was it not? She stared at Henry's sweeping signature. Traced his name with her fingertip, aware of the utter and absolute silence of the room. Her heart pounded in her breast so that she wondered why the salon's walls didn't reverberate in response. At last she looked up at her sisters, still seated across from her, and blinked away the wash of tears.

"Well," Helena said, "that *is* a surprise."

"But a delightful one!" Louise cried. She shot to her feet, plopped her little niece in Helena's lap and rushed across the room to pull Beatrice up and into an embrace. "And do you love him? Above all, do you love him, Bea?"

"I think… Yes, yes I really do." She laughed out loud. "He is such a sweet man. Such a wonderful, warm, safe feeling man. But exciting too! We enjoyed each other's company. I do think he is absolutely perfect for me. It's as if no man ever before or will ever again be as right for me as Henry Battenberg."

"Oh, bosh!" Helena groaned. "Is *that* what you think marriage is about? All romance and cuddles? Well, let me tell you—no man is perfect. The sooner you realize that the better. All you can do is to hope that you get one who doesn't beat you or the children, who will give you a little of his time now and then but otherwise leave you in peace."

Louise glared at her. "Do shut up, Lenchen. Why spoil the dream for the girl? If she's in love, let her enjoy being in love. It's a difficult enough world without you or Mama crushing whatever little happiness we can find in our lives."

Beatrice watched Helena pout and bounce the baby on her lap, while her older child tugged at her skirts for attention. But Helena wasn't done with her.

"The problem is," she said, "can you trust this man? I'm sure we'd all like to believe he's sincere."

"Lenchen, please—"

"I'm just being protective of my little sister, Louise. Don't berate me for caring about her happiness and warning her. I mean, how well do any of us really know this Henry Battenberg? His brother once made overtures toward Beatrice then backed off. Maybe Henry will do the same. I don't want to see her heart broken again."

Beatrice winced. Was that possible? Henry might not honestly and deeply enough care about her to stay interested for more than a few weeks or months?

"Neither do I wish to see her hurt," Louise said calmly. "But let's not assume the worst. Liko clearly has thought this through. He has timed his proposal—and it certainly seems to be that—hoping for a positive response. And he's even asked Beatrice first, rather than putting her in an awkward position in front of Mama." Louise released her embrace, took Beatrice's shoulders between her hands and moved her slightly away to better look her in the eyes. "The question is, how do you feel about all of this, Bea? Do you really and truly love him? Is marriage what you want?"

"I know it would mean making many changes in my life," Beatrice said. "Some, I'm sure I will like very much. Others make me a little nervous, or even afraid."

"As well you should be," Helena huffed. "Can you imagine what Mama will say to this Henry if he actually pleads his case for marriage to Baby? Why, she'll go through the roof. She'll never allow it. Never in a million years."

Louise stamped her foot at her sister. "Stop that, Lenchen! If you and I have the right to marry, then Bea ought to be allowed to have her own life, her own husband, her own family. She shouldn't be deprived simply because she's the last girl in the family, or because having her here to care for Mama is a convenience to us, her brothers and sisters."

Helena stared at her, open mouthed. "A convenience? You make it sound as if we're all so careless of her feelings. As if we're *using* Beatrice. That's not it at all."

"Oh yes it is," Beatrice snapped before she could stop herself. She cast her eyes down at the lush Persian carpet beneath her feet. "Louise is right. As long as I'm here, providing Mama with constant companionship, serving as her helpmate, she pretty much leaves the rest of you alone. All you have to do is visit now and then, like this, for a few days or weeks out of each year. You can then go on with your own lives. *I* am the one who has stayed and taken up the burden of her happiness. *I* am the one who will always be alone." She couldn't stop a sob from working its way up through her throat.

Louise put an arm around her. "No. You don't have to always be alone. Love will find a way; it always does. Mama will have to give in if you are persistent. If Henry pleads his case well, and you insist upon having him, she will give her blessing. Eventually."

"So sayeth the Almighty Louise!" Helena burst out bitterly. She was jiggling the baby on her knee so violently the child's teeth would have been chattering, had she any. "Can you claim your own marriage has been in every way fulfilling?" She rolled her eyes when Louise didn't immediately answer. "I thought not. We've all heard the rumors about your husband and his dirty little escapades with young m—"

"Enough!" Louise shouted, blushing furiously.

"The point is—Bea could go to all sorts of trouble, destroy her relationship with Mama over this man, break both her own and Mama's hearts...and for what? She has everything here at the palace she could possibly need."

"Everything," Beatrice said, "except a family of my own. Except happiness."

"And sexual fulfillment." Louise crossed her arms over her chest and raised a single eyebrow meaningfully at Helena. "Let's not forget that delightful benefit of producing a family."

Helena made a disgusted face. "Louise, please. You don't have to use such filthy language."

"*You* were the one who brought up sexual preferences."

"Please, sisters, don't let's argue," Beatrice pleaded. "I'm desperate. I need your help. What do I *say* to him? I do love Henry, I'm sure of it. I'm just so very afraid of what Mama will do to the poor man if he comes to claim me."

Helena looked as if she was going to say something more, but Louise shot her a final glance, sharp as a Scottish dirk. "Tell

Henry that you return his love," Louise said, "if that's how you feel. Encourage him to come for you. Two are always better than one when it comes to confronting Mama."

"An *armed battalion* is more like it," Helena muttered.

Louise ignored her. "In the meantime, for I'm sure it will take him a week or more to make arrangements for the trip, talk to her. Tell her that you want to marry Henry Battenberg. If big brother Louis was good enough for her beloved granddaughter, Henry is good enough for you."

"I don't know," Beatrice sighed.

Louise put an arm around her. "Of course, she'll be all bluster and denial at first. That's just the way she is. She didn't really want Helena or me to marry, not after losing Vicky and Alice to foreign husbands."

"It's true," Helena added, sounding less combative now that things had been decided. "Something changed in her after Papa died. She suddenly decided she had to protect us from men, or some such crazy notion."

"You can't let her stop you from being happy, Bea," Louise said.

"I don't know that I can be that brave," Beatrice whispered. Even now she could feel her stomach souring, and one of her attacks of raspy breathing coming on. "I'm not as strong as you, Louise. If Mama doesn't want me to marry there will be little I can do to change her mind."

"We'll see about that," Louise said firmly. "When you are ready to speak to her, I will go with you if you like." She pulled a lace-edged handkerchief from the sleeve of her blouse and blotted the tears that had pooled beneath Beatrice's eyes. "Now write to your sweet Henry and tell him what is in your heart."

13

Before Gregory left for London, he needed to tackle one final matter back home in Scotland. Her name was Margaret Graham.

He'd visit his voluptuous, red-tressed mistress at her father's cottage. After enjoying her generous company for a few hours while the men were in the fields, he would break the news to her of his upcoming absence. He'd give her as little real information as possible—he was off to make his fortune, to provide for the future for both of them, he'd say—but reassure her he would soon return for her. After all, what if Wilhelm's crazy plan didn't work? Then he'd be back where he'd started, in Aberdeenshire, but without the pleasure of the most beautiful woman in the shire. For he never doubted Meggie would find herself another man if she suspected he'd left forever.

He collected his horse from the stables of the manor house that had been in his family for generations. He rode the three miles down the hillside, into the vale. It was a glorious day, as stunning as any he'd known in the Highlands. Rusty-brown dirt fields basking in the sunlight, crops beginning to sprout, spring flowers a riot of color amongst the yellow-green virgin grass, a sky as blue as a songbird's melody is sweet. Nothing about it foretold anything but good fortune.

When he arrived at Frank Graham's cottage on the usual day of his trysts with the farmer's daughter—Meggie wasn't waiting outside for him on the stoop. Puzzled by this, he left his horse, mounted the slab-granite steps worn hollow in the middle by a hundred years of footfalls, and pushed on the plank door. It didn't budge. He knocked.

"Who is it?" Meggie sang out, far too sweetly.

He scowled. "You know damn well who it is, girl." If anyone else had been at home, he was sure they would have called out to him. Why this sudden coyness? He put his shoulder to the splintery wood and, forcing the rusty latch, shoved his way inside. "What's going on, Meg?"

She sat at the rough-hewn oak table in the middle of the room, a candle burning on a chipped saucer at its center, sending shimmers of gold through her thick mane. In her cupped hands she held a mug. He smelled whisky.

She raised her drink to him as if in a toast as he stepped through the doorway and into the room. "Come to say goodbye, have ye, love?"

Startled, he hesitated. This presented him with a dilemma.

Until this moment, he had said nothing to Meg or anyone else about his plans. How she'd discovered he was leaving he had no idea. Gregory suddenly felt the need for caution. If the wrong person discovered his true mission, his future—if not his very life—would be in jeopardy. The role Willy had assigned to him—seducer of a royal princess—flirted with treason. Aside from that, the emperor-to-be would be furious with him for leaking their plot. He'd seen the consequences of the prince's temper. He didn't at all relish being the object of that Hessian rage.

"What are you talking about, woman? Who's been filling your head with gossip?"

"None of your concern, now is it? I have me own friends. I have ways of knowin', Greggy. If you intend to leave me I'll not be taken by surprise."

"Who says I'm leavin' you?" He intentionally gentled his voice and reached to pull her up out of her seat, into his arms.

She struggled away and stood behind the ladder back of the chair, eyes flashing at him. "I want the truth, you little turd," she snarled. "I heard from one of the maids at the big house—

you've booked one-way train passage to London. She saw the ticket. Least you can do is be honest with me. We were to marry, or so you said. After your da passed. You said he would never allow it but you promised we'd marry when the old man was gone. So now, what do you say about that?"

He tried to move around the table toward her, but every quarter turn of the circle he made, she matched, keeping furniture between them.

"And I *will* marry you, lass. 'course I will. Just a trip to London, that's all it is. Nothing permanent."

She squinted at him, hands propped on her hips. "And the return ticket?"

"Don't know how long my business there will take, now do I? How can I buy the ticket home until I know when it's for?"

"Business," she said, casting him a witchy eye, albeit a pretty one.

"Aye. All business, nothing more. Legal matters. I'm doing this for us, Meggie. If everything works out I'll have my fortune made in no time. Then we will marry." It came as a blessed relief to him that her reaction suggested she knew nothing of his ambition to gain the virgin princess's bed.

Now he needed to keep her in the dark about his real purpose. And, if he succeeded in his mission and won both Beatrice's heart and the old queen's trust, what then? Meg would be furious if he went off and married another woman, no matter who she was. She'd make trouble for him. He'd probably have to pay her off to keep her from spreading details of their past.

The good news was—he was pretty sure she could be bought. Her family had always lived the hard-scrabble life of tenant farmers. They'd none of them be above accepting a bribe when all they had to do was keep silent. And he'd happily pay, out of his wife's royal coffers, to keep Meggie's pretty lips sealed.

"Darlin', be reasonable. What sort of fortune can I make for us here?" He swept a hand around him as if to indicate all of Scotland.

She winced and cast her eyes down at the dusty floorboards,

looking less sure of herself. "I don't know, Greg. You wouldn't be lyin' to me, would you? You wouldn't do that to me."

"'course not, my darlin' girl. How long we been together? Two years? Three?"

"Since before you went off to school in Germany, I'll remind you." She scowled at him.

He laughed. "I was just teasing you. Come on now. I'm here to tell you about my journey. And I'll be back sooner than you think. Now, what's the use of a trip to London if I can't bring my girl back a present?"

Her eyes brightened at that. "A bit of Honiton lace would be wonderful. Enough to make an elegant collar for church."

"Easy enough done," he said cheerfully. "I thought you were going to ask me for jewelry. But if it's lace you want—"

"No. Oh, no!" she squealed. "A ring? Oh Greg, a pretty love ring. I saw one once, in a shop window in Edinburgh. Three circlets—one of white gold, one of yellow gold, and one of rose gold—intertwined like woven flower stems. The shop woman said they was all the rage in London. You'd do that for me?" Her green eyes sparkled. She danced around the table's edge and flung herself into his arms. "It would make a fine engagement ring."

He regretted having put ideas in her head. "Now, how would that look? You waltzing around the village with a gold ring on your finger. And all the county asking, 'Who's the lucky man? When's the wedding day?' We can't have that, now can we? Not while my father's still breathing."

She sighed and turned away from him, flinging her long red curls over her shoulder. They shimmered in the candlelight and, as always, he felt compelled to reach out and knot his fingers through their enchanting tangles. He brought his face down into their soft nest and breathed in the scent of her—all woman, all his for as long as he wanted her. In her impoverished circumstance, she'd find no better than the third son of a minor noble. But if he wasn't here to satisfy her lust…

He brushed his hands up her bare arms. "Oh, Meggie,

my beauty, my love. I'll be the happiest man on earth the day I'm free to marry you." His hands wandered down from her shoulders, along the swell of her breasts to her waist, smoothing over her hips, gathering her skirt in greedy handfuls. He slipped his fingers beneath the layers of petticoats and felt her fine, strong thighs.

She looped her arms around his neck and threw back her head in invitation. "Oh, you," she cooed, exposing her throat to his kisses. "I never can say no to you, Greggy."

"I know," he said.

14

Beatrice sat at her escritoire, pen poised above the ivory sheet of vellum. Responses to Henry's proposal had tumbled through her mind like colored glass shapes in a kaleidoscope, all night long. By morning's first light, she had slept not a wink but, oddly enough, didn't feel tired. In fact she felt invigorated, more alive than ever before.

A future—she had a *future* now! And it wasn't the bleak one irrevocably attached to her mother. Marriage to Henry Battenberg was personal, precious, *all hers*.

She'd never viewed the world, at least not since she was a tiny girl and before her father died, as a place of joy. Life for her had always been a grim, gray place of weeping and sad remembrance. Neither the present nor the future could ever live up to the joy the royal family had shared while Prince Albert had been alive—that was her mother's sad mantra. They were trapped in a limbo of deep and inescapable loss.

It wasn't until this very moment that Beatrice was struck by the realization that this unending cycle of grief might have become her mother's preferred existence. Victoria actually seemed to *enjoy* the complexity and variety of funereal ethics and trappings—the black bombazine gowns, the mourning pin clipped to her bosom encasing a lock of Albert's hair, the high collars and severe hair dressings. Even the wearing of a black veil when going out in public seemed to please her sensibilities and had became part of her usual costume.

She supposed her mother found all of this comforting, in a strange way. But the rest of the family was forced to choose between suffering along with her, or retreating into their own lives and putting themselves at sufficient geographical distance from the queen and her Court. As her sisters had done.

What would happen to her mother if she married Henry?

Beatrice stared down at the half page she'd already written. Victoria would have no one close to her. Of course there were her ladies in waiting and the rest of the Court. Never was there a shortage of bodies rushing about the palace. A staff of hundreds was required to feed, clothe, entertain and comfort the queen, as well as run the government. But that wasn't the same as family. Would her mother fade away to nothing after her last daughter deserted her?

Overcome by a wave of guilt, Beatrice crumpled the note and pushed it aside. She cradled her aching head in her hands. A traitor, that's what she was. How could she accept Henry's proposal without first telling her mother of their intentions? It was the least she could do. It was what she *should* do.

And yet, the very thought of presenting her mother with news of her engagement terrified her.

"Marie. Are you there?" She'd heard her lady step discreetly through the door and into the bedchamber moments earlier. But the young woman had said nothing, as if seeing her busy at writing and not wanting to disturb her.

"Your Highness." The French girl stood and stepped away from the princess's dressing table, where she'd been sitting with needlework in her lap. She observed Beatrice's face with concern. "You did not sleep well last night?"

"No." Beatrice smiled and only when she saw the puzzled look her lady gave her did she realize her happiness at a sleepless night couldn't possibly make sense to her. "I have good reason though. I was thinking of Henry Battenberg. It's fortunate he isn't here to see me now, or he'd never— Well, never mind."

"Your gentleman admirer from Germany, is he? The one who writes you letters."

"Yes." A bubble of laughter escaped from her lips. Happiness was such a rare thing for her. To think: She actually had an admirer. More than that, *a suitor*. This would take some getting used to.

A thrill rushed through her as all sorts of wonderful possibilities sprang to mind, chasing away her momentary gloom. Travel. A lover who was devoted to her alone. Children. A home of her very own without her mother always lurking and ready to snatch every decision away from her—from choosing her clothing to declaring how Marie must dress her hair for her. From determining when she must wake in the morning and go to bed each night, to whom she would allow her daughter to socialize with.

Freedom. That's what she must grasp for herself and why she couldn't let this last chance pass her by.

"Marie?"

"*Oui*, Your Highness."

"Has my mother been asking for me this morning?"

"*Pas encore.* It is a little early even for her."

"Yes, I suppose it is." Beatrice traced a fingertip around the leather-framed blotter on her desk. "But I suspect she will be at breakfast soon."

"Do you plan to join her as usual?" Marie asked.

"Yes. Would you be a dear and run off to Cook. Ask if there is something a little special to accompany my mother's favorite Scottish oatmeal. Perhaps fresh fruit or a sweet of some kind?"

"*Certainement*, Your Highness."

As soon as her lady left, Beatrice drew a deep breath and tried to calm her whirring thoughts. She must present her case to her mother in the best possible light, when the queen was in a rare, sunny mood. Maybe during a carriage ride?

She turned toward her bed to see that Marie had lain out a simple dark navy-blue dress—a favorite of Beatrice's because it allowed her a hint of color without irritating her mother's sensibilities. In most lights the fabric looked nearly black. But even this subtle nod to the living she dared not risk today. She must at all costs gain her mother's blessing. Although she'd come to hate its dreariness, she would wear black today.

Because her future with Henry was at stake.

~

The staff had drawn open the heavy velvet draperies along the west wall of the breakfast room. Through the windows streamed a pure, white light that only seemed to favor London in the spring, and then only after a good rain washed the coal ash out of the air. Beatrice was so involved in her own thoughts she hadn't even realized it rained during the night.

She entered the room to find the queen already seated. "Good morning, Mama." She kissed her mother's wrinkled cheek, cool and dry as parchment.

"It is morning, that's true. Whether or not it is good remains to be seen. The pressures I struggle under…if my people only knew." Victoria sighed deeply.

"What pressures are these today, Mama?"

"The Prime Minister is most annoyingly persistent. He nags me to make an appearance before Parliament."

"I see."

"Not satisfied with that, Mr. Gladstone would also have me out among the people to celebrate the opening of a new mill. I have no idea why the man is so insistent. He claims I am not popular with the working people, and this hurts the government. Have you ever heard anything quite so ridiculous?"

"Perhaps he is just looking out for the Crown's best interests. Popular opinion these days seems to matter." Beatrice didn't want to come right out and remind her mother that lack of popular support had caused more than one European monarchy to fall in recent years. Frightening her mother certainly wouldn't serve her purpose on this particular morning.

"You too then? I'm supposed to *perform* for the entertainment of commoners? To put on a show as if I were a trained monkey? Ludicrous."

Beatrice gave up. She had more important fish to fry this morning than taking up Gladstone's cause. "How were the pastries? I see you've already tried one. They look especially fine and a nice addition to your oats. Apple and fig, are they?"

Victoria broke off a piece of flaky dough and popped it into her mouth. "They are good. Quite. I don't know what inspired Cook to include something I hadn't requested, but I'll have to let her know it was most appreciated." The queen sipped her coffee. "Such a busy schedule today. I just pray I have the strength. I'll need you, of course, for the full day, Baby. We shall both be drained, I'm sure, by the evening."

Beatrice took a deep breath to steady her nerves. "Before we get too busy there is one thing I would like to talk to you about."

"Really? And what is that, my dear?"

"You do remember, when we were at dear little Vicky's wedding, visiting with the Battenberg brothers?"

"Of course I remember them." Victoria chuckled her eyes crinkling at the corners. "And I expect every other woman attending will remember them as well. Such a striking clan they are. I don't suppose you are aware, since you were so very young at the time, but their papa was quite the dashing fellow in his youth. He would have had my hand if he'd had his way." The queen simpered girlishly behind fluttering fingertips. "But then your father came along and swept me off my feet, and I'd have no other. The poor duke, I suspect I left him with a broken heart. Still, he did marry well and produced that marvelous family. I do hope little Vicky is happy with her husband."

"Oh I'm sure she is. She and Louis seem very much in love."

"Love." Victoria released an onerous groan. "I sometimes wonder if it is all worth it."

Beatrice tensed. She couldn't afford to let her mother slip into a maudlin cloud of self-pity at just the moment when she needed her to be thinking positively and feeling her strongest.

"Mama, speaking of the Battenberg boys, I received a letter from Henry. He's the third eldest."

"Yes, of course, I know Henry. He was sweet to spare a dance or two for you, wasn't he?"

Beatrice bit down on her lower lip to stop herself from saying something she'd regret. She concentrated on keeping her tone level, absolutely devoid of emotion, despite her quivering heart. "Yes, very sweet he was. He is. Actually, we have been in communication since the wedding."

Suddenly, it was as if Beatrice could see the inner workings of her mother's mind. Like complex, whirring clockwork. Gears spinning, gyrating, clicking into place. Churning out implications even before Beatrice could state her mind.

"Of what sorts of communications are you speaking, dear?"

"Letters." She swallowed once, then again. "Henry and I have kept up a friendly written correspondence. I like him very much, Mama. He is such a gentle and intelligent man. And it appears his affections lean toward… *me*." She held her breath and waited for the not-so-subtle hints to sink in.

Her mother's tiny, glittering eyes flitted about the room. She put down the uneaten half of a brioche, straightened in her chair, and lifted her head to look directly into Beatrice's eyes.

"What sorts of affections are we discussing, Baby?"

There was nothing for it now but to come straight out and boldly state her intent. If she stammered vague suggestions that she was seeking her mother's approval for Henry to visit, without coming to the real point, the queen would surely cut her off cold.

Be strong, Beatrice. Be firm. Louise's encouraging words.

Beatrice cleared her throat, focused on her mother's stern face, and burst into a breathless rush of words. "I speak of the affection between a man and a woman—an intimate attachment only possible and proper within marriage." There she'd said it. But now she felt the compulsion to quickly add qualifiers and avoid giving her mother any chance at all to speak before hearing all she, Beatrice, had to say. "I think Henry a fine man. As fine as I've ever met. And although we have spent only a little time together, at the wedding, I knew immediately he was different.

I sensed that he cared for me in a special way." She felt sick to her stomach, short of breath, but carried on. "Mama, I want to marry Henry Battenberg."

Beatrice looked up from her clenched hands to her mother's face, watching for the first telltale signs of a reaction. She was prepared for anything—good or bad. When she saw the corners from mother's lips tip upward in the beginnings of a smile Beatrice felt an immediate, glorious wave of relief. Could it possibly be this easy? Had she assumed the worst for no reason?

But the smile immediately stiffened. Victoria let out a dry laugh.

"My child, you are so very innocent. A few compliments from a man, a smile and a dance. They mean nothing. Henry's father has brought him up well. He is a charming young man and was simply being kind to you, knowing you had no escort and few chances to dance."

"No!" Beatrice objected, her throat going hot with rage, eyes burning. "That's not it at all. I mean, I thought at first he was just being nice to me. That's his temperament, I agree. He *is* kind. But after we went riding the second time and—"

"You did what? You went riding with the man? When did this happen?"

Oh lord, Beatrice thought. *Here we go*. She fought to keep her voice from cracking. "The day of the wedding, Henry accompanied me on horseback out from the castle."

"No!" the queen roared. She straightened in her chair, seeming to grow six inches taller. "That is not possible. It's your foolish imagination playing tricks on—"

"I didn't dream it, Mama," Beatrice cut her off. "During the weeks we were there, everybody, including you, was busy doing their own thing. I was at loose ends, wanting to relax and take some air. Henry was very accommodating."

Something altered in the queen's expression. Her chest heaved with a great, unexpressed emotion. Her eyes darkened and turned brittle. "That was a foolish and dangerous thing for you to do, Baby. Just imagine what might have happened, had he been less than a gentleman. And if anybody had seen? The scandal would have been most difficult to explain."

Beatrice shuddered, struck by a sudden wave of desperation. What compelled her mother to always rob her of any precious moment of joy? "But we were entirely proper in everything we did and said." *Except for the kisses.* And she certainly wasn't going to mention those to her mother.

"Are you mad, child? To invite such behavior at your niece's wedding. Do you have any idea how many young women get themselves into trouble at weddings?"

"No, I suppose I don't." Anger, at the unfairness of it all, filled her until she could barely sit still, hardly speak. She balled her fists on the tabletop to stop them from trembling. "But, Mama, I *do* see how many young women have a wonderful time, dancing and laughing and enjoying the attentions of young men at weddings. Which is an experience *I have never before enjoyed!* I can't tell you how happy I was to finally find someone who thinks I'm pretty, who tells me he loves the sound of my laughter and the cleverness of my wit."

The queen pinched her lips and rolled her eyes. "Such nonsense. Henry was pulling the wool over your eyes. He is a far cleverer young man than I'd suspected. I should have kept you away from him."

"But you didn't, Mama, did you?" Beatrice was shouting now. On her feet and shouting. And she didn't care. "And now that I've discovered how much I enjoy Henry Battenberg's company and how deeply I care for him—it's too late, isn't it?" Beatrice felt fire in her veins. She had never spoken to her mother in such a way before. But she simply couldn't hold back. Before her mother could say another word Beatrice added, "I know that Henry is serious because he wrote me a letter asking for my hand in marriage. Or rather asking for my permission to ask you for permission to come and request my hand. He wants to do this properly, you see. Even though I would have told him in a heartbeat, 'Yes, yes, yes!' he still wants your blessing. And so he will come to London, to see you and—"

"No! Absolutely not. I do not wish to see him, and neither do you."

Beatrice felt the air rush from her lungs leaving her nauseated, disoriented. She couldn't speak. Couldn't draw even a whisper of a breath.

"Now that that's settled, you'll write one last letter and tell youngerrH Battenberg that under no circumstances will you ever consider marrying him. That will save him a trip. And save me the uncomfortable task of having to tell him myself."

Could this really be happening? Beatrice heard her mother's words as if from a great distance. As though reaching her from another room, another continent…another century.

"Mama," she gasped, "I am twenty-seven years old. From the time Papa passed on—"

"Don't you *dare* bring my precious Albert into this argument. He would never have allowed you to—"

"Never have allowed me to marry?" Beatrice shook her head violently. "Oh, I think you're wrong. I can't recall much from those years, but I do remember him waltzing me across the ballroom, calling me his littlest princess, and telling me I would be a beautiful queen someday. As there were eight heirs to the English throne before me, it seems clear he wasn't speaking of my becoming Queen of England. He meant for me to marry a king. Well, Henry isn't a king and never will be, but he isn't a commoner either. He's very special, born of a distinguished noble family, and I like him so very much."

Her mother rested back in her chair, closed her eyes, looking weary with their quarrel. "He will see you into your grave, Baby. It's what men do, you foolish girl. If I let you marry him, he would demand physical acts of you. Acts you could only find disgusting, shocking. And the pregnancies—so many babies inside of you, until you are so weakened you will die a wretched death, before your time, like your poor sister Alice." Beatrice opened her mouth to object. Her sister had died of diphtheria, not in childbirth. But the queen rambled on before she could get in a single word. "At the very least, you will be made an insignificant member of a family that ignores you. Husbands take away your freedom, stifle your individuality. They force a woman to live in places not of her choosing. Once a woman marries, she loses all of her rights. She loses herself."

Beatrice jammed her palms down on the table edge and leaned over the white expanse of damask toward her mother. "And what rights do I have now? I have no freedom so long as I live with you, Mama. You allow me nothing of my own. Nothing! No decision is made without your consent. You never listen to me. Never let me do or experience or feel anything that you don't want me to." Hot tears coursed down her cheeks. "You've robbed me of my childhood, my friends, of any hope of happiness. And now you warn me that my life could be so much worse. *How?* Tell me that. How could it be any worse?"

Her mother's sour gaze fixed on her face. The queen remained silent, indomitable, unmoved.

Beatrice let out a wild shriek of frustration. A wash of tears blurred the room around her. She kicked the chair back and out of her way. It toppled over with a crash, the sound of her fury echoing through the palace. And she didn't care, didn't care about anything at all.

Beatrice gathered her skirts and rushed from the room.

15

Victoria looked up from the correspondence on her desk at a soft knock on her door and sighed. It had taken hours and three cups of tea to calm herself after the scene with Beatrice that morning in the breakfast room. What was she to do with the child?

The knock was louder the second time. It was about time. Beatrice would be coming to beg her forgiveness for her outrageous behavior. Victoria hadn't yet decided whether she would forgive her or withhold her pardon, at least for a while.

"Yes?" she snapped.

Far too many demands were being made upon her strength and her time. If it wasn't the prime minister, it was squabbling MP's, gossiping ladies of her court or—worse yet—news of another political disaster in Ireland, Europe, or the Dark Continent. Lately she'd begun to wonder if Britain might even lose its grip on India, the jewel in her crown. And the horrid situation in Khartoum? Major Gordon and his staff had been trapped during a siege in the Sudan for weeks. If Parliament didn't act soon and send a rescue mission—well, the inevitable bloodbath was too awful to contemplate.

The door swung open, and Major-General the Right Honorable Sir Henry Ponsonby, secretary to Her Majesty, entered her office. He approached the paired desks set in the center of the room and waited patiently for Victoria to invite his communication.

She lifted her gaze only as far as dear Albert's desk, across from and facing hers. Her staff knew to keep it precisely as he'd left it: a clean blotter, his favorite pen, a full inkwell, the lovely crystal-and-silver oil lamp she'd given him when he complained of his eyes tiring from strain. All there as if he might stride into the room at any moment with a "breathtaking morning, my dear—don't you think?" And a kiss on the cheek. Always a kiss. Then they'd knuckle down to their day's labor over stacks of documents. Together.

Always together. Tears came to her eyes.

She'd leaned on Albert so completely that his absence, even these many years later, left an aching void in her life. An emptiness beyond his disappearance from their bed—in a shared bedroom, even though this raised eyebrows in court. It was thought proper for husbands and wives to have their own discreet sleeping areas except during occasional times of intimacy.

Yes, even in her role as monarch, Albert had been her guiding light. Relieving her of decisions when she'd felt overwhelmed by the demands of her reign. Taking on the distasteful duty of meeting with dignitaries whose personalities or requests she found unpleasant. It was Albert who made tolerable the uncomfortable task of being seen by and speaking to her subjects.

With him by her side, she had felt strong and capable, except for those times when carrying another child or recovering from yet another birth temporarily robbed her of her vigor. Without him, even the simplest decisions and tasks took on a crushing weight that left her head pounding.

Oh, my dear, beloved Albert, today is one of those most despised days.

Beatrice, their youngest, whom she had believed would remain always faithful to her, had struck her a wicked blow. Even now, hours later, as she had struggled to complete the letter of thanks she owed the duchess of Kent for a recent visit, she felt appalled by Beatrice's traitorous behavior. Had she known the girl was cavorting in the woods with that sneaky Henry Battenberg she would have put a stop to it. She would have sent her guardsmen to drag the silly girl back to the castle so that she could talk sense into her. But events of the day had distracted her. She still felt ill at the thought of her son-in-law, the Grand Duke, and his mad plan to marry his mistress. How dare he even contemplate bringing a woman of such reputation into the family!

"Oh, my dear Alice," Victoria whispered to herself, "I'm glad you aren't here to know of your husband's betrayal and your little sister's foolishness."

"Ma'am?"

Victoria looked up to see her secretary standing before her desk. She'd entirely forgotten him in the fervor of her emotions. She pressed the back of one hand to her throbbing forehead.

"What is it then, Ponsonby?"

"The master of the royal mews wishes to speak with you about an important matter concerning the stable boys. Shall I tell him he must return…at a more opportune time?"

Her secretary had echoed her favorite, and most frequent, response to those who wished her attention. She was well aware that if she sent them away enough times, they'd likely give up trying to bother her. But her precious horses she never wished to ignore.

"Is one of my horses ill or injured?" The very thought of her animals in distress pained her.

"I am unaware of the nature of his concerns, Your Majesty."

"Nevertheless, the matter must be critical for him to interrupt his day and come in person. Send him in immediately."

Victoria stood up from her desk, feeling suddenly restless. At first she had resented the men she'd brought in to replace her beloved John Brown as master of the royal mews, finding each of them inferior and sending them away, one after another. But Elton Jackson had proven gentle and adept at managing her horses, a stern taskmaster over the palace's squadron of grooms and stable boys, and he kept her precious animals healthy and content. She had grown to respect him.

Before the man could cross the room, she held out a hand

to stop him. "Which one is it? Who is sick or hurt—I can't bear to hear it is one of my favorites."

"No, no, Your Majesty. Please, mum, don't distress yourself," he said, his weather-roughened face flushing. "It's not about one of your horses I come."

She took a deep breath, relieved, then immediately irritated. "Then why are you here, Mr. Jackson?"

He blinked sheepishly at her. "You said you wished to personally approve all new staff to the mews."

"Yes?"

"I've found a replacement for the boy who had the accident last week."

She scowled, trying to remember. "He took a fall while exercising one of my horses?"

"No, mum. It was in the city while running an errand. A carriage done run him down. Nearly killed the lad. It was terrible bad."

"Such awful drivers we have in London." Victoria tsk-tsked. "You've seen that he has a proper doctor and treatment?"

"Of course, mum."

"Good." She wouldn't want it said that she didn't care about her people. "But he won't be back to work in the stables?"

"Not for a very long time, if ever. His leg's broke and a shoulder dislocated. Lad's no good for horses now."

"But you have a satisfactory replacement?"

"I believe so, mum. He's from up north. Very good with the horses. Scottish lad. Comes from the county round about your Balmoral. If you approve I'll start him right away, break him in to our routines, see how he fits. If you'd like me to bring him to meet you—"

She waved him off. "I'll go for a carriage ride soon and see him then."

"Very good, mum."

"You'll watch him closely, won't you? Start him with the calmer horses until you know he can be trusted."

"I will." The stable master bowed and looked toward the

door as if waiting for permission to leave.

"What's the boy's name, Mr. Jackson?

"Gregory, mum. Gregory MacAlister. May I be excused, mum?"

"Wait," she said, frowning at the familiarity of the name. "I think I know him…or his father perhaps. James MacAlister. He's a minor noble, a landholder from Aberdeenshire, is he not?"

"That he is, mum."

"Are you sure you have the name right? Why would the son of a lord seek a low job as a stable hand?"

"He's a third son—a bit of a waster, I should guess." He gave her a toothy, tobacco-stained smile. "My expectations are the father's thinking to teach the lad a lesson. Make him work a bit for his meager share of the inheritance. The boy will never have the title for hisself, or the land, since he's got two healthy older brothers."

"You think so? Punishment? Then he might resent his duties and shirk them. I can't say I like this, Mr. Jackson."

He shrugged and kept his eyes down, looking increasingly nervous to be forced to converse for so long. "May be the family is in worse financial straits than they're letting on, Your Majesty. It happens. He might be here to truly earn his own way."

Perhaps, she thought, *it was just that simple: the old lord getting rid of a son who was a drain on the family's resources.* Victoria was only vaguely aware of giving her stable master a wave of her hand to dismiss him. When she looked up out of her thoughts, Jackson was gone.

A young man from up north. Well, that would be a change from the local farm lads they'd depended upon in recent years. *Refreshing to hear a Scottish brogue again at Buckingham.*

Or maybe not. Victoria shook her head. She just hoped hearing and seeing the Aberdeenshire boy wouldn't make her sad. How she missed the Scot's company and strong physique. She'd always felt so safe around him.

16

Henry Battenberg read Beatrice's letter in disbelief. Twice. By the third reading the bad news finally sank in.

He pressed a fist to his chest in shock and disappointment. It wasn't until Vicky leaned over and kissed him on top of his head that he became aware his brother Louis and his new bride had entered their father's dimly lit library.

"Little brother," she teased, "are we so unimportant to you that you cannot look up from your work?"

Henry slowly lifted his bleary gaze from the little square of ivory parchment, neatly lined with Beatrice's familiar script. "Not work," he said. "More like reading my own obituary."

His brother laughed. "Liko, come now!" He turned to Vicky. "Henry, the romantic, we used to call him. What is it now? Have you broken another heart and she pleads for your lost kisses?"

Henry bit his tongue to stop himself from flinging back an angry retort. It was always his older brothers who had cut a wide swath through the ladies in his father's domain, and beyond. But it wouldn't do for him to remind Louis of that now—not with his wife standing at his side.

"It's from Beatrice."

"Oh, how sweet of Aunt Bea to write to you," Vicky cried. "Will you answer? She'd be so pleased, I'm sure. Such a lonely life she leads, shut away with her dull old mother."

Her husband stared at her in feigned shock. "How dare you speak of the queen of England with such irreverence."

"Oh, I'm not saying anything her entire court doesn't think. I love *Grand-mere* of course, but she can be such an old-fashioned, bossy thing. Don't you think, Henry?"

"I wouldn't know," he said glumly. "I haven't had many chances to be around her."

"But you were around Beatrice a great deal during our wedding week," his brother said, giving him a sly wink, "were you not?"

Henry caught Vicky casting her husband a sidelong look of puzzlement. "Around Aunt Bea?"

"To Henry," Louis said, with a wicked grin, "she's not 'aunt' anything. She's the same age as he. The l-o-o-ovely Beatrice. Mysterious goddess of mourning. Me thinks Henry is smitten."

Vicky clapped a hand over her mouth and stared at him wild-eyed. "He is *not*."

Henry quickly folded the letter and shook it at her. "I fear I am. And all for naught."

"Why do you say that?" Louis snatched up the note before his brother could tuck it away into his frockcoat pocket.

"I say there, give it back," Henry shouted. "That's personal."

"Don't I always look after you, little brother? I want to see what this wicked woman has done to shatter your dreams. Up to her old tricks, is she? She spurned me, and now she's tossing you over. We'll teach the wench a lesson."

"Give me that!" Henry dove over the desk, reaching for the letter, but his brother was quicker. It disappeared behind his back. "You'll teach her no lesson. The poor girl is beside herself with grief."

Vicky was shaking her head in obvious confusion. "I don't understand. What's going on? What's happened? Somebody please tell me! She's my dearest aunt and I must know."

"Now, now, my precious, don't be concerned until we discover what has transpired to so upset Bea and destroy my brother's usual cheerful countenance." Louis stepped further back from the desk, even as Henry sank disconsolately into the chair and let his head fall forward on folded arms.

"Oh, dear," Vicky murmured a few seconds later, and Henry guessed from the crinkling sound of paper that she was reading the note along with Louis. A moment later she let out a gasp. "Henry, you asked for her hand in marriage?"

"I did."

"And she's saying no?"

"In effect, yes."

"But why?" Vicky asked.

"Because," her husband answered, saving Henry the painful trouble, "the queen refuses to let her marry my brother."

"But Henry is ever so perfect for Beatrice," she objected.

"You didn't finish the letter. Here. She explains…albeit in perplexing detail."

Henry heard his brother's steps approaching him but he didn't look up. A hand rested on his shoulder. "The woman is a fool."

"Beatrice is *not* a fool." Henry shot to his feet, ready to lash out physically in defense of his love. "You take that back, sir. Brother or not I'll thrash you within an inch of—"

"Not Bea, you idiot. The queen. She's a fool if she thinks she can keep her last child to herself forever. Maybe that's the way it used to be—hold back the youngest to care for the aging parents when there was no one else to do it. But she's the queen of England, for God's sake. She has hundreds of staff, servants, and the court, all loyal to her and ready to do her bidding. Why does she need to make an old maid of her daughter?"

"She isn't an old maid," Henry grumbled, his protest weaker. All the fight had suddenly gone out of him. "But you're right about one thing. It makes no sense."

"Listen to this," Vicky whispered, "she says here, 'Mama is so delicate in both health and spirit, so in need of my attentions.'"

"Ha! Delicate?" Louis railed. "I should be so delicate. That woman is a force to be reckoned with."

"But she *is* getting along in age," Henry said. "She may have few years left." He could only hope.

Louis laughed. "Victoria will live to be a hundred. If Bea

waits until then to marry—if she herself lives that long—no man will have her. Not even you, Henry."

I would, he thought. *I'd want her even in our old age.* "But what can I do? Beatrice says it's off. We're done. She believes her mother will never change her mind."

"Oh, Henry, no-no-no." Vicky, cheeks pink with excitement, rushed toward him waving the letter in his face. He grabbed it back from her. "You must persist! You really must. Beatrice may say it's impossible, but if you love her as I love my sweet husband and he loves me, then you must soldier on. She may find the strength to stand up to her mother if you are there to support her."

"But if the queen says no—"

"Vicky is right," his brother said. "This is only the first mention of an engagement. If you prove yourself worthy to the queen as a husband for her daughter, and if Bea proclaims that she can never be happy without you in her life, how can the queen deny her last and favorite child? Victoria may be ruthlessly selfish, but if she fears Bea will withdraw her love from her, if she refuses to let her become engaged to you, she may come around."

"Not just engaged—married," Henry said firmly. Yes, marry the girl, the sooner the better. A long engagement meant frustration, sexually and otherwise. He wanted Bea in his bed, not a long-term correspondence from hundreds of miles away and open-ended engagement.

"Engaged first," Vicky said. "Your brother is right. That's the first step. It takes *Grand-mere* a long time to get used to the tiniest changes. If you make yourself part of Bea's life, if you're frequently in London and present in Court, then the queen can't help but be won over." Her eyes sparkled with encouragement. "Truly, patience will win her hand."

"You really believe this?"

"We'll help," Louis promised. "We'll be your seconds, there to patch you up after each royal parry, after each cruel thrust from the queen. If you stand strong, you cannot fail, brother."

Henry sighed. It was good of Louis and his sister-in-law to be there for him. But when he thought about other examples of the queen's determination—more like, her supreme pigheadedness!—he felt little real hope. Years ago, hadn't she insisted on parading to her Accession Day celebration even after her Secret Service officers and Scotland Yard warned her of a plot against her life? And they'd been right. The day had been a disaster the likes of which London would never forget.

But he would try. By God, he would try to convince the woman that her daughter should be his—for the sake of his own happiness and for his darling Beatrice.

17

Beatrice barely had time to breathe. In the days following the posting of her bitterly sad letter to Henry, her mother seemed to need her at every turn—from dawn until dusk, and often late into the evening. Even Ponsonby wasn't able to keep up with the queen's sudden burst of energy and demands on his time.

In many ways, it was good to see her mother so busy. The gout that had returned to cause her such wretched pain in her foot didn't stop the woman from attending official functions she normally would have refused. And she was more open to social occasions, all of which seemed to require her youngest daughter's company. Victoria then decided it was time for the royal seamstress to fit her for two new dresses to replace the worn black gowns she most frequently wore. While the woman was at Buckingham Palace with her swatches and sketches, she also measured Beatrice for a new gown and a riding outfit. Bea became suspicious that all of this activity was intended to keep her so busy she wouldn't have time to think about Henry.

It didn't work. Henry Battenberg's image haunted her all the day long, and he flitted through her dreams at night.

Falling into bed after a late night of theatre with her mother at the Royal Opera House, Beatrice waved off her lady's offer of warm milk. "I'll have no difficulty sleeping tonight, Marie." She closed her eyes and rested her head back against the satin pillow. "I've never been so exhausted. Do you suppose she's bribing me?"

"*Pardon*? Who bribes you, Your Highness?"

"The queen, my mother. First she nearly kills me by keeping me so occupied I hardly have time to think, then she buys me two new outfits of far more extravagant material and detail than she has allowed me in years." Beatrice pushed herself up wearily onto one elbow. "And the riding suit is plum, Marie. Not black. *Plum.*"

"Very dark. Not a red-plum or cardinal, like other ladies wear."

"No, but that's not the point. It's definitely a *color*. She knew how much that would please me. I could see it in her eyes when she chose the swatch from the seamstress's samples."

"She wants you to be happy." Marie winked at her.

"No, she wants me to be *content*. There's a huge difference." If Beatrice was content, she imagined her mother reasoning, she would continue to do as Victoria commanded and forget about marriage. Forget Henry. That was clearly her mother's intent.

"Why is she so against my marriage? She and Papa were so happy. She must remember what it's like to be in love. Why does she deny me the chance to be as happy as she once was?"

Marie sat on the bed beside her and smoothed the hair out of her eyes. "*Ma Cherie*, after your father is gone, she feels such pain. *Non*?"

"Of course she did. She still does. She mourns him every day."

"Just so. She feels the agony of his absence. And so, perhaps, she tries to save you from the greatest sadness. *Oui*? She is trying to protect you."

Beatrice rolled away to her side, and squeezed her eyes shut. "I think you're giving her the benefit of your sweet nature, Marie. I might have believed Mama was acting in my best interest before Henry came along and we fell in love. But now…I'm not so sure. Maybe she *believes* she's protecting me. But I think she's just looking after herself."

Marie sighed. "What will you do, Your Highness?"

Beatrice started to open her mouth to say what she'd been

thinking all day. About her options. About following her heart. But, as loyal as she believed Marie to be to her, the woman also had pledged her allegiance to the queen. And Beatrice knew, in the mind of each and every member of her mother's Court, a mental line had been drawn, past which they would never step. If it came to choosing sides between their monarch and one of her children—Victoria would always win.

And so, Beatrice kept silent, pretending to drift off to sleep.

After Marie turned down the gaslights and left the room in darkness, Beatrice sat up in bed. Her heart beating wildly, she puzzled over her future.

Dare she defy the queen? Dare she even consider the impossible? If she ran away to be with her lover—that is, the man she wished could be her lover, because she and Henry had only ever kissed and shyly touched. Hands. Faces. His fingertips trailing through her hair. Not making love, of course. Just tender gestures and words. But she could imagine more. And those thoughts thrilled her. If she ran off to be with Henry, it wouldn't be the first time a princess had escaped to marry the man she loved. *If* he'd still have her after receiving her letter, knowing they'd both be defying the queen—a dangerous thing to do.

She bit down on her bottom lip at this thought. Having read what she'd written, Henry might think her so immature and naïve, still tied to her mother's apron strings (As if Victoria ever would wear an apron!) that she no longer interested him. But if he *did* still want her—could she really turn her back on the queen and her own country, run away to the Continent and into Henry's arms? Was she brave enough, impulsive and daring enough to do *that*?

Tears seeped from beneath her eyelashes. Maybe not. Years of grief imposed on the entire family by their father's premature death and their mother's obsession with mourning rituals had crushed all the life out of her. It was a miracle Henry had seen anything of interest in her.

Even if she had tricked him into caring for her—for a few hours, days, or even weeks—it was only a matter of time before he recognized her for what she was. A drab, bashful, awkward, boring female who was past her prime.

What man could possibly find a woman like that appealing—let alone loveable?

~

The next morning Beatrice woke from the deepest sleep she'd experienced since leaving Darmstadt. Her cheeks and eyelashes were crusty with salt from her tears, but her head felt clear. She rose from bed before Marie appeared to draw open the draperies of her bedchamber. She felt a different sort of energy than she'd ever felt before, something akin to—courage.

She also sensed an urge toward mischief that she hadn't indulged in since her very earliest childhood when she'd tried Nurse's patience with her pranks.

Louise, of course, had been the truly naughty one. The defiant child who refused to be controlled by their parents or nurses or tutors. Lenchen was the peacemaker, and Alice always seemed caught in the middle of sisterly intrigues. Crown Princess Vicky had been the haughty one, who took on airs and always, always got what she wanted just because she was the eldest and her father's protégé. Albert had been determined that his eldest daughter would rule a grand nation, even if it was through the man she would one day marry.

But *she*, Beatrice, had been the entertainer. The little girl who charmed everyone with her dances and silly rhymes and songs, making them smile and laugh and praise her cleverness. All of this before she turned four years of age. She truly was the blonde, blue-eyed darling of the English Court.

How times had changed.

Now, for the first time, Beatrice wondered if it was partly her own fault that all the joy had disappeared from her life. What would have happened if she'd been more assertive like Louise, more demanding like the Crown Princess...and resisted her mother's insistence on gloom, black garments, dull mourning jewelry, and solemnity?

Louise had counseled her to stand firm, to not give up on having Henry, even in the face of disapproval from their mother. But Louise herself had married a man chosen by the queen. Beatrice was certain her sister didn't love Lorne, now the Duke of Argyll. She'd never understood their relationship but, of course, had never asked Louise why she had agreed to marry Lorne when her sister seemed capable of withstanding their mother's bossiness in every other situation. Someday maybe she'd uncover Louise's secret heart. But for now, it was all she could do to work on her own problems.

Stand firm, she thought. And again came that urge to do something just a little daring, a little wild.

If she, Beatrice, was to do battle with her mother for the right to marry the man she loved, she'd have to become a stronger, more independent woman. Beatrice sat on the edge of her bed and wondered how one went about changing one's life. How could she become a different, better sort of woman? She tingled with excitement. Yes, she must analyze this process of redesigning oneself.

Louise made independence seem so easy. She opened herself to the world, traveling with or without Lorne as the mood moved her. She went out among commoners, attended women's suffrage rallies, visited hospitals and women's shelters. She had even opened a consignment shop where women with no other means of supporting themselves could sell their handmade items; for many it was just enough to keep them off the streets. Louise seemed afraid of nothing—not even Irish separatists who, years earlier, launched a violent plot against the royal family.

Beatrice thought for another moment. If only she could recall just one time in her life, as an adult, when she hadn't felt timid and hopelessly awkward. Then she might be able to repeat that moment. She'd practice being brave.

It came to her all at once, the memory so poignant and

vivid she laughed out loud with joy.

Yes! She'd felt strong, in control, even bold and playful when she'd ridden with Henry at Darmstadt.

Well, she couldn't have Henry, at least not just yet. But she could go for a ride. The royal stables had horses aplenty.

A soft knock sounded on the door, and Marie peeked around the corner before stepping inside. "Ah, Your Highness is awake. *Bon.* The queen, she is asking for you."

"Please tell her that—" Beatrice took a deep breath. "—that I am busy."

Marie stopped in the middle of the room and looked at her as if she had grown an extra head. "You are *busy*?"

"Yes. I will be engaged for the next two hours, at least. It's been a while since I rode out into the park." She pushed up off the bed and strode toward her wardrobe closet. "It's too bad I don't have the plum outfit yet. The old one will have to do. But at least it fits. And, in black, I won't stand out among the other riders on Rotten Row."

Marie reached out, as if to touch fingertips to the royal forehead to test for fever, but Beatrice stepped away. "Your Highness, is well?"

"Am I?" Beatrice laughed again. "I don't know if I am yet, but I'm working on it. I'm working on a lot of things." She looked at the young woman who was as close to her as any friend she'd ever had. "Will you go now and tell the queen? Then I'll need your help dressing. I'll be back in time for lunch and available after that to help my mother however she requires."

"*Oui*, Your Highness."

Beatrice watched Marie go and felt a trifle cruel. Her lady would likely be on the receiving end of the queen's anger once she learned Beatrice wouldn't be joining her for the morning. She'd find a way to make it up to the girl later.

18

"My apologies, Princess, but I don't think it's wise."

Beatrice looked up at Elton Jackson and tried to remember exactly what Louise always said to members of their mother's staff when they balked at giving her what she wanted.

She straightened her back, whacked her riding crop smartly against the palm of her gloved hand and narrowed her eyes at the man, trying to project an image of royal indignation. "I intend," she said, "to ride out each day from now on, for healthful exercise. Will you bring my horse out to me, Mr. Jackson? Or do I need to go fetch her myself?"

"But, Your Highness, your mother will be—"

"Her wishes aren't, at the moment, your most pressing concern. Your job is to see that one of your grooms saddles my mount and delivers her to me as quickly as possible. Any setback will delay my return to the palace. Which means I shall be late to join my mother. And you know how irritated the queen becomes when she's kept waiting."

The man closed his eyes for a moment as if weighing the consequences then glanced back at the stables. "Right, Your Highness. I'll get to it. Do you prefer Tarff?"

"No, I'll take my new pony, Lady Jane." "I'll do it," a voice called from the shadows inside the barn.

Beatrice squinted against the sunlight to see which of the grooms had volunteered to bring her horse to her. A young man stepped out from the building with bridle in hand. "Leave it to me, Your Highness." As quickly as he'd appeared, he dissolved back into the shadows of the mews.

She tipped her head to one side, surprised at his accent, a pronounced Scottish brogue. Although he was wearing the livery of a stable groom, she thought she'd caught a glimpse of chain and tassel, such as the Scots wore about their hips.

"Who is that? I don't recognize him."

Jackson turned toward the paddock. Another horse had been brought out, and a groom was stretching the animal's legs by leading it in circles on a long lunge line. "The fellow's new. Here to replace Tom Feigel."

"Has Tom left us? Didn't he have a good temperament for horses?"

"One of my best, he was, Princess. But he had a bad accident and can't work no more. I told the queen 'bout him, and she approved of the new boy. He's older than many of them we get from the farms round about, but the advantage is he has a good deal more experience with fine horse flesh. From up north he is."

"Yes," she said thoughtfully, "I could tell. Has my mother met him yet?"

"Expect she will soon enough."

Beatrice's gaze strayed toward the dim interior of the barn. "I think I'd better go and see how he's getting along, since he's new on the job."

"You don't need to—"

But she was already striding in that direction, shutting out the stable master's objections. She was tired of listening to people tell her what to do, or not do. After all, she wasn't a child any more. She needed to remind the staff of that.

She turned to the right. Three stalls down, she saw the young groom talking gently to the mare, easing a bit into her mouth. His voice was so soft and low that, at first, she didn't realize he was actually singing to the animal in his buttery Scottish accent. He cupped the horse's muzzle with the palm of one hand and stroked her gleaming brown neck.

Beatrice stopped and watched, mesmerized. When he'd finished tacking her horse he led the mare out of her stall. The horse followed along with him docilely.

"She likes you," she said.

The young man looked up sharply, as if surprised to see her there. "She's a sweet lady, she is. I think she's missed you, Princess. Seems ready to go for a ride."

"Well, I'll be spending more time with her now." She felt sorry for having neglected her horses of late, but her mother had kept her so very busy. And anyway, they did most of their riding at Windsor, where the royals had more privacy along the trails. "Here, I'll lead her the rest of the way." She held out her hand for the reins.

"Very good, Your Highness. I won't be a minute."

She frowned as she watched the groom dash back into the recesses of the stable. "A minute for what?" she called to him. "Isn't Lady Jane ready?" The horse appeared saddled, bridled, stirrups adjusted. Nothing missing that she could see.

"She *is* ready," he shouted back, "but I need to get my horse. He's further back."

Beatrice shook her head. What was this all about?

She found Jackson in the yard, one boot braced on the rail of the paddock fence, watching his groom exercise the sleek thoroughbred she'd seen earlier. "Your new boy behaves as if he intends to accompany me."

"Princess, you can't go out into the park unattended. You know that."

She did, of course. They never went for a drive in the carriage without at least two footmen, armed in recent years. When Brown was alive, he sometimes took her mother out alone, for a trot on her favorite mount. He had been a formidable man and protection enough.

But, in Darmstadt, Beatrice had found it so refreshing to roam woods and field on her own, and then with just Henry. She hadn't wanted an attendant along today. She yearned for another taste of that same privacy and independence. Aside from that, she more than half suspected her mother used staff to spy on members of the family and Court.

"I will be fine on my own."

Jackson looked horrified. "There are those, Princess, would like nothing better than to—"

"I know…wreak havoc on the Crown and bring down the government, using my family's vulnerability to do so. But surely, not on Rotten Row!"

Elton Jackson removed his tweed cap and wrung it in his hands. His whiskered, leathery face contorted with concern. "Please, Your Highness, let the lad go with you. He'll be most respectful, won't pester you at all. If you've any trouble with your horse, he'll at least be there to help."

"I've never had trouble of any sort with Lady Jane." The man was being insistent to the point of irritation. But she could see little point in arguing, out here in the middle of the yard for all to see. "All right then. I see him coming now. Help me mount. I'll let him tag along if it makes you feel better, Mr. Jackson." She sighed, resigned to the trade off. The groom's company for a few precious hours of freedom from her mother.

As soon as he'd seen her safely up onto her saddle, the stable master glanced behind him at the younger man, now astride a magnificent black Arabian. She thought she saw a worried look flash across Jackson's craggy features. Beatrice knew this particular horse wasn't popular with the family, due to his unpredictable temperament. He'd thrown more than one groom, but her mother insisted upon keeping him because John Brown had purchased him as a foal, for the queen, not long before he died.

Just then, something else seemed to catch Jackson's eye. Beatrice followed his gaze to a well-dressed couple, approaching on foot from the far side of the yard. At this distance, she recognized neither of them. Jackson quickly excused himself and rushed toward the pair, waving them over to the opposite side of a shed before Beatrice could get a closer look at them.

Odd, she thought, *what are two strangers doing on palace grounds?* But movement closer to her robbed her of the fleeting thought.

She turned to see the new groom walking his mount up to hers. He stood the horse and waited patiently, erect in his saddle, gaze cast at a servant's respectful mid-distance, not meeting her eyes.

"I hope you know how to handle that beast," Beatrice murmured as she turned Lady Jane toward the gates. "Otherwise I'll be the one helping *you*."

He laughed pleasantly. "I can handle myself with any beast, four legs or two. Don't you worry about me, Your Highness."

His bravado was both off-putting and charming, in a strange way. Strong, hard-willed men appealed to her mother, but they had frightened Beatrice as a child. Now that she was an adult they still made her wary. She noticed the groom had strapped on a sword. She was about to object to the necessity of having an armed escort, but then Mr. Jackson might insist on a pair of the queen's Beefeaters attending her. She'd be made a spectacle of and have to endure the stares of everyone she passed in the park.

"I prefer riding alone," she said when he started to bring his horse alongside hers. "But since it seems you must do your job, I'll thank you to give me some distance."

He nodded but she sensed a smile not far from his lips. "As you wish, Your Highness." He let her lead the way across the yard, then out through the tall wrought-iron gates with their gold-encrusted coat of arms, and from there across the road and toward the park's entrance. As a child, she'd wondered if those spiky, black gates had been meant to keep commoners out, or royals in. Some days, she still wasn't sure.

Beatrice rode sidesaddle, as her mother had always done and insisted upon for all of her girls. Only Louise had eventually refused the polite convention and chose to straddle her horse, horrifying the Court and amusing the gentility of the city. *If I had Louise's pluck,* she thought, *I might even now be on my way to join Henry.*

But what if she was wrong and Henry didn't love her enough to marry her in spite of the queen's disapproval. Or, perhaps even worse, didn't love her enough to stay with her always even if they did marry? If she cut her connections with her own family, and he later cast her aside for another woman, would her mother take her back? Or would she, Princess Beatrice, become one of those thousands of desperate women she'd read about in *The Times*, roaming the streets of London without home or income? Begging for money to feed themselves. Poking through garbage. Selling their bodies in exchange for a safe place to sleep.

"Princess?"

"Hmmm?"

Startled out of her dark thoughts, she turned toward the voice and suddenly remembered where she was and who had spoken. The groom. On his horse just behind her. And in front of her stood a horse-drawn omnibus loading passengers. She had missed the park gate and nearly run her horse into the back end of the thing.

"Oh, sorry. I was miles away in thought." She laughed, embarrassed.

"Not a problem, Your Highness. Come then, follow me. I know another way."

He led her across a strip of grass, between two ash trees whose lowest branches forced them to duck down against their horses' necks, and then they were in among thick foliage. Just when she thought he'd got them lost, they came out onto the carriageway that ran parallel to Rotten Row, the riding path traditionally reserved for the nobility.

"Oh, I see, well done." She laughed nervously, looking around, pleased that they hadn't yet attracted the attention of other riders or occupants of the open carriages passing by, who seemed more intent upon themselves being seen than in watching her. "I'll have to remember that short cut."

He nodded at her and smiled. She noticed, for the first time, his reddish gold hair, slightly longer than was fashionable in the city, so that it brushed his collar. His eyes, she could now see from this close up, were a gray-green, as alert as a fox's as they scanned the wide path and nearby woods. He sat his mount with confidence as they rode at a relaxed pace.

"What is your name?" she asked.

"Gregory, Your Highness." "Gregory." It suited him. Regal. A name of popes and kings.

"Most everyone calls me Greg. Fits my current situation better, I expect."

He was modest after all. "And I understand you are a Scot?"

"Grew up in Aberdeenshire. Lived there all of my life, ma'am."

Somehow, they'd come to be riding side by side again, and she didn't object. Conversing comfortably with him while he followed her would have been next to impossible.

"Why did you come to London, Greg?" She knew her mother would never have carried on a relaxed conversation with a commoner or member of her household staff. Somehow it made her feel more liberal and modern to show a personal interest in the man.

"Adventure, I guess you'd say. There's little for me to do up north. My two older brothers care for the farm and surrounding land, and the manor house, of course."

She stopped her horse abruptly and stared at him. "What sort of fantasy is this?"

He laughed, his eyes dancing as if he'd known his last words would surprise her. "No fantasy, Princess. I'm not a peasant, you know."

"No, I didn't know. I assumed, like most of the boys who come to work in the royal mews, you were a tenant farmer's son."

"Well, we do run a proper farm on the estate, but we have a foreman to do the hiring and handle most of the actual labor. No, my dad's a Lord, James MacAlister, and we're an old landed family. He used to hunt with your father after your parents took over Balmoral and rebuilt her."

She still felt confused by his unorthodox background. "Then you haven't sufficiently answered my question. Why come to London and why work in the queen's stables?"

"Why not?" He shrugged and grinned at her, revealing a captivating dimple in his right cheek. "What is the third son of a lord to do with his life except educate himself (if he's wise), gamble and drink (if he's not), and hunt? I was tired of living off my father's stipend. Besides, I wanted to be useful. I love horses, and I'm good with them. So why not do something I enjoy?"

"You could breed a stable-full of your own in Scotland," she suggested.

"Ah, but there's another part to that equation." He blushed and averted his eyes, and she realized she must have hit on a sensitive topic.

She asked anyway. "Which is?"

"Investing in fine horse flesh costs money. And keeping a large stable even more. My family has struggled to hold onto our property for as long as I can remember. My grandfather lost most of the family's fortune back during Crimean War."

And then she understood. It was a tragic and familiar tale these days. Working as an equerry for the queen, Gregory would never earn enough to make a difference in his family's future, but at least he wouldn't further drain their resources. She felt badly for him and sensed his discomfort, talking about his family's financial ruin.

She changed the subject. "So, do you enjoy working in the Royal Mews?"

He settled more solidly on his saddle and smiled. "Aye, I do, ma'am. I'm already very fond of many of the horses."

Without warning, his mount danced skittishly at a dust devil whirring in the dirt path just ahead of them. The horse snorted, eyes rolling, looking as if it were about to bolt. Beatrice gritted her teeth and tightened her grip on her own reins, afraid the ebony Arabian might spook her mount. But Greg skillfully settled his horse with a firm rein and a subtle motion of his hand along the powerful horse's neck.

He whispered into the black's twitching ear, "There now, fella. There now, naught a thing to fear. 'Tis just the wind singin' to ye."

And as if by magic, the animal's eye lost its panicked look. It snorted once more, snuffled softly then became serene and walked on.

"How did you do that? Beelzebub is the terror of the stables." For he was aptly named after the devil himself.

"Giving a horse a name like that shows how little you know him. He's a proud fellow, just misunderstood."

She studied the young groom, curious to learn more about him and his talents. She'd tell her mother about his masterful handling of the horse. It would impress her. The queen might arrange a quick promotion for the lord's son.

Beatrice was still lost in thought, focusing on her gloved fingers curled around the leather reins as they ambled pleasantly along the path, when a hand shot out and tightened around her arm. She flinched at the sudden pressure, cried out in shock and looked up into Gregory's eyes.

The groom's expression had altered from gentle affection for the animal he rode to a mask of anger—eyes wide, lip curled to reveal a slash of white teeth. Her first instinct was to back Lady Jane as far and quickly away from him as possible.

"Sir!" she cried, trying to wrench her arm free. "Release me!"

But he held tight then shocked her further by dragging her off of her saddle. He swung her up and onto the stallion's saddle in front of him, her back pressed tight against his chest. Before she could protest, he'd spurred his mount to a wild gallop, carrying her away.

19

Beatrice screamed for help but dared not continue struggling for fear of falling off the big horse while they were moving so fast. From behind them, she heard shouts. *Good*, she thought, *someone has sent up an alarm*. The police, palace guards, maybe both would hear and come for her.

But when she craned her neck around to look past the groom's left shoulder, behind the black's straining flanks, no one was chasing after them. Instead, she saw two men in grimy rags attempting to drag Lady Jane into the trees.

The truth of the situation suddenly dawned on her, all the more horrifying with the realization that she was not the one in jeopardy. "Horsenappers!" she screamed. "They have her. Stop them!"

"I will," Greg growled, leaning even harder forward and into her, nearly crushing her between his muscled chest and the horse's neck as he urged Beelzebub to even greater speed. "First, I see you safe, Your Highness." His breath rasped in her ear. "They would've knocked you from the saddle."

The heat of the man's body radiated through her. She felt his heart hammering against her shoulder blade, his breath hot and moist on the back of her neck. She gasped for air and clung to the black's flying mane.

She'd heard of such outrageous assaults, but not here in the most posh part of London. Horses, dogs too, stolen from the wealthy then ransomed for princely sums. Thieves were so brazen they sometimes grabbed a leash right out of a dog walker's hand and simply outran them, or snatched up small pets by leaning down from the back of a galloping horse. But the thieving of horses was most often done from an unguarded paddock or stall. Few were daring enough to attempt it in a public park.

It took less than two minutes for the groom to race his horse back down Rotten Row, across the cobbled street and on toward Buckingham's gates. Two guardsmen stood, arms at the ready, staring with obvious concern and confusion at the demon horse and its riders, speeding toward them. They raised their weapons. For a moment, Beatrice feared they might fire on them.

"The princess!" Greg shouted, bringing the animal to a hoof-clattering halt before them. Beelzebub's chest heaved like immense bellows beneath her, nostrils flaring, snorting. Dust rose up in gritty brown clouds from dancing hooves. The Scot handed Beatrice down to the guards. "See she's safe." He gestured with his chin to the yard inside the gate. "Thieves got her horse."

A soldier gave out a shout of alarm. An ear-piercing whistle blew. Before Beatrice could catch her breath or get out a word of thanks to her rescuer, she was surrounded by crimson-jacketed guardsmen who hustled her back inside the palace gates. She pivoted, trying to peer out through the iron grille then beyond the line of trees. But all she could see was the back of the brave groom, bent low over the glistening black Arabian, mane and tail flying as the pair disappeared back into the park.

Moments later, a dozen mounted guardsmen chased after him, leaving her in a billow of dust, surrounded by growing confusion from staff who, having heard the commotion outside, began to spill into the yard as if pouring from the spouts of the castle's many doors.

Beatrice was only vaguely aware of questions shouted at her. She shook her head, unable to answer, incapable of focusing on anything but the line of trees that screened whatever drama might be happening beyond them. Everything had occurred so very quickly. One minute she'd been enjoying a pleasant ride. The next, Gregory was whisking her away and out of harm's way, apparently having foreseen menacing signs she'd missed.

"*Mon dieu!* Your Highness, are you hurt?" Marie appeared at her side, wrapped an arm around her trembling shoulders.

Beatrice turned into her lady's comforting arms. "It was terrifying. My poor horse. And the groom—those terrible men might attack him."

"In the park? How can this be?"

Beatrice was shaking so hard, her knees going all porridge-y, she could barely stay on her feet. "He was so brave, Marie. And I...I didn't even realize what was happening. But he *knew* what they were up to, clever boy. He must have seen the men, two evil rogues who meant to steal my Lady Jane."

"Thank goodness he was with you, Your Highness."

"If I'd agreed to take a pair of guardsmen, they might have been deterred and not tried." She felt idiotic now for insisting upon riding alone. London City was *not* Darmstadt! "Perhaps they thought I was without reliable escort." The stable master had been right. If she had gone alone, she might have been badly hurt...or worse. There was no knowing how desperate or violent her attackers might have been, had Greg not been there to speed her away from danger.

"Come, Princess. We will go to your chamber, and you will lie down and rest. I shall bring chamomile tea and biscuits to calm you."

"No." Beatrice resisted, pulling out of the woman's arms, planting her feet firmly and willing herself to stay upright though she ached to collapse right there on the ground. "No, I must see what has happened to Greg."

"Greg?"

"Gregory MacAlister, the groom. He was the one escorting me. I can only hope he hasn't been injured on my behalf. And Lady Jane. Poor thing, she looked terrified. I'll never forgive myself if they've harmed her."

"At least come and sit out of the sun, away from all this

madness." Marie drew Beatrice protectively out of the crowded center of the yard and into the relative shelter of one of the tacking sheds. More and more guardsmen took to their mounts and rode out at breakneck speed. Now that it was obvious Beatrice was being looked after by her lady-in-waiting, other staff gave them space. The two women sat on a wooden bench, clutching each other's hands. Waiting.

Beatrice thought her heart would never stop racing even as the yard quieted, the dust settled, and curious members of staff and court retreated back inside the castle at the direction of the Master at Arms.

Beatrice squeezed her eyes closed and recalled how quickly Greg had reacted to the unexpected danger. That fierce expression on his face and the strength with which he'd pulled her from her horse, forcefully but with care enough not to hurt her. He'd somehow sensed it was the animal the thieves were after, and she would be in their way and at risk. *What a brave, brave man.*

"Please, please don't let him be hurt by those wicked men," she whispered.

"They are coming back!" Marie shouted, pulling her hands free and jumping to her feet.

Indeed, when Beatrice opened her eyes she could see a wave of red jackets and tall fur helmets on horseback. She searched the cluster of men for the ebony stallion and the much more petite Lady Jane, but saw neither. Her heart lurched.

Then, as the troupe approached the spiked palace gates, the outer ranks of guardsmen split, revealing the young Scot on Beelzebub, leading Lady Jane by her reins.

Beatrice shot up off the bench. "He's done it! Do you see, Marie? He's rescued her too." She gasped for breath, feeling weak and dizzy and exhilarated, all at the same moment. "Oh, how gallant! Does the Scot look injured? Is he leaning a bit heavily to the left in his saddle?"

Marie laughed. "Your Highness, I'd say he looks as fit as any man. *Maintenant, tout est bien.* Please. Let me take you inside to a soothing bath."

"No, I must thank him and see my horse."

"The stable boys, they will take care of Lady Jane."

"I must find out what happened." She pushed away from the woman and strode shakily, but with determination, across the yard. The guardsmen, still on their horses, parted for her. She arrived at Gregory's side just after he'd dismounted. His expression was solemn, his face flushed and coated with a sheen of sweat and dirt.

"Did you catch them? Have the guardsmen got the two of them?"

Gregory spun around to face her. "No. I'm sorry; they were too late. I had one of the villains down on the ground, but the other was making off with your horse. I had to choose. By the time I caught up with him and retrieved Lady Jane, the first man was off and running. His partner slipped away when he saw the guardsmen coming across the track."

"Oh," she said. "I'm sorry." He glared at the ground, looking disgusted with himself. "I should have had them. I should have—"

"Oh, no, it's not your fault!" she cried. "You did all you could. And what is most important, you kept me from harm and my horse from injury, or from being sold to some cruel costermonger for a dray nag."

She stepped forward, wanting to fling her arms around his neck in gratitude but stopped herself, suddenly aware of Marie and a flock of stable lads watching. Stepping back, she lifted a hand in a gesture of gratitude. "Thank you."

Elton Jackson approached and thumped Greg on the back. "Well done, lad. I heard what happened. Nasty business." He seemed not to want to look Beatrice in the eye, as if he might be tempted to say: *Told you so, didn't I?* "Boys, take the princess's horse back to her stall and clean her up good. Oats for her. She needs a bit of pampering after her fright."

Before they took her away, Beatrice stepped up and rested her forehead against Lady Jane's velvety muzzle, hoping that would somehow convey how grateful she was to have her safe. When she lifted her head, the stable master was ordering her brave rescuer back to his chores.

She sighed. Greg was the one who could use a hot bath and a reward of some kind. But then, maybe he thought he'd just been doing his job.

Well, he'd done it just fine.

She finally let Marie guide her away from the mews. Her mind circled round the excitement of the morning. The day had started out so well, with such hope—but might have ended in tragedy. She would write to Henry and tell him of her adventure. He might still find her life interesting. She hoped he'd write back. Even if they couldn't marry, she still wanted to be his friend. His very closest friend.

20

Gregory kept an eye out for a chance to speak with Beatrice again. And to let her see him as something more elegant than a stable groom. But he found few acceptable excuses for a man from the mews to enter the palace proper. In the end, he was forced to wait for the princess's daily rides.

When she did come, sometimes it was at an unexpected hour, and he was raking out stalls or brushing one of the queen's prized Windsor greys. Then Jackson called up the captain of the guard and asked for two men to be assigned to accompany Beatrice. After the incident in the park, she didn't object to an armed escort.

Several weeks later, Gregory's patience was at an end. He had to establish a special relationship with the princess, something more intimate than the trust he'd earned after the horse napping incident. Already Wilhelm had sent two terse messages, demanding an update on his progress. Gregory had little to report to the prince. He was at a loss for what to do when, without any effort from him, the problem was handily resolved.

He heard Beatrice talking with Elton Jackson after she returned from a ride with her military guard.

"I feel so much safer with your new groom MacAlister. He acted so swiftly the day of the attack, and I daresay those two men are still on the loose. From now on, please free him of his duties to ride with me."

And, of course, what else could Jackson do but acquiesce

to the princess's wishes?

The next day Gregory had Beelzebub saddled before Beatrice appeared. While taking down his choice of bridles, one of the youngest boys came to him, wearing an impudent grin. "Another letter for ye. From yer sweetie, no doubt. Stinks a perfume it do." The boy thrust it at him then ran off laughing before Gregory could cuff him on the ear.

Gregory swore then stuffed the note, unread, into his vest pocket and went to saddle the princess's mount. Meg had written him every few days since he'd come to London. He'd only once returned a brief letter to her, assuring her that he was well but far too busy with his duties to correspond regularly.

Her message was always the same. She fretted about his health. She missed him. She needed to see him. Girlish romantic nonsense. But the last few letters had taken on a more worrisome tone. She insisted he return to Aberdeenshire, saying she had news for him she couldn't deliver by post.

Meg was being a bother, and ignoring her didn't seem to be working. If she kept up this harping at him, she'd become a true liability and might even ruin everything. He didn't know what to do.

After some thought, Gregory decided he had no choice but to make the journey home, on excuse of someone in his family being ill. He needed to impress upon the girl how important it was that he pay attention to what he was doing in London. "Can't always be dashing off silly love letters to you," he'd tell her. He'd not compromise on this point. After all, his future depended upon this escapade on behalf of Wilhelm. If he pleased the young prince by successfully wooing Beatrice, he'd be set for life.

At first Gregory had thought Willy's plan a very long shot indeed. But now that he'd met Beatrice and saw for his own eyes how vulnerable she was, and how open to his influence she could be, he'd begun to believe the prince's plot might actually work.

And if it did? Never again would he have to worry about money. Crown Prince Wilhelm's assets were astounding even now. But once he became emperor, unlimited riches would be at his disposal. Wealth with which to reward those loyal to him. In addition, Gregory would receive an annual allowance from the Crown, as husband to Victoria's youngest daughter.

The elder MacAlister sons might never have enough money to hold on to the family estate. But if he, Gregory, was able to support the family and their lands—his father, brothers and everyone else in the shire would respect him.

Bolstered by that thought, Gregory led the two horses into the sunshine-bright yard. Beatrice had arrived and was waiting beside the exercise ring. She turned and smiled at him. "Good. Then we're off." Her eyes drifted down to his belt and the gun holster at his hip. "I hadn't noticed you wearing that before."

He tugged the bottom of his jacket around to hide the pistol. "After our little adventure, I thought it best. Mr. Jackson made it a rule that whoever accompanies a member of the royal family, they will be armed. A sword is only good close up."

She nodded. "Hopefully word has already gotten round to the undesirable elements of London that I have competent defenders, and we won't be assaulted again. But I thank you for your caution." And with that she turned her horse toward the gate and they began their ride.

He followed her into the park. As soon as they were on the raked path, the horses moving at a relaxed walk, he brought the black up alongside her mare, a casual move toward intimacy she no longer objected to. She normally talked very little. Today, as on many others, he had to remind himself to keep to his place by not speaking to the princess unless she first addressed him. It would not do to be too forward, break with protocol and make her suspicious.

After they had ridden for twenty minutes in silence she turned her head toward him and asked, "May I impose upon you for your opinion, Mr. MacAlister?" Her eyes sparkled shyly at him.

"You may ask anything of me, Your Highness. I am happily at your service."

She cleared her throat and looked away into the distance, as if uncomfortable meeting his gaze while she posed her question. "You see, I have no living father to ask for his advice. And my brothers would never give me a straight answer. They think me silly and naïve. But you treat me as a real and thinking person. I feel secure in asking your opinion."

"I'm glad of that, Princess."

"You see, I need a male perspective. And I am going to be quite frank so that you may be the same in your answers." He gave her a nod of agreement. She continued. "While in Germany, I met a very special young man. We had an understanding and have written to each other ever since."

"I see."

He, of course, knew she was speaking of Henry Battenberg. Court gossip extended not just to the royal mews but throughout London. Everyone had heard, by now, that the princess was infatuated with a dashing young prince from the Continent. But most of the gossip came down to this: A marriage would never happen, if for no other reason than Victoria was set against attaching yet another of her daughters to a German. Her ministers had long advised against such a match, because they, not to mention the English people, feared losing their monarchy to foreigners.

"My mother," Beatrice was saying as they rode on, "has discouraged our correspondence. But a friend is a very precious thing, don't you think? And I don't wish to lose Henry's friendship." She nibbled her bottom lip. "I will, of course, discourage intimacy that isn't proper between a man and woman who are not married. But I wonder if you could tell me, Gregory—" She turned to him with wide, innocent eyes. "—is it possible for a man to have a purely platonic relationship with a woman? A friendship that is warm and close, such as two men have." She blinked, looking flustered when he didn't immediately answer. "What I mean is, can he still *like* her and not expect more than she can reasonably give without damaging her reputation and hurting her family?"

It was a better opening than he ever could have hoped for.

He put on a solemn face. "I do think friendships of that sort exist, between a man and a woman. But," he said, measuring his words carefully, "they are rare. It would depend upon what the woman expected from the man. What degree of loyalty does she require?" He paused to let her mull over his meaning.

"Yes, loyalty," she said as if tasting the word for hidden flavors. "But I think the word you are really searching for is honesty or perhaps even fidelity. What you are trying to say, in a delicate way, has to do with jealousy perhaps?" She glanced at him. "Are you saying that if a woman is unwilling, or unable, to give herself physically to a man, she must then accept that he will find satisfaction in the arms of another woman? Or women."

He lowered his eyes to the gravel passing beneath their horses' hooves. He had to be careful not to venture into territory that would offend her or make her wary of him.

"It's such a sensitive topic, Princess. I don't know how to put it to you. But yes, the man would undoubtedly be tempted to look for satisfaction elsewhere." He immediately added, "I'm sorry, I have no right speaking to you like th—"

"No, no. You put it just right. I'm not in the least affronted. This is what I needed to hear. The *truth* about how men think. I'm grateful for your candor, Gregory." She drew a breath and looked around her, and he could see how hard she was thinking about this. "Men need physical relationships. Yes. I understand from my mother that women are not the same and do not require similar experiences or maybe—" She brought her horse to a stop as if by running out of words she'd also run out of path.

He angled his mount up alongside her. "If you'll pardon my boldness," he said, keeping his voice low so that others moving past them along Rotten Row wouldn't hear, "but I think that people are people. Although a man's needs may, at times, seem more urgent to him, women also have needs." Her eyes widened at this, and he wondered if it was the first time she'd heard anything but her mother's version of sex education. "However, Princess, it's my experience that men far more often fail to control their desires, and therefore their fidelity is less often sure." *There, the seed of doubt is planted.*

"Oh," she said, her eyes beginning to glisten with emotion. "Then if a woman wants to continue a friendship on a purely platonic level with a gentleman, she must be prepared to release him of the obligation to remain as pure as she. That's what you're saying? Or at least she must accept that he will eventually … wander?"

"If he truly cares for her," Gregory said, trying to catch her eye, "he will abstain from affairs with other women. But it is the nature of the male animal to seek a mate." He noticed with pleasure that she blushed at this. Before she could react further, he hastily tacked on another apology, "Your Highness, I really shouldn't be talking to you like this. I've overstepped the bounds of decency."

"You are not at fault." She rested a gloved hand over his. "Please don't blame yourself when I asked for the truth. It is good to know someone in London will speak honestly to me." Tears threatened, but she blinked them away. "You can't imagine how frustrating it is, to be a grown woman and treated as a child, or an imbecile."

"If I may be so bold as to speak my mind one more time?"

"Oh, please do." She sniffled but managed to hold back her tears.

He finally caught her soft blue eyes with his. HH"Your Highness is not just an adult. She is a beautiful and intelligent woman. Any man would be a fool not to—" he shook his head and looked away, as if disgusted with himself. "No. This is totally inappropriate. I beg your pardon. I can say no more."

He was aware of her studying him, her gaze fixed on his face as she puzzled over his compliment. *Another seed planted. Good.* She now knew he found her attractive. And a moment earlier she'd, no doubt, imagined Henry Battenberg humping away atop another woman. It didn't matter whether or not Battenberg had been faithful to her up until this point. It was the future she would fear.

Silence cloaked the rest of their ride. *Perfect*, he thought. He'd accomplished a great deal in less than an hour, on horseback no less. Now all he had to do was start a few well-worded rumors to feed off of the princess's doubts about her would-be lover.

~

Back in the royal mews, after Gregory had helped Beatrice dismount, escorted her across the busy yard and through one of the doors leading into Buckingham Palace, he whistled his way back to the stables. "You lads, take up these horses and brush them down."

As official escort to the princess he'd acquired a sheen of respectability and jumped to a higher pecking order. He was now a Senior Groom, no longer expected to perform the same drudgery as the younger boys.

Gregory strolled back toward the groom's equipment room to exchange his good riding boots for working clogs. He unstrapped the pistol from around his hip to return it to the armory. In doing so he felt the crackle of paper in his pocket. He pulled it out. His mistress's latest letter.

Might as well read it now as later. He leaned against a post in the shade of the stables.

Me Dearest Greg,

I didden wish to bring you this news x-sep for when I could hold your brawny self in me arms and kiss you and show you how happy I am. But you been so busy as to not answer me letters or to come home as I begged you. So now I can wate no longer.

I carry your child, my darling. Even though you been gone for near two months, I know it is your babe as I have no other man in me life, nor ever will, my love. I know what you is doing in London is portant for our future. So I do not now ask you to come home as it will be at least four months before our child is born. I just want you to know that he (or she) is yours, just as I shall always be. There will be no prouder day in my life than the one we're free to proclaim our love by marrying before God and our frends and family, at St. Edmonds in the village.

I long for the day you come home to me. But, if you cannot come away from the job you are doing, cood you send for me? All I need is mony for a train ticket and a little more for room and bord in London, and I will run to your side. Please tell me that you want me to come.

Yours everlasting,
Margaret

Gregory crumpled the letter in his fist. He stifled the rage building inside his chest. Silenced the scream of frustration working its way up through his throat. Swore, and swore again. She was going to spoil everything.

21

Helena and Louise extended their visit at Buckingham Palace another two weeks. Beatrice had no trouble figuring out why. She had overheard them in the queen's garden. "Bea is in far too fragile a state since her hoped-for engagement didn't take," Louise said. "She can't be left here alone to deal with Mama."

Helena nodded in agreement. "We must find a way to cheer her, if we can't help the situation in any other way."

But attending teas or the theater with her sisters hardly replaced the exhilarating future she'd glimpsed for herself with Henry Battenberg before her mother forced her to reject his proposal.

It was a Saturday, about a week later, when she received a message from Louise, asking that Beatrice meet her and Helena in the drawing room. Helena was already there, divested of her children who were in the nursery with the nurse who traveled with them. Helena looked up from where she was seated with a lapful of embroidery.

"Louise send word I should meet the two of you here," Beatrice said, "for a surprise of some kind. What is it? Do you know?"

Helena smirked at her. "It's a secret, I guess."

"But you do know, don't you?" Beatrice smiled. It was good to see that somebody in this house was happy and enjoying herself. "What is it? Is her statue of Papa finished? Has she set a date for the installation and unveiling?"

Louise had achieved one of her most cherished dreams—to become a professional artist. Not only did she paint magnificently, she was capable of sculpting the most amazing and life-like images of people, from life or portraits. Prince Albert's full-body likeness in marble would be placed in a prominent location when it was done. But, so far, Beatrice hadn't heard where or when.

"All I'm allowed to tell you is that you need to wait here." Helena's expression became more serious. "Actually, I'm glad we have a chance to talk before Loosie comes with…with the surprise. I've heard rumors in Court that you should be aware of."

Beatrice waved her hand as if chasing visible clouds of gossip from the air around them. "You know I never pay attention to their ridiculous chatter."

"I know, dear." Helena pressed a hand over Beatrice's clasped fingers. "But this is something that affects decisions you must make very soon."

"What are you talking about?"

"Sometimes knowing what others believe, even if it isn't completely true, can help you sort out what's real from what isn't. I just don't want your heart broken." Helena hugged her.

Beatrice pushed her away impatiently. "Just tell me quickly, so I can laugh it off and be done with their nonsense."

Helena lowered her voice, even though no one else was in the room with them. "Unfortunately, Mama's insistence on discouraging Henry Battenberg was overheard by several of her ladies. Now, apparently, everyone in Court knows about your fondness for him."

Beatrice laughed. "That's old news. I hate being talked about, but there's nothing I can do. By now you'd think they'd have tired of that story and found something more exciting to whisper about."

Helena pursed her lips. "That's just it. They have. The new gossip has to do with Henry, back in Germany." She shook her head mournfully. "It's being said that, even as he was wooing you in Darmstadt, he had a mistress. And he still keeps this woman for his own pleasure."

Beatrice closed her eyes and shuddered. Of course she'd feared something like this was coming. Hadn't Henry been entirely too generous, too handsome, too nice to have remained true to her, even if she hadn't turned down his proposal?

She felt sick to her stomach; her head spun and vision blurred with wretched crimson swirls. She had thought she was prepared to hear something like this. Gregory had warned her; it was the nature of man to seek a mate. Sometimes, apparently, over and over again.

And yet she hurt. The pain of knowing another woman had stolen the joy that should have been hers was almost unbearable.

"I think I will go to my room now." She started to stand up.

Helena pulled her back down on the loveseat beside her. "Oh, Bea, I'm so sorry. Of course it may not be true. He may not be the sort of man who needs that sort of companionship."

"Oh shut up, Lenchen. Not be the sort of man who needs *sex*? Is that what you're saying? Of course he needs it. Why wouldn't he? He's a virile, gorgeous, and healthy man."

Her sister blanched whiter than the bleached lace doilies lying across the armrests, and it was only then that Beatrice realized what she'd just said. "Don't talk like that," Helena snapped. "Such language! You're beginning to sound as bad as Louise."

"But I'm tired of being proper," Beatrice cried. "Tired of avoiding subjects that are important in our lives. I should have listened to Louise long ago, ignored Mama and followed my heart. What is wrong with me? *I wanted Henry!* But I let Mama badger me into rejecting his proposal. And now he has found someone else."

"But isn't it better to discover this now, if it is true?"

"Stop it."

"No, listen." Helena held onto Beatrice's hands and looked into her eyes. "If he already had a woman while we were in Darmstadt, he was deceiving you even then. And if that part isn't true, but he has a new mistress, then it appears he took very little time to mourn the loss of his dear Beatrice before finding a replacement." She shook her head. "How disloyal is that? You would think the man might have taken some time to recover from your rejection before leaping into the bed of another woman."

Beatrice held back her tears, mortified. "You're right. He should have done. Oh God, my life is ruined."

Just then the door to the salon swung open and Louise stepped through. She wore a broad smile and opened her mouth as if to say something wonderful, but then took in the situation. Beatrice looked up at her from within Helena's comforting embrace, aware that her tear-streaked face must surely reflect her breaking heart.

"Oh my, what tragedy have we here?" Louise glanced back over her shoulder and made a stopping motion with her hand behind her.

Helena's voice was cool when she said, "A healthy shock of reality is all. She needed to know how things stood before you —"

"What have you told her, Lenchen?" Louise's voice stretched taut with sudden anger.

"Nothing but what she needs to know."

Beatrice sniffled. "Please don't fight, you two. I feel miserable enough as it is."

"I've just opened her eyes to the ways of men," Helena said. "She'll be all right soon enough."

"I won't. I won't be all right. Ever!" Beatrice moaned. "Mama has destroyed my life. And I let her do it, fool that I am."

"Oh, is that all?" Louise said breezily, her expression mellowing. "She does that every day of the week to one of us. You ought to be accustomed to her imperious bullying by now, Baby." She cast Helena a damning look but then, remarkably, Louise's eyes twinkled with delight. "Now, dry your pretty eyes, Baby. Here is your surprise."

Beatrice forced herself to look toward the doorway,

knowing in her heart that whatever appeared there could not possibly cheer her up. A figure moved into the space behind Louise. Louise stepped aside. A man in a beautifully tailored dark blue frock coat stepped forward and into the light of the room.

Beatrice's heart exploded into a thousand pieces. "Henry!" she gasped.

"Hello, my darling. I simply couldn't stay away." He smiled at her—that beautiful, perfect, intoxicating smile paired with eyes that shone as warm and blue as a tropical sea.

"You beast!" Beatrice shrieked and, gathering her skirts, ran from the room in a flood of tears.

22

"What have I done?" Henry asked, honestly bewildered.

Helena glared at him. "What every man does—makes a mess of women's lives." She refused to look at him and instead turned to Louise. "I think it was a terribly tactless thing for you to bring him here, now that we know his true nature."

Henry turned to Louise. "Know what? I thought you said Bea wanted to see me." He had run into the Duchess of Argyll and her sometime traveling companion Stephen Byrne in Germany. The American Civil War veteran had served on the queen's Secret Service until Her Majesty tossed him out of her employ and her country.

"She did. She does, I'm sure of it." Louise turned to look down the hallway as if Beatrice might have left a visible wake marking her dramatic departure. "I don't know why she's acting this way. She was broken hearted when Mama forced her to write and reject your proposal."

"I know why," Helena said, folding her arms over her chest.

"Enlighten us," Louise said, and Henry had never heard her sound so severe.

"It is because of *his* women." Helena jabbed an accusatory finger in his direction.

Henry shook his head, more confused than ever. "My women?" "Most certainly. There you were at your brother's wedding, whispering honeyed words in my sister's ear, promising her your heart, and God only knows what else, and all the while you were…you were…*fornicating!*"

Louise stared at her sister in horror. "Lenchen!"

Henry shook his head violently. "I wouldn't…I never—"

"Well, it's true, Helena insisted. "Everyone says he had a mistress, even while we were in Germany. Since then he's kept this woman, or got himself a fresh one, showing not one bit of remorse for losing my sister's affection."

Louise let out a long sigh. "I dare say you haven't a shred of evidence. And here dear Henry Battenberg himself stands, as steadfast as any man, coming all this way to see Beatrice. Tell her, Henry."

Henry felt as if he'd been shoved into a meat grinder and rendered a bloody pulp. Who could have imagined princesses being so brutal? He sat down heavily in the nearest chair and shook his head.

"Henry," Louise said, "you must tell me this isn't true. Are you involved with another woman?"

"I did have a mistress. Yes."

"You see!" Helen yipped triumphantly.

"*Did,* not *do.* I had been spending time with a young woman, a merchant's daughter. But after reacquainting myself with Beatrice at the wedding, I realized I was wasting my time when I could have Bea's love. I broke it off with the girl the next time I saw her, which was the night after my brother's wedding. I haven't been back to her or with another woman since. I'm determined to win the woman I love."

"Well said." Louise applauded.

"So he claims." Helena glared at him. "But does he speak the truth or is he just trying to trick us into believing him?"

Henry groaned and clasped his hands together in front of him, in supplication. "On my honor, I have been true to Beatrice, even though she refused my proposal. I know she only did it because of the queen."

"You can bet on that," Louise muttered, pacing the floor. "But now we need to convince Bea that these rumors have no basis."

"I'm not sure that's a good idea," Helena said.

Louise ignored her sister and turned toward the door. "I'll go talk to her."

Henry jumped to his feet and rushed to stop her. "No. Please. I appreciate your willingness to intercede for me, Duchess. But it's up to me to speak to Bea and explain. She can't take another's word for my loyalty to her."

Henry left the two women in the salon, loudly debating the Battenberg honor. He wondered what it was about this family that had enticed both his brother and himself to become involved with them. Certainly Louis saw for himself financial benefits and a boost in social status when he wed the queen's granddaughter. He took after their father, a practical man. But he believed Louis also cared for Vicky.

The one impractical thing the grand duke, their father, had ever done was to marry their mother. She was not of royal or even noble lineage, and their engagement had caused a monumental scandal years back. Then his father had dug up a discarded title and somehow found (or manufactured) a link through his wife's family to it. Before long the aristocracy forgot their silly rules and accepted her into their ranks. By the time his sons came along, the duke had learned his lesson and began planning early for his boys' future wives.

But Henry didn't give a whit about the prestige of wedding the Queen of England's daughter. He didn't see Beatrice as a royal ticket to wealth and fame. He saw a gentle and lovely young woman who smiled and laughed far too infrequently, whose eyes he'd delighted in making sparkle. Simply put, he loved making her happy. He couldn't understand why others failed to recognize the qualities he had discovered in Beatrice.

But now, because of vicious rumors, and her damn obstinate mother, he was about to lose her.

He couldn't let that happen.

He ran as fast as he could, not even sure where to start looking for Beatrice. Once he reached the family quarters, and he had only the vaguest memory of which wing that was, it would be a miracle if a servant didn't challenge him and demand to know where he thought he was going. He choked back a hysterical laugh. He must be insane chasing after the woman this way.

Insane or in love. Maybe a little of both.

Of course he'd been attracted to other women in the past. His experiences with them sometimes had been exciting and flattering, but they'd meant nothing. Suddenly he'd found the woman whose temperament, intelligence, and appearance all appealed in the most profound ways to him. He couldn't lose her. He just couldn't.

But he almost ran over her.

Henry broke his sprint and leapt over a billow of dark-colored skirts plumped up in the middle of the hallway floor. He immediately recognized them as a downed Beatrice, sprawled on the marble tiles.

"My darling, did you fall?" He spun around and came back to her, stooping down to lift her chin and brush the hair from her eyes. "Are you all right? Did you hurt yourself?"

Beatrice shook her head, sobbing. "Just go away and leave me alone. I can't bear the thought of…of you and another wo-wo-woman."

"Bea, sweet Bea, there is no one but you." He lifted her chin again to make her look into his eyes. He kissed the center of her puckered, pink forehead. "I promise you. I solemnly swear that I want no woman but you. Will have no woman other than you for as long as there is any chance we can be together. And I do believe we *will* find a way. Please trust me."

"Oh, Henry!" She lifted her tear-blotched face to him.

He kissed away the salty moisture from her cheeks, stroked a finger down her nose to its tip and lightly touched the petal-soft bow of her lips. Down here in the floor with her, where they sat, her skirts pooled around them and not another person in sight, he was suddenly overcome by the urge to enfold her in his arms and lie down with her. Right here. Holding her for as long as it took for her to feel the stirrings of his heart and know how desperately he wanted her.

This very moment.

On the floor.

Oh, Lord! He had to distract himself from that kind of thinking.

"This is a two-way street, my dear. You must learn to trust me. And somehow, I must learn to trust *you*, my Beatrice."

She frowned at him. "Trust me in what way?"

He shrugged. "How will I ever convince myself that this beautiful woman won't run off with the next dashing courtier who flirts with her?"

She giggled and covered her mouth with one hand. Her eyes flashed at him with delight. "Oh Henry, no one ever flirts with me."

"You see why I worry? You don't deny you would run off with the rogue. And—" he put up a finger to stop her from interrupting him "—I expect there have been many young men who have attempted to flirt with you, Princess. But your good breeding has enabled you to pretend they don't exist and thus discourage them."

"More likely my mother has done the discouraging, though I have no proof." She sighed but looked a good deal happier as he took her hands and pulled her to her feet. "Oh Henry, she really is determined to keep us apart. I think she's decided that I shall never have a man in my life."

"How cruel and selfish that is." He should have bitten back the words, but he couldn't contain his frustration and anger.

"I don't know that she intends to be mean to me," Beatrice said, "or to any of our family. I think she's just afraid."

"Afraid of losing you?"

"One way or another, yes. Childbearing was never pleasant for her, or so my sisters assure me. She thinks she's saving me from pain, or from myself, or…I don't know. Somehow I must convince her that what I most want and need in all the world is you."

His heart swelled. Henry took her in his arms and kissed

her as he had never dared to kiss her before, until she melted in his arms and the world around them disappeared.

He slipped his hand up along the soft swell of her breast. His insides went volcanic at the mere suggestion of her warm flesh beneath layers of clothing. He stroked his fingertips gently around the pleated curve of her silk bodice. When he possessively cupped her breast through her dress's bodice, she drew a soft breath of acceptance and pleasure.

Beatrice's lips parted. He deepened their kiss but got only a quick, sweet taste of her before she drew back with a gasp. "Oh my!" Here eyes flew wide, shimmering with surprise.

"I'm sorry," he said quickly. "I'm too bold."

"No. Oh no. I do so very much like this." She smiled. "Again, please."

He had to remind himself that it was very possible she'd never been kissed before Darmstadt. At least not like this, not with passion nipping away at both of them, spurring them toward the ultimate intimacies.

"Bea, oh Bea. Another moment touching you like this, another kiss like the last, and I will be lost."

"Lost?" She shook her head, looking truly puzzled.

He looked down at the front of his trousers ruefully. "Your Highness, you—how shall I say this without offending?—you *arouse* me."

"I do?" Her eyes sparkled. Blue chips of sapphire.

"You do. Nearly beyond my ability to control this…this situation." He laughed when she stepped back and looked down as if to observe the effect of her feminine powers.

"Good," she said, beaming at him then whispered, "I shall hope to inspire more of this arousal in our marriage bed."

He laughed out loud, thrilled with her, then took her hand and led her back—with no little reluctance—to the safety of her room.

23

Gregory bought the train ticket at Paddington Station. It wasn't for Meggie; it was for him. Round-trip.

He spent the day-long trip north, slouched against the itchy horsehair seat. Buried in the dismal gray fog of his own mind, mixed with coal cinders the size of large beetles that swept in through the open windows of the railcar, depositing soot on anything they hit, including him. Miserable, he tried to ignore the filth and slept when he could. Most of the time he brooded about what he would say to encourage Meggie to be patient and keep her mouth shut.

Buying her silence before now had never been a problem. A promise of a someday wedding. A little gift and snuggle. She was spirited and gave of her body freely, but only to him—which was what he liked best about her. They had been sweethearts since childhood. It was her increasingly serious side that might become the issue now. In recent years she'd grown more and more possessive. And now there was this—a child.

A baby made everything different. Would becoming a mother alter her allegiance? Make her less amenable to his desires and plans. Make her more impatient for a ring on her finger.

He had to talk to her and see where her mind lay.

But first he had to go home to assure himself that gossip of Meggie's condition hadn't reached his father. If that happened, there would be bloody hell to pay.

Old Jerry from the estate was there to meet him at the tiny

station with one of the wagons they used on the farm. No fancy barouche or phaeton now; those had been sold off along with much of the art that had graced the walls of the manse. An hour later Gregory jumped down from the splintery bench-seat. It was almost dark now, the day gone with the long journey. He left Jerry to handle his bag and started toward the main entrance to the house. A figure stepped out through doorway as if the person had been waiting for him.

It wasn't his father as he'd at first feared.

"Andrew!" Gregory laughed nervously. His eldest brother had made it clear years ago that he wanted little to do with him. Andrew was high-minded, solemn as a preacher, and too proud by half, in Gregory's estimation. "I'm flattered. Have you been watching for my arrival?"

"I have." His brother's cool gaze took him in without revealing any real emotion. "I wanted to speak to you before you saw Father."

"Is he not well?"

"He's in good enough health, and I want to keep it that way."

Gregory eyed him suspiciously. "If you think you need to protect him from me—"

"Come this way," Andrew said, walking away and toward the library before Gregory could finish his sentence. Maybe this meant their father wasn't at home. The library was where the old man spent most of his days, immersed in his private studies, or hiding from bill collectors.

Gregory followed along.

As soon as they were inside the dim room lined with shelves of leather-bound volumes, Andrew shut the door. He didn't, however, move to any of the deep-seated leather club chairs in which Gregory had learned the pleasures of books. Despite his wildness as a youth—and some would argue, later in life—he adored reading and was a decent student.

"I've had to step into a situation on your behalf," Andrew began, "and I don't mind telling you, I detest the whole business."

"What situation is that?"

"Your little tart from the other side of the village came a-visiting two weeks ago."

Gregory's heart lurched to a stop. "Meggie came here?"

"To see the laird. To tell him he would soon be a grandfather."

A sharp bark of a laugh burst from Gregory's throat. "The nerve of the wench." He waved a dismissive hand. "She can't prove who the father is."

"A whore, is that what you'd make her out to be?" Andrew's eyes flamed with contempt. "Greg, you and I both know you've been all that girl has thought about since she was twelve years old. You may treat her like a tramp, but she hangs on your every word and breath, and always has."

Of course. He knew that. How could he not? He saw it in her eyes every time they were together. Even when she was angry with him, there was tenderness behind her words. She couldn't pass him by without letting her fingers graze some part of his body.

"True enough, she thinks a good deal of me. But I've been gone for months now, and you know how these farm girls are, needing a man and taking their pleasure where they will."

"That sounds more like a description of my little brother to me." His brother's lip lifted in a sneer.

Gregory balled his fists at his sides, wishing for an excuse to crack Andrew's jaw. The man might be a good six inches taller, but he wasn't a fighter. It would take a lot to get his older brother to hit him first. "You've sown your own wild oats."

"There's a time and a place. And you've taken chances far too long. Now you'll have to pay for your carelessness."

"And what does that mean?"

"It means, Meggie came here meaning to tell Father, but I was lucky enough to intercept her."

Gregory let out a breath of pure relief. So Andrew had somehow talked her out of approaching the laird. Excellent. "What did she say? And you—what did you tell her?"

"She said you had stopped writing. Said she'd asked you to let her come to London but you refused. I expect she's beginning to panic, to feel desperate."

Gregory sensed what was coming, felt fate being forced upon him, suffocating him. It was as if his brother was pressing a cushion over his face. His only defense now was a show of fury at the injustice of it all.

"Well, what would you have me do, Andrew? I'm employed by the queen, damn it. I have responsibilities. There's no place for Meggie in Buckingham Palace or over the stables where I live. Grooms aren't allowed to keep wives or mistresses on the grounds."

"You need to *provide* for her," his brother said, leaning over him as if to drop his words from a height to add weight to them. "And for the baby. I know some men refuse to acknowledge their bastards, but Father has always been of a different mind. And so am I. She's not a bad girl, and you're clearly not material for marrying up in aristocratic circles. I think you'd do her just fine."

"But haven't you been listening? I can't marry her. *I can't*—" What would he tell Wilhelm? The prince would be past furious. He'd challenged men to duels—two that he was aware of—and killed both.

"So you have a London woman too, is that it?" Andrew laughed and shook his head. "You just dig yourself in deeper and deeper, don't you? Everyone knows you've been promising to marry Meggie for years."

"No!" Gregory protested. "Now just you wait here—"

"Even Father knows you've kept on seeing her, despite his telling you, years ago, to leave her be. Now you've taken yourself off to London to break it off with her because of the child, is that it?"

"It isn't. Of course not. I just—"

"Your timing couldn't be better."

"I didn't *know* she was with child before I left!" This was preposterous.

But his brother was right about one thing—the timing was atrocious. If he married Meggie he wouldn't be free to carry out Wilhelm's plot. Word would get out that he had a wife. He saw his future plunging down a black, black hole.

Gregory muttered, "I was shocked when she wrote to me. She totally blindsided me. But I came home to make the necessary decisions, you see, to make things right for her." He tried out a thin, encouraging smile on his brother.

"You did?" Andrew still looked skeptical.

"Yes, of course. I know you think I'm a worthless clod, but I do have a heart. I do care for Meggie."

Andrew's shoulders lowered a notch. "Then you intend to marry her after all?"

"I'll talk to her and see what she wants to do. If we don't marry, I'll make sure she's taken care of." He met his brother's eyes. "You haven't told Father yet?"

"No. Of course not."

Gregory nodded and went to the butler table to pour himself a whisky. Then, as an afterthought, another for his brother. He handed Andrew the glass. "Please don't tell him just yet. Let me do that—man up, and all that." He smiled, and actually got a whisper of a smile back for his effort.

It was at that moment he knew exactly what he had to do. He knocked back the whisky, and his stomach immediately settled.

24

Ponsonby had taken to his bed.

"It is nothing I can't work through. Just a sniffly cold," the queen's dignified, silver-haired secretary told Beatrice earlier that day when she stopped him outside of her mother's office.

"You may be able to work, but what if the queen catches whatever you have?" Aside from the very real possibility of contagion, Beatrice knew how terrified her mother was of illness of any kind. Hadn't the doctors assured them that Prince Albert's fever indicated he had a mild case of the flu? Hadn't they promised that, with bed rest and fluids, he would be on his feet again in a week?

But he hadn't recovered. And it wasn't influenza. It was typhoid fever. When he'd rallied for a few days, seeming to prove the physicians right, then suddenly died—it had been a shock to them all.

"You should go to your bed and stay there, Colonel, until you're feeling better. I have acted as my mother's secretary before, and I am capable of doing so again."

Ponsonby wiped at his swollen, watery eyes and blew his nose. "If she needs me—"

"I will send someone. I promise. Now go."

She watched him shuffle out of her mother's outer office, leaving her alone with the day's schedule. This wasn't how she had hoped to spend her day. In fact she'd depended upon her mother being so busy and well tended by Ponsonby that she,

Beatrice, would be free to go riding with Henry, or perhaps take a carriage into the country for a picnic. She wasn't even sure that her mother knew Henry was in the city. He had decided it would be more appropriate for him to stay at one of his friends' clubs in London, instead of asking for a room in the palace.

Of course, sooner or later they would have to make his presence known to the queen. In the meantime, Beatrice relished keeping Henry to herself. Her secret love, here with her in London. The mere thought of his nearness sent ripples of happiness through her. As long as Victoria believed Henry to be miles away across the channel, Beatrice wouldn't be subjected to her mother's rants about the dangers of men, childbirth, and anything else the queen dreamt up to stand in the way of her happiness. Victoria's fantasies of disaster knew no limits.

The first thing Beatrice did after Ponsonby left the office was to write a note to Henry, letting him know that their plans for the day had changed. She suggested she see him that evening. They could go wherever he liked. *La Bohème* was at the Royal Opera House, and the aging but still fabulous Jenny Lind was giving a rare private performance at the Royal College of Music, where she had taught singing during her declining years. Or they could dine at any of the many fine restaurants in the city—*Simpson's* in The Strand, or *Wilson's* where the queen acquired her oysters, either would be lovely. She didn't care what they did or where—as long as she was with Henry.

No sooner had she handed the letter to one of the palace couriers than Mr. Gladstone arrived at Ponsonby's desk, his own secretary in tow. "Go right in, Prime Minister. The queen's expecting you." Beatrice knocked lightly then held the door open for the two men. She couldn't help staring at the slim valise the secretary carried. She'd never forget that time, years ago, when a man had smuggled terrifying contraband into the palace in a case no larger than that. How vulnerable they all were, even here in a fortress like Buckingham Palace, protected by guardsmen and servants. One could never be sure of one's safety.

She shook off the sudden chill of fear, scolding herself for falling prey to her mother's imaginary dangers, and gathered up a stenographer's pad and pencil.

Victoria had chosen to move from behind her desk to an upholstered chair. Her bad foot rested on a needlepoint-covered stool. Beatrice pulled over a straight-backed wooden chair beside her mother's plump form and sat down while the PM wished the queen a speedy recovery from her gout.

"Thank you. It comes and goes, you know," Victoria said. "The pain is less today than many others." She sighed. "Best we get down to business while I'm still relatively comfortable. Your message yesterday mentioned a most grave situation you wished to discuss. I assume you mean the siege in Khartoum. Have you come to your senses and now agree that we must intervene to rescue dear General Gordon?"

Of course Beatrice had been following news in the *London Times* of the uprisings in both India and the Sudan, and the growing fear for the lives of British citizens in those countries. Her mother had sent one of her most trusted ministers to deal with the situation in India. Some suggested evacuation of the entire country. But India had become home to many British subjects, and the queen considered it one of the most valuable assets of her empire. She would no more order her people out of India than she would suggest they vacate Wales or Scotland.

The prime minister observed the queen solemnly. "Parliament is still against sending men to fight the Sudanese rebels, thus further involving our government in what appears to be a civil war. No, I fear the issues I wish to address are closer to home though no less treacherous."

"Are we to guess at your meaning, sir, or will you enlighten us?" The queen's tone was not in the least playful. Beatrice knew she resented having lost Benjamin Disraeli, her previous prime minister, to whom she had become very close. Disraeli would have charmed her; Gladstone was a dour-faced old man who saw humor in nothing.

He coughed into his hand but, to his credit, didn't otherwise react to the queen's starchy attitude toward him. "Your Majesty, it has come to our attention that the German Emperor is about to turn over nearly all of his duties to his son, that is to say to your son-in-law, Crown Prince Frederick."

"Fritz has been quite open about his father's failing health. This is not unexpected."

"Yes, of course, Your Majesty. But we have heard from reliable sources in Potsdam that Frederick himself is in poor health."

"I know all of this!" the queen snapped. "My son-in-law has a throat cancer. Of course he's not well. Why are you telling me things I already know? Haven't I worried about Europe's future every month of my reign? The Continent is a mess—a cesspool of revolt, violence, and corruption. Thank God our country has not succumbed to the same problems."

"Precisely, Your Majesty." Gladstone glanced toward his secretary, whose expression remained unreadable. Beatrice thought neither man looked at ease. "We, your ministers, are concerned that, should the unthinkable happen, should both the Emperor and his son Frederick pass from this life within a few months of each other, your grandson will then become Emperor." He paused to study his clasped hands. "Unless something is done to stop him."

Beatrice stared at the man, her mouth falling open in shock. Was he suggesting that her mother put pressure on her daughter's husband to name an heir other than his eldest son? To skip over young Wilhelm, his first born, entirely?

Beatrice turned with an aching heart to her mother.

The Queen stared into the distance. Silent. As if she hadn't heard a word that had passed Gladstone's lips. At last, she turned her head to fix the man in her coldest, most disapproving glare. "What you are suggesting is impossible, sir. I will not tamper with the sovereignty of another nation. The line of succession is sacrosanct. If I were to act to keep Willy from his throne, what precedent might that set at the time of my own death? Who might then contrive to wrest the crown from Bertie, from my own son?"

Gladstone shook his head grimly. "There have been rumors—" he drew a deep breath, and Beatrice thought she could see pain in his aging features "—that your grandson might use his position and power to bring about regrettable changes in Europe. That he might even attempt to encourage yet another war to gain territory for his empire, forcing nations on the Continent, and their allies, to take sides. The entire world would likely be thrown into mayhem. We cannot allow this to happen." He stood up and started to pace. "Wilhelm is young and capricious and unpredictable. Without the wisdom of his father to temper his whims—"

"Capricious? Unpredictable?" Victoria huffed. "You're being far too diplomatic, sir. Willy is insane. I've never doubted it. His temper tantrums, cruelty, and selfishness are dangerous. I won't argue with you on that point." The little queen drew herself up in her chair and met the PM's worried gaze. "But let me be clear—there is very little I can do to stop him from taking up the crown when his father dies, short of murdering my own grandson. And I shan't participate in such a plot."

Beatrice was writing as fast as she could. Should she even be copying down this conversation? She couldn't believe what she was hearing. In recent years, Ponsonby had taken over so many of the secretarial duties she hadn't needed to be included in the most sensitive political meetings. She didn't mind because, most of the time, they bored her to tears. But this was critical. Not just to Britain but, it seemed, to all of Europe.

"Surely Willy would listen to you, Mama," Beatrice whispered close to her mother's ear, "as you've ruled for so long and gained so much experience."

The queen shook her head mournfully. "Your sister gave birth to a tyrant. No one believed me when he was a child. Now the world will see."

Beatrice's stomach twisted with worry. She had always felt sorry for her nephew. His crippled arm, his awkward attempts to hide his defect. And yet he was quick witted and often brilliant when it came to his studies. She had told a young Willy how proud she was of him for his mind, and he'd seemed pleased. But he'd rewarded her compliment by tossing her favorite muff out through the carriage window as they rode through muddy London streets.

"We will wait and see what transpires," Victoria said. "If he comes to the throne within the next year or two, perhaps I will have some influence over him. I will try, God knows. But if Bismarck continues to alienate him from Britain, then we may have a problem."

Gladstone shook his head. "All of the world will have a problem if his threats and bellicose posturing become a reality." He paused as if to think through his next words. "Your Majesty might be wise to consider how far she is willing to go, to stop him."

Beatrice watched her mother's face. She looked ten years older than she had at breakfast that day. But she also looked ready for a fight. "I assume this morning's conversation between us shall remain in your confidence."

"Absolutely," the PM agreed. "The utmost discretion is called for. In fact, the fewer people who know about this, the better. The foreign office suspects Wilhelm may have planted spies in London. I wouldn't be surprised if he attempts to infiltrate your Court."

Beatrice stopped writing. "Should I not even be taking notes on this subject?"

The queen and prime minister exchanged looks.

Her mother said, "These will go into my private files. They are absolutely secure. And none of us in this room will discuss the matter with anyone who doesn't absolutely need to know."

Gladstone nodded solemnly. "Even so, think twice before you trust anyone with what is in your heart, Your Majesty. The least sign of weakness on your part, or England's, might encourage aggression."

25

Beatrice left her mother's office late that afternoon, still shaken by the prime minister's words. A war. Hadn't they had enough of that?

The Crimean War had robbed Britain of thousands of her youngest and finest young men. Women whom she personally knew had gone to the front to nurse the wounded and come back with stories of working for a tough-minded young woman with the oddly delicate name of Nightingale. The horrendous tales they brought home had reduced Beatrice to tears. Unarmed men had been slaughtered by the hundreds because there weren't enough weapons to go around. And because their officers were untrained, inept, and foolishly proud. Most of these officers had bought their way into the upper ranks with their families' money. They knew nothing of war; it was all a romantic adventure, a game to them. But the game pieces they played with were human beings, whose lives they carelessly ordered into impossible battles.

Did people never learn? Hadn't history demonstrated innumerable times the price paid for greed and violence? If it wasn't a war between nations, tribes, or religions—then it was a revolution. More fighting. She hated it all! The thought that her nephew might someday have a hand in creating yet another hell on earth, with thousands more dying, was just too much for her to bear on her own. She desperately wanted the company of Henry Battenberg—gentle, level-headed, beautiful Henry. The man she'd come to love.

She had arranged to meet him in the palace garden at dusk. Her mother was so preoccupied with the Prime Minister's fear of subversion within her court that she hadn't objected when Beatrice told her she planned to go with friends to the opera that evening.

Henry was waiting for her in the gazebo. When she came up the steps he turned, azure eyes flashing his joy, rushed to her, and they embraced. Being held in his long arms was the only salve she needed. She pressed her cheek to his chest and felt as comforted as if she was sipping from a cup of warm Dutch cocoa.

But that peace lasted but a minute. Then she felt other, stronger emotions. The exhilaration of a gallop across sun-spangled poppy fields. The first heart-throbbing notes of a Viennese waltz. Standing there enfolded in his arms, his lips pressed to her, she thought: We are lovers. *Lovers!* Or soon would be.

Such was her bliss at that moment, she would have done anything for him. Anything at all to make this man happy. But she suspected that might require a little more of her physically than an occasional hug or kiss. For she felt that particularly satisfying firmness below his sword belt that he was taking no pains to hide from her. She blushed at the thought of his arousal and felt a secret thrill. Maybe, after all, the sexual act wouldn't be as bad as Mama suggested. Maybe it would be glorious.

"We'd better not tarry," he said, taking her hand in his. "I can't trust myself to be a gentleman when we're alone like this. You are so deliciously enticing." He nuzzled her neck, which tickled and made her laugh with delight. Henry cleared his throat and smiled at her apologetically. "Anyway, the opera begins at eight o'clock, and will last until after midnight if the reviews are accurate. Let's go along so we don't miss the overture."

This, too, was a new experience for her. She had never attended the opera, ballet, or theater with anyone other than family members. Always closely watched. Always protected from possible male predators, even her own brothers, by the women in the family. And now here she was, alone with a man who excited her beyond her wildest dreams.

"I've arranged for a barouche from the royal mews," she said, managing to keep her voice from quivering with anticipation.

"I'd hoped you would. I released the hansom cab that I took to get here." He held her away from him for a moment and looked her over. "You grow more beautiful every time I see you. How is that possible?"

She laughed, unable to come back with a witty response. She held his words in her heart. *I'm beautiful. He desires me.* Never had she believed she'd hear such words from a man.

The carriage ride to the opera house took only minutes. They held hands all the way. Soon they were seated in the royal box. Alone. For no one else at Court had come tonight. Beatrice wondered if, somehow, Henry had arranged it to be so.

She looked around, feeling like a different woman entirely. A more independent woman. A woman with a future and a say in her own life—who had private, delectable sensations bubbling up through her body. Her body felt ten degrees warmer, all over. Her heart felt lighter than ever before. Here she was, like any of the grand ladies from her mother's Court, escorted by one of the handsomest men in Continental society.

She sensed people taking notice of them, perhaps guessing at their relationship. Did they have any idea that she and Henry were an engaged couple? Well, at least pledged to each other, engaged in their hearts. Or did the nosey old things assume she and Henry were illicit lovers? She didn't care. Let them gossip. She couldn't have been happier.

During intermission, Henry sent the footman stationed at their box for Champagne and a tray of cakes. After the man left them, Henry took her hand in his and placed it on his knee, as if encouraging her to lay claim to him. When she glanced down at his lap, out of curiosity, he lifted her chin to make her meet his eyes. She blushed, realizing he must have known what she was looking for.

He smiled and gave a subtle nod of his head. The message: *Yes, that's what your touch does to me.* "Tomorrow, my love, I am going to your mother," he said. "I have requested an audience with her in the morning, and will ask for your hand then. I am prepared to reassure her in every possible way that I will be the best of husbands and will in no way interfere with the affection shared by the two of you."

Her pulse escalated, tripping over itself—joyful one moment, timid and fearful the next. "Henry, I can't promise her reception will be pleasant."

"The queen may say what she likes. But I intend to reassure her that I will bring you to London or Balmoral or anywhere she chooses, as often as the two of you like. I see nothing standing in our way, once she realizes she isn't really losing you, dear girl."

Beatrice shrugged. "I don't know. She's unpredictable these days, and she sounded so very firm when she said no to our engagement the first time."

"And if she says no again, what will you do, Beatrice?" He looked at her pleadingly. Was he asking if she dared ignore her mother's wishes? Was he asking if she would leave her family and run away with him?

Tears came to Beatrice's eyes. She shook her head. "I just don't know."

It was as if she'd thrown a bucketful of water on his flame. He gently pulled his hands away from her and started to turn away.

She seized his arm in desperation. "Henry, please. You have to understand. I'm all she has now. It's not just that she's my mother. She's the queen of England. If I desert her, I can't say what that will do to her ability to rule our empire. She's under so much pressure. There are things happening now that vex her so and need her full attention. A great many people depend upon her. If I leave her—"

"Stop. You need say nothing more." His expression had waned from teasing to dismal. His eyes dulled, blue to gray. His lips pinched together in regret.

She swallowed over the salty taste at the back of her throat. "Are you angry with me?"

"I—no, not angry. Disappointed." But the light had left his beautiful eyes, and it was all her fault. He went on, his voice sounding strained, "I believed if you loved me enough, even if she refused her blessing, you would come away with me. I thought—oh, hell, Beatrice. Yes, I'm angry. *Furious* that we're both made so helpless by an old woman."

"An old woman who happens to reign over a good part of the world." She said it as soothingly as she could, willing away his fury.

"Yes." He gave her a thin, wavering smile, as if even that had cost him. "I know now what I must do. I will go to her and plead my case. I must convince her. Because you see, my darling, I don't wish to return to Germany without you."

When he kissed her this time, her heart melted—a little snowball held in his palms and now nothing but a puddle. Never in her life had she felt so exquisitely alive…or so very vulnerable and frightened.

26

Gregory hadn't told Meg which day he'd arrive in Aberdeenshire. That bought him at least one night at the MacAlister manse before he saw her. Now that he'd learned the lay of the land from his brother, he lay awake considering his options—none of which were pleasant. By dawn, though, he'd decided on the wisest course of action.

The next morning Gregory set out on horseback for the Graham farm. He found Meg in the vegetable garden behind the house, down on her hands and knees in the moist Highland dirt, sowing potato eyes. He rode past, without alerting her to his presence.

Continuing on across the stony fields he finally spotted her father and brothers. The younger men stopped working to look up at him, wary aggression in their eyes. So they knew. She'd told them. The laird's son had impregnated their little sister. No doubt the only thing that kept them from killing him on the spot was the old man, who wouldn't want to lose two sons to a nobleman's wrath.

Gregory dismounted and strode up to the old man, cap in hand as a perspective son-in-law should do. "Mr. Graham. I've come to ask your daughter Margaret's hand in marriage, sir." He looked the old man dead in the eyes. "I want to make an honest woman of her, if she'll have me."

Alvin Graham's posture altered—spine straightening, shoulders shooting back. The farmer's sons exchanged surprised looks.

"Will you give us your blessing, sir?"

Meg's father chuckled. "Well, I'll be." Grinning, he stuck out his hand and pulled Gregory in to thump his back. "Good on you, son. Yes, ye'll have me blessings and congratulations too. When will the day be, young sir?"

"If it's all right with Meggie, I want our wedding to come as soon as possible," he said solemnly. "I'm needed back in London but wish to marry here in my home county before I return to the city. With Meggie at my side, of course. If we announce bans tomorrow, and the priest will do us a service next week, I'll be most pleased."

"Yes, yes!" The old man's eyes glimmered. "She'll like that too, I'm sure. Ye'll be off to tell her now?"

"I will."

Her brothers offered their good wishes too, although he wasn't convinced they were as heartfelt as her father's. Then Gregory rode back the way he'd come and found his woman where he'd left her in the dirt.

After he told Meg of his conversation with her father, she threw herself, weeping, into his arms. "Oh, my sweet, sweet Gregory. You've made me so very happy," she cried.

"You'll be happier still on our wedding day, I hope."

"Oh, Greggie. I do so love you."

"And I love you," he said, holding her. He pressed his lips to the top of her head. "'til death do us part, my sweet."

The proposed wedding date, although just five days after bans were announced, was approved by the priest. Gregory explained to anyone who remarked on the odd timing that he was anxious to be back in London, as he didn't want the queen's stable master to lose his good opinion of him. And then, of course, he'd need to find appropriate accommodations in the city for his wife.

Early on the morning of the wedding, Gregory took two of his father's best riding horses down to the farm and found Meg with a garrulous flock of women from the village, in the tiny, hot farmhouse kitchen, cooking up the wedding feast.

"You've been working all week," he said. "Don't wear yourself out, love. Come, let's go for a ride and let the ladies who won't be wearing a veil handle the food."

They all encouraged her, accompanied by laughter and warnings to not allow the groom favors before the wedding night, despite general knowledge she already carried his child.

"But this is the kind of work I don't mind at all," she objected, clinging around his neck while kissing his nose, his forehead, his lips. "Seems I've waited all of my life for this day."

He smiled at her patiently but said nothing as he helped her onto the chestnut gelding he'd brought for her.

They rode out across the moor, brilliant with wild flowers thrusting their sunny faces up at a cloudless sky.

She shrieked with joy. "Oh I'm so glad you suggested we ride today, Greggie my darling. It's glorious, the air so sweet with blooms and a sky like one big ribbon of blue satin." She threw her head back and laughed.

"It is fine," he agreed. "Quite fine." Gregory looked across the wide open turf. The land seemed to stretch out forever to the east, to the north was the manor house, but to the west and less than half a mile away, the woods lay. Little sunlight would penetrate the green canopy to brighten the few trails.

Meggie wanted to race to the edge of the woods. He let her win and kissed her as a prize. "Let's ride a ways into the forest," he suggested.

"Oh dearie, I know what you have in mind now." She wagged a finger at him. "There'll be none of that on the night before my wedding."

"I promised I'd wait to make love to you again until after we'd said our vows, and I meant it."

She gave him a skeptical look. "That doesn't sound like you at all, Greggie."

"I'm a new man with a new life ahead of me."

She beamed at him.

"One more race," he said, "through the trees and to that big oak just where the path splits. You know the one."

She laughed and kicked her heels into her horse's ribs. The animal leapt forward even as she shouted over her shoulder, "I'll win this one too!"

He watched her run her horse as if the devil himself was after her. In a way, he supposed, she was right. But he doubted ol' Lucifer ever felt a spasm of guilt as he did now. Still, it had to be done. There was no other way.

She was waiting for him at the oak and had already jumped down from her horse by the time he arrived. She stood holding the gelding's bridle, nuzzling his nose against her cheek. "You did good, old man. Want to rest for a minute?"

He wasn't sure if she was speaking to the horse or teasing him.

Gregory swung his leg over the saddle and slid down to the ground. He looked around, saw what he needed. Stooping, he picked up a stone the size of a croquet ball. He passed it back and forth between his palms, studying the rusty and amber veins of quartz running through it. "I would have won if I hadn't been distracted by your horse's gait." He pointed at the animal's right rear hoof. "I think he's picked up a stone in his shoe. Looked to me like he was hobbling a bit."

"Oh no," she said, "I would've noticed."

"I'll check it for you anyway." He took a step forward. "We don't want him going lame on the ride back."

"I'll do it." She picked up a sturdy stick then bent over and lifted the horse's hoof, bracing it between her knees as if she were shoeing it. She peered down at the iron shoe and ran the tip of the stick into the groove, prying out dried mud. "Just dirt, no stone. He's fine, like I said."

Gregory tightened his fingers around the rock and brought it down as hard as he could on the back of her skull. The crack of bone and whimper that burst from her lips sickened him. Her glorious red hair flew wild as she tumbled to the ground.

Standing above her, he could tell she was still breathing. He set the stone on the ground near her head, its bloody side turned up. More blood spilled onto it from the gash in her head. Gregory knelt beside her. She groaned once and whispered something that might have been his name.

"It's all right," he said. "I'm here, my love."

He wasn't supposed to feel anything. He'd told himself over and over—once he'd made the decision and acted, it would be like putting down a lame pony or an ailing loyal dog. Sad but necessary. But it wasn't at all like that. Tears burned his eyes.

"I'm sorry. I've no choice, you see. Sleep well, my angel."

He closed his hands tenderly around her smooth, white throat, tightened his fingers. With a little more pressure and a sharp jerk, he snapped her neck. At last, she lay still.

Gregory sat back on his heels and closed his eyes, forcing himself to breathe slowly, evenly, though his heart pounded with condemning ferocity.

A fall from a horse, that's what it must look like. And he couldn't take her back with him. Couldn't let her brothers and father see him with her body, on chance they'd suspect him.

His mind spun and reached for the next step.

And then he knew how it had to go. Return to her father's cottage alone, with just the one horse. Pretend they'd become separated and he'd lost her. Ask one of her brothers to come with him and help look for her, because he was worried. She took too many chances while riding, he'd say. He'd seen her jump a stone wall recklessly many times. They'd been racing, and she'd outrun him. He lost her in the woods, spent over an hour searching. Scared, really scared now.

He'd make sure someone other than him found her. He'd play the grief-stricken groom on the eve of his wedding day turned tragedy. It wouldn't be hard. Gregory almost wished he hadn't done it. Hadn't killed her. But if he'd had to choose again, he'd have changed nothing. There was so much at stake.

27

Beatrice looked around at the other guests as they arrived and were introduced to the queen at the Duchess of Devonshire's garden party. She had to remind herself to breathe, as if this essential bodily function wasn't something that nature took care of without conscious effort.

She and Henry had agreed to stand before the queen today, here at the party, and declare their engagement. They'd discussed the strategy at length. It seemed a good idea to have witnesses—as many and as important as possible. By making their intentions public, they would also make it more difficult for Victoria to simply dismiss their engagement.

Henry would, of course, come by separate carriage to the Palladian-style mansion. It was one of the grandest homes in all of London, designed by William Kent over a hundred years earlier, standing majestically on Piccadilly. Henry had agreed to arrive a stylish thirty minutes or more into the party so that most of the guests would have already had a chance to greet the queen. That would leave the stage free for them to make their announcement.

While Beatrice waited for him, she took extra care settling her mother into the most comfortable chair in the shade of the duchess's rose arbor. She sat beside her mother, making sure she had plenty of tea and a selection of the nicest biscuits, while steering conversation toward light topics. When two members of parliament, whose political views always irritated Victoria, started to approach the queen, Beatrice left her seat and boldly headed them off.

"The gout has put Her Majesty in a most negative mood, sirs," she said. "If you have expectations of turning her to your side, you may want to wait until she is in less pain."

They scampered like pigeons shooed away after the bread crumbs were gone. Pleased with the results, she returned to her seat beside the queen.

And then, suddenly, there was her Henry, striding through the garden gate, elegant in his military uniform. Wide shoulders capped by epaulets, tucked waist, polished black boots, dazzling smile. Her pulse quickened with adoration as he made his way across the garden, nodding to those courtiers and noblemen he knew. Women turned in the midst of lively conversation to ogle him or whisper to each other behind plumed fans as he passed. Never had it been more obvious to Beatrice that she wasn't alone in admiring him.

She didn't mind. Other women's interest made her all the more proud that he had chosen *her*.

When Henry was no more than twenty feet away, his eyes met Beatrice's. She read hope and excitement in their steady blue gaze. He looked so very brave, a soldier going to battle, determined to emerge victorious. And *she* was the prize of this war, the sought-after spoils.

Admittedly, she had failed to make her wishes understood when she'd faced her mother at breakfast that other day. But Henry wasn't the sort to become awkward or tongue-tied. He knew his way around the elegant courts of Europe. Surely he would charm the queen as thoroughly as he had her daughter.

"I wonder what *he* is doing here," her mother said and, when Beatrice turned to see who she was talking about, Victoria's stony gaze had fixed on Henry. "The duchess can't have invited him. She has an aversion to foreigners."

"Wasn't her mother French?"

"I can't recall. But the French and Germans are entirely different, my dear. There are already far too many Germans scurrying about England."

Beatrice felt a bubble of panic begin to form low in her chest. "What a funny thing to say." A nervous laugh escaped her. Why was her mother talking like this when her eldest daughter, the Crown Princess, had married a German who would likely make her an empress any day now? If that wasn't enough to make any mother happy, what was?

The woman's moods seemed to swing on a pinhead. But it was too late to wave Henry off. He had started toward them with a smile on his face. Hoping to avert disaster, Beatrice dashed forward, all too aware that her mother was watching, and dragged Henry by the arm behind a nearby privet hedge.

"We have to wait," Beatrice gasped. "I don't understand why she's acting like this. She adores flowers, being outside, garden parties." She chewed her bottom lip. "I've rarely heard her sound so cheerful and calm as she was this morning, but now, suddenly she's—"

Henry pressed a white-gloved finger across her lips. "No sense panicking. We've made our decision. The stage is set. We shall bravely advance according to plan." Henry pecked her on the cheek.

Beatrice held her breath as Henry rounded the hedge, after giving her hand one final squeeze of reassurance then releasing it. He approached the Queen, stopped and bowed.

"Your Royal Majesty, how very well you look today. I gather you have recovered your health since returning from Darmstadt."

"My health is of no concern to you, young Herr Battenberg." The Queen flashed a suspicious look at her daughter then turned back to Henry. "Baby told me of the presumptuous letter you wrote to her. I hope she hasn't let you down too hard. But I know how young men are—intrigued for the moment by one woman, then off to experiment with others."

Henry's smile froze. "Not I, madam. Once I declare myself to a lady, I never waver."

"Then you speak from the experience of having proposed to *other* young women?" Victoria raised a meaningful eyebrow.

Henry looked horrified. "No, never. My love of your daughter has been unique, constant, and I can honestly say I have no desire to ever love another. That is why I have come today to speak with you."

The queen lifted her chins and stared down the length of her nose at him. "Then, sir, you have wasted a trip. My daughter understands that a union between the two of you is impossible. She has other obligations that are much more important than becoming a wife."

"Mama, please—" Beatrice rushed forward, shaking her head, hoping Henry wouldn't take the queen's words to heart. She stood by his side to face the queen. Already she felt a heavy sadness crushing her chest, and an overwhelming sense of doom. A lump rose in her throat, making it near impossible to speak. She forced the words out. "Please give him a chance to speak."

If Victoria heard her, she gave no sign of it and continued talking. "I have made my position perfectly clear, Henry Battenberg. Beatrice will not leave my side. Even if I were able to spare her, I would not want for her the degradation of being converted into any man's servant for his wicked pleasure and the breeding of his children. Her fate will be a much more exalted one, which she fully understands. She has no desire to become any man's wife."

Henry stood silent, shock etched into his features.

"How can you say such things, Mama?" Beatrice wailed, ignoring the muffled gasps and whispers of guests around them. "What you want and what I need to be happy are very different. You can't speak for me!" She lurched forward, prepared to throw herself to her knees.

Henry put out his arm to stop her. "Your Royal Majesty, my respect for your daughter is such that I would never make demands upon her to harm or offend her in any way. I treasure Beatrice, will cherish her forever and—"

"Enough!" Victoria pushed herself to her feet. Although barely five feet tall she seemed to rise above them all. "You

178

presume too much. Beatrice doesn't know what she wants. She thinks she needs what her sisters have—a man. But ask them if they are happy with their choices. My dear Alice died, exhausted by her efforts to provide her husband with still more heirs when she'd already given him eight. Helena grumbles constantly about her husband's impossible behavior. Louise flits all over the globe without her husband; one can quite easily guess what *that* means. And my eldest, the Crown Princess, has bred a crippled monster who will one day become emperor. Marriage, and all it entails, is far too dangerous for my Baby. I won't allow her to be turned into a brood mare."

"But I am prepared to—"

The queen cut him off with a slash of her arm. "All of this aside, disturbing rumors have reached our ears. Rumors involving *you*, Battenberg. As often as they are repeated I expect at least some are true." She took a deep breath, puffing out her bosom. "I command you to leave us. We wish to never see you again."

Henry stared at Beatrice, visibly stunned. Beatrice was no less so. Hadn't Louise promised her that persistence would pay off? If anything, their situation had worsened!

Henry lunged forward raising his hand in a combined gesture of objection and pleading. Immediately, the two nearest guardsmen stepped forward, their faces cramped into belligerent expressions. Each one grabbed an arm.

"Mama!" Beatrice shrieked. The day had gone horribly, disastrously wrong, and she feared there was no way of fixing it.

"I will persist, Your Majesty," Henry shouted, struggling against the soldiers' grip. "I will prove to you I am worthy of your daughter. I *will* make her happy."

"That will be difficult," Victoria murmured, her voice stripped of emotion, "as you are no longer welcome in this country." She spoke a little louder, as if to make sure the departing nobleman, and everyone else in the garden, heard her. "Henceforward, Henry Battenberg, you are banned from setting foot in England. Guards, escort the gentleman from our presence. He needs to attend to his travel arrangements."

A whimper of anguish escaped from Beatrice's lips. She shot a look of remorse and apology at Henry, wanting to run to him, to cry out before everyone that she loved him, would follow him anywhere. Anywhere at all! But Henry moved his head slowly side to side, subtly warning her as though he knew her intent.

Helpless, she watched as four more of the queen's guards surrounded the young man and marched him out the gate. Guests had already begun slipping away, but now they seemed to melt into the foliage by the dozens—behind hedges, down garden paths, putting as much distance as possible between themselves and the queen's temper.

Beatrice spun back around. "Mama!" She very nearly growled the word. "How could you do this to me? How could you humiliate me in front of Henry and all of society this way? His only desire is to make me happy."

Victoria pursed her lips and lifted one shoulder in dismissal. "Foolish girl. Don't you understand? You're only important to him because you are a queen's daughter. I'm saving you from terrible grief when he throws you over, which he most certainly would do."

"No!" Beatrice screamed, stomping her foot so hard she jammed the heel of her shoe into the packed dirt between stone pavers. "He would never do that to me." She looked toward the gate through which Henry had disappeared moments earlier and pulled her heel free from the crack.

"I know your mind, Baby. Do not consider running off with that man. I will make it very hard on him. You will be his ruin, just as he will be yours."

Beatrice let out a screech frustration. "Oh!" And then, she bolted.

She snatched up handfuls of her skirts and ran across the garden, weaving between the last fleeing guests. The duke and duchess had positioned themselves at the main gate, as if in a last ditch effort to see off a few of their guests with decorum.

She ran past them. When she reached the street, Henry had already secured a hansom cab and boarded. The driver lifted his whip to urge the horses forward.

Beatrice launched herself in front of the team, waving her arms. "Stop! Stop your horses."

Henry peered down at her from the open side of the carriage. "Beatrice, what are you doing?"

"I want to be with you," she cried, swallowing the flood of tears she'd forcibly blinked from her eyes but couldn't entirely defeat. She rushed around to the carriage door. "I want to go with you to Germany. Now! Please, Henry. We'll be married. There's no way she can stop us."

He reached down and pulled her up inside the cab with him but signaled the driver not to leave yet. "There are many things she can do to stop us, my darling. You of all people shouldn't underestimate her."

"But what shall we do? I can't lose you. I love you so much. I'll die if we must part." She fell into his arms.

"No, you won't. We'll both be miserable but we won't die. The thing of it is—" He pressed her cheek to his lapels and stroked her hair "—if my father knows the Queen has refused to give her blessing, he will be furious with me for stealing you away behind her back. He won't dare defy the queen. He will cut me off straight away. There will be no money from my family for us to live on. And you know there wouldn't be a shilling from your mother."

"Oh, Henry." Was that what her mother had meant by saying she'd make things hard on him? On them both, it appeared, as he'd explained the consequences.

"I can't ask you to live under those conditions—ostracized by society, scraping up a bare living as we can."

"But we *would* survive somehow. At least we'd be together." She looked up into his troubled eyes and could see he was thinking.

"No," he said at last. "What we must do is exactly what your sister suggested before. We must give her time and be persistent, wear her down. I will return to Germany to appease her. But we will write to each other as often as we can and stay true to our vows of loving no other. And I will find a way, somehow, to convince your mother that she can trust me, and that she'll be able to see you as often as she likes. After we're married, we can spend half of every year in London, if that is your wish and hers. She will tire of fighting us if we are brave and wait her out."

Beatrice sighed, wrapped her arms around him, and squeezed as if to never let him go. "I will be bereft of you, Henry. I want to be *with* you, not separated by an ocean."

"Be brave, my darling." He kissed her forehead when she blinked up at him. "I will be true to you, no matter how long it takes. Trust me, as I trust you."

She sniffled. "I do trust you. I do. And I will write every day with news of her moods and tell you of the slightest sign that she might be weakening in her resolve to keep us apart. Maybe you can go to your father and ask if he can speak to her. He and my father were dear friends. She has a soft spot in her heart for him. Perhaps he can sway her where we cannot."

"I will talk to him. But now you must let me leave, before the situation worsens. Your mother might change her mind and decide I should not leave." He tipped his chin to indicate the two guardsmen who now stood on either side of the two horses hitched to the carriage, hands holding the bridles. She understood. Under no circumstances would they allow the coach to leave with her in it.

Her mother's lady-in-waiting came to the steps of the carriage. "Princess, your mother has asked me to let you know that she needs you. Now." The woman's expression seemed sympathetic, but Beatrice knew if she made any attempt to leave with Henry, the woman would order the guards to stop her.

"Safe travels, Henry. I'll wait for your letters." Beatrice kissed him on the lips. "They will be like breathing to me."

28

Victoria blotted the ink, folded the note in half, and handed it to Ponsonby. "Please give this to one of the pages, for Beatrice."

Her secretary looked down his impressive hawk's-beak nose at the single sheet of paper in his fingertips. "No seal, Your Majesty?"

"Wax isn't necessary. It's just a list of tasks I wish her to attend to. I'll give you the details later, so that you may instruct her."

"I see." But he didn't move yet. "Might I suggest that it would be simpler for all concerned if the princess stopped by your office, enabling you to speak with her directly?"

"I'm not speaking to my daughter. She has behaved vilely toward me. Notes will do just fine for the time being. She doesn't deserve my words, foolish girl. Such trouble she's become. I never expected her to take the course of her sisters and attempt to desert me."

"I'm sure the princess would never—"

"Ponsonby, you are an excellent secretary and your military record is impeccable. But you know nothing of young women's temperaments and fantasies."

"Yes, ma'am."

"Baby must learn to be responsible. She best serves Britain and our family by doing her duty to the queen. Until she apologizes for her behavior and graciously accepts her duty to us, we shall not waste words on her."

Ponsonby bowed once, and retreated without further comment.

Victoria stared after the man. He hadn't exactly argued with her, but she'd felt his censure in those steel-gray eyes. Was she the only one who recognized the folly of Beatrice's attachment to Henry Battenberg? And what about her blatant disloyalty to her mother? That alone deserved punishment. She hadn't been surprised at Louise's behavior during her twenties; the girl had been difficult from early childhood. So rebellious and headstrong, more trouble than any of her four brothers. But Beatrice had been a delight and dear Albert's favorite. And after he was gone, the child had been a constant comfort to her.

These sudden changes in the youngest princess were most disturbing. Not to be tolerated, and certainly not to be encouraged. She must remain firm with the girl until she outgrew this treacherous, wicked phase. The adolescent years had, perhaps, arrived a decade late for Beatrice.

Victoria glanced down at the next document on her desk, a letter from the Prime Minister that needed a quick and carefully composed response. But she couldn't think clearly she was so bothered by all that was going on in her life. If Beatrice left her, she would be alone. All of her family gone. She just couldn't face such a bleak, unloved existence. Surrounded by Court and servants—that wasn't the same as being with your family.

When Victoria and Albert had first started having babies, the act of motherhood had seemed such a wretched nuisance to her. How could she function as the ruler of a nation if she was forever pregnant and popping out infants? But somehow she had managed, with the help of nurses, governesses and tutors. Albert himself had taken on managing the children's education. But now that she *wanted* her family, needed them around her to support her later years, they were all too busy in their own lives to bother. Beatrice, she had believed, was different. Beatrice was clearly uncomfortable in society. She never seemed to do or say the right thing in pleasant company. Didn't she understand she would humiliate herself if she married into a flamboyant family like the Battenbergs?

With a sigh, Victoria finished the document for the PM, as best she could, and left it for Ponsonby to send off with a messenger.

The queen repaired to her room to change into her riding habit and then sent off one of her ladies to inform the stable master she wished to ride. An hour later, accompanied by two attendants, she made her way down to the royal mews. Her ladies would ride with her, and they'd all be accompanied by a mounted pair of soldiers from the Queen's Guard. She'd also requested the most recently hired groom join their party.

The stable master was waiting in the yard with her guardsmen, the party's mounts all tacked and ready for them. The air smelled of horse flesh, damp straw, and oncoming rain. She hoped it would hold off until they returned from their ride.

Elton Jackson bowed and gave her a shallow smile, but as she talked to him, his gaze flitted here and there around the courtyard in a distracted way she found annoying. "Is there a problem, Mr. Jackson? You seem inattentive to your duties, sir."

Her remark seemed to shake Jackson out of his preoccupation. "Not at all, Your Majesty. Just keepin' an eye on everything little thing, you know." He chuckled, shrugging. "These young grooms—never know what they'll be up to next, and the stable lads are forever into mischief and causing me worries."

"Much like any family, I suppose," she said. At least here was someone who understood her dilemmas. "Where is your young groom? I hope he won't keep us waiting long."

"About that, ma'am, wouldn't you rather I send a more experienced gillie with your party?"

"No. As I requested in my message, I'd like to get to know your new man. My daughter told me weeks ago how bravely he defended her. I haven't had a chance to thank or even meet him. I think this would be the perfect opportunity. Don't you?"

"Of course, ma'am. I was only thinking of your—"

At the sound of another horse approaching, Jackson broke

off, the muscles of his weathered face bunching as if struggling to keep from frowning before he announced with pointed enthusiasm, "Ah, here he is now, Mr. MacAlister. All mounted up and ready for you."

Victoria noticed with mild surprise that the young man rode the notorious Beelzebub. Had Beatrice said something about that? She couldn't recall. After John Brown purchased the animal as a colt, so close to his own death, she hadn't at first been aware it had arrived in her stables. Only weeks later, when she was beginning to recover from the bitter loss of her cherished Scot did she notice the horse in one of the stalls. She took its presence as a mystical sign that her old friend was still watching over her. She was pleased that today she'd be riding alongside the magnificent animal.

"Good. We're all here now. Let us go." She motioned to the young man on the black, beckoning him forward. "We'll get to know each other a little as we ride."

One of her guards took the advance position and another followed behind her two ladies.

"Do you enjoy an early morning ride," Victoria asked her young escort.

"Why, yes, Your Majesty, the earlier the better." He bowed his head in deference as he matched his mount's pace to hers.

What a nice, deep Highland burr. His accent sounded so very pleasant to her ears. If she closed her eyes she could almost imagine John riding alongside her, making her feel safe. She could easily see why Beatrice had taken to him as her bodyguard. A strong, good-looking man servant—that's all any woman really needed. The shackles of marriage, pain of childbirth, and bitter disappointment in grown children who deserted you in your declining years—who needed that?

They rode in silence for a good ways. The morning dew still clung to the grass; few riders chose to be out on Rotten Row at this hour, giving the queen's party the luxury of privacy they wouldn't have had later in the day. Still, she would rather have been up north at Balmoral this time of year, walking her horse across the rolling meadows, never coming across another soul, feeling all of Scotland was hers and Albert's. Then hers and John Brown's. Or even, simply…*just hers*. But with Parliament in session she needed to be here in London, at least that's what her ministers insisted upon.

"Are you enjoying your work in the royal mews?" she asked the young man.

"Aye, Your Majesty, I surely am."

"Gregory, is it?" She was good with names, even as she felt herself slowing down physically. A sharp mind, that's what her doctors said about her.

"Yes, ma'am, Gregory MacAlister."

"And you're from the shire around Balmoral?"

"I am, ma'am. Born and raised in bonnie Scotland, and proud I am of it."

Bonnie Scotland. Bonnie lass. John Brown had used phrases like that most often when he'd had too much to drink and broke into the ballads of his homeland. Some of his tunes were drinking songs, others love poems set to music. He'd melted her heart. She hummed to herself, remembering one he'd altered to suit her—

> *I love a lassie, a bonnie Hielan' lassie,*
> *If you saw her you would fancy her as well:*
> *I met her in September, popped the question in November,*
> *So I'll soon be havin' her a' to ma-sel'.*
> *Her father has consented, so I'm feelin' quite contented,*
> *'Cause I've been and sealed the bargain wi' a kiss.*
> *I sit and weary weary, when I think aboot ma deary,*
> *An' you'll always hear me singing this…*
>
> *I love a lassie, a bonnie bonnie lassie,*
> *She's as pure as a lily in the dell,*
> *She's sweet as the heather, the bonnie bloomin' heather,*
> *Victoria, my Scots bluebell.*

The melody seemed to linger on in her memory, like the last, fading notes of a church organ.

"Are you musically inclined, Gregory?" she asked after they'd ridden on a while, turning her head just enough to keep him from seeing her touch the back of her gloved hand to still moist eyelashes.

"Not at all, I'm afraid, ma'am." "How disappointing." She sighed. Nothing so moved her as a fine baritone.

"O' course, I now and again belt out a ditty or two with the boys in the barns. But that's nothin' but noise to royal ears that's heard the likes of fine musicians."

"Sing me one of your ditties, Gregory," she said. "Don't be embarrassed."

He appeared resigned to pleasing her. "I'll do my best, Your Majesty."

She waited patiently, the horses walking on while he searched his memory for a good tune. At last he shifted in his saddle, sat up straight and tall, and began in a clean, vibrant tenor:

> *O these are not my country's hills,*
> *Though they seem bright and fair;*
> *Though flow'rets deck their verdant sides,*
> *The heather blooms not there.*
> *Let me behold the mountain steep,*
> *And wild deer roaming free—*
> *The heathy glen, the ravine deep—*
> *O Scotland's hills for me!*
>
> *The rose, through all this garden-land,*
> *May shed its rich perfume,*
> *But I would rather wander 'mong*
> *My country's bonnie broom.*
> *There sings the shepherd on the hill,*
> *The ploughman on the lea;*
> *There lives my blithesome mountain maid,*
> *O Scotland's hills for me!*

The throstle and the nightingale
May warble sweeter strains
Than thrills at lovely gloaming hour
O'er Scotland's daisied plains;
Give me the merle's mellow note,
The linnet's liquid lay;
The laverocks on the roseate cloud—
O Scotland's hills for me!

And I would rather roam beneath
Thy scowling winter skies,
Than listlessly attune my lyre
Where sun-bright flowers arise.
The baron's hall, the peasant's cot
Protect alike the free;
The tyrant dies who breathes thine air;
O Scotland's hills for me!

Victoria closed her eyes, soaking up the tune, and felt the comforting rhythm of the horse beneath her. She let the animal follow the path without direction from her hands on the reins. The young man's voice wasn't professionally trained, but it rang out clear and strong. The song brought her back so many years.

A thought came to her: *If I were younger...*

But no. She had no wish to fall in love again. To trust in a future with a man she loved, only to have it all stolen away by fickle fate—such a waste of emotion. Why didn't anyone understand that this was what she wanted to save Beatrice from? How much wiser it was to never surrender one's heart and body.

"I can tell you have a tender soul," she said. "Singing as you do with such sincerity. Do you miss your homeland?"

"I do, ma'am. But I am honored to be in your service."

"When we next travel up to Balmoral, you will come with us. You can then visit with your family."

"That's very good of you, ma'am. They will be most

189

grateful, as will I."

She smiled. How pleasant it was to have a riding companion who didn't argue with her and pout, like Beatrice.

When they returned to the palace, Gregory was first off his horse and beat the captain of the Queen's Guard to offer his assistance to the queen as she prepared to dismount. He held up a hand to her, and she realized the dear boy didn't understand she would need more help than that.

"I am still able to mount on my own, with the assistance of a step, but must be lifted to the ground." She was mildly irritated that Jackson hadn't adequately briefed the young man.

"Have no fear, ma'am." Gregory MacAlister reached up, his strong hands firmly but gently gripping her substantial waist. Her eyes widened, suddenly in fear of falling should she be too heavy for him. But he lifted her as lightly as if she were a fluff of goose down to the ground.

"There you are, safe and sound. Shall I escort you inside, ma'am?"

She beamed up at him. He made her feel a young girl again. "Yes, yes that would be appreciated." She would let the stable master know how pleased she was with his selection and ask that Gregory MacAlister's duties be arranged that he might accompany her in the future.

29

Beatrice wrote to Henry the very next day after he was officially banned from English soil. His long letter in return assured her of his devotion and faith in their ability to overcome all obstacles to their marriage. Four days later, a second letter came, apologizing for the time that had passed, hinting that Henry had been working on a plan to win over her mother all the more speedily. Then she waited for days that turned to weeks for another letter. But although she wrote to him every single day, excited to hear more about his plans, no more letters came.

"Men are such terrible letter writers," Helena said on her next visit. "They are like children, too easily distracted by whatever is in their line of sight."

What if the thing within Henry's line of sight is another woman? Beatrice began to worry.

"He loves you," Louise assured her sometime later when she was passing through London on her way to Brussels, where several pieces of her sculpture were to be exhibited. "He's probably just busy and will write you a long, newsy note when he has a chance."

But after still more weeks passed, when no letter had come, a malicious suspicion wedged its way into Beatrice's mind. She and the queen were still not speaking. Had her mother found another way to punish her?

At breakfast the next morning, Beatrice laid the generous damask napkin across her lap, sipped her coffee from the egg-shell delicate Limoges cup, then set it down to confront her mother. "Mama, are you interfering with my personal correspondence?"

Victoria started at the sound of her voice and stared at her, lips clamped shut so tightly they turned white. She drew closer the pad of paper and pencil she kept always with her for communicating with the daughter-to-whom-she-refused-to-speak. She wrote on the pad then slid it across the tablecloth toward Beatrice.

One word: *Why?*

Beatrice huffed with impatience. "Because Henry has not written to me, and we'd promised to stay in touch...as friends."

Her mother pointed toward her paper pad. With a groan and roll of her eyes, Beatrice shoved the tablet back across the table. Her mother wrote. Beatrice reached out and retrieved the pad as soon as Victoria put down her pencil.

The message: *I would never do such a thing. And, no, I did not instruct any of my people to keep letters from you.*

Beatrice closed her eyes and swallowed. She had actually hoped it was her mother's doing. But among the many things the queen was capable of, lying was not one of them. She might ignore or refuse to acknowledge issues that were important to people around her. Or she might use subterfuge or creative trickery to get what she wanted. But she wouldn't lie to a person's face. If accused, she would simply admit her guilt and proclaim her actions justified.

Therefore, if her mother, or one of her agents, hadn't intercepted Henry's letters, then he must have simply stopped writing. For one reason or another, Henry Battenberg, the only man she'd ever loved, no longer wished to communicate with her.

She didn't understand men. Not at all.

But it seemed to her that, if his love for her was as strong as hers was for him, he would have wanted to answer her letters and share his days with her. She left the breakfast table, having eaten nothing, aware of her mother's gaze following her from the room. She didn't want to turn to see her mother's face. If

Victoria's expression showed relief or, worse yet, joy—that would only add pain to her already broken heart.

~

Hours later, Marie met Beatrice in the princess's bedchamber with an envelope. Beatrice's heart leapt. "For me? From Germany?"

"*Oui*, Princess, for you but—"

"Let me have it." Beatrice laughed, and the sound reminded her of happiness. Of wind chimes and spring blooms and summer's warmth. "I've been so looking forward to—"

As she turned the envelope over she saw no wax seal with the imprimatur of the Battenberg crest.

"But this isn't—"

"No, Your Highness. I tried to tell you, it's not from Germany. I think it's a message from within the palace."

But it wasn't her mother's writing. This was the spiky, forceful hand of a man. Curious, she untucked the neat folds that kept the page from opening flat. She glanced down at the signature.

Gregory MacAlister

She frowned. Why was a stable groom writing to her? This was highly irregular.

She looked at Marie, but the girl looked quickly away. So she knew who this had come from. Perhaps Gregory had given it directly to her to deliver. How else would he have managed to get a letter to one of the royal family but by intercepting one of the staff?

Marie busied herself in the room with unusual industry. Beatrice went to her dressing table and sat to read the young man's message.

Your Highness:
   I hope you do not think me too forward, but I am concerned for your well being. You were very quiet when we rode together

last week and looking very sad. And this week you have not ridden out at all. I hope I have done nothing to upset you. Please tell me I am not the cause of your staying away from the mews and your Lady Jane.

I am ever your loyal and admiring servant,
Gregory MacAlister.

"How sweet," she murmured.

"Your Highness?" Marie's pale reflection hovered behind her when Beatrice looked up into her dressing table mirror.

"That new groom from Scotland. He is concerned for me."

Marie gave a half shrug of one shoulder and averted her eyes. "*Mais oui,* but we all are concerned for you, Princess."

"But he—" It was hard to explain. "—he didn't need to do this, to show it in this way. He's not part of the family or even the Court."

"No."

Beatrice observed Marie's pinched face. "You don't like him, do you?"

"It is not for me to like or dislike members of the queen's staff—"

"You don't though, do you? Why? Has he given you cause to distrust him or to even hate him?"

Marie hesitated for a breath. "No." She looked away again. "I can't say there is."

Beatrice shook her head. The jealousies and intrigues within the palace were endless. She had thought Marie, so level-headed ordinarily, would be above the gossip and maneuvering for favor. Perhaps she felt threatened by Beatrice's glowing reports of her rides with Gregory. She had found him a pleasant companion who made her feel safe when outside of the palace grounds.

Maybe the girl had a crush on him. He was, after all, terribly good-looking and virile in his kilt. It seemed odd that the stable master allowed him to exchange the traditional royal livery for his clan's tartans, as he sometimes did. Very possibly the queen had countermanded Mr. Jackson—feeling as fond as she did about everything Scotch. She'd literally draped Balmoral castle in Highland relics, fabrics, furnishings, and tableware.

"Help me change," Beatrice said. "I've decided to ride today."

Marie looked indecisively toward the tall wardrobe on the far side of the room.

"Did you hear me, Marie?"

"*Pardon moi.* I will get your things for you."

Beatrice wondered if the young woman's distraction was due to something as simple as homesickness. Or an ill relative she wished to be with but was afraid to ask permission to travel home for a visit. Or maybe she was herself ill. Beatrice felt a twinge of guilt for not being more sensitive to people around her. In the two years since Marie's arrival at Buckingham Palace, she had been an ideal companion and helpmate. Beatrice would ask her again what troubled her later.

Although she'd fully intended to take her usual ride through the park, by the time she reached the stables she had changed her mind. She felt restless, eager for adventure, but mostly annoyed with Henry. How could he promise to write, swear that she'd always be in his mind and heart when he'd been true to his word for so short a time? Two sweet letters then he'd fizzled out. Was she that easy to forget? To dismiss from his life?

The stable master was waiting with Lady Jane. "No," she said, waving him off, "my plans have changed." She felt daring, dangerous, alive. Anger pricked her toward action. What kind of action didn't seem to matter. She was overdue for an adventure. She was tired of being Beatrice-the-Meek. Beatrice, life-long companion to the queen. *Baby.*

The littlest princess had been the obedient shadow to the queen for far too long.

"I want a carriage, Mr. Jackson."

"A carriage, Your Highness?"

"Yes, you know, one of those things with four big wheels," she snapped. "I want to go into the city. To *shop!*" She thought of Louise, who often went out among commoners and visited commercial establishments of all sorts throughout London. Her mother thought Louise unseemly. Beatrice yearned for a taste of her sister's wildness.

"I want to…to *buy*…things." Everything she wore or owned had been brought to her at one or another of the family homes—Osborne House, Balmoral, Buckingham Palace, Windsor. But ordinary people were free to leave their homes whenever they felt like it, to procure whatever items they felt like having—food, tools, clothing, gifts. Why shouldn't she?

"It will take some time, Your Highness," he said cautiously. "Bringing round the carriage, hitching up the horses, fetching a driver and footmen and—"

"Just, please, do it," she said through clenched teeth. Why should how long it took make the least difference to her? What else did she have to do but wait for her mother's next idiotic note with a new list of chores? As if she were one of the queen's staff or, worse yet, a common servant.

She paced the dusty yard, muttering to herself. Whether or not she heard from Henry ever again, as of this moment she was taking her life into her own hands. "Chasing off Henry isn't going work, Mama."

"What's that, ma'am?"

She spun around, horrified to realize she'd spoken out loud. "Oh, Gregory. Nothing. Just thinking to myself…loudly." She let out a choked laugh. When she reached up with her gloved hand to massage her forehead, the tips of her fingers ran into the brim of her riding hat and veil. She tugged both off in frustration. She was stupidly dressed for going into shops. She ought to be wearing a town dress and pretty flowered hat, not riding gear. What an idiot she was.

"Is something wrong?" the groom asked.

"No. Yes. I don't know." She let out an involuntary whimper. "I had thought to go riding and, of course, ask you to escort me. But then I changed my mind in favor of visiting shops in the city. Now I'll have to go all the way back to my room to change. People will think I've gone mad if I walk into a dress shop in riding boots, jacket and—" She swept her hands down the sportswoman's skirt. *Hopeless.*

Gregory stepped back and gave her outfit a long, studious inspection. "More like they'll decide you're a trendsetter and want to copy you. Next week every lady of any worth will be shopping in foxhunting regalia."

She laughed. "Not really."

"Certainly, Princess. Don't you know that's what London ladies do? They see you, or one of your sisters, in a gown and rush off to their seamstresses, saying, 'Do me up a copy, Duckie.'"

His pretend Cockney accent was atrocious, but she laughed anyway. She felt her mood lighten. "Honestly?"

"Word of honor." But he couldn't keep a straight face. He broke into a wide grin. "So you'll go into some shops and to bloody hell with what society thinks. Do you know which ones you'll visit?"

She shook her head dolefully. She was familiar with the bookstore where she and her sisters always browsed. When a member of the royal family visited, the owner closed the shop to give them privacy. But she didn't know many other commercial establishments, other than the few her mother rarely frequented and referred to.

"Maybe this is a foolish plan." She sighed.

"Not foolish at all. You just need a guide. I'll be happy to escort you, whether on horseback or in carriage."

She tipped her head and really looked at him this time. He seemed serious. It was more than brazen of him to suggest an outing together. Then again, it made sense for her to take along a man she could trust, who already had proven a brave protector. Besides, others of the staff would be with them—a driver and one or two footmen. Although they were no doubt reliable, she felt relaxed with Gregory in ways she didn't feel with them.

"Yes, please, if you don't mind coming with me. But I warn you, I'll be going into ladies' shops. Places stuffed full with dresses, petticoats, plumy hats, lace gloves, and such." He'd undoubtedly feel embarrassed, poor man.

"Delightful," he said, his eyes twinkling at her. "And we'll make the first stop a dress shop where I know they have rack dresses. You can buy a change of clothes there, latest style, and no waiting on a seamstress."

"Really—that's possible?" He nodded. "But aren't ready-made dresses very…common?" The word was out of her mouth before she could stop it. "I'm sorry, that sounds so rude."

"Well, common can be plain but well-made. If you're still concerned about going out into public and not attracting a lot of attention—"

"Oh yes." She clapped her hands, suddenly understanding what a perfect plan it was. "Of course you're right. A more casual outfit would be perfect for going out in the streets unrecognized, wouldn't it?" Didn't the queen herself sometimes travel incognito? This day truly was turning into an adventure. She couldn't be more thrilled.

As soon as the carriage was ready, they took off. Gregory suggested a little shop on Marylebone Street. The owner immediately called his wife out of the backroom. She showed Beatrice her stock and made suggestions then helped her try on several outfits, while Greg talked politics with her husband, who had turned over the open sign while his royal customer made her selections.

Back in the carriage, now crowded with boxes holding her discarded riding outfit and several new garments, they set out again. Greg—he'd asked her to call him Greg—suggested they stop for tea in a café, and she was surprised by the delicacy of the cakes and the quality of the Indian tea served with little cubes of Demerara sugar. Then on to two more shops for a hat and gloves and adorable ankle boots—also, miraculously, ready-made—with dainty heels and lace inserts.

She was learning so much, and the young groom proved the most pleasant company. How freeing it was to venture out into the city *on her own*. She decided she must do this more often and continue learning about all of London and its people.

After they'd returned to Buckingham, and she'd arranged for all of her purchases to be brought to her room, she turned to see Greg moving off toward the stables. "Wait!" she cried.

He turned with a shy smile, still walking away from her but backward, hands tucked casually in his pockets. "Hope you had a good time, Princess."

"I did. Thank you so very much. I've never really...you see—" She couldn't seem to find the right words to express her gratitude. For the first time in weeks she hadn't thought about Henry, hadn't felt a pitiful sad lump of a girl.

"New experiences," Greg said. "They're always fun."

"Not always. But this one was. I hope I can do it again sometime soon. Would you—I mean, if your duties allow—"
"Be your escort again? Of course," he said cheerfully. "I'm at your service. Good day to you, Princess." He doffed his cap and walked off, whistling.

She watched him go. How she wished it had been Henry she'd just spent the afternoon with. How she wished and wished and wished. And yet, it seemed that might never be. She must be realistic. Her mother's opposition had discouraged her suitor far more, it seemed, than it had her. Perhaps to the point of his giving up on their engagement entirely.

30

Henry paced the floor, flung open the balcony doors, strode outside into the cold then turned back into the gold-and-ivory salon of his family's house.

"For God's sake, son, will you stop this infernal pacing?" Prince Alexander of Hesse glared at him. "You'll send us all to Bedlam."

Although the asylum and London were a far stretch from Prussia, the phrase for driving a person mad had become just as popular on the Continent as it had in England.

Alexander turned to his other son, Louis, who, thankfully, was a good deal calmer than his younger brother. He felt that maturity must, in part, be due to his marriage to the queen's granddaughter two months earlier. "What is wrong with him?"

"Little Liko's in love." Louis grinned.

"For all the bloody good it does," Henry grumbled.

"With whom?" their father asked.

Henry didn't answer, didn't want to say her name when even thinking it brought heart ache.

Louis answered for him. "My wife's aunt. Beatrice."

The prince stared at Henry. "It can't be. She's a nice enough woman but—all this dramatic chest heaving over *her*? Bea is as plain as the day is long."

"She isn't plain, she's just...refined, quiet. I like her. At least I did. Now that she refuses to answer my letters I'm not sure where her head is at, or mine for that matter." Henry swung around to face his brother with a hopeful thought. "Maybe she's ill. She can't write because she's taken to her bed." But he wouldn't have wanted her to be truly sick, seriously languishing. "If so, I must go to her immediately!"

"She's not ill, Henry. And anyway, you know you can't set foot in England, at least not as long as the queen feels about you as she does. Face it, you've been dumped. Beatrice did it to me years ago, now it's your turn, dear brother. Time you moved on."

Henry felt his face flush with heat. The mustache he'd recently grown, to make him look older, itched on his upper lip. He clenched his fists at his sides and lurched toward his brother. "You don't know her. She isn't like that at all. Take it back!"

Louis stiff armed him away. "I know her well enough to know she isn't ill. Beatrice has twice written to my wife in the past month. Vicki read her letters to me…in bed." He wriggled eyebrows at Henry, clearly gloating at the implication. "Believe me, Beatrice is hale and hearty. Been riding a good deal, I hear. Seems there's a new groom in the Royal Mews who has become her regular escort—a Scot."

Henry's heart turned to stone. "No. She wouldn't…she's not like that."

"What you see is what you get, dear boy. It's her way, apparently. Tease and invite the attentions of a man, then back off as soon as he shows serious interest."

Alexander harrumphed. "Have you ever thought, Henry, that Beatrice might be content in her spinsterhood? She's been the queen's constant companion since the age of four when Albert—"

"I know all of that." Henry shook his head violently. "And, no, I don't think she's content. I think she is ready for marriage. And *I* want to be the one to marry the girl."

Louis studied his younger brother, and it seemed to Henry it was with compassion, or else pity. "Henry. Think about this. HenIf the woman isn't committed to you enough to write a few letters in her spare time, I can't see that she's ready to take on marriage or—"

"Or," the prince broke in, "the breeding and raising of children. That particular young woman will always be distracted by her mother. The queen is everything to her. I doubt she'd agree to live anywhere but wherever Victoria chooses to be. Fighting an uphill battle, Henry, that's what you'd be doing if you became engaged to Baby."

Henry cringed at the family pet name. The woman he'd ridden with at Darmstadt, who'd greeted him so passionately in London, she wasn't childish or selfish. She'd lit up when he was around her. And when he'd kissed her, she'd responded tenderly, inviting more. He just didn't understand what had gone wrong. Had more vicious rumors about him reached her? Rumors she'd been unable to ignore?

There was, of course, no truth to them, if any still floated around. He'd broken off all attachments to other women. He'd stayed away from the brothels too. Maybe she thought him not exciting enough.

Alexander was speaking as he poured himself a brandy. "The fact is, whether or not Beatrice is prepared for marriage, the queen isn't. I seriously doubt she will ever change her mind where Bea is concerned. She wants to hold onto her last daughter, her last child. In a way, it's natural and understandable."

"It is *not!*" Henry shouted, causing his brother and father to exchanged shocked glances. "It is most definitely selfish. She is robbing Beatrice of a life of her own."

His father's voice turned gentle. "My dear boy, Beatrice has always lived in a pampered, astonishingly wealthy world. Maybe she has had second thoughts and doesn't want to lose the prestige, glamour, and many benefits that a life in Court entails."

He hadn't thought about it like that, and now his father's words made him sad. It was true, he could never offer Beatrice all that her mother could, in terms of wealth and social connections. Their marriage would be a step up the social ladder for him. Did she consider it a step down for her? Was she holding out for marriage to a king or crown prince? She had every right to do so. But if she wanted to be loved and have a family of her own, as he'd believed she did, he could happily give her those things.

Henry sank into the blackest of moods. He couldn't have said how much time passed as he sat there immobile before the rustling of his father's newspaper roused him. "Awful situation that," the prince muttered.

Henry sensed the comment was meant to apply to a situation other than his. "What is that, Father?"

"The Sudan of course. Victoria must be out of her mind with concern."

He had thought of nothing but the queen's daughter in months. Why would a faraway African nation concern him? Then he recalled. General Gordon, hero of the British expeditions to China, had been sent to negotiate the evacuation of British citizens after a dangerous uprising in northeastern Africa. Gordon had kept a modest military contingent with him and a civilian staff sufficient to aid his mission. He had negotiated with the Caliph for months, trying to convert him to Christianity even as the Caliph attempted to convert Gordon to Islam. Relations had been tense and grew even more explosive when the Caliph's men kidnapped and beheaded a number of British citizens.

"What has happened now?" Henry asked, his heart not yet invested in the conversation.

"Gordon's people are still under siege in Khartoum. The rebels have surrounded the city, and no supplies can get through."

Despite his preoccupation with his own future, Henry's blood fired up. "Then reinforcements must be sent to break through the barricade."

His father shook his head. "Gordon is one of Victoria's favorites. She's been fighting with Parliament for weeks to get the government to authorize a rescue expedition."

"Good for her. I'd volunteer to serve." Maybe that would impress the queen. He could imagine himself slashing away at infidels with his saber, arriving victorious at the walls of Khartoum to rescue Gordon, bringing the general and his grateful people home to England.

Louis laughed and pushed a glass of brandy into his hands. "Henry, drink up and forget about it. You're such a romantic. Do you think an old military veteran like Gordon incapable of getting himself out of this fix?"

The prince sighed and folded his newspaper closed. "The English think they are all-powerful. That attitude will be their downfall. And Gordon's too, I fear."

"I can't fathom it," Henry said. "Why not send in troops?"

"Prime Minister Gladstone is as set against intervention as the queen is for it. Nothing will happen without Parliament's blessing."

"But if a voluntary expedition crossed through Egypt to the interior…" Henry felt his father's eyes boring into him. "No, seriously, if I let it be known I was mounting a rescue mission—"

"Henry, don't be ridiculous." Louis said.

"What? It would prove to the queen I am of value and deserve her daughter."

"It would get you killed, son." Alexander gave him a stern look. "You have no idea what you'd be up against. The Caliph's men are without mercy. They will defend their country and punish without mercy anyone who tries to take it from them."

"But surely, if Gordon and his people surrender—"

His father looked grim. "No one will leave Khartoum alive. Take my word for it. It's too late for them. Don't do it, Henry. It's a suicide mission."

~

Later that day, Henry thought about his ruined relationship with the queen. He'd approached her from a social angle, as a good man, as a reliable husband for her daughter. But what he should have done was to first make of himself a man after Victoria's own heart. If a man didn't appeal to her, she wouldn't find him deserving of her daughter. And Victoria clearly respected military men. Strong men. Daring men. He could be all of those things for her. Then he would return to ask again for Beatrice.

His only worry was not knowing why Beatrice had stopped writing to him. Maybe it was her way of letting him down gently, without final words of farewell that would be painful to both of them. Whatever her motive for silence, he had to find out.

But first things first. He had an invasion to plan.

31

Beatrice studied her reflection in the cheval glass before heading outside to the royal mews. Her new plum riding dress fit beautifully, emphasizing her womanly curves—perhaps more pleasingly than her mother would have preferred. But, so far, the queen hadn't remarked on the addition to her daughter's wardrobe. Months had passed since the queen started her silent treatment—refusing to speak to Beatrice about even the most mundane matters. They sat at meals in silence. They walked out into the garden in silence. If one or more of the ladies of the Court, a visiting dignitary, or Ponsonby was in the room, Victoria carried on a light-hearted conversation with them as if nothing at all was wrong. She just didn't include Beatrice in their dialogue.

Beatrice tried to coax her mother into a chat by bringing up her favorite topics. Sometimes she intentionally antagonized her by mentioning Gladstone, commenting on the desperate situation in the Sudan, or pointing out the blighted blooms in the garden. Nothing persuaded the queen to speak a word to her.

Having lost that battle with her mother, Beatrice threw up her hands and spent her time where she pleased—mostly in the riding academy, a long, narrow building that was part of the royal mews, and out riding with her usual escort, Greg. By staying busy, she kept her mind off of Henry's desertion, as best she could. But the sting of his rejection was difficult to ignore.

After weeks spent in and around the stables, she began to

sense that something wasn't quite right there. Occasionally, she glimpsed strangers, as she had once before, in small groups of two or four—some well-dressed and obviously of high social standing, others quite clearly of the middle class. They seemed to come and go, quite mysteriously, without any obvious reason for their being inside the palace gates.

She asked Greg about them one day while she was brushing Lady Jane's smooth russet coat. He shrugged, looking uncharacteristically petulant. "Not my responsibility, now is it, Your Highness?"

She stared at him, confused, and was about to demand an explanation when he changed the subject. "Her Majesty informed Mr. Jackson she would be traveling to Osborne House in two weeks, accompanied by—" he looked pointedly at her "—*the princess* and a reduced Court."

"Really." She quirked a brow at him. This was the first she'd heard of the trip. True, they traveled annually to the family estate on the Isle of Wight. But she and her mother usually discussed dates and made plans together. Apparently the queen took for granted that her daughter would meekly follow along, even if abused and ignored.

"You didn't know, Princess?" Greg asked.

"No," she admitted, more than a little embarrassed. When he'd gone off to his other work, she pressed her cheek along the curve of Lady Jane's long, smooth neck, trying not to think about how hurt she felt. "When you love someone," she whispered to the mare, "you show it with tender, respectful gestures." *By letting the person you love make their own decisions. Or, by writing promised letters.*

She felt desperately unloved.

Beatrice spent another hour in the stables, relishing the pungent musky-sweet smell of the place, comforted by the contented whinnies and snuffles of the animals. She could hear Gregory and the younger lads working here and there in the stalls, caring for the horses. Eventually Gregory came back to check on her.

"Sorry, ma'am, I shouldn't have said."

"Said what?"

"About Osborne House."

She shook her head. "No, it's all right, Greg. Better that I know the queen's plans, however the news comes to me. My mother has become forgetful at times." She wondered if Marie also had been informed, so that she might start the process of packing for both of them. But wouldn't her lady have said something to her?

On the other hand, Marie's moods had been unpredictable of late. The young woman kept to herself whenever Beatrice didn't need her. She rarely smiled these days. Perhaps she was ill and trying not to let on? She'd have to insist upon an explanation. Beatrice picked up the curry brush to give Lady Jane a few more strokes before leaving the mews for the day.

"The queen," Greg said in a low voice, "doesn't appreciate you as she should, ma'am."

Beatrice's eyes flashed to him in disapproval.

"Another thing I shouldn't have said?" He stepped closer and looked down at his hands when she didn't answer. "Pardon me, Princess, but it's true. You give your mother everything, all of yourself, holding nothing back. She should treat you with more respect."

"It's not for you to say," Beatrice said, although she of course agreed.

"Nay, it's not. But sometimes, the way I feel about a person, it just comes out."

What was the Scot saying—the way he *felt*? About her? She turned and looked up into his gray-green eyes, no longer averted as appropriate for a member of the queen's staff. His hand came to rest over hers where she held the curry brush against her horse's flank.

Pull away, she told herself.

It was unthinkable that a commoner should touch royal flesh. But wasn't Gregory MacAlister also the son of a lord? Wasn't he more than a mere stable hand?

"Greg," she said.

He lifted his hand but didn't move it away. Ever so lightly, he traced around each of her fingers with one of his own, like a child drawing his own handprint. "I hate seeing you so sad, Princess. Because of your mother. Because of that ungrateful Battenberg. If I can cheer you in any way…" He looked deeper into her eyes. She wanted to look away. She couldn't.

Her heart beat wildly at his touch, at his words. What was he suggesting? Was he offering comfort only—a simple expression of compassion? Or was there something more ardent, more physical suggested by his touch?

She slid her hand out from under his. The brush dropped into the straw at her feet. "Thank you," she said weakly. "But I'm fine."

Suddenly disoriented, awash in emotion, Beatrice turned and walked quickly away. Her knees wobbled. She felt the straw under foot shift, the floor tilt. Around her, the plank walls shivered as if electric.

"Princess?" he called out from behind her. "Are you all right?"

"I'm—yes, I'm fine." Don't stop, she told herself. Keep on walking.

~

Gregory watched the queen's daughter weave down the alley of the dim barn and out into the sunshine. He laughed to himself. Girl didn't know it but she was his.

He had seen it in her eyes. They had dilated nearly all-black at his touch. She'd trembled and reacted to him with unmistakable sensual awareness. He'd waited patiently for such signs these months as they'd ridden together, as he'd gently urged her to open up to him.

At first he'd worried that she might cling to her hope of Battenberg coming for her, but the missing letters did the trick.

She no longer seemed to believe the Prussian loved her. He just hoped his agent had destroyed their correspondence as they'd discussed. Without the princess's letters ever leaving London, and Battenberg's missives intercepted before they could reach Beatrice, communication had been completely severed between the two. Moreover, his spies assured him that, whatever had transpired between the pair in Darmstadt, or later in London, their relationship hadn't yet progressed to the bedchamber. Kisses and hand holding maybe, but Beatrice was still a virgin.

Which meant she knew almost nothing about sex.

Which meant he could use her naiveté to his advantage.

And now? He'd wait and let today's little encounter sink in. Let Beatrice think about touching hands, about how much she missed Henry's kisses and how nice it would be to be kissed again—by someone conveniently close by, someone she'd learned to feel safe with, and who knew how to please a woman.

In the meantime, there was this bloody job in the mews to get rid of. He needed to move up in the world, and fast, if he was to woo a princess, the task set for him by Wilhelm. That's where he needed the help of the queen.

"Letter for you." It was one of the youngest pages at Buckingham.

Gregory snatched it from him on seeing the familiar wheat-colored vellum Willy favored for their correspondence. No royal seal, of course, but distinctive enough to attract the curiosity of mischievous pages.

Before the lad could move away, Gregory pinched him on the ear, hauling him back. He scowled down at the sod. "Haven't been taking a peek, have you, boy?"

"No, sir. Not a bit."

Gregory studied the simple blob of wax that had not yet come free.

"I better not catch you tamperin'."

"Wouldn't do that, sir." The boy looked honestly frightened. "Got it up at the palace and brought it straight down to you, sir, as the butler directed. I wouldn't be peekin'."

Gregory released his grip, giving the brat a rough shove meant to be remembered. "Better for your health if you don't," he called after the boy as he scurried off across the yard.

He peeled open the flap, unfolded the page. Just four words, in German: IS THE DEED DONE?

The emperor-to-be was growing impatient.

Gregory cursed and stuffed the letter inside his pants waist. This was the third time Wilhelm had asked for a report, each request briefer and more urgent in tone. He knew from experience how dangerous his old school friend could become if kept waiting.

But winning the heart and trust of a virgin princess required subtlety, perfect timing. Surely Wilhelm didn't expect him to slam her down on the ground and take her! Still, it appeared he'd have to speed up the process, if he didn't want to risk Wilhelm sending one of his brutal envoys to reinforce his message.

32

The next morning, still in her night shift, Beatrice looked up from her dressing table at the tap on her bedroom door. "Come," she said, and watched in the mirror as her lady-in-waiting stepped through.

Without turning, Beatrice studied the reflection of Marie's profile in the mirror. Far too pale. The young woman's face was strained with concern, her pretty hazel eyes distant. Beatrice spun around on the tufted silk stool to face the girl. As soon as Marie saw that she was being observed, she produced a porcelain smile.

"Your Highness, shall I arrange your hair for you?"

Beatrice drew a deep breath. "Not just now. Come and sit with me for a while, Marie."

The young French woman frowned. "But you must go to the queen. No?"

"The queen can wait," she said firmly.

Marie frowned but pulled a chair from the closest corner and sat. "You wish to talk to me about something important? You look so *sérieux.*"

"Yes, I fear it is serious." Beatrice hesitated. She had the feeling that the answers to the questions she was about to ask might result in more, rather than less, turmoil in the royal household. But she could no longer avoid seeking the truth. "You know that I have continued to write to Henry Battenberg, though less often."

"Of course."

"I need you to be honest with me." Her lady's eyes widened, the skin across her cheek bones tightening so that it looked as if it might split. Beatrice continued, "Has my mother interfered with my mail?"

"The queen? Do you mean, does she *steal* your letters?"

"Exactly. Have you witnessed anything that would indicate she or someone under her orders has taken my letters or destroyed them?"

Tears welled up in the woman's eyes. "But it so very sad, to suspect your own mother."

Beatrice let out a dry laugh. "When things go wrong I always suspect my mother." Even though she had asked her straight out and the queen had denied it. "Answer me, Marie, have you noticed anything that might indicate she is tampering with my correspondence?"

"No. No, I'm sure that is not possible." The woman shook her head violently. "Her majesty would never—"

"Then I don't know what to think." Beatrice was near losing her mind with frustration. "Is it possible she's enlisted the help of Ponsonby or someone else she trusts in Court?" She looked steadily at the girl.

Marie choked out a sob. "*M'accusez-vous?*"

"No, of course I'm not accusing you. Just answer my question."

"No, Princess, the queen—she has given me no reason to think she has taken your or Herr Battenberg's letters."

Beatrice studied the girl's stricken face. Now came the real question: "Then if it's not guilt over keeping a secret for the queen, why these dark moods of yours?"

Marie sniffled and brushed away her tears. "I suppose I…" Her gaze flitted around the room, as if to capture words on the wing. "I am worried for you. I see your loneliness and sadness, and it is only right that I feel sad too as you are my—"

"Oh, good grief." Beatrice pushed to her feet and walked across the room. "Stop it! Just stop it this instant. Hasn't this family seen enough fretting and mourning? It doesn't suit you, Marie. Don't let the queen do to you what she's done to me." She reached out and pulled the younger woman into her arms and held her there for a moment. "Please. Let's not shut ourselves off forever in a shroud of black bombazine and tears."

"*Oui*, m'lady." Marie gave her a brave smile as they separated. "I will try."

"Good. Now, I shall treat myself to a lovely ride in the park with Greg. He, at least, is always cheerful. Will you fetch my riding clothes? The plum outfit again, please."

Marie opened her mouth as if to say something more, blinked twice as if undecided, then turned toward the armoire.

~

Henry greeted each man as he arrived at the first meeting of *The Second Sons*. He had chosen Paris as a central location, well-suited to most of the young men he hoped to attract to the cause, and the turnout was even better than he had hoped for. Young noblemen from across the Continent answered his call to arms. Now they crammed themselves into a spacious private room in the chic *Restaurant Durand* at Place de la Madeleine. The establishment was favored by esteemed writers, including Émile Zola, as well as prominent politicians, artists and journalists. Today Henry would introduce his daring rescue mission to Khartoum.

Louis stood beside him as he waited for silence. He had promised to support his younger brother's plans to round up volunteers, but made it clear he would not be among those sailing for Egypt or marching across desert sands to the interior of the Sudan. Louis's young wife had extracted a promise that he would not risk his life so soon after their wedding and with a child on the way.

The first order of business, as always, was food and drink. Henry had ordered the staff to prepare tables with absinthe glasses and the traditional slotted spoons.

Seated before his own glass, Henry began the elaborate ritual by placing the spatula-spoon atop the rim of his glass, half-filled with the emerald green herbal liquor. He set a single sugar cube over the slots then drizzled cool water over the dissolving cube and into the glass, awakening and sweetening the exotic wormwood oils.

"And thus we set free the illusive green fairy," he murmured as the clear green liquid slowly turned hazy then morphed into a mysterious opalescent cloud of liquor. At this moment, he always felt a bit like a wizard, conjuring a spell. Looking around the room, he saw others just as entranced by the ritual blending of the intoxicating drink, brought back by soldiers from exotic lands.

"Gentlemen," he said, raising his glass when the transformation was complete, "we the second, third, and fourth sons of prestigious families, have at last found our calling." The room settled around him as the few men still standing took their seats and raised glasses in a salute.

Then all was quiet. They waited for him to speak.

"I realize my message to you has provided few details of the mission I propose. It was little more than a call to arms, to those of us who find ourselves in similar circumstances. Not being first-born sons, we have little chance of inheriting our fathers' titles or property. But that isn't to say that we lack worth. And, in at least one way, we are fortunate to be free of the burden of being heirs."

"Yes, all of that money weighs down my brother terribly!" a man standing at the back of the room shouted.

"Such a burden," muttered another.

Laughter spilled through the room.

Henry smiled and nodded. "Yes, our elder siblings have the purse strings in hand. But we are free to adventure where we will. To find fame and our own fortunes." He had their attention now, he could tell.

"Are you about to lead us on a new Crusade, Henry of

Battenberg?" a count's son from Milan asked, chuckling.

"Yes, Emilio, I am." Now was the time for seriousness, and he paused to look around the room, his gaze suitably grave. No smile. Shoulders pulled back hard in his frock coat.

There was a buzz of interest and speculation around the room.

Henry set down his drink and held up his hand to silence them. "I propose an expedition, not of the religious nature, but of the humanitarian sort. Our brother in arms, General John Gordon, along with British soldiers and innocent civilians of assorted nationalities, are about to be slaughtered. And no one is doing a bloody thing about it. Not the queen of England, not the British Parliament or any of the governments whose people are trapped in Khartoum. The caliph will not grant his hostages safe passage through the Sudan and Egypt. Negotiations have failed, and these people *will* be murdered by the caliph's soldiers unless someone does something, immediately."

"We all know the dreadful situation, Henry," a man said from a seat near the frosted glass doors. "It is lamentable, but if the English won't step up and send their navy to squash the rebellion, what are we on the Continent to do?"

"What men of honor anywhere in the world would do for a comrade in distress—go to his aid. *This*—" Henry raised his voice as he brought his fist down on the table with a crash "—is the humane, the honorable thing to do. The civil war there has already killed thousands. Gordon, hero of the British Expeditions to China, went there as a goodwill gesture to help negotiate a peace between warring tribes. He got caught up in the middle of a nasty business. We, as the untitled sons of the civilized world's finest families, can either stay at home—drinking, gambling and womanizing our lives away or—"

"Sounds good to me!" came a shout.

A flurry of appreciative laughter followed, but Henry didn't let it rattle him or break his rhythm.

"—or we can go to Gordon's rescue. I propose we sail for Egypt, however many of us are brave enough to form a relief party. We are brothers-in-arms, linked by the common cause of decency. We shall prove our manhood on the battlefield, for a just cause."

Henry had no idea whether he would end up with a handful of volunteers, none at all, or a veritable army. But he'd had his say and, after a few moments of stunned silence in the room, he sat down and waited. If he succeeded in mustering a force and freeing Gordon, the queen would have to acknowledge him worthy of her daughter's hand in marriage. That is, if he didn't die on desert sands.

As the seconds ticked by, he began to think his speech had aroused not a single soul to action because no one had spoken or moved since he sat down. Perhaps the absinthe had been a mistake, making the men lethargic instead of inciting them to valor.

Then, as if it had been agreed upon ahead of time, first one man, then another, then a half dozen slowly rose to their feet. The liquor he'd swallowed belatedly burned in his stomach as his hopes plummeted. They were going to walk out on him. He closed his eyes in defeat and lowered his head.

Suddenly, a voice from the center of the room jerked him to life. "To arms! To arms, Second Sons!"

"To arms!" the room exploded with voices.

Henry opened his eyes to see nearly the entire room on its feet. By God, he had his army!

33

Beatrice walked down the steep flight of wooden steps built into the chalky cliffs. Below Osborne House stretched the pale beach of her childhood. The sea that day was a slick, gray-green, nearly as peaceful as a lake. The fishing fleet that left the island early each morning hadn't yet returned. Spare nets draped over long poles above the high-tide mark, looking like laundry hung out to dry. Wooden-hulled skiffs and wherries in paintbox colors had been carried up and away from high-tide mark for repair or paint. She looked out across the lazy sea and breathed in the tangy salt that came off the spume as each wave ground noisily into the gravel on the beach.

The island had served as the royal family's summer retreat throughout her childhood, a haven for the nine little royals to run as wild as they ever were allowed to run. One July, Albert decided his sons and daughters needed to learn how the daily work of their staff and servants was done, where the food on their table came from, and how the ordinary person provided for himself. Albert gave each of his offspring jobs. He built for them a Swiss cottage on the property that was to be their laboratory. He supervised them as they tended a vegetable garden, baked bread, polished silver, mopped floors, and laundered clothes.

To Beatrice, barely more than a baby, it had of course all been play. She was allowed only the simplest of tasks. But she remembered that summer as the happiest days of her life. Too soon after that, their beloved father had died. Then came the bleakest, most morbid months of mourning. How she had survived those years, when even the weakest smile or timid laugh was discouraged, she'd never know. She'd lost all hope.

Until Henry came along. In his arms, she'd have happily died. No vision of heaven could be sweeter.

How brief that bliss had been. She sat on a twisted chunk of driftwood and remembered all of it. Every precious moment.

After a while, feeling calmed by the sea's soft music and silky breezes, she sighed and turned around to walk the long way up and over the dunes, back to the house. Above the rush and retreat of the waves, she heard voices and looked up.

A pair of figures stood silhouetted on the bluff high above her, against the cornflower-blue sky. A woman and a man—she was able to tell that much—but she could make out neither their words nor their features to identify them. She watched in shock as the taller figure, in jacket and trousers, lurched forward and struck the woman with his open hand, hard. She staggered backward, nearly falling before catching herself against a bench.

Beatrice gasped, clapping a hand over her mouth to keep herself from screaming. Instinctively, she sensed that by revealing her presence she might put herself at risk.

She looked away for a moment, trying to slow her racing heart, trying to think what to do. By the time she reached Osborne's gates and the guards on duty, the couple most likely would have moved on.

Indeed, when she did look back, the bluff was barren. And she had no idea in which direction the two might have gone—together or separately.

Beatrice's first instinct was to avoid running into either of them. They'd obviously been having an argument. It had turned emotional, violent. She told herself she shouldn't become involved in any way. The woman would be embarrassed and might not thank her for interfering; the man possibly still angry and unstable.

But wasn't it her duty to see that no harm came to anyone on the family property? The pair might be strangers, townspeople.

But, more likely, they were either local staff or members of her mother's retinue, having traveled with them from London.

Beatrice hurriedly retraced her steps, climbing the cliff steps as quickly as she could. She rushed to the approximate place on the bluff where the two had stood. She looked around. No one in sight. Nothing moving. Gardens, cliff-side paths, even the beach below appeared deserted. Her stomach clenched. She felt suddenly queasy at the remoteness of the place. The salt air that had earlier seemed a breath of freshness, now came to her as a poisonous effluence. She covered her mouth and nose with her handkerchief and ran, fast as she could, back to the house.

The incident haunted her throughout the day. She considered asking around to find out who the quarrelers might be. But because of the glare of the sun in her eyes, and the distance at which she'd stood below in the coarse sand, she was unable to describe either of them. So what was the point? A man and a woman arguing. They could have been anyone. Because the queen kept her busy with correspondence throughout the rest of the day, she had little opportunity to question even Ponsonby.

By the time she returned to her bedchamber, Marie, with the help of two maids, had finished reorganizing and cleaning the room. They both changed from day dresses into silk tea gowns. While Marie arranged her hair in neat plaits, coiled around her head, Beatrice described the incident she'd witnessed.

"Have you heard of any serious disagreements among our ladies and gentlemen of the Court, or within the staff?" Beatrice asked, looking up from her seat at the dressing table.

For a second, the two women's eyes met. Then Beatrice's gaze settled a few inches lower, on a smudgy shadow on the French girl's left cheek. Was it her imagination or did she see a heavier application of powder to that side of Marie's face?

Marie snapped her head around as if suddenly aware she was being studied. "There you are, Your Highness. Done. Lovely." Her forced smile was as rigid as a mannequin's. "If I may, I'll go lie down now. I have a little headache."

"Wait." Beatrice held out a hand. "What is wrong with

your cheek?"

"*Rien.*" The woman's nervous laugh failed to reassure. "It's nothing."

"That's a bruise, isn't it?"

"I—the trunk lid. I was careless and let it fall just as I was bending to take out a dress."

Beatrice searched her lady's wandering eyes, certain she was lying. Had it been Marie on the bluff, arguing with a man?

"Please, Princess…I don't feel well."

"No. What's wrong? You're not telling me something."

Marie blinked. "I cannot. *S'il vous plait.* I am fine. You needn't be concerned. A little accident is all it was."

Beatrice stood up and looked at her levelly. "You and I will sit in this room, straight through tea, dinner, and the entire night, if necessary, until you tell me how you hurt yourself… or *who* hurt you."

Marie's panicked gaze flew in desperation around the room. At last she looked back at Beatrice. "*Mon Dieu.* You saw us arguing. "

"I was standing on the beach. So that was you—the woman he struck?"

"*Oui.*" The poor girl's cheeks burned with shame.

Beatrice swallowed back her anger. "It's not you who should be embarrassed. Tell me who the monster was. I shall have him dismissed. No! Punished, severely."

There was a quick flash of confusion in her lady's pretty eyes, then a suggestion of another emotion that might have been relief. "He won't bother me again," Marie said softly. "He …I angered him. I'd made a promise to him but then changed my mind about keeping it. When I told him he went into the rage."

"Who? Who is *he*?" Beatrice shook with her own brand of rage.

Marie drew a shuddering breath. "He's gone now. Back to London," she said quickly. "He won't hurt me again, I'm sure."

"How do you know? His behavior was outrageous. Who is to say what the vile man might do to you the next time you meet? Tell me who he is and I will protect you."

Marie hesitated then seemed to give in. "The stable master, from Buckingham."

"Mr. Jackson? But why would he strike you?"

"I know something about him, and I threatened to tell the queen."

"I don't understand. Explain."

Having made her decision to unburden herself, Marie now spoke hurriedly, as if to be done with the conversation that so troubled her. "He lets people into the Royal Mews who shouldn't be there. Outsiders. They pay him a fee. He calls it his Private Royal Tour."

"Tourists?" Beatrice was astounded.

"Yes. Of course, he knows if he's found out, it will mean his dismissal. I suppose I felt sorry for him, so I agreed to keep his secret. But now—*mon dieu*." She stared at the floor. "If I hadn't taunted him, hadn't told him I'd go to the queen and reveal his illegal business, he wouldn't have been so angry and lost his temper."

Beatrice eyed the woman skeptically. Was she even now telling the truth? Something felt wrong about her story.

"I will find out if this is true. If it is, the queen will hear of it and your tormentor will be dismissed. Striking one of our ladies is unforgivable. But letting strangers inside palace grounds is a serious security risk to all of us."

"I know," Marie whispered meekly. She swiped at her tears with the sleeve of her dress. "May I please go now?"

Beatrice sighed. "Yes, get some rest. We'll talk more about this later."

"Thank you, Princess."

Beatrice watched the woman step through the doorway that separated their two rooms. Some of the story made sense. A man who had taken advantage of his position in the queen's employ had been found out. Well then, he certainly might threaten anyone who had the power to expose him. Now the stable master would most certainly be dismissed. Beatrice would insist upon it!

But why had Marie agreed to keep secret his shady business in the first place? She'd proven herself absolutely loyal to the royal family from her first day in Court. Had the fellow paid for her silence? Most likely. Had they been romantically involved? That seemed far less possible. Elton Jackson wasn't educated or attractive, and must be at least twenty years older than Marie. To Beatrice's knowledge, Marie had no lover. She'd confided in Beatrice that she'd been married once, but after her husband died she had no desire to remarry. She'd come to England in hopes of starting a new life. Since then she claimed to have turned away all serious suitors, saying she knew the queen preferred unmarried women around her, which was true. But what about the rest of her story?

Something was missing. Or twisted around to conceal a worse, more damning truth. She'd have to discover what Marie was hiding. And to do that she'd need help. Someone who was better than she at digging up secrets.

To her relief, it struck her that she already knew the perfect man for the job.

34

Louise had remained behind in London, unwilling to spend long days isolated with her mother and youngest sister on the Isle of Wight. True, if she'd made the trip, she could paint to her heart's content *en plein air*; the coast was beautiful this time of year. But her current projects all involved sculpting, and she needed her studio in Kensington for that.

Her husband John Campbell, the 9th Duke of Argyll, known to the family as Lorne, had been appointed by the queen as the Governor General of Canada, and he was still in Ottawa. They often traveled independently, and sometimes lived separately for months at a time. The arrangement was as much his choice as hers. But the bitterness she'd once felt at having been tricked into a loveless marriage by her mother—that, at least, had been spent. She and Lorne were friends now, nothing more or less, although in the eyes of the law and the public they remained man and wife.

If she'd had a healthy marital relationship, she'd never have sought or accepted a special friendship with Stephen Byrne, known in certain circles as The Raven. As it was, the former agent for the queen's Secret Service perfectly suited both her physical and emotional needs.

"Wonderful," she said, smiling when she'd read Beatrice's letter asking Louise to contact Stephen on her sister's behalf. "I love having an excuse."

Her lover had arrived in London three days earlier. They'd

of course met, discreetly, his first day there. But she'd had her art exhibition to prepare for, and Stephen was on a mission connected to his most recent assignment—providing intelligence and protection for Mr. Grover Cleveland, who was running for the U.S. presidency. After the assassination of President Lincoln and then President Garfield, no one wanted to chance losing another of the country's leaders. And so, she and Stephen had agreed to take care of business first then rendezvous in Bath for a leisurely spa vacation together at *The Royal Crescent*. She dashed off a note to him at his hotel.

Later that day, her maid peeked in through her studio door and announced, "A visitor, Duchess. Mr. Byrne." The girl smiled mischievously. "Will you see him?"

"I will," Louise said, putting down her sculpting tools and wiping her fingers on the moist rag she kept for quick cleanups.

As always when they came together, a pleasant feeling of lightheadedness seized her. Years had passed since they'd met in the most dramatic of fashions. But her attraction to the man never lessened. Which seemed odd, because she hadn't at first even liked the flamboyant American with his trademark leather duster and black Stetson. And yet, how could a woman not feel admiration for the man who had risked his life to save hers? These days, her gratitude just added richness to the sensual appeal of the man.

And into her studio he strode.

The look of him lit up her world. His touch melted it.

"Stephen," she held out her hands to him.

"Princess." He always thought of her as Victoria's daughter, never as Lorne's wife.

Stephen Byrne passed up the invitation to kiss her fingertips, instead drawing her into his arms as soon as a backward glance assured him the maid had left the room. His mouth lowered over her lips. He kissed her long and deeply and satisfyingly. She returned his passion in equal measure, but then pressed her palms to his chest to break the embrace that surely would have resulted in at least a good hour draped sweatily across her upholstered studio divan.

"We have Bath to look forward to," she said breathlessly. "Let's not get ahead of ourselves."

"Why not?" His ebony eyes sparked with equal measure of lust and amusement. "From ahead or behind, I think you're the loveliest creature that ever—"

"Stop that now!" Laughing, she swatted at him playfully. "There is a time and place for everything. And at the moment, my sister needs our help."

He raised a brow at her. "Which one?"

"Baby."

"Really. I've never known Beatrice to get into trouble, the little mouse."

"It's not *she* who is in trouble, at least I hope not. There appears to be a blackguard among my mother's staff. Bea's lady in waiting has been assaulted by the queen's keeper of the Royal Mews. He's running a little side business at Buckingham, allowing tourists into the stables for a fee."

"Clever devil."

"I suppose *you* might see it that way, rogue at heart that you are." She plucked playfully at his shirt collar. "But the fact is, he's giving strangers permission to roam the Queen's private property, and if the wrong person got into the palace—"

"You're right. It can't be allowed. Does she have proof?"

"No. That's where you come in, Stephen. All she has is Marie's word." She went to her desk, pulled open the center drawer, and retrieved the letter Beatrice had sent, asking for Stephen Byrne's help. "The girl claims to have known what the fellow was up to and promised to keep silent, for reasons Bea doesn't understand. When Marie finally rediscovered her conscience and told him she was going to report him to the queen, he struck her and threatened her life. Bea thinks the fellow's truly dangerous, but suspects there also might be more involved than what her lady admits."

"Let me see." He reached for the letter without releasing Louise, taking only a moment to scan the words. "He's no longer at Osborne House? He's returned to London?"

"So Bea says. Shall I go with you—to make sure you can get into Buckingham?"

Some of the palace guards, who had been on duty when Stephen Byrne was fired by the queen, years ago, were still assigned to the gates. Although he'd been pardoned since then, they might have selective memories.

"No, best I do this on my own." He kissed her again. "I will have a chat with the queen's stable master. Answers soon."

She winced. Stephen's version of a "chat" with a troublemaker often entailed physical encouragement. And bruises. And, more often than not, bloodletting.

Well, whatever it took. Beatrice's letter made it sound as if serious skullduggery was afoot. Things needed sorting out before the queen returned to London. Particularly if whatever the stable master was up to posed a threat to the family.

"Be safe then," she said. "Will I see you tonight with your report?"

"If I personally deliver my news, you may not be rid of me until morning." He caressed her throat with the rough pads of his fingers, grazed his lips along their path, inhaled the scent of her.

She closed her eyes and shuddered with delicious pleasure before stepping back out of his arms with reluctance. "Bath cannot come too soon."

"Bath," he said, "may need to be a state of mind."

~

His black leather duster flapping open like great wings, The Raven left Louise's studio. He chose not to hire a hack and instead took to London's streets in long strides, giving himself time to think.

He agreed with Beatrice's concerns. If the stable master was carrying on a clandestine business under the nose of the queen, it was only a matter of time before palace security caught up with him. Then the man would be sacked, at the very least. This much made sense. But if a sharp-eyed lady of the court had become aware of the man's mischief before the captain of the guard, why would she agree to protect his secret instead of turning him in?

He arrived at the palace, flashed his identification and was pleased to be admitted without fuss. He stopped the first stable boy he saw crossing the mews. "Boss is in the tack room, across the yard there."

"I know where it is," Byrne said. It was as good a place as any for an interrogation.

He walked into the dim interior, smelling of leather, saddle soap, and dun—and pulled the door behind him shut for privacy. A short, wiry man with gray whiskers and hard eyes turned to face him. His eyes lit in recognition.

"I 'member you." Elton Jackson didn't smile. "If you're of a mind to take out one of the queen's horses, you can think again, son. She's gone to Osborne House, and I've no authorization for—"

"Was the queen happy to see you on the island?" Byrne interrupted. "I shouldn't think so, as you were supposed to remain in charge here." No beating around the proverbial bush. The stable master scowled at him. "What you goin' on about?"

"You followed the retinue there, intending to confront one of the ladies—a French girl named Marie. Why did you attack her?"

The older man exploded like a keg of black powder. He came at Byrne, both fists up, jabbing at his face. Byrne ducked and swung out a leg, knee-high, tripping the fellow. Once he'd got him down on the straw-covered boards, Byrne pinned him, face squashed into the floor, his knee wedged nicely into the hollow of the man's back.

"Now let's talk civilly, sir, or there will be a lot more than the wind knocked out of you."

"Are you crazy, man? I been here in London all month long.

Ain't seen Osborne in years."

"You can prove this?"

"Plenty of my lads will tell you, to their disappointment. I've laid into them more 'n once these past days. Can't be in two places at once, can I?"

"No, you can't." To his disappointment, Byrne believed the man. At least on this count. But if he hadn't been the one to strike Beatrice's lady, who did? The princess couldn't have imagined the attack. He focused on the rest of the lady-in-waiting's story. "Word is out that you sometimes welcome company at the royal mews." He removed his knee and allowed the man to roll onto his back then sit up.

Jackson took a moment to catch his breath. His rheumy eyes turned wary, the cornered animal. "Aye, and is there a crime in the occasional friend dropping by where I live and work?"

"How often do your friends show up?"

"Now and again."

"How many? Two at a time, four…by the trolley load?"

"I tell you I don't know what you're goin' on about."

"Let's stop playing games, sir. You're running tours through the property. It's earning you a tidy supplement to your wages, isn't it?"

The man's eyes went dead. "Listen, there's no harm in letting a few curious folks see how royals live. I meant no harm."

"Sending someone to threaten and assault a witness to your little business—that's doing harm."

"Me? Who told you that? I never touched nobody." A suspicion came alive behind his eyes. "Oh, I see how it is now. Mr. MacAlister's been tattlin', has he? Well, he'll be sorry, he will."

"Who is MacAlister?"

The man laughed. "You don't know nothin', do you? He's the only one who figured out my tours-for-tips. At least I thought he was. He said he'd not tell if I—" His face turned chalky white and he sputtered to silence, lips clamped shut.

"Go on."

Nothing.

Byrne grabbed the man by his shirt collars with both hands, and hauled him up onto his feet. "You two had a deal. What did he want for his silence?" When no answer came, he lifted the stable master clear off his feet and dangled him above the ground.

The old man choked and sputtered. "Put me down. I got breathin' troubles, I do."

"I know a way to cure that." Byrne felt his control slipping. If his temper got the best of him, it would be bad for the old man. And bad for him, too, because he'd have no answers for Louise.

"Please, I'll tell you all of it, just leave me be."

Bryne set Jackson down with forced gentleness. He brushed off the man's rumpled jacket. "There. You're still in one piece. For the time being. Now talk."

The stable master cleared his throat. "It was this way. A young gentleman, he come up to me in the pub one day, a few months back. Buys me a pint, says he's from Scotland, third son to a lord, penniless and looking to work at a fine house with horses. Says he knows I'm in charge of the Royal Mews and would I like to hire him."

"And?"

"I told him to bugger off, we got no openings. I had all the grooms I needed. He says, 'Then let someone go, I'll make it worth your while.'" He looked up at Byrne. "Right then, you see, I knowed he meant no good. I says to him, 'Off with you. I don't trust your type.'"

"What did he say to that?"

"He says, 'Then I'll teach you to trust me.' But he says that word, *trust*, with a bloody sneer on his face."

"Words, they're just words."

"So I thought. So I did nothin'. Then two days later, one of my top lads, he's in the city on an errand for me, and a farm cart runs him down. Breaks him up so's he can't work no more."

"Let me guess," Byrne said. "You get another visit from

the Scot."

"Very next day. And he says, cool as a Highland brook, 'Now you got an opening, old man?'"

"Why didn't you contact Scotland Yard?"

"Because—and ain't you slow on the uptake, Yank?—he tells me I best not let on how he got the job on account he'll spread word about my extra income and how I'm comin' by it. Tit for tat. So what choice do I have?" He stood up straighter and faced Byrne. "Thing of it is, he's better with the horses than any of my other lads. He's a hard worker too, even if he comes from a father who's a lord, or so he claims. And not many days on the job, he up and saves Princess Beatrice's life and her horse's too. So, I say: What's the harm in keepin' the lad on?"

Byrne had a wicked bad feeling. "He saved the princess how?"

"Princess Beatrice was out ridin' Rotten Row. Horse thieves fell on her. Gregory acted fast, got her out of there and back inside the gates to safety then went back for her mount."

Byrne smiled briefly before the dark thoughts closed in again. At least some of this puzzle was coming together. But what did this rogue intend to gain from his job in the stables? Why had he gone to such lengths—maiming a man—just to take a job obviously beneath his station?

Jackson was staring at him. "What you thinkin', Raven? You looks like you found a spider in yer boot."

Far worse than that, Byrne thought. "This Gregory destroyed an innocent man's life, nearly killed him." He gave Jackson a pointed look. "You don't believe he could rig a fake horse-napping?"

The man's face fell. "Bloody hell...you don't think he'd hurt the princess—"

Byrne rolled his eyes. Louise wasn't going to like this. The queen would like it even less.

35

Precious days passed as the remaining preparations were made for the Khartoum mission. A ship had been secured, with crew. They would sail out of the port of Taranto, low on the Italian boot, making the voyage to Alexandria as short as possible. No one could say how much longer General Gordon might be able to hold out against the siege, without food and military reinforcements. The few reports that came back from the Sudan were not encouraging.

On the morning of their departure, Henry watched with a mixture of satisfaction and terror as one man after another boarded the cargo-steamer, *Armistice*. Faster even than the fleet clipper ships of his youth, it would speed them across the Mediterranean in record time. They were finally on their way, or would be in a matter of hours. Henry wondered—was he signing his volunteers' death warrants, or leading them to fame and glory?

The day before, he'd received an official-looking letter from Queen Victoria herself. She'd commended him personally, as well as his international force of mercenaries, for their bravery and dedication to a cause close to her heart. "Where Parliament has failed me," she wrote, "Henry Battenberg offers himself as my champion."

It was a formal document, making no mention of his petition for Beatrice's hand, or her banning him from English soil. But her acknowledgement of his dangerous mission meant she had been, and would continue, thinking about him in positive ways. She might not wish Beatrice to marry, but if her daughter insisted upon it—what better mate for her than a hero of the soon-to-be-famous Khartoum Campaign?

As he paced the docks, trying to calm pre-seasick nerves, keeping a weather-eye on the gritty skies that threatened to blow into a gale, a messenger approached him at a run. "A letter for you, sir. A courier from Calais just arrived with it."

Calais? That meant it had come across the channel from England. A good luck message, no doubt, like so many others he'd received in recent weeks as newspapers carried word of *The Second Sons'* adventure.

He had given up expecting letters from Beatrice. Whatever he had done to offend her, whatever he had failed to do that had rendered him wanting in her eyes, he would rectify with this trip. But when he saw the royal seal embedded in red wax his heart leapt.

Miracle of miracles…could it possibly be from Bea?

But no. Closer inspection of the seal revealed the message had come from the Duchess of Argyll, Princess Louise. Of course, it was like her to send a personal note of support. He tucked it inside his jacket. He would save it to share with his men as they sailed across the Mediterranean.

Henry turned back toward the gangplank, leading from the wharf and up to the ship's deck. The last of the freight, including food, weapons, and ammunition, had been loaded and stored in the ship's hold. He was about to climb the wooden ramp when a man he recognized as one of their party came shouting down the docks, waving a newspaper high above his head.

"Bloody hell," Henry muttered. Discipline would need to be the first rule of order. The fellow should have been aboard hours ago; he'd very nearly missed the boat.

As the figure drew closer, Henry began to make out his shouted words. But only three mattered.

"Gordon is slain!" Gasping for breath, the young man stopped in front of Henry and thrust the newspaper at him.

"It's all here. The caliph's forces took Khartoum two days ago. They've killed everyone inside, to the last man, woman and child. Slashed them to pieces. A blood bath."

Henry gripped the nearby wooden piling to steady himself. "Lord, save their poor souls."

"What do we do now, sir?"

The men, at least some of them, would demand revenge for the massacre. But what was the point? Gordon and his people were all dead, and the outrage of civilized nations around the world would be brought down on the caliph. Too late by far. But the murderer would pay, one way or another.

"Sir?" the man with the newspaper persisted.

Every last ounce of strength seemed to drain from Henry. He felt sickened by the images in his mind—the cruel slaughter, blood of innocents mixed with that of the illustrious Gordon.

"What now?" Henry repeated, feeling utterly deflated. "We all go home."

~

It was as Henry lay in his hotel bed in Taranto that night, sleepless, sick at heart that they hadn't sailed in time to save Gordon's people, that he rose from bed to take Louise's letter from his jacket and began to read. At first, his mind didn't fully register her words…and then he realized that, of course, she had written before news of the massacre reached England.

Dear Henry,

I hope this finds you well. We hear that you are busy mounting your expedition, and I wish you well. The Queen, at first, seemed surprised but then, in her own inscrutable way, pleased. I hope you are not doing something rash simply to impress my mother. It is such a terrible risk, going into that harsh, hot land. We hear nothing but horrendous stories of wickedness and bloodshed.

I don't know what will happen to you over there. And I still have no idea why your correspondence with Beatrice has been interrupted. (You wrote to complain that Bea wasn't answering your letters, but she swears she has been and you are the one who has stopped.)But there is another matter of deep concern. It appears that one of the grooms—a Scot named MacAlister—has used trickery, and perhaps even violence, to gain employment in my mother's staff. He also has won the attention and trust of my sister and, according to the stable master, is becoming a favorite of the queen. I don't know the nature of his relationship with my sister, but I'm convinced he is up to no good, already having seriously injured a former groom and, we suspect, may have assaulted my sister's lady-in-waiting.

I just wanted you to know that Stephen Byrne and I plan to travel to Osborne House, where the queen and my sister are now, to discover this man's intent. I have already sent a warning on to Bea. We will leave as soon as Mr. Byrne is free from his duties at Scotland Yard, on behalf of his own government. If I have my way, Mr. MacAlister will be immediately released from the royal staff and arrested. Had you not been engaged in such a brave and serious venture in the Sudan, I'd ask that you come at once to the Isle of Wight, to undo what this most suspicious man has done to interfere with your friendship with my sister.

I hope this reaches you before you sail for Khartoum. Godspeed, Henry.

   Your loyal friend,
   Louise

Henry reread the letter two more times, shocked by the audacity of the groom. He folded it away and took a deep breath to steady himself, but it was useless. He couldn't imagine what the fiend intended to gain from his wicked exploitations of his job and relationship with Beatrice. But he sensed that Bea was sure to suffer.

With the expedition rendered useless and cancelled, there was no reason he couldn't go to her. The Queen might still hold a grudge against him and wish to send him away again. But, by God, he would protect his Beatrice from the scoundrel-interloper and send him packing.

Although it was after midnight, and Henry had gotten precious little sleep for two days, he left his bed, made arrangements with the porter to send most of his luggage back to his father's house and went in search of the quickest transport to England.

36

Beatrice crumpled the letter and threw it over the cliff. "The nerve of her!" The wad of mauve writing paper floated for a moment on top of a wave before disappearing beneath the water. She couldn't believe Louise had taken it upon herself to meddle in her personal life—not again, not after all these years.

When Beatrice was little, Louise had bossed her around. That was to be expected of older sisters. But they were both adults now, and Beatrice saw no reason to listen to Louise's vaguely hysterical warnings of doom.

What had the letter said? She was so upset now—her heart pounding away in her breast, her head foggy with irritation— she hardly remembered. Something about Louise and her companion, the American agent, arriving at Osborne House, posthaste. Something about an emergency and needing to speak with her urgently. And what was the nature of this so-called *emergency*?

Louise had written only that her baby sister was not to listen to or spend any time whatsoever, accompanied or alone, with handsome Gregory MacAlister from the queen's stables. She promised to explain all when she arrived.

How ridiculous was that? Had Louise even mentioned the far more disturbing fact that the stable master himself had roughed up and threatened her poor Marie? No. Not one word of response to her news about the man's diabolical behavior or about the arrest that Beatrice had assumed would ensue once

Louise told Stephen Byrne so that he could pass it along to the Yard. Clearly her sister didn't listen to a word she said.

That was the trouble with Louise.

She had messed up her own life—thrusting herself into the avant-garde lifestyle of an artist, mixing with commoners if only to infuriate their mother, marrying the *wrong* man—and now she wanted to stick her nose into everyone else's business.

"Not fair!" she wailed at the sky, fists clenched so hard they hurt.

Beatrice sat down hard on a flat rock well back from the crumbly cliff's edge. That was the heart of it. Life just wasn't fair. Here she, the youngest in the family, gave her all to their mother, while Louise tripped gaily around the world. She frequented spas and resorts where (coincidentally?) Stephen Byrne also booked a room. If anyone had asked Beatrice's opinion, she would have said her sister's friendship with The Raven was questionable at best. And yet, despite Louise's dubious lifestyle, Victoria turned a blind eye to her sister's improprieties.

Well, she wasn't about to let Louise choose *her* friends for her. She simply had no right!

Henry had abandoned her, evidently having found other interests on the Continent. She'd read about his campaign. All of the newspapers called his grand venture selfless and brave. But he hadn't bothered to write to her any of the exciting details. Hadn't bothered to reassure her that he still loved her and intended to return for her. All she could assume was that, like every other man she'd ever met, he had all-too-quickly become bored with her.

Footsteps approached from behind. A man's, she thought automatically, at the sound of heavy boots striking the gravel leading away from the garden and toward the sea cliffs. She turned to look over her shoulder, expecting to see one of her mother's guards. But it wasn't.

Beatrice smiled, pleased that she was about to ignore her sister's unexplained warning.

"Greg. How are you?"

"Very well. The better for seeing you, Your Royal Highness."
He reached out a hand, offering to help her to her feet. When
she swayed ever so slightly in an unexpected gust of wind, his
arm closed around her waist to steady her. For just a moment,
she looked up into his face and saw a telltale twinkle in his eyes.
She drew a sharp breath, felt a sudden warmth tingle through
her fingertips.

She had seen a similar look in Henry's eyes. And now,
because of those heady, intimate days spent with the German
prince in Darmstadt and, later, in London—she understood
exactly what that look meant.

Lust. It was the way a man looked at a woman when he
wanted her, as Henry had said he wanted her.

But he no longer did. That was the bitter truth. And here
was another man who—miraculously—welcomed her into his
arms. It was almost too much to hope for. To be found attractive
not by one man in her lifetime, but by two!

Nevertheless, she slipped out of Gregory's grip with an
embarrassed laugh. Perhaps he was just being a little playful,
teasing her. That would be like Greg, as sweetly easygoing as he
always behaved when around her. But she turned back to look
at him again, she saw a deep longing that told her she wasn't
imagining is intentions. Still, propriety should be observed. Out
in the open as they were now, they might be seen.

"Please don't do that, not here," she said in as calm a voice
as she could manage.

"I'm sorry, Your Highness. I meant no disrespect. You
must know I am your loyal servant, as I have been since the first
day we met. Do you remember that day?"

She smiled. "You saved my life."

"Aye, I did, my bonnie princess." He reached out and
clasped her hand in his. "And now I know that was a selfish
deed, because I wanted to save you, *for myself.*"

Beatrice felt her cheeks go hot. She took a step back,
slipping her fingers free. "Please don't say such things, Gregory.
It's not right. Not proper. My mother would be horrified."

Just saying those words of denial did the exact opposite of what she'd intended. They sent a delicious thrill through her. To defy her mother, to do something so totally unexpected that the Court could only imagine Louise doing—such behavior made her feel independent, strong, blissfully free.

But a different emotion blossomed across Gregory's handsome face—anger. At her? "The queen wouldn't want me courting her daughter—because I lack a title? Is that what you're saying? I'm every bit as good a man as her John Brown was." He thumped his chest with one fist. "Victoria chose Brown as her unofficial body guard. Some say for more than that. Born of the same county in Scotland, we are. But I'm at least the son of a laird. Brown wasn't even that."

Beatrice clutched her hands in front of her skirt, held wide by the stiff hoop underneath its many layers. "Please don't be angry, Greg. You are a wonderful friend. So very kind to me. I do appreciate your loyalty." She started walking back toward the main house, suddenly feeling uneasy with his volatile emotions.

He strode alongside her, shaking his head, his mouth working as if trying to rid it of a sour taste. When at last he spoke it was with strained urgency. "Of course I am loyal to you. But it's more than that, these feelings between us. Don't you sense how drawn we are to each other, lass?"

She felt a flutter in her heart, or was it her stomach? Could this be love again—so soon? She really liked the way his arm felt around her. She wanted to be touched. What woman didn't ache to be loved? If her first choice for a mate didn't work out, was it so very wrong to look for love elsewhere? Louise had done it—and found herself a lover. Gregory might be her last chance. Ever!

Louise's warnings be damned! Her sister wasn't the one who'd stayed behind to care for their mother all these years. When Victoria's mourning had extended season after season, with no end in sight, Louise had thrown up her hands and said, *No more!*

"You're an idiot, Baby, for pampering Mama and kowtowing

to her every whim."

But Louise wasn't the one who spent every day with the woman, witnessing her everlasting sadness. Seeing the overwhelming grief in her eyes whenever she looked at Albert's desk in her office. Caressing the wedding veil she still kept closeted in her room. How could Louise be so cold-hearted as to withdraw her sympathy from the Queen? And then to encourage her other sisters to do the same, saying that only by no longer humoring the woman would they ever break their mother out of her ridiculous mourning rituals.

Beatrice felt Louise's measures far too harsh, and so she'd continued to stand by Mama. But now, she wondered if there might be a better alternative. A way she could love and support her mother, but also enjoy the companionship of a man who would be her mate.

She snuck a quick look at Greg, walking along beside her. He was a brawny Scot, terribly good looking, though in a rugged way. No, she didn't love him yet, but maybe she could grow to love him. People did. She'd heard other women say that they hadn't been in love with their husbands when they married them. The caring and pleasure in his companionship came later as he proved his devotion and gave her children.

Maybe that's the way it would be for them? Her and Gregory.

"I would like to learn more about your family, Gregory," she said as he held open the rear garden gate for her and they passed inside. She barely glanced at the crimson-jacketed guards who stood their silent vigil. "About your growing up in Scotland. And what you hope to make of the rest of your life."

He looked pleased. "I will tell you my whole story, Princess, whenever you like."

And with those words, she felt a return of hope. Like a lovely golden globe it rose before her, shining, holding within it the one thing that mattered—*Happiness*. Maybe she didn't need to live a life of solitude after all.

Her mother had said she liked Gregory and was grateful for his services to both of them. Beatrice knew the queen also appreciated his not being a foreigner like her eldest sisters' husbands.

Beatrice reached out and shyly touched his sleeve. He gave her a cocky grin.

37

The day edged toward dusk, the western sky a band of fire opal as Marie Devereaux set out from Osborne House. She'd had to wait until Beatrice finished dressing for dinner and went downstairs to dine in private with the queen, before she could leave. Now, because she didn't want to be stopped by the guards, she took the narrow stairs into the tunnel that led beneath the garden and toward the sea. The cavern stank of decay and mould. Cobwebs, thick and cloying, draped across the passage every few feet, so that she had to wave them aside with one arm, protecting her face from their sticky filth with her other. Clearly, the tunnel hadn't been used in a very long time. Beatrice had mentioned its existence one day, along with a story of its design as a secret escape route for the monarch, should the house ever come under attack.

She came up at the other end, into what appeared to be an abandoned boat shed, now used for gardening tools. She followed the path along the ledge, high above the fishing fleet's beach. Below and stretching out seemingly forever, the vast gray-blue ocean lay. Already the lower rim of the sun's disk was brushing the horizon; in minutes, night would fall. Charcoal clouds raced overhead, driven by a gathering wind. The air smelled of rain, crackled with the warnings of an oncoming storm, pricking at her skin.

She'd best get back to the house before the sky broke wide open. But first, she had to do what she'd come to do—put an end to this wicked business with Gregory MacAlister.

An hour earlier, Marie had been cutting flowers for the vases in Beatrice's room. Gregory whispered to her as he'd passed her in the garden, "Apologies owed." He flashed that caramel-warm smile of his. "Meet me at the stone bench overlooking the beach?"

She'd felt relieved that he no longer seemed angry or violent. Maybe he really was sorry for hitting her. Maybe he had decided to give up his insane plan of interfering with Beatrice's and Henry's courtship. All of Beatrice's letters that were supposed to go to Germany, Marie had kept back from the courier. All of Henry's notes from the Continent she'd taken from the royal mail sac and pocketed. She was ashamed for her actions. But the alternative—refusing to do as Gregory demanded—had seemed unthinkable at the time. The consequences were just too awful to contemplate.

She'd lied to Beatrice—telling her the old stable master had followed them from London and struck her. She'd been desperate and it was all she could think to say at the time. So foolish.

Now, despite the terrible personal cost she'd pay, Marie had decided she must confess all to her princess. Luckily, she'd foreseen the need to protect herself and had collected evidence that would ruin Gregory MacAlister, should he threaten her again. Tonight she'd free herself from him—come what may.

Marie stood beside the rough-hewn granite bench overlooking the ocean. Wave after ferocious wave smashed over the rocks below. The dark sea boiled tonight, but she shivered in the chill of the salty spume as it feathered up over the bluff from below. A bad night it would be, windows rattling, wind howling. Nasty. Evil.

"You beat me here," a cheerful voice shouted above the sea's crash.

"I did." She spun around and checked his eyes to gauge his mood. They were a soft undefined hue, devoid of emotion, showing no sign of the fury she'd seen in them the day he'd hit her. The bruise on her cheek had taken days to fade, he'd struck her that hard. "It is cold. I want to go back to the house, Gregory. I have something to say. But first, why is it you wanted to meet here—an apology you said?"

"Yes. You see, I was out of control. I didn't mean to hurt you. I honestly didn't."

He sounded sincere. She studied his eyes again; they revealed nothing. "*Ecoutez moi*, Gregory, it is just as well we are talking tonight. I cannot do this anymore. You don't need me anyway." A flicker from his eyes, just that and nothing more. A warning? She rushed her words. "Henry and Beatrice have stopped writing to each other. The romance, it is dead, if that is what you intended. You said this was necessary to protect the princess, but I do not believe that. I refuse to be involved in your mean tricks any longer."

He shrugged. "I had a feeling you'd back out. Must be your Catholic upbringing. Put the fear of God in you, did it?"

"*Oui. Exactement*," she murmured. The way he was looking at her made her squirm. Her stomach churned. "I don't deserve Beatrice's trust, not after what I have done. I won't say anything bad about you, I promise. I'll tell her it was my mischievousness. I'll say I was jealous, not having a man of my own."

"And will you also tell her that you were never married but had a lover? A priest no less, who gave you a child—the bastard you've keep hidden away in Paris."

She stared at him in disgust. "No! Your threatening to leak my past to the Court was the only reason I helped you." Fury flared in her veins, throbbed in her temples until her whole head hurt. This was the sort of reaction from him she'd feared. But she wasn't without a weapon of her own, a threat she would make good if forced to it. "If you dare to reveal—

He held up a hand to silence her. His voice came to her so low she could barely hear him above the cacophony of wind and sea. "Marie, if your adultery is revealed, Beatrice will have no say in your fate. The queen will know you've lied to her about your past. A childless widow, you claimed. But you were a priest's whore. You won't be allowed near Beatrice again. Victoria will ban you from the Court, from London most likely." He grinned. "Fornicators need not apply."

"You're a wicked, wicked man." She was too quick for him. Her hand flew out, slapping him hard across his mocking face. Spinning around, she started to march away.

She managed two steps.

His long arm shot out, fingers latching around her arm. "Don't. You. Turn your back on me!" Gregory roared. His eyes brimmed over with sooty hatred. "The thing of it is, *ma chere* Marie—" He hauled her back toward him, as if he were reeling in a trout on a line. "—I don't trust you. I never have. But I thought that knowing your secret would keep you honest."

"There is nothing honest about stealing what doesn't belong to you!" she shouted.

"You fucked a priest! You stole from God. Don't play the innocent with me."

He ground his teeth and gripped her harder the more desperately she struggled. "But you're right about one thing. I no longer need you."

He swung her around to his other side. The ocean side. Her feet landed barely a foot from the crumbling shale edge. She gasped, looked down, closed her eyes against the dizzying sight—black rocks, crashing surf. Hell.

"*S'il vous plait, non!*" she screamed. "Please. You can't mean to kill me."

"What's to stop me?" He used his body to block her escape, to shove her still closer to the edge. Chips of stone fell from beneath her slippers and sprinkled over the edge and into the abyss. "They'll find out." She sobbed, shaking her head violently. "They'll know it was you."

"I bloody well doubt that." His hands loosened on her arms, but she knew he wasn't letting her go. He only wanted to make sure she didn't take him with her.

Before she could even think how to save herself, his fists came up to center on her chest…and pushed.

She screamed. Arms flailing, hands clutching for his jacket, she sensed her left foot had already slipped over the edge. Her right foot shot forward seeking firm ground, missed.

Marie felt herself go weightless.

But, in the second before she plunged, she saw something amazing. Reflected in Gregory MacAlister's eyes, she glimpsed her own face, lips lifted in a secret smile of triumph.

Don't you know a mother will always protect her child?

"You'll hang!" she screamed into the snarling wind. "I *kept* them, you bastard."

Even as she plummeted, his silhouette shrinking against the dying light of the stormy sky, she wondered if he'd heard her. It didn't matter. He'd never find the damning evidence she'd hidden. But Beatrice, or one of the maids, would. And her child? She'd made certain her little girl would be cared for—better than Marie herself ever could, had she lived.

It was a rapid descent. The rocks came up fast. A single vicious jolt of pain when her body broke across them, before the chill of the incoming waves mercifully numbed flesh and bone, taking away her last breath.

Then Marie was away…away with the angels.

38

It grew dark early. All day long clouds had rolled in, blanketing the sky. Building thicker, higher, blacker. Then came the wind across the Solent, the normally calm body of water separating the island from the English mainland.

Beatrice sat with her mother in the salon. They were still not speaking—at least the queen wasn't. But the queen summoned her daily nonetheless, expecting her to be nearby. As if she might, on a whim, decide to readmit her to the human race.

Ponsonby entered the room, his white hair no less perfectly groomed than any other day, although an hour earlier Beatrice had seen him outside in the yard, among swirling leaves, dust and the first stinging rain. He been talking with two men she recognized as coming from East Cowes, the nearest village. His black jacket and trousers now looked as if they'd been brushed within an inch of their life.

"Yes, Ponsonby?" Victoria said when he stopped in front of her chair.

"Your Majesty, I fear it will be a bitter, mean night. We'd best have the men secure the shutters."

"We've weathered worse at Osborne House," the queen said without looking up from her correspondence. "But yes, if you think it wise. Get boys from the stable to lend a hand. Put that strong young man from Scotland in charge of them. He's quite capable."

"MacAlister, ma'am?"

Beatrice smiled a little, hearing his name. Yes, he was strong. Yes, he was capable. Her mother's trust in him gave her another taste of hope for the future.

"Yes. Gregory." The queen looked up at Beatrice, sitting nearby and drawing her mother in profile on a sketch pad. "I'm glad we brought him with us, Baby. He's useful and most pleasant. Mr. McAlister reminds me of—"

"I know who Gregory reminds you of, Mama. But he's not John Brown."

It suddenly struck her that the queen had actually spoken to her. To *her*, directly. Without the usual intermediaries—*Tell my daughter I wish for her to...*

For months there had been no verbal communication between them, only the endless notes passed by staff and servants. Now, suddenly, the woman was talking again, as if nothing had happened. No apology. No explanation. Just carrying on a seemingly normal conversation.

At least, this was a sign her relationship with her mother might be saved.

Beatrice lifted her gaze to the heavens in relief. Why was being a daughter so difficult? She decided the best thing to do was not to comment on the restoration of civility. Perhaps her mother had decided the proper penance had been paid?

"A younger version of Brown perhaps," her mother said.

"Yes. But a darker one." The thought came to Beatrice out of nowhere. Maybe it was the weather—so very oppressive with the storm coming on.

"Really? You think so? I see him as more fair—at least his hair is a lighter color."

"That's not what I meant." What did she mean? She liked Greg. More than liked actually. He was intriguing, a bit of a mystery. And the few times he'd touched her she'd reacted— not unpleasantly.

But sometimes when they rode out together, and he wasn't aware she was watching him, she imagined seeing the shade of the man. His ghost. His soul. She'd heard it claimed that, out of the corner of one's eye, one might glimpse the true nature of a person as a pale, shimmering sort of aura—the personal essence they hid from the world. Strange, really, that she should think of that now. She wasn't normally prone to superstition or mysticism. She hoped she wasn't turning into a dotty old crone, inventing apparitions, obsessing over the trivial or nothing at all.

Beatrice drew a few more lines then gave up with a sigh. "I'll never be another Louise." She set down drawing pad and pencil with a discouraged sigh.

"Thank the Lord for that," her mother muttered. "As fine an artist as she is, your sister gave me more trouble than all the rest of you girls together."

Beatrice frowned at her. "You never really told me what came between the two of you. Something happened, didn't it? Something terrible when she was young."

"Certain matters are beneath discussion," the queen said with a sniff.

It was always this way. The most intriguing gossip about events in their family, Beatrice was deprived of knowing. "We must protect our innocent Baby," she'd heard her mother say more than once to one or another of her relations.

Was she forever to remain Baby in her mother's eyes? In the eyes of the world? Beatrice felt a surge of rebellion. "I'm going for a walk." She stood up.

"In the dark? With this horrid weather so near?"

"You've dragged me out in worse at Balmoral." Miserable carriage rides in the freezing Scottish drizzle. Oh how her bones had ached!

"But that was in daylight and in a covered carriage," her mother protested.

Suddenly inspired, Beatrice decided to use one of her mother's own arguments. "Yes, and sometimes a little fresh air *is* necessary. I remember hearing that from you often enough, Mama, when you wished to escape a meeting with one of your least favorite ministers."

The queen laughed. "And what do you have to escape from

but a warm, well-lit room?"

"Oh, please," Beatrice murmured under her breath. Then, a bit louder, "I'll take Marie for company."

~

Beatrice returned to her room. When she didn't find the French girl there she tapped on the connecting door that led to her lady-in-waiting's smaller room. There was no answer.

Annoyed that Marie had disappeared and would now need hunting down, Beatrice took her cloak from the chiffarobe, wrapped it around her shoulders and ran down the stone steps to a side door that led directly into the garden. Wasn't that where the girl had said she was going? To cut fresh flowers before darkness closed in. Or had that been earlier in the day?

When she stepped out into the evening air, the wind rushed at her, fiercer than she'd expected. A gritty spray stung her face, even though it wasn't yet raining very hard. She pulled the fur-lined hood over her head to protect her hair. Marie had pressed hot waves into it and arranged it; she would be annoyed to have to do it all over again before dinner.

The wind played impossible tricks, sucking her breath away even as it struck her full in the face. She gasped and looked back at Osborne House. The staff had made short work of sealing it up tight, shutters latched, their sturdy slats blocking the glow of gaslights from behind scores of windows. She turned her back on the immense stone structure. She hungered for adventure, not a crypt.

No one was about now, although it wasn't late. Even the staff from the stables and the kitchens in the lower level of the main house looked to be tucked up for the night. Strangely, their absence cheered her. She felt daring to be out here alone. She felt awakened from a long, unnatural sleep.

Beatrice walked briskly through the garden, along the path that skirted the Swiss cottage where they'd played as children, to the top of the wooden stairs that led down to the beach. The rain had stopped, at least for the moment. Without the light of moon or stars, she couldn't see the sand below. For all she knew, the storm tide was running so high that the ocean had devoured the beach entirely.

She stood looking out over the black sea until the dampness in the air permeated her clothing and prickled her skin. Clearly Marie wasn't out here. Beatrice took the long way back, through the garden and around to the front of the house. She was goosepimpled and chilled to the bone by the time she reached the entrance foyer.

Their butler rushed at her from his station. "Princess, are you all right?"

"I'm fine." She laughed plucking her hood off. "Why does everyone in this household fuss so over a little weather?" She felt brave, fearless—having ventured out when no one else would.

An amused spark lit the old man's eyes. "Yes, Your Highness. If you pardon me, you are so like the queen. How she loves a good storm."

I am not like her! she wanted to scream, but didn't.

He took her cloak from her. "I'll ring for your lady, shall I, when this has dried?"

"Yes," she said distractedly. "I'm sure I won't need it until tomorrow."

He nodded his gray head. "The locals say tomorrow will be a day to not venture out at all."

"We're well provisioned," she said. "I shouldn't worry about spending a cozy day or two indoors." But the idea of being cut off from the mainland was a bit unnerving.

When Beatrice reached her bedchamber she found it as empty as when she'd left. This time she didn't knock on the door connecting her room with Marie's. She flung it open in annoyance and marched straight in, prepared to scold the girl for her neglect. Instead, she stood stock still and looked around. The bed wasn't mussed from having been lain upon—so Marie hadn't taken a nap and overslept. A Bible rested, as it always did, on the bedside table beside a carafe of water and clean glass. The room was in perfect order.

It wasn't at all like Marie to neglect her duties, or to be absent from Beatrice for long periods of time. The stone mansion was spacious, but there were only a few places the French girl was likely to spend any time: the library, gaming room, one of the smaller salons where they both liked to read. And outside, the garden through which Beatrice had just now passed. But Marie had often commented that she didn't enjoy strolling the grounds unless the weather was fair, so there was small chance she was walking for pleasure in the deepening gloom and wicked wind tonight.

Maybe she'd gone to the kitchen to fetch something to eat?

Beatrice arrived at the basement level of the house and approached the community room where the servants took their meals. The door was shut. She hesitated, but then there was no other way. At her knock, the clatter of pots and clink of glassware stopped, as did all conversation.

Mrs. Herrington, Osborne's cook, came to the door and opened it. "Your Highness?" She craned her neck to look up and to her right, checking the service bells. "I didn't hear you ring."

"I didn't," Beatrice said. "I was wondering if Marie was with you."

The woman frowned. "Why no, would there be a reason? She didn't miss lunch, did she?"

"No, and I realize dinner will be served soon, but I'm having trouble, well...finding her."

The woman chuckled then immediately sobered. "I'm sure she ain't doin' anything improper, Your Highness. Not Marie. I might worry 'bout some of these local girls hired on temporary for the queen's stay. Flirting with the staff gentlemen, if you know what I mean. But not Lady Marie."

It hadn't occurred to Beatrice that Marie might find someone here on the island that she liked better than anyone in London. After all, she had been acting odd lately. Perhaps her behavior had something to do with a man?

"Never mind. I'm sure she'll turn up. If you see her, please let her know I've been looking for her."

"Of course, Princess."

Beatrice climbed two floors of thickly carpeted stairs, passing only a few maids scurrying silently along the high-ceilinged corridors. Somehow she still half-expected to find Marie—contrite, offering a breathless explanation in French for her absence—when she arrived at their rooms. But when she opened the door to Marie's room, the girl still was not there.

Beatrice tentatively stepped inside, leaving the door open between the rooms. She crossed the blue Persian wool carpet to Marie's bedside table, opened drawers and shuffled around inside, searching for anything that might tell her where the girl had gone. Nothing out of the ordinary there. She picked up the Bible and bent back the spine to splay open the pages, shaking the book. A sheet of paper fell from between pages to the floor. Instinctively, she looked over her shoulder to make sure that no one had entered the room behind her. She hated the idea of being caught snooping. But what else was she to do?

She picked up the paper.

It was a letter, addressed to Marie at Buckingham Palace.

Beatrice immediately thought of all the letters she'd written to Henry. Notes of love that he'd ignored. Who had written to Marie? The girl had kept the letter. It much be important to her.

With only a twinge of guilt, she unfolded the plain white sheet. The writing was in French, but that wasn't a problem. All of Victoria's children had been taught French, as well as Latin and German, from the time they were very young.

She told herself she'd only read a little. She easily translated the words:

Charlotte is well. Cheerful little soul as ever. Quite the good girl.

Suddenly ashamed for prying, Beatrice refolded the note without reading further and stuck it back where it had been. Marie's sister writing about her niece? No, her lady-in-waiting had told her she had no family. She had no living parents or siblings. A friend then. How nice.

Beatrice returned to her room and sat on the canopied bed, feeling a little at a loss. She couldn't remember a time when she'd had to dress or undress herself. She wasn't entirely sure she could reach all of the tiny buttons down her back and hoped there was a button hook handy if Marie didn't return soon. The dampness of the fabric, from being out in the elements, was becoming uncomfortable. She shivered. Maybe she should summon one of the upstairs maids to help her? But that thought just increased her sense of uselessness. Surely she was capable of changing her own clothing.

When another half hour had passed, and she knew the queen would soon expect her for dinner, she started tearing off her soggy clothing as best she could. She dried herself and, with much struggling, managed to get herself loosely laced into a fresh corset and her pale blue dinner dress.

39

Henry Battenberg had been to sea with the Prussian navy. Thus, sitting in his private compartment in the train heading southwest from London and across the English countryside, he only had to look at the threatening sky to know a squall was in the making. He also knew the risks of getting anywhere safely by water in a bad storm. A ship might get caught in open water during a storm and successfully fight its way into the nearest port, but no captain in his right mind would deliberately choose to set out in raging seas.

By the time he transferred to a hired carriage and was racing toward Southsea and the ferry docks, the sky had turned a slimy greenish-black with bloody streaks. *The color of putrefying flesh*, he thought. The air felt as if the oxygen had drained out of it, leaving him short of breath. His shoulders ached with tension. Pressure built in his head. And then the rain started in earnest. And didn't stop.

He could only hope that Louise and her American had already made it to Osborne House.

Henry rapped on the roof of the carriage to get the driver's attention. "How much farther is it?"

"If the rain stops, another two hours, sir. If it don't, we'll be on the road the night long."

"No-o-o," Henry groaned.

"Chances are you'll have a good long wait afore a boat goes out from Southsea, if that's your plan, sir." And hadn't he already told himself as much?

"I'll make my own chances, thank you," Henry growled. "Just drive."

But fellow seemed unfazed by his passenger's curt tone. "You'll be better off, sir, finding shelter. Not six hours ago I picked up a couple from the station, bound for the queen's house on the island."

Henry's heart leapt with hope. Louise and Stephen Byrne! "You got them to the boat, and it sailed?"

"No, sir. The gent, he were smart enough to know not to try. Wind was blowin' up fierce. I left them at the inn in the village."

Henry swore then made a hasty decision. "Take me to the inn."

"That I will, gov'ner."

Henry threw himself back against the seat cushion and stretched his legs out, crossing his boots over his traveling bag on the floor of the carriage. His trip had been pell-mell, every step of the way from the docks in Dover. But he'd been reassured by his belief that Louise would have reached Beatrice by now and made sure she was safe. Something must have held them up.

The most maddening thing about this mess was realizing all that he *didn't* know. A flirtation with a groom wasn't the end of the world. But his last communication with Louise made it sound as if there was something more threatening about the man than his being a cad. She'd also implied that the letters Henry had sent Beatrice still hadn't reached her. How was that possible? He'd sent dozens.

At the inn he paid his driver and gave firm instructions. "Soon as you see the least sign of clearing, get yourself back here. I'll pay you double your usual fee to deposit me at the docks the moment the sea's calm for travel."

The man winked at him. "Other folks made the same arrangement. Looks as I'll be doin' a profitable-good business."

Disgusted by the driver's greed in the face of his passengers' troubles, Henry rushed inside. The space between carriage door and the inn's portico was only twenty feet. Nevertheless, he was soaked in the driving rain by the time he burst into the candlelit pump room. He looked around for the innkeeper.

From behind him came a female cry of delight edged with hysteria. "Henry! Oh, God, what are we going to do?" Louise threw herself at him and hugged what little breath he'd left out of him.

"Your Highness, tell me what is going on," Henry said. "Your note told me so little."

"I'll let Stephen explain. He's a bit calmer and more up to date on things. Have you two formally met? His Serene Highness Prince Henry of Battenberg—Stephen Byrne, formerly of President Lincoln's security detail, American civil war veteran, and my mother's one-time Secret Service agent."

Henry raised a brow. "Quite a résumé."

"Quite a title," Byrne responded with a wry smile.

Henry did not ask what role Byrne played in Louise's life, but he sensed an easy companionship between them. Perhaps spiced by something more, upon which he was too much the gentleman to remark. But he couldn't resist one question. "What brings you to England, Mr. Byrne?"

"I enjoy travel," the American said. "Except when it's required by an emergency involving someone I care about. I've known the royal family for over a dozen years now—" He pointedly looked away from Louise. "—some better than others." She blushed anyway, and he continued, "Beatrice is too nice a person to be involved in the intrigues of those who would harm the Crown."

"I agree." Henry leaned toward Louise and lowered his voice, as others were in the room and he sensed their interest. "Waste no time. Tell me, what has happened."

Louise put her hand on his arm as yet another man burst through the door, wet from cap to boot and shaking off rain like a big dog. "We don't know for certain yet, Henry. But come. Let's find a quiet corner out of the way of the door and more travelers fleeing the storm."

They took command of a heavy table near the fire where the couple must have been sitting before Henry arrived. He saw a black leather overcoat that must have been Byrne's, laid over the back of one of the chairs.

Louise sat and beckoned to her companion. "Stephen, hot tea and biscuits until something more fortifying is available, don't you think?"

"I'll see to it," and he was off toward what Henry assumed was a kitchen.

Louise looked up from beneath thick lashes. "Someday I'll tell you the story of the most remarkable circumstances under which Mr. Byrne and I met. For now, it's unimportant."

"Understood. A private matter between the two of you." He cleared his throat. "You are safe with him?"

"Utterly," she said, and gave him a dazzling smile.

"Good. Now, about Beatrice."

"A little from me, then the rest from Mr. Byrne," she said, smoothing her skirts, eyes lowered. "First, I must ask why you have forsaken my sister."

He hadn't been prepared for such a question. "Forsaken her? I told you, I wrote to Bea of my dreams, my plans for our life together, with such tenderness…but it was for naught. It was she who stopped responding. I was confused at first, then realized it was unkind of me to press her for a commitment if she was reluctant. Clearly she was reacting to the queen's refusal to bless our union. I felt it was kinder to let my supplications lapse, rather than cause her more pain."

"I see," Louise said, with equal weight to each word.

"But now in your own letter, you made me feel I still had a chance. I had hoped by mounting the expedition to Khartoum I might change the queen's mind about me and then I could try again to ask for her blessing. Do you not think that's possible?"

"I think," Louise began slowly, "there stands more in your way than my mother—which is saying a great deal when one considers that the queen is a force to be reckoned with on her least aggressive days."

Henry didn't even attempt a smile. There hadn't been the least hint of humor in the duchess's tone. "This stable boy Bea has developed a fondness for—he can't be a serious threat."

"He's more than a boy or regular staff, Henry. I've met him. He's the son of a Scottish lord and a very charming young man indeed. Perhaps too charming."

"Are you talking about me again?" Stephen Byrne had returned with a serving girl in tow. He carried a pewter tea service, and she a plate of plain looking biscuits that Henry hoped weren't too stale. He was starving.

"You're not charming as much as a rogue," Louise teased the American. "Come sit with us, and let's bring Henry up to date. I was just beginning to explain Mr. Gregory MacAlister."

Louise poured dark, steaming Darjeeling tea all around. Henry watched Byrne's face harden at the name. The American didn't take up a biscuit or touch his tea cup. All business, it seemed.

"From what I've been able to learn," Stephen Byrne began, "MacAlister is a penniless third son of landed gentry struggling to hold onto their land. He also has a very interesting but questionable past."

Henry polished off a second biscuit that gave him a shot of energy, though the pastry was lardy and none too tasty. He sipped his tea and his stomach felt marginally fortified. "Questionable in what way?"

"As long as the family had money they sent their sons to schools on the Continent. Gregory MacAlister and his two brothers schooled at the University of Bonn. It appears one of Gregory's closest companions during those years was a young Friedrich Wilhelm Viktor Albert of the House of Hohenzollern."

Louise added, "Better known as Willy in our family. He's my nephew and the queen's first grandson."

"Yes, of course," Henry said. "I know him but haven't spent much time in his grandfather's court. He'll be emperor soon enough, I assume. Good Lord, the Scot ran with a rich crowd!"

"Yes. He also managed to run wild whenever he was at home in Scotland. The father had a job keeping his son out of trouble. Gregory nearly was imprisoned after beating and almost killing one of his father's staff." Byrne's eyes fixed solemnly on Henry's. "Guess who he ran to for help?"

"Wilhelm?"

"Right. So they've stayed in touch, swapped favors. Probably a good deal more to it than I could dig up. But it seems less than a year ago Wilhelm visited Scotland on a hunting trip and spent three days as MacAlister senior's guest. It was soon after that Gregory decided to leave Scotland and come to London to work in the queen's stables."

"Not likely a coincidence," Henry muttered, feeling a bit ill. Oh, God—Bea was at the mercy of this rogue?

Byrne nodded his head. He turned to Louise. "Do you suppose Willy influenced your mother to give MacAlister a job because he needed to get out of another sticky situation at home?"

Louise leaned back and sipped her tea thoughtfully. "I seriously doubt it. Mama hasn't trusted my nephew since he was a child. She can't abide temper tantrums, and he threw them repeatedly when he wasn't given his way. Still does, I understand, although with more serious consequences for those who provoke him. No, she wouldn't listen to anything he says."

Henry said. "Then it doesn't make sense. This Gregory has been living the life of a wastrel, you say, for years. Why would he stoop to the hard life of a lowly stable boy now? Why not run through the rest of his father's money?'

"As I've said, maybe he became involved in another incident, like the attack on the boy that chased him to Germany," Louise suggested. "Did you find anything like that, Stephen?"

"Not exactly. What I did find was this." He took a swallow of tea, but glanced toward the bar as if longing for something stronger. "I made a quick run up to Aberdeenshire. He had a regular lady friend, a farmer's daughter. Those in the village said the girl spread it round that it was only a matter of waiting until the old man died before they married. And then suddenly, Gregory appeared to no longer care about waiting. He announced their engagement, and they were to quickly marry."

"And?" Henry didn't like the sound of this.

"Day before the nuptials, the pair ride out on horseback. She falls and is killed."

"Convenient."

"Henry!" Louise gasped.

"I'm sorry, but it seems an unlikely match and not of any profit to him who needs money to sustain his high living."

Louise pinched her lips together. "Maybe it really was an accident, exactly as it seems. Maybe the poor man was so distraught over his bride's death, he couldn't stay in the country where she'd died. It's a sad story."

"Sad for her," Byrne said grimly. "I am more inclined to think the Scot was clearing the deck." He glanced at Henry. "To put it in naval battle terms. He couldn't very well have this girl knocking about, questioning him about working at the palace, expecting him to come home to her. Not if he had higher designs—such as marrying someone else."

"Not marrying my sister!" Louise burst out in hysterical laughter. "That's preposterous. My mother would never allow it."

"Surely not," Henry chimed in.

Byrne looked from one to the other of them but settled on Louise's face. "Can you think of no situation when your mother might grudgingly endorse her daughter's marriage to a man socially beneath herself?"

Henry watched Louise flush a violent red then just as quickly pale. She reached out to squeeze his arm. "Please, no, Stephen. Don't even think that."

The American kept a steady eye on her and, as if by habit and without thinking, reached out and covered her hand with one of his own. There was such tenderness in the gesture, Henry looked away, at a loss for what Louise had meant. "The queen may be stubborn," Byrne said, "but she's capable of learning from personal history."

When Henry looked back, Louise had closed her eyes and was visibly trembling.

What? What are you talking about? Henry wanted to shout at them but contained himself. Obviously an intimate message of sorts had passed between the two of them. He waited, holding his breath until Stephen Byrne turned to him.

"Gregory MacAlister has a black streak in him, Henry. He nearly killed one man for a minor offense. The fellow accused him of cheating at gambling. Also, it's my theory he intentionally ran down the groom whose place he took in the royal mews. Then, let's say there's at least a chance he had a hand in dispensing with his fiancée to free himself to marry better. He wants a quick fortune—how better to achieve it than by marrying the queen's daughter? It may seem an insane fantasy to us, but to him it's a promising plan. If he's anything like Willy, his school-days pal, he's ruthless and capable of anything."

"But murdering a woman he's made love to in cold blood?"

Byrne rested a hand on his shoulder. "Henry, I've witnessed far worse. And if the man is willing to go this far to get what he wants, what do you suppose he'd do if he has set his sights on Bea and she refuses him?"

Louise closed her eyes and shuddered.

Henry looked at her then at Byrne, panic welling up inside of him until he could barely breathe. "The queen would never agree...not to marriage."

"Unless," Byrne prompted.

"Unless," Henry said, his voice dropping to a hoarse whisper, "Bea was with child."

"Exactly."

Henry's mind raced ahead. "If Beatrice refuses the lout, as I believe she most certainly would, he might—" He cast Louise an apologetic look, unable to go on in her presence.

Byrne was less discreet. "Seduce her. And, if necessary, he might even use force to get the deed done."

Louise let out a whimper. "I should have warned Bea by being more direct in my letter. Poor kitten."

"You told me she'd not have believed you," Byrne reminded her then looked at Henry. "It's my fault. I shouldn't have pressed Louise to wait the two days before we left London."

"You had no choice," she groaned, "your mission, Stephen. It is I who should have come directly, without waiting for you."

Henry dropped his head into his hands. "Stop it, both of you. It's water under the bridge now. We're here within reach of her but trapped by the storm. All we can do is wait it out and hope she is doing the same, in the safety of Osborne House."

Louise sighed. "If only she hadn't suddenly developed a mind of her own. That's all your fault, Henry." She gave him a weak smile. "You've given her a life to look forward to, a reason for fighting for her independence." Her tone sounded controlled, strong, but when she reached for her tea cup, Henry noticed her hand was shaking.

"We'll just hope that by tomorrow the worst of the storm will have passed. Then we'll commandeer the first ship willing to venture out."

Byrne nodded. "Right you are, Henry." He took the cup out of Louise's unsteady hands and pulled her close. She turned toward him and buried her face in his shirt front.

Henry looked away again, feeling utterly helpless. He'd never forgive himself if anything happened to his Beatrice.

40

Beatrice felt agitated nearly to the point of madness, her nerves prickly-raw and head achy. She paced the length of her bed chamber, incapable of sitting still. Maybe it was just the storm, she reasoned. Hour after hour, all evening long, the winds had blasted and battered the house, rattling windows, cracking two of them on the ocean side, despite their being shuttered. Branches scraped against the outer stone walls, sounding like claws trying to get inside. At her.

It seemed as though they were under siege.

And that, of course, made her think of Khartoum and the terrible suffering and loss there. Which immediately reminded her of Henry. The man she'd loved, *still loved* though to no avail.

He'd evidently moved on with his life, throwing himself into manly adventures, mounting a rescue force to travel to Egypt. A mission that, everyone now knew, never had a chance of succeeding because there simply wasn't enough time. The sad news had come by way of courier less than twenty-four hours ago. Gordon was dead.

Even though Henry no longer loved her, she'd been terrified for him, agonized over the risk he was taking. At least now he was safe. *God forgive me,* she thought, *for being glad it's over. Those poor people.*

Outside, the storm seemed to gather ever more strength, and she jumped at the sound of slate tiles clattering off the roof. Beatrice snatched up a piece of needlework as she rushed out of the room. Anything to keep her hands and mind busy while she sat with her mother. The queen would be expecting her in the smallest parlor on the first floor.

Beatrice flew down the stairs, her mind turning to another concern.

Still no Marie. If Marie had wanted to leave her duties for any reason—boredom, romance, homesickness—why hadn't she felt able to confide in her? What if the queen asked why the woman wasn't attending her? Beatrice didn't want to cause the girl unnecessary trouble by complaining about her neglected duties. And yet, sooner or later, she'd have to inform the queen.

As if the storm and disappearance of her lady weren't enough, Beatrice admitted that she also felt troubled by Gregory MacAlister's compliments and increasingly ardent attentions. What was she supposed to do with the man? What would Louise do in a case like this? Run off with the handsome Scottish lord's son to make Henry jealous? Ignore Greg and boldly dash off to Prussia to confront Henry in person? Forget both of them and take Marie with her to tour the Continent on a ladies' holiday? If she could locate the girl, that is.

How had her life come to be such a complicated mess?

In the parlor her mother sat exactly in the middle of the room, midway between the blazing fireplace and the shuttered, creaking windows, as if seeking the one spot in the room that provided the ideal temperature and lack of drafts. Beatrice chose the settee closest to the crackling logs and rested her feet on a stool to point them toward the fire. Her body welcomed the heat. It felt as if she were transforming from solid to liquid. She closed her eyes and pictured the French *cote d'azure*, sunny Naples, Spanish beaches with their pretty striped cabanas. Heavenly.

"I must say I'm impressed," her mother said.

Beatrice cracked open her eyes and picked up the untouched needlework from her lap. "By what, Mama?"

"By *whom*," the queen corrected. "The Duke of Battenberg's son—Henry."

Beatrice's heart leapt. Not four months earlier Victoria had tossed Henry out of London, forbade him from returning to Buckingham or the city. Beatrice tried to sound casual when she asked, "Why is that?"

"He, at least, tried to save those poor people. Parliament never lifted a finger, but young Henry—he did make the brave attempt. His intentions were laudable."

Beatrice widened her eyes. "I suppose," she began tentatively, "the more we learn about a person, the easier it is for us to like them." Her mother always took a long time to feel comfortable with new people. Nonetheless, this long overdue, positive attitude toward Henry came as a shock to her.

"To like, or to detest them," her mother corrected. "But I'll admit, the boy surprised me. I didn't think he had it in him. I believe I shall reward him, even though he wasn't successful. It wasn't his fault, after all." Beatrice put down her stitchery. "How reward Henry? A medal? A title or special honor?" *My hand in marriage?*

Her mother's tight-lipped expression revealed nothing, but her eyes sparkled darkly with mischief. "I shall consider my options in the upcoming weeks."

Beatrice gave up trying to interpret her mother's mood. She closed her eyes for a moment on a wave of bitter-sweet emotion. It was too late now for her to stand at Henry's side as anything but a friend, if he let her do even that. But she could feel happy for him. Whatever honor her mother might have in mind for him, it would bring him respect in society and help build beneficial contacts.

"Oh, Mr. MacAlister, good!" her mother's high-pitched squeal of delight startled Beatrice out of her melancholy. "I hope my summons didn't take you from your duties."

Gregory MacAlister hesitated in the doorway but stepped inside the room at the beckoning wave of the queen.

"Not at all, Your Majesty. I've just come from the kitchen. Cook gave me hot tea and a fire to sit in front of while I dried out."

"Ah yes, you were out checking on the safety of my horses.

The animals are well?"

"They are, ma'am." His head bowed, he shot a sideways glance at Beatrice.

She gave him a weak smile.

"Do you expect the weather to pass soon?" the queen asked.

"No, ma'am, I'd say it'll get worse before better. Least that's what the local boys are saying."

"Oh, dear." The queen breathed deeply, her button eyes fixed on the window that would have overlooked the stables if it hadn't been shuttered fast. "I worry that my dears will be frightened or the roof fall in on them. It's quite old, you know. Albert would have had it replaced years ago if…" Her voice dropped away.

"If it will make you feel better, I'll bed down with the ponies for the night," Gregory said.

"You'd do that?" Her plump cheeks fairly glowed.

"If it would comfort Your Majesty."

Beatrice tilted her head and studied him. Such a physically powerful man, yet so gentle and thoughtful. Always eager to assuage her mother's anxiety. And yet… Why should she doubt his sincerity? Any member of the staff would do as much, wouldn't they? But she couldn't help wondering at the depth of his rich brogue and his always just happening to be close by whenever they needed him.

She'd liked that he took a personal interest in her own safety, until the moment when he'd told her of his attraction to her. That was both flattering and exciting, yes—but she'd also felt uncomfortable with the idea. Didn't she trust him? She supposed she should. But when she heard him speaking to her mother, so intent on pleasing her, he reminded her more of a jackal than a trustworthy hound.

Beatrice shook her head, wishing away dark thoughts. Perhaps she was just in one of her moods, thinking ill of everyone when she should be much kinder. Or maybe it was the effects of the storm. Or because Marie was still missing, and she was growing more and more frightened by her absence with every passing minute.

She bit down on her lip, thinking for a moment before she spoke. "Gregory, there is another problem for which we might need your help before we all settle in for the night."

Her mother snapped her head back from the window and lifted a brow in question but said nothing.

"It's probably nothing at all, just some confusion about my lady-in-waiting's whereabouts." The queen scowled at her, silently demanding explanation, but Beatrice directed all of her attention toward the groom. "I haven't been able to find Lady Marie Devereaux, though I've looked for her since late this afternoon."

"Impossible," the queen bit off. "The girl can't just have disappeared."

"Yes, Mama, but—"

"And now the weather is so fierce she can be nowhere but sheltered here in Osborne House."

"But she isn't, or seems not to be." Beatrice blew out a breath in irritation. She imagined her mother preparing an accusation, though how she could blame *her* personally for losing her lady was beyond her. "I've looked everywhere. From the kitchen to the ballroom and both of our bedchambers. It's possible she might have gone off to one of the nearby villages on the island and got trapped there by the storm, but she's never left me without permission. She's nowhere to be found, and no one has seen her since before the storm broke."

"You must let that young woman go when you find her," Victoria said. "This is inexcusable behavior."

Beatrice shook her head. "It's not like Marie to neglect her duties. I worry that she might have had an accident and be lying unconscious somewhere in the house. Maybe in a wing or room that's not in regular use. Or somewhere outside on the property. What if she did go into one of the villages and was trying to get back before the storm…and something happened along the way? An accident of some sort."

"Beg pardon, ma'am," Gregory said, looking solemnly at

the queen, "but I think the princess is right to be alarmed. We should alert the staff, search both the mansion and the grounds." He turned to Beatrice. "I believe I saw her out walking not long before the storm struck. She seemed in a hurry, as if late to meet someone."

"Did she now?" The queen sent a piercing glare toward Beatrice. "Do you know of any assignations between your Marie and—"

"Of course not. She'd have told me." But then she recalled the French girl's odd behavior in recent weeks, how unpredictable her moods had become—sometimes distracted, other times sulking or just sad. "I'll alert the house staff. Gregory, perhaps you can instruct the grooms and the gardener's men to keep an eye out for her. We can't have them out searching for her in this gale, but as soon as it lets up—"

"I will, Your Highness. Right away."

"A good lad he is, that Greg," her mother commented, as soon as he'd left the room. "Just hearing his bonnie brogue comforts me in my loss of John."

"It's not John Brown we should be thinking of now. It's Marie." Had she actually said that? Scolded her mother.

But Victoria seemed not to have heard her. She was gazing at the photograph of herself on her favorite horse, with Brown standing steadfastly beside her, one big hand on the bridle. Her mother's Highland protector. To be sure, after Beatrice's close call with the horsenappers, they'd both viewed Gregory as her protector. Yet something about the intimacy of his speech and manner, and the way he looked at Beatrice, felt terribly out of place.

After alerting the butler and housekeeper so that they too could inform their people of the missing Marie, Beatrice rushed back upstairs to her lady's chamber, head throbbing worse than before. Massaging her temples, she rapidly scanned the room. Nothing had changed. No piece of furniture or article within the four buttercup-yellow walls had been moved. She crossed to the nightstand and took the letter from the Bible.

Propriety be damned—this time she read it all, top to bottom:

Cher Marie,

> *Charlotte is well. Cheerful little soul as ever. Quite the good girl.*
>
> *The nuns say she is an angel. Do you suppose they know of her paternity? As to Father Pierre, you would think he doesn't realize the child is his. He turns a blind eye when she passes by with her classmates, not even a blush for his shame.*
>
> *She learns well, is clever enough to write letters to you on her own soon. I will send one with my own as soon as she perfects her letters. She wishes to be perfect for you. Soon we will travel to Lyon to visit my brother's family. There she will have playmates; his children are close to her age.*
>
> *The money you have left for us, and continue to send, provides well enough. There is no need to worry. A longer letter with more news next time.*
>
> *Yours fondly,*
> *Adele*

Beatrice wasn't so much shocked as she was puzzled. So, her lady-in-waiting had a child. It must still have been a baby, left in the care of this woman, when Marie first came to Court. The queen had selected her as her youngest daughter's companion. Thinking of it now, Beatrice felt embarrassed. *She* should have been the one to choose the woman who would play such an intimate role in her own life. But then her mother always had made the important decisions for the family.

Beatrice gritted her teeth. Something had to change. She couldn't live like this any longer. She must take a stand. But first, there was the missing Marie.

The girl had been utterly loyal to her until this day. Now she, in her royal capacity, must be loyal to Marie and assume nothing evil of her. Having read the full letter, Beatrice now understood why Marie had kept her child a secret. Victoria would have dismissed her immediately, had she known. One of "her girls" giving birth to a babe out of wedlock was bad enough. That it had been a priest's child was ten times worse.

Beatrice stood very still, looking around the room, her heart rate ratcheting up, notch by notch. She'd already discovered one secret hidden here. There likely were others.

She focused on the mahogany chest of drawers across the room then rushed to it. In a frenzy, she began pulling everything out, drawer by drawer, onto the floor.

41

Gregory pounded another nail into a pine board, reinforcing the shutters from inside the stable while the wind did its best to tear them off from the other side. The sound of the gale was horrendous, like a monstrous steam locomotive barreling down upon the island.

Whack. *Words!* Whack. *Her words!* Whack. *Words lost in the howling wind.* His hammer hand telegraphed pain up his arm with each violent strike.

What had the bitch shouted at him as she fell?

Marie Devereaux was taunting him, that was clear enough. But he'd caught only a few words, ripped from her lips by the wind. Even more troubling was that final defiant glare she'd given him. She'd actually seemed pleased. How could that be? She was about to die and she *knew* it!

He plucked another nail from the canvas carpenter's pouch at his waist, impaled the slat, putting so much force behind the blow, the wood split. "Bloody hell!"

So what now? Assuming he'd never know what the girl had said, dare he proceed as planned?

If he didn't follow through, he'd have Wilhelm to answer to. Strangely, the German prince's wishes seemed less important now. Gregory's reason for wanting Beatrice had changed in the past couple of weeks. Willy required a spy; Beatrice was merely a means to an end, as far as he was concerned. Any connection within the royal household would have done. But Gregory needed her because she was his ticket to the life he deserved. A life of privilege and ease as a gentleman. A life of unimaginable wealth that required nothing more than charming a fat old woman and her daughter. After a while, he'd be relieved of even those obligations. Once the queen made him part of the family, they'd be hard put to kick him out without creating scandal.

Whack. *You're worrying over nothing.*

He thought about the way he'd handled Beatrice's, and the queen's, concerns over the missing French woman. He'd acted suitably worried, pretended to be as much at a loss for an explanation as they were. They hadn't seemed in the least suspicious.

But his mind kept replaying Marie's parting words, the few he was absolutely sure he had heard above the storm surge: *You'll hang!*

Well, of course the woman had wanted to lob one last pathetic, futile threat at him. Aside from those two words, he'd understood only one more: *kept.*

Kept what? Kept her promise to him? Or maybe, she was saying she'd kept her child safe. Well, that was laughable. Once the money she sent for her bastard's maintenance stopped, there was little chance the brat would end up anywhere but in a workhouse, or on the street with the rest of Paris's orphans.

Clearly, Marie hadn't confided in Beatrice or the queen that she had a child, or that he had blackmailed her into helping him. If she had, the women would have confronted him.

"Mr. MacAlister, sir, all is nailed down that can be."

Gregory looked out from his darkest thoughts and down the wooden ladder on which he stood. Two junior grooms stood at its foot. "Good lads. Go on then, catch yourselves a sleep. But be ready to wake and calm the horses if necessary."

"Yes, sir," the younger one said, looking more excited than frightened.

"And the search, for the missing lady, sir?" the older boy asked.

"Not yet. If the storm weakens during the night, we go out

at dawn. Until then, we'll see nothing in this devil's soup."

The boys took off. Outside, the wind's scream pitched higher. It reminded him of Meggie's wail of pain when he'd felled her with the rock. He shook off the stab of guilt. The Frenchie meant nothing to him. But that other memory was the price he'd pay his life long. Meggie, he really had loved her. Still, he'd do it all over again if it meant he'd get the princess as his prize.

He climbed down the ladder, looked along the dim alley between stalls. Horses snuffled nervously. Somewhere far back in the barn, one of them repeatedly kicked a hoof against a rail, setting up a hollow rhythm that sounded like a drum beat in a funeral dirge. All the animals were edgy, ears pricked, eyes rolling. Horse hell.

Gregory put away his tools and strolled over to the stable door that faced the stone mansion. He rolled the door open a crack on its iron tracks, and peered across the yard in the direction of Osborne House. The rain slanted away in solid blasts, a gray wall that completely blocked out the house. Not so much as a single chimney, tower, or gable visible.

He looked behind him. The lads were mostly all busy, bedding down. Gregory pulled up his coat collar, tugged his cap down low over his ears, and launched himself at a run, into the storm and toward where the house should be, if it hadn't blown away.

He was less than six feet from the servants' entrance before he saw the stone foundation loom up before him through the maelstrom. He caught himself against the building's wall. A sentry came to alert and shouted a challenge. The man looked miserable, standing out there in the downpour in helmet and what looked like a tarpaulin slung over his shoulders. Gregory identified himself and signaled that he wanted to access the kitchen. The soldier waved him inside, looking envious.

Gregory shouldered open the door; the wind caught it and slammed it shut behind him. Breathing hard he stood for a moment, listening to the house. Not a sound. All had gone to their beds. He stood dripping on the stone floor, thinking about what to do next.

Beatrice's bedroom was two floors above the basement kitchen. Marie had told him that's where hers was as well, just next to the princess's. But exactly which room it was, he didn't know.

He removed his boots then his Macintosh and hung it on a peg by the door with others belonging to staff. Miraculously, his shirt had remained dry. His pants were soaked through from cuff to knee, but there was nothing to be done about that. In stocking feet, he stealthily moved through the servants' parlor to the back stairs used by the staff so as not to be seen while carrying out their daily tasks.

When he reached the floor dedicated to the royals' rooms he padded silently along the plush crimson carpeting. The low flames of the gilded gas sconces cast a murky, mustardy light on a long row of closed doors. He was suddenly terrified that, whatever door he chose, it might be the wrong one. If caught, he had no excuse for being here. None at all.

So much was at stake. He couldn't afford to make a foolish mistake now.

He froze, debating whether to take the risk and just start opening doors.

It was at that moment Gregory saw a tiny square of color stuck to a door on the left side of the hallway. Soundlessly, he moved closer. A note. He pulled the paper free.

Marie, please come to my room and wake me, regardless of the time. HRH Princess Beatrice

He smiled. Puzzle solved. This was Marie's room. If she'd kept anything she had hoped to use against him, he'd find it.

~

Beatrice startled at the sound of the door latch clicking open. *Marie? At last!*

She stood up from where she'd been sitting on the edge of the bed, sorting through papers she'd found in a box in the bottom drawer of Marie's dresser. Her heart soared with hope then just as quickly crashed when she saw it wasn't her lady at all.

"Gregory, what are you doing here?"

Her mother's groom visibly flinched, apparently not having seen her until she spoke. "I-I was just…" He looked over his shoulder into the hallway, as if wanting to turn back the way he'd come, then glanced down at the piece of paper in his hand. He laid it on the fireplace mantle. "I beg your pardon, Your Highness. I thought—"

"This is Marie Devereaux' room. Whose were you looking for? All of the grooms are rooming in the loft over the stables, are they not?" He must have known he didn't belong in this part of the house because she was sure she saw a flash of guilt in his eyes.

"Yes, Princess, of course." His gaze swept the room then snapped back to fix sharply on her. "The queen," he said.

"What about the queen?"

"She asked that I search for Mademoiselle. Don't you remember?"

"Yes, search the grounds and island, after the storm passes." She narrowed her eyes at him, wondering at his brazenness, daring to enter the private domain of the royal family without permission. She was certain her mother hadn't given it.

"And since we can't search outside for hours," he continued, "and your lady has been missing this long, I thought it important I begin right away. Inside the house." His eyes skipped around the room again, seeing to take in its dishevelment—clothing, books, papers, tossed and piled here and there, marking the trail of Beatrice's frantic hunt. "I thought, well, if there's any place we might find a clue to where she went, we'd find it in her room." He smiled.

She considered his excuse and, at last, let out a held breath. "Yes, of course, exactly what I thought." She waved an arm across the mess. "As you can see, I've done my worst with this room, but I've found—" she hesitated, thinking of the letter revealing the child "—I've found nothing."

"Nothing?" His expression—half pleased, half vexed—puzzled her. "Really. Not a hint at where we might find her?"

She breathed in, out—and felt a crinkling sensation against her chest. She'd tucked the note from the child's caretaker in France down inside her dress bodice, to make sure she didn't lose it. "Sadly, no clues at all."

"Ah well." He studied her for a moment then stepped closer. "You must be exhausted, Your Highness. If there's anything more to find, though I doubt there is as you've given the place a good tumble, why not let me give it a try. You should rest."

Beatrice bit down on her bottom lip and looked around the room again. She'd searched everywhere, hadn't she? Surely if anything was worth finding, she'd have come across it by now. "Well, look if you like. Poor Marie, I'm becoming so worried about her. What if she's out there in the storm even now, injured and helpless?"

"Then we'll find her in the morning." He stepped closer and shook his head in sympathy. "How bad can it possibly be? If she twisted an ankle and can't walk back to the house, I'm sure she's smart enough to shelter somewhere until she can be found. A little soggy and cold, but she'll survive."

"I hope you're right." Beatrice said, thinking she indeed was tired and would go to her room. She must have been standing much nearer to Gregory than she realized because, when they both turned at the same time, her breast brushed his chest. He reached out and closed a strong hand around her arm, stopping her.

She looked up at him, not surprised this time but ready to reprimand him for breaching protocol, again. The soft longing in his eyes stopped her. "What is it Gregory?"

He frowned. "Have you ever wished with all of your heart for something you believed was beyond your reach, Princess?"

"What?" She laughed. "This is a new side of you. Have you turned poet?"

278

"Please, Bea, don't mock me."

He bent still closer, bringing her focus to his mouth, a sensuous mouth. She felt enveloped in his manly scent—the freshness of the outside air, sea salt, horse flesh, leather. Beatrice shut her eyes just long enough to regain her composure and quell the little shiver of arousal.

"Gregory." She laughed nervously. "One of us needs to leave this room."

"I just want you to know, Your Highness. I will always be your defender, your champion, no matter how you feel about me." He rushed on before she could interrupt. "But I am only a man. I can't control the passion that wells up inside of me whenever—"

"Stop," she said firmly, suddenly embarrassed. "I appreciate everything you've done for me. You saved my life that day in the park. And you've done a lot to make my mother happy, because of her attachment to her horses. But—"

"But you would never accept me as your lover?"

Her breath caught in her throat. Hadn't she at least once fantasized such a thing? Knowing Henry was lost to her. Despising the idea of living out the rest of her years, a lonely virgin?

"No," she said, suddenly sure of herself. If love waited for her, somewhere, sometime, it was with a man other than Gregory MacAlister. Her mind might become muddled at times, but her heart spoke clearly to her. Feeling relieved, and generous in light of her decision, she determined to hurt his feelings no more than was necessary.

"Dear Gregory." She removed his fingers from around her arm and touched him lightly on the shoulder. "Can we not just be friends?" Hadn't Louise set her an example, befriending commoners, believing they were every bit as worthy of her friendship as people with titles?

He gave her a fraction of a smile although no light touched his eyes. "Friends then," he said stiffly. "Of course, Princess. And you still have my promise of loyalty."

"For which I'm grateful." She lowered her hand from his shoulder. "Now, if you like, continue the search—here and elsewhere in the castle. I shall see if I can get some rest and plan on joining the search party as soon as calmer weather calms makes it safe for us to venture out. In the meantime, if you do find her—"

"I will send her directly to you," he promised.

"Good." She was halfway through the door to her own chamber when he spoke again.

"I'm glad you at least trust me."

Beatrice cast him a final smile over her shoulder.

When she'd shut the door behind her, she stood for a moment with her back pressed against the heavy wooden panel. It felt reassuringly solid.

Odd, she thought, remembering the slip of paper he'd laid on the mantle in the other room. *Why did he take the note off the door?*

Beatrice slid the bolt home on the connecting door then did the same to the hallway door. She stepped close to the dying embers of the fire Marie would have prevented from going out during the chill night. Suddenly, she felt terribly cold.

~

Gregory looked around the room. Beatrice had torn it to pieces. "Kept," he muttered. "Kept…kept…kept *what*, my little French traitor?"

There was only one thing he could imagine might have given the doomed woman the strength to laugh in his face. *The letters*. He had instructed her to burn them. What if she hadn't?

But if they'd been in this room, and if Beatrice had found them, surely she would have been so angry she'd have said something about them. No, if Marie had indeed stashed them away, either they were somewhere else or they were still hidden here, in this room.

But every drawer had been emptied. And even the drawers themselves were pulled free and turned upside down, stacked in the corner of the room, as if Beatrice had thought to make sure nothing had been glued to their bottoms. The linens were torn from the bed. The desk emptied out. Chairs tipped over onto their sides. Framed pictures on the walls lifted to the floor. (The princess must have stood on a chair to haul those down. Impressive!)

In short, everything Beatrice could reach or was movable had been inspected.

Everything she could move, he thought again.

His gaze fixed on the immense, oak wardrobe standing against one wall. Although its doors were open, contents spilled out, it must still be too heavy for the princess to shift. But the French witch? He remembered the strength of her grip, moments before he'd shoved her off the ledge. Was it possible?

Going to it, then bracing one shoulder against a back corner, he eased the thing forward of the wall a few inches. An equally exhausting effort shimmied the other rear corner forward. He was rewarded with the sound of something with a bit of weight hitting the floor. Gregory grinned, knowing before he saw it.

He got down on his knees and stretched out an arm along the floor, close to the wall. When his hand came back out it held a packet of letters neatly tied up with a red ribbon.

"Foolish girl," he breathed. To think she believed he wouldn't find them.

Now that he had these, nothing remained to tie him to her death. Or to Willy's mischief. All he had to do was burn the letters. And woo a naïve princess. If necessary, he'd force the issue, though cleverly of course. The woman was so pitifully inexperienced, she likely wouldn't realize what he was doing until it was too late.

42

"Go to bed, Henry." Louise touched his arm, flashing him a sympathetic look when he glanced up drowsily at her. He felt so very helpless. Where was Beatrice at this very moment? Was she safe? Had she heeded Louise's warning in her letter?

When he'd asked Louise if she thought her cautionary words would be enough to keep Beatrice safe, the Duchess of Argyll had said only, "If Bea's in the mood to listen." Not terribly reassuring.

"I can't sleep," Henry said now. "I've tried."

Outside, the wind slammed anything it could rip free from trees or buildings against the inn's outer walls. Every now and then the innkeeper, looking as exhausted as Henry felt, shuffled through the room, checking the shutters, staring mournfully at the ceiling, which had begun leaking hours earlier. "Thatching's likely blown off," the man had muttered.

Two more men caught in the storm arrived and unceremoniously curled up in opposite corners of the fireplace wall, and fell asleep.

"Nothing to be done until the squall blows itself out," Stephen Byrne said. "We should all get some rest."

"How can you sleep through this noise?" Henry held his aching head. "And knowing poor Bea is trapped on the island with that monster."

"We can't be certain he's done anything worse than flirt with the woman you love," Louise said, managing to actually look a little amused at his pain. "Every young woman deserves to have at least two gentlemen fighting over her, once in her life."

Henry lifted his head to roll his eyes at her. "You can't call the Scot a gentleman, if he's made improper advances toward your sister. Never mind that he's murdered his fiancée. "

"No," she said, looking grimmer. "No, I wouldn't do him the honor if what Stephen has discovered is true." She sighed. "I admit that it looks bad for the fellow, even if all we have is hearsay...not a shred of proof."

Henry slammed his fists down on the tabletop. "You would defend the bastard?"

"I suggest you not take that tone with Her Royal Highness," a deep voice came at him from behind. He'd forgotten Stephen Byrne had remained in the room, hunkered down on a settee near the inn's door. Their unofficial sentry.

Henry turned to see the American, now looming over him, wearing an expression he'd only ever seen on a man in combat. Dangerous. Deadly.

Henry drew a steadying breath. "I'm sorry." He turned back to Louise. "I apologize, ma'am. Truly, I don't know what's come over me. I'm just so terrified he'll hurt her, as he may have done that woman in Scotland."

"If what we suspect is true," Louise said, her voice gentle but threaded with determination, "I don't want him anywhere near my sister either. But until this storm passes the coast, there's little we can do."

"Yes, of course." No matter how hard Henry tried to control is anxiety, his heart refused to stop racing.

They all three sat up with coffee until Louise seemed unable to keep her eyes open despite the hot drink. She leaned against Byrne on the oak settee, and he coiled a strong arm around her and pulled her into his chest. When the innkeeper passed through the next time and gave him a look, Byrne merely met the man's reproving eyes, and the man scampered away as if the American had pointed a gun at him.

Henry couldn't have said what time it was when he too fell

unconscious. The next thing he knew a strong hand was gripping his shoulder, shaking him. "It's time, Henry. We're away."

He blinked his eyes open and stared up into The Raven's face. "What?" He looked around. The two most recent travelers had gone. Only then did his brain get the message: *Silence.*

"The wind has stopped," Henry said.

"Right, but it's still raining. I don't know if a ferry will run in this. We might find a captain from the fishing fleet willing to take us to the island. It will be dawn soon. We should get down to the docks."

"Yes, absolutely." Henry staggered to his feet. "How will we—"

"Louise has arranged to borrow the innkeeper's cart and horse, and a tarpaulin to keep us as dry as possible. I'll drive," Byrne said.

With little in the way of luggage they were away within minutes. Exposed to the elements, they were shivering in ten minutes, for the tarp did nothing to keep sudden spits of rain from blowing in beneath it. Henry's skin felt clammy, his overcoat sodden, but he didn't complain. All that mattered was reaching Beatrice and seeing her safe.

"Do you know how far it is to the docks?" Henry asked Byrne.

"They say three miles due south."

"So if a wheel doesn't get mired in this muck they call a road, maybe an hour?"

"More likely two. We can't move very fast in this."

Louise let out a hopeful little cry. "Oh, my, look!"

"What is it?" Byrne asked.

"The sky," she said. "Do you see, to the south? Doesn't it seem to be clearing?"

"By God, it does," Henry cried. "Maybe by the time we reach the water, we'll have a blue sky overhead."

Byrne nodded. "And less wind. Bad for a sailing barge, but better if we can find a steamer."

No one seemed to be around the town wharf when they

first arrived. Finally, they located three fishermen at a pub two streets away from the water. One told them that a couple of the larger boats had already gone out. "I'm givin' it a coupla more hours. Still pretty rough out there."

"Too rough to cross the Solent for the price of three days' catch?" Byrne asked.

The man looked interested but only pursed his lips thoughtfully.

"A week's catch," Henry upped the ante.

The man smiled. "Give me an hour to make her ready."

"How long to reach the queen's house, once we reach the island?" "Relax," the fisherman chuckled, "I'll have you folks there for luncheon with Her Majesty."

43

"I don't care who else is looking for Marie," Beatrice said, letting the heavy velvet draperies fall away from her fingers. "I'm going out too."

The sky over the Isle of Wight was clearing. Already she could see tattered patches of silky indigo blue, and the wind had dropped to a breeze that hardly moved the leaves in the trees outside the salon's tall windows. Safety seemed no longer an issue.

"Why do you insist upon trudging through muck and mire, Baby?" Victoria shook her head in exasperation as Beatrice turned toward the hallway door. "The island will be a horrid mess of puddles and downed tree limbs after the storm. Let the men handle the search."

"We need as many people looking for Marie as possible," Beatrice said.

"You don't intend to go out alone, do you?"

"No." Exasperated, she turned to face the queen, her hand on the gilded door latch. "I suppose I'll ask one or more of our men to accompany me. On horseback. We'll cover ground more quickly that way."

Victoria rolled her eyes. "You'll feel quite foolish when you discover the girl has simply run off with a villager."

"That's not like Marie at all, and you know it, Mama."

"I wouldn't have said so before yesterday, but given the suddenness of her disappearance, it seems the most logical explanation." She sniffed into her handkerchief. "The French are flighty and prone to unrealistic passions."

It was, of course, a distant possibility. A young woman as attractive as Marie should have had a flock of admirers. But now Beatrice knew the reason why her friend had kept to herself. The child. And probably the pain of a broken heart following her affair with the priest. Had she expected her lover to leave the Church for her? Had he forced her to abandon her homeland and seek asylum in England, to protect his honor? There were so many questions she longed to ask Marie. And she would…if only she could find her.

Beatrice rushed out of the salon and up the stairs. She'd need serious riding gear.

She ran into Ponsonby on her way to her room. "Will you send word to the stables that I require two men to accompany me on the search?" She flung the words at the old man as she raced past on the curving stairway. "Have them stand ready with the horses. I'll be down in the yard in ten minutes."

From the stiffening of Ponsonby's shoulders in his black frock coat, she sensed another lecture coming on. "Princess, is it wise to—"

"I don't want to hear it!" she snapped.

Determined to get to the bottom of her lady's mysterious absence, she excused herself for her burst of temper and concentrated on speedily casting aside dress and petticoats for leather and wool that would stand up to a rough and sloppy ride.

Outside in the mews, she checked the sky again. The shroud of black clouds that had covered the island for forty-eight hours had lifted, and the sun shone brightly. Her mother was right though. Puddles everywhere. Impromptu streams of fast-running water crisscrossed the property, and flotsam and jetsam lay all about. The fields would be treacherous with mud, some trails through the woods impassible. It would make more sense to put off the search, *her* search at least, until the next day when the earth had soaked up at least some of the moisture. But Beatrice couldn't abide the possibility of Marie lying on damp ground somewhere, helpless and cold, unable to walk on a twisted ankle, or unconscious.

She rounded the corner of the stables and found Gregory already mounted, holding the reins to her horse. Attached to his saddle were a leather satchel and a rolled blanket. Medical supplies, she assumed.

She looked around. "Where is our other man?"

"Those who can be spared have already left." Busy adjusting his stirrups, he didn't look at her. "We'll catch up with them soon enough."

Feeling only a little uneasy striking out alone with the ardent Mr. MacAlister, she sighed. Surely he'd behave himself under the circumstances. "Fine. It's probably best we spread out anyway. Which way did they go?"

He hesitated, as if trying to remember. "Half of them toward the cliffs. They'll take the high road along the shore."

"And how many are off toward East Cowes?"

"Four. And three more took the bridle path through the fields. We can cover the woods." "Isn't it less likely Marie would have ventured into the forest during a storm—being that's away from the house instead of toward it?" she asked.

He shrugged. "If she was already out walking there, she might have imagined it wiser to seek shelter where she was, rather than try to cross open fields, exposed to the worst of the wind."

Beatrice drew a breath at another jolt of fear on behalf of the woman who had never been far from her side for two entire years. "Right then, let's go." She waved off a young page who stepped forward to give her a leg up onto her horse. She set her left foot in her stirrup and easily swung herself up, expertly negotiating the twist of her body and swish of long leather skirt necessary to land in proper position on her side-saddle. She hooked her right leg over the first pommel and secured her left leg over the lower pommel in case she had to jump the horse over downed trees. "We'll take the southern path, work our way up the hill then loop back through the densest woods to the house."

"Yes, Your Highness," Gregory said.

She led off at a slow trot, not daring to run her horse across the uneven ground, riddled as it was with treacherous gulleys and sinkholes into which her mount might catch a hoof, and snap delicate leg bones. She repeatedly called out Marie's name, in hopes she'd hear a response. Gregory followed suit, bellowing loudly, although she sensed he put less faith than she did in getting an answer.

They searched through a stony glade, rode up and down a series of sparsely treed hillocks, continually calling out for Marie. Beatrice's heart grew heavier with each passing minute. Where could she be?

At last, riding side by side, they entered the thick of the woods.

As worried as she was, Beatrice couldn't help marveling at the forest around her. It smelled fern-fresh and green, bursting with life after the torrential rains. How clever nature was. Clearing out stale air and dust from the earth. Washing it down to give life a new start. Too bad her own life wasn't like that. What wouldn't she give for a new beginning? How her heart ached for another chance to be with Henry. Her dear, brave, lost-to-her-now prince.

"We need to stop and rest the horses," Gregory said, pulling her thoughts back to the moment.

"They can't already be tired," she objected. "We've only been riding a little over an hour."

"It's harder on them than you think, stepping though this mess. Risking injury to one of the queen's animals isn't worth it."

"But we've hardly covered a quarter of the woods between Osborne and the town."

Gregory smiled, his eyes sparking with something that almost looked like amusement. "We'll do it carefully, so as not to miss the poor lass. If she's on the island, Princess, we'll find her."

"Yes, I suppose you're right. I am just so terribly worried." She considered telling him about the child and the priest. But that was something from Marie's past that the girl had meant to stay a secret. She'd honor her friend's privacy.

Only then, as Beatrice slid down from her saddle to the mossy ground, did another idea strike her. Maybe that was where Marie had gone. To see her child. The little girl might have taken ill. Marie couldn't very well have asked permission to go to her child when, as far as the queen was concerned, no child existed.

She turned and saw Gregory taking down the blanket roll from behind his saddle. "What are you doing?"

"If we're going to rest, we might as well do it in comfort. I won't have you sitting on cold, damp ground."

She gave him a tentative smile as he spread out the blanket. "How very thoughtful of you."

He produced a flask. "Thirsty?"

Actually, her throat did feel dry from all of her hallooing for Marie. She accepted the leather-encased container from him, anticipating a cool wash of water down her throat. But when she put her mouth over the opening she caught a whiff of something pungent and drew back. "What is this?"

"Scotch, to fortify and drive away the cold."

She shook her head. "Not for me. It will just make me sleepy. You go ahead, if you like." John Brown also had a fondness for strong drink. One of the Scot's habits her mother liked least.

"A biscuit then?" he offered, popping open a tin he produced from the leather satchel.

Pursing her lips, she studied his innocent smile, and shrugged. "Thanks." She took a wafer from him and sat on the blanket. But her nerves pricked at her, little nudges toward action. *Move. Ride. Go!* a voice urged her.

She hastily munched the crisp, buttery-sweet shortbread. "I can't believe you packed a picnic, Greg. This hardly seems the time." Part of her admitted pleasure that he cared so much for her comfort. Another, much more insistent, grew irritated and impatient. The man was taking this search far too lightly.

Beatrice watched the horses drink from the nearby stream. They snuffled softly, shook their manes, drank some more. They didn't look in the least fatigued. Neither was she.

Beatrice dusted the crumbs from her fingers and was about to push herself to her feet, when the Scot startled her by sitting down close beside her. She flinched as his hip bumped against hers, hard, knocking into her just enough to interrupt her attempt to stand. He stretched out on his back. Hands folded behind his head, he closed his eyes in repose. Glittery patches of sunlight filtered through the branches overhead, down across his strong masculine features.

"What do you think you're doing?" she said.

He seemed not to have heard her.

Beatrice looked around her in exasperation. *The lazy turd!* Only then did she think about how far they were from the house—at least two miles. They hadn't seen even one other person—soldier, staff, or villager—from the search party. Clearly, this was ground that should be thoroughly scoured.

Never mind. If she had to continue on her own, without the blasted groom, she would.

She tucked her feet under her hips to stand up.

Gregory's hand shot out. Rigid fingers clasped her wrist. His eyes flashed open, fixing on her. "Don't go, Princess. Let's talk a bit while the horses recover." His voice was soft but insistent.

She stared at him—her earlier wariness swelling to alarm. "The horses aren't even breathing hard." He didn't respond. "Talk about what, Greg?"

"Us." He smiled.

Before she realized what he intended to do, his other hand clamped the back of her neck. He dragged her down on top of him.

His kiss was hot and moist and adamant. His mouth tasted briny, with a sweet aftertaste of tobacco, and the liquor he'd just swallowed. Beatrice recoiled. But her body betrayed her, responding with an inner heat to the intimacy of finding herself atop a man's hard chest, his ribs pressing into her breasts, his arms locked around her. She became aware of the thunderous pulse of her own heart.

Despite the possibility that she felt excited by their closeness, she was compelled to remind him that his behavior was, simply put, outrageously inappropriate.

"Gregory—"

He pulled back a few inches, touched a finger over her lips. "Hush. Hear me out. You may still think you need to save yourself for Henry Battenberg. But he doesn't deserve you."

Was the man mad? First, he took physical liberties with her. Now he spoke of her private life as if he deserved to have a say in it. She opened her mouth to chastise him, but his finger pressed so firmly over her lips, she imagined the tender flesh bruising against her teeth. It was an obvious warning.

Still, Gregory's tone remained calm, almost mesmerizing. "If Battenberg had been a real man, he would have stood up to the queen and not deserted you. He'd have taken you with him back to Germany. He is a coward. I am not." His eyes suddenly blazed with dark intent. "I will stand by you no matter what, Princess. You *must* trust me."

"Trust you in what way?" She gasped as he traced one finger down the line of her throat.

Suddenly, a woman's instinct took over. The heat that had shot through her body at his surprise embrace seeped away, leaving her as chilled as if she'd been lying on frozen ground. She sensed their roles had altered without her realizing it. He was predator, she was prey.

Beatrice desperately wanted to get away from him, even if she didn't fully understand what he expected of her. But she could tell from the intensity of his gaze that he had no intension of letting her go.

She wiggled just enough to force her arms up and create a small space between them. "Gregory, I'm uncomfortable. Let me up." The muscles in his arms hardened. She felt the strength in his body. As long as he ignored her wish to be released, she knew she had little chance of escape. And the idea she might overpower him was ludicrous.

Her mind raced. *What to do? What to do!*

He was talking again in that sing-song voice, no doubt

meant to reduce her to limp acquiescence. "A man who loves a woman *shows* his devotion, my sweet Beatrice. Words are nothing. It is his actions that prove him worthy. I will never neglect you as Battenberg has done."

His hands slid down her body, skimming over tweed riding jacket and suede skirt, raising up chills as they went. She wondered if he interpreted her shivers as pleasurable. They were not.

"Stop!" she shouted.

"Let me prove myself. Let me bring you the happiness you deserve."

"I don't know what you're talking about. Now release me!"

Inexperienced as she was, she knew now that Gregory MacAlister wasn't the harmless flirt she'd at first assumed. She had to get away from him. Any way she could.

Beatrice lashed out at him, striking his chest, shoulders, face with her fists. Putting everything she had into her assault.

Nothing she did fazed him. "It's time," he whispered in her ear.

She stiffened and pushed away from him with a shriek of protest.

He rolled them both over, putting her back against the mossy undergrowth off the edge of the blanket. He pinned her wrists above her head to the damp forest floor. She could feel the moisture seeping through her clothing. His body seemed to take on extra weight, so heavy now the breath was crushed out of her.

"Stop, Mr. MacAlister. Stop…this!" She tried to scream the words but was barely able to force them out in puffy half-breaths. "No!"

His gray eyes darkened. He kissed her throat. "I will, my sweet. But first we shall bind ourselves together. And don't pretend it will mean nothing to you. I know you, my innocent flower, and I know your mother. Once her Baby is no longer a virgin, the queen will tolerate nothing less than seeing you married. To any other man, you'll be ruined, an embarrassment.

You'll have no one but your loyal Gregory."

To her horror she realized his lower regions had swollen, hardened. Forcing himself on her excited him.

She had, of course, been aware of Henry's masculine reactions to being close to her. He'd admitted his arousal, and she had been flattered, thrilled. She'd looked forward to discovering ways to please him, to lovingly surrender and joyfully provide for him a wife's gift of her body.

This was nothing like what she'd felt with Henry. There was a word for this.

"Rape hardly recommends you as a husband!" she gasped.

He was laughing now. *Laughing* at her! "Not rape, my dear. You teased me. Insisted on having my company alone on our many rides. Remember? Everyone in the mews knows that. Princess Beatrice specially requested me. And there are those who will swear you threw yourself shamelessly at me."

Her eyes widened with horror. "That. Is. A. *Lie*!"

He kissed her throat again and shrugged, looking pleased with himself. The truth behind his arrogance struck her like a fist to her stomach. Whether he had started the lie or paid others to do it for him didn't matter. Gossip flew unchecked through her mother's court. Within days, no one would remember who first told the tale of her obsession with the handsome groom. Society would accept it as the truth.

In that moment, she believed the manipulative Scot capable of anything. No matter how twisted or cruel.

"I hate you!" she screamed.

"Trust me, my darling," he breathed between her lips. "I will be gentle. Unless you fight me, the pain will be brief, the pleasure delicious."

With a burst of strength, she wrenched one hand free of his grip. Before he could duck away, she'd dug her nails deep into his cheek and dragged them down the side of his face. Blood seeped from four jagged trails of flesh.

"Witch!" His eyes narrowed in stark warning. "Don't you *dare* disobey me."

Dare? she thought. Her body tensed, from head to toe. She'd spent her entire life doing what others told her she must do. She'd never been able to choose for herself. But now… *now!* She refused to let Gregory MacAlister make the most intimate decision of her life for her.

No man will take my maidenhead—without my willing it!

While he was distracted, sliding off of her in their struggles as he tried to recapture her free arm, she got one leg out from under him, crooked her knee and jerked it up, *hard*, into his crotch.

He let out a low, agonized groan and fell off of her, clutching himself. Her wrists throbbed, her chest ached, but she rolled away and onto her feet. She lifted the hem of her skirt and ran for the horses, not risking a glance back over her shoulder to see if he was following her. Or how much of a lead she had on him.

44

Henry was the first off the *Nancy Ann*. He leaped the four feet between the deck of the fishing trawler and splintery dock, his boots landing with a squelchy thud on the sodden wood planks. He caught a line thrown by Byrne and tied off the boat with a naval man's snug cleat hitch.

In the distance, he could just see the crenulated stone towers of Osborne House. Not directly atop the chalky cliffs but perhaps a quarter mile back from the shore. The sky had cleared, the sun peeking out from behind the few remaining sooty clouds. He thought to run on ahead of the others except he'd be turned away by the guards without Louise there to identify him. It had been many years since he was an invited guest to the island, and he surely wasn't expected now, as he was still *persona non grata* with the queen.

He paced up and down the dock, scanning the waterfront while he waited for the duchess to disembark. Byrne was tossing their luggage up onto the wharf. Luggage that Henry couldn't have cared less about. All that mattered to him was seeing Beatrice unharmed and safe.

He turned to observe the condition of the beach while he waited. The storm had kicked up a snarl of glistening emerald seaweed, small and large branches of twisted driftwood, and black bladder-kelp along the sandy shore. A half dozen green and red wooden boats from the fishing fleet remained beached, high above the water's edge, and appeared not to have suffered from the storm. His impatience growing, he was about to shout at Byrne that he would run on ahead of them and take his chances with the queen's guard, when he caught sight of a cluster of men huddled around something much smaller than a boat, smaller even than any of the men themselves.

One of them pointed toward the *Nancy B.* The others turned as one to observe the three strangers. A fellow in a wool cap broke from the group and ran toward the wharf.

"Do you know this chap?" Henry called out to the captain.

"Bryan Axelrod, one of the islanders, sir. A mackerel fisherman like me."

Perhaps it was an unusual sea creature that had washed up and the young man was looking to make a few coins by offering to show it off to tourists. Well, Henry had no time for that nonsense.

"Ho there!" Axelrod hollered. "Are ye from the queen's house?"

"We're on our way there. Why do you ask?" Henry heard steps on the dock behind him and turned to see Louise and Byrne coming along. At last!

"A sad state of affairs, sir. A woman's body washed up on the beach."

Henry's heart stopped. *Beatrice? No! Oh, God, no.* His heart hammered in his chest. *Tell me something to prove it's not her!*

The fisherman continued talking, "She ain't from round here. Not an island woman, no sir. Way she's dressed, we figured she might be from the queen's household."

"A maid maybe?" Henry guessed. *Please let it be!*

The man winced. "More likely, one o' the Court. Seein' how she's dressed so fine."

Henry felt the world implode around him.

"What's all this about?" Louise demanded, stopping beside them. She tucked a strand of hair back under her straw hat but the breeze tugged it loose again.

"There's been a terrible—an accident." Henry swallowed. Then swallowed again, barely able to speak. "A woman has drowned. They've found a body. Not sure whose. There." Unable to force another word from his stiff lips, Henry pointed down the beach.

Byrne peered over Louise's head. "You're sure you can't identify her, sir?"

"Nay. As I was tellin' the gentleman here, we think she may be from Osborne House. Not an hour ago, men from the queen's house came along this way, searchin' for a young miss. If this is her—" The fisherman shook his head. "Trouble is, we don't want to upset Her Majesty until we're certain."

"I see."

"If you could send someone down from the house, sir?" The man looked pleadingly at Stephen Byrne.

"Yes, of course."

"No!" Louise said. Henry jerked his head up, shocked at the sharpness of her response. "I know everyone in the household. Let me look at the body. I'll tell you if the poor thing is one of ours."

Henry stared at her. "Surely you can't be serious, Duchess. A drowned body? You can't think to submit yourself to the distress of—" *And if it is Beatrice, her sister?*

"Don't even try, Henry." Byrne rested a hand on his shoulder and shook his head, even as Louise took a determined step around the men then off the dock. One corner of the American's lips lifted in a weary smile. "She won't listen."

"Indeed, *she* won't," Louise called back over her shoulder. "Let's get this sad business over with."

Louise marched off down the strip of storm-ravaged sand, leaving the men no choice but to follow her. When they arrived at the corpse, the protective little group of males around it parted and stood reverently back, caps in hand, whiskered jaws clenched, eyes downcast. Henry stared down at the tragically bloated face of what he assumed was a young woman not much over twenty years. Although her clothing was stained with sea water, and brown sludge from the cove's bottom, he could still discern the quality of the garment. The fisherman was right.

This was no village girl.

But all Henry cared about—God forgive him—was that this was not his Beatrice. Wrong hair color. Wrong features. Wrong everything. Assuredly, thankfully, *not* her. He thought he might weep with gratitude.

Beside him, Louise gasped. "Oh, no!"

Henry spun to face her. "You know her?"

"This is Marie Devereaux, my sister's lady-in-waiting."

Byrne stepped forward, gripped her arm and whispered into her ear. "The effects of desiccation. They can be distorting, misleading."

"No. No, I'm absolutely sure it's her. Poor dear. How could this have happened?"

"Then what about Beatrice?" Henry burst out. "You don't think the two were together when—"

"I should hope not," Byrne said, his eyes black fire. "Come. We'll send someone for your bags, Louise. We need to tell the queen as well as Beatrice. And find out what's happened at this bloody house to bring the poor girl to this state."

Before Byrne had finished speaking, Henry was racing for the only steps he saw, leading up from the beach. Louise and Byrne followed close behind. By the time he reached the top, he was winded from the long climb, bent over at the waist with a painful stitch in his side. He peered up at the gray-stone house with its many wings and outbuildings. He'd forgotten how immense the place was. No quaint beach house this.

They rushed along the path and up to the gates where Louise ushered them swiftly past guards, through a garden and into the central vestibule. A butler met them. He seemed rattled by their unannounced appearance.

"Your Highness," he said, bowing, "we weren't informed of your arrival. I apologize that you weren't met properly."

"The storm," Louise said, "there was no way to reach you. Don't fret, Sampson. Listen, I need to see my sister immediately. And Mr. Byrne has some rather disturbing news for the queen as well."

The butler frowned. "The queen is resting in her room. I wouldn't wish to disturb her. The storm kept everyone awake last night."

Henry turned to Stephen Byrne. "Maybe that can wait. But Beatrice—"

"Yes. Bea is our priority." Louise turned back to the butler. "My sister is in her room as well?"

"No, ma'am. She has gone out on horseback with the others to search for Lady Marie. The girl has gone missing."

"I'm for the stables!" Stephen Byrne barked, disappearing out the door.

Henry lunged at the servant. "Where?" he shouted. "*Where* exactly is the princess now?"

The man fell back a step, looking bewildered. "I'm sorry, sir. She's searching for Marie is all I know. I can't say which way she went."

"But she wasn't alone, was she?" Louise asked.

"Certainly not, ma'am. She took one of the grooms with her."

Henry's heartbeat tripped. Dare he ask? How much worse could this get? His gaze met Louise's eyes—hers wide and flaring pale blue fire.

"Which one?" she cried. "For God sakes, which groom went with Beatrice?"

"The young Scot, ma'am—the man the queen brought with her from London." The butler looked from her to Henry, obviously flustered by her alarm. "Mr. MacAlister. They left together, a little over an hour ago."

Henry cursed. "We need horses. Now!"

"Come with me." Louise gathered up her skirts and bolted for the door. "If any are left, Stephen will be throwing saddles on them by now."

45

Beatrice bent low against her mount's straining neck as she raced down the narrow riding path, twisting through the woods. She ducked beneath branches bent low or snapped off in the storm, praying the animal wouldn't stumble on the uneven ground and go down. Ahead she could see one of the massive felled oaks they'd walked their horses around on their way into the woods. She heard the Scot's horse behind her, its lungs heaving like huge bellows, its hooves striking the ground faster and faster, louder and louder as it gained on her.

Gregory had stopped shouting promises not to hurt her. She hadn't believed him anyway. He must know by now she'd never trust him—not as a friend, never as a lover.

She steeled herself for the jump, locking her leg around the jumping pommel on the sidesaddle. Woman and horse sailed over the trunk. Looking back over her shoulder, she saw Gregory's mount easily clear the log too.

By the time she reached the edge of the forest and burst out into the open field, Beatrice could feel her horse's fatigue through the twinges of his muscles and its labored breathing. Still, she urged her mount onward, knowing she would be safe only when she came within sight and hailing distance of her mother's guards at Osborne's gates. Only if they saw her before Gregory caught up with her.

Even though her horse strained to obey the urgent signals of her crop—*Run! Run! Run!*—her peripheral vision revealed the Scot's mount edging up alongside her. She switched her whip to her left hand. Gauging the approximate position of the man's face, she let loose with a vicious swipe.

A loud crack was followed by a cry of pain and cursing. She felt the crop torn out of her hand. But before Gregory could make use of it against her, his horse balked and broke stride, slowing down as if confused by the scuffle.

She'd bought a little time, yes, but only seconds. Beatrice knew her own horse might drop from exhaustion any moment. Osborne was in sight now, thank God. But she was still too far away for the guards to see or hear her. Or, at least, to realize anything was wrong.

And then it happened. The miracle she'd been praying for.

A pair of riders appeared in the distance, off to her right and across the field. She shouted and waved her arm above her head. When they didn't seem to see her, she turned her horse away from the house, toward them, and rode as she'd never ridden before.

~

Byrne saw the rider first. "There!" he shouted. "Who is it? The fool—what is he trying to do, break his horse's neck and his own as well?"

Henry's heart leapt as the familiar shape of the bold rider became evident. "It's her! Bea." How could Byrne not recognize her? But of course, *he* hadn't seen her ride like this before—glorious, breathtakingly wild and free, racing across the poppy fields at Darmstadt.

Henry's pulse triple timed. He stood in his stirrups, unable to take his eyes off of her. The princess's hair had flown loose from pins and braiding, and spread out behind her in lush, wind-torn waves. Her face, even at this distance, appeared flushed pink with exertion. She leaned forward in the saddle, strong and confident.

The woman was nothing short of magnificent. His heart soared.

But there was something different about this ride. A desperation he hadn't seen before.

"Another rider. Fifty feet behind," the American called out. "Is it MacAlister?"

"Can only be," Henry ground out between clenched teeth. He kicked his horse into a gallop, aiming for a point of interception with Beatrice.

The groom must have been so intent upon catching up with the princess, he seemed at first unaware of the other riders' approach. When he finally looked their way, Henry saw a flare of vicious anger in the man's eyes, then the fear came. He'd been closing fast on Beatrice's laboring horse. But now, seeing he had witnesses, he tugged at his reins and veered away from her.

"He's making a run for it!" Henry shouted.

"You see to Beatrice. I'll manage the joker." Byrne tugged his Stetson down over his forehead and, leather duster flapping, took off after the man.

As soon as Beatrice saw that MacAlister had given up chasing her, she slowed her horse and brought it, wheezing and snuffling, to a stop in the middle of the field. By the time Henry reached her, she was slumped forward over her mount's neck. Milky froth dribbled from the animal's mouth. Its eyes rolled in lingering panic and confusion.

He spoke gently to the animal so as not to spook it as he dismounted, but all of his attention was on Bea. "Darling, are you all right?" He reached up and lifted her from her saddle, only then remembering she always rode sidesaddle. How she'd stayed on through that insane ride seemed nothing short of a miracle.

"Bea?"

She turned in his arms at the sound of her name.

"Henry!" Tears came to her eyes. "Oh, I'm so very embarrassed that you should see me in this state."

He couldn't help laughing at that. "My darling, are you hurt?" He set her feet on the ground and pulled her tenderly into his arms. "Did he—"

"No, I'm fine. Truly." She smiled up at him. "I'm so glad you're here. Even if you no longer want me as your wife, I'll be forever grateful that you've—"

"Hush," he said. "Stop talking nonsense. I shall never stop wanting you—as wife, as companion, as my everything."

Her eyes widened, and he thought he saw tears shimmer behind her lashes. He would have said, and done, much more, but then Stephen Byrne appeared, leading two horses behind him by the reins, and walking Gregory MacAlister ahead of him, through the tall grass.

Henry didn't even think about what he was doing. He released Beatrice, stepped forward and bashed the man in the face with his fist, bringing an immediate spurt of blood from the Scot's nose.

"You fiend! I will kill you here and now."

~

After another minute or two, Beatrice had recovered her breath and cleared her head enough to think, *I really should stop him.* Truly, violence had never excited her. And yet…she took wicked pleasure in seeing Gregory pummeled by Henry Battenberg and brought, literally, to his knees.

She looked at Stephen Byrne but he'd turned his back on the pair to study the sky, as if considering the improving weather. He allowed Henry ample time to punish the Scot and, when Henry had got Gregory down on the ground, pleading for mercy between kicks and punches, the American casually let the horses' reins fall and inserted himself between the two men.

Byrne braced a hand against Henry's heaving chest. "Enough. The rogue will be well punished by the queen's magistrates."

"I didn't. Do. Anything!" Gregory gasped, jabbing an accusing finger toward Beatrice. "She…she asked me…begged me. Came on to me, a cat in heat!"

"Shut up," Byrne said. "I'm not talking about your attacking the Princess. You have other crimes to answer to, sir."

Beatrice stared at Stephen Bryne. What was he talking about?

Henry rubbed his raw knuckles then slipped an arm around her waist. "Dear heart, I'll explain everything back at the house."

46

Days after Beatrice learned of Gregory MacAlister's probable murder of two innocent women, all to pave his way toward marrying into Victoria's family, Beatrice still felt on edge and haunted by everything that had happened. How could she have trusted Gregory, a stranger, charming though he was, and so easily lost faith in Henry? Victoria herself seemed so unsettled by the Scot's treachery that raising the question of marriage, again, seemed imprudent.

"Never you mind," Henry assured Beatrice. "I'll wait until the time is right. For as long as it takes." At least the queen hadn't objected to Henry Battenberg's presence in England. She even asked if he would stay with them at Osborne House, then asked to hear about his ill-fated rescue mission to the Sudan.

But would there ever be a right time to petition the queen, so long as the very mention of marriage triggered her mother's need to revisit her tragic losses? Beatrice's only comfort was to imagine her someday wedding day—a bittersweet fantasy. It saddened her to know Marie wouldn't be there to dress her for the most blessed day of her life. Perhaps only the death of her own mother—something she truly did not wish for—would permit her to marry Henry.

Meanwhile, questions remained unanswered about Gregory MacAlister's motives for forcing himself on her when she didn't succumb to his advances. The Court's gossipmongers assumed he'd simply become infatuated with her to the extreme. But

Stephen Byrne's investigations indicated a conspiracy of sorts. Something to do with his old school chum, Prince Wilhelm—Beatrice's unstable royal nephew.

Of course, Gregory had admitted to nothing. But, the more Beatrice thought about all that had happened, the more she suspected the Scot really had been involved in both his mistress's and Marie's deaths. It broke her heart that Marie's little daughter was now without a mother and, presumably, without financial support. She was determined to find the girl and make sure she was well cared for. No return address appeared on the letter she'd found in Marie's Bible. But she asked Stephen Byrne, after he delivered Gregory in shackles to Scotland Yard, to continue on to Paris and search for the child.

Beatrice prayed the British court would make certain Gregory never again walked the streets of London a free man.

Now, sitting in her bed chamber, she closed her eyes for a moment to rally her spirits. How blind she'd been to his ruse. How little faith she'd had in Henry and their love, to let that wicked man come between them and cause such misery. If any good had come out of the experience, it was that she was a wiser, more worldly woman. Happier, saner days must lie ahead.

"Jenkins?" she called out to the maid who had stepped in to fill Marie's shoes for as long as they were on the Isle of Wight. Clara Jenkins was a local girl, whom Beatrice had chosen for her sweet and simple manner. "Will you bring me my pearls? They're in the smaller of my trunks, in a quilted jewelry case of their own."

"Yes, Your Highness." The girl made a nervous curtsey, then scurried away toward the niche where the luggage was stored. Five minutes later, she poked her head around the corner, her cheeks flushed with embarrassment. "I'm sorry, ma'am. I don't know what I'm looking for. A quilt you said?"

Beatrice took pity on her. "Never mind. I'll show you then you'll know next time."

It took her less than two minutes to locate the satin pouch that protected the precious pearl choker with the diamond clasp—a gift from her mother on her sixteenth birthday. No doubt it had last been put away by Marie. But when Beatrice untied the delicate ribbons that secured the outer flap, a folded sheet of paper and two envelopes fell onto her dressing table.

Beatrice frowned at the stationary's familiarity—one letter from her own supply of hand-made paper, the other with Henry's family crest pressed into the unbroken wax seal.

She dismissed the girl to give herself privacy then, with trembling fingers, unfolded the sheet of paper that accompanied the two envelopes. The writing was in Marie's hand:

For Her Royal Highness, Princess Beatrice,

If you have found this and I am not with you to explain why these letters are in your hands, then it is because I am no longer able to confess in person my deep sorrow for having deceived you. You see, I have a little girl, and elle est très belle and most precious to me. But because she is a child of shame, I could not admit to you—and never to the queen, of course—that I had been so wicked as to conceive a baby out of wedlock.

But now this shame has been doubled by my attempts to keep my secret. I helped Gregory MacAlister play a very mean trick on you. At least he said, in the beginning, that it was a harmless joke, taking a few letters—yours to Henry, and his to you. Then he claimed it was for your own good—to prevent you from falling in love with a man the queen would never let you marry. He said it would break your heart. I believed him. How could I have known what a terrible man he was?

Later, when he told me to destroy all of the correspondence entrée vous, letting you neither send yours nor see Henry's, I told Monsieur MacAlister I could not continue to deceive you. But he'd learned my secret, and he threatened to tell the queen about my child. His silence could be bought only by my doing as he commanded. For months I was so terrified that I did what he asked. But my guilt has become too painful to carry any longer. And so I will go to Gregory tonight and tell him I will no longer do as he says. I am convinced he is evil and a very dangerous man. I expect I may have paid the ultimate price, if you are reading this.

I know I do not deserve your sympathy or help. But I ask of you two favors. Please, protect yourself and your family by insisting upon his dismissal. Secondly, I beg you to consider rewarding my earlier, faithful years by seeing to my daughter's welfare, in whatever way you think is best. I pray you won't allow her to be cast, motherless, into the streets of Paris.

My heart goes out to you, Your Highness and ma cher ami. I beg your forgiveness. I would have given my life for you. Perhaps I already have.

My daughter's name is Sophie. She lives with her nurse in Paris at the address at the bottom of this letter. Bless you for understanding that all I've done—whether resulting in good or ill—has been out of love.

Fondly,
Marie

Beatrice looked up from the letter, now lying in her lap, limp and moist with her tears. *Poor, poor girl.* Byrne was already, or soon would be, in Paris. She would get word to him of the child's address. It pained her that, even with Marie's incriminating letter to show the magistrates in London, there was still no actual proof that Gregory had murdered Marie, or his mistress, although Beatrice knew in her heart he had done it. What if they dismissed the murder cases?

He'd still face charges of assault against a royal. And she wouldn't back down from her statements on that count, even if she had to appear in court herself and reveal every single embarrassing detail. If found guilty of attempted rape, his punishment would be swift and harsh. Two or more years of imprisonment at hard labor. But was that enough?

Her heart hardened.

One way or another—in payment for Marie, and for the misery he'd caused others—she'd see that justice was done.

47

Gregory found it amusing, how easily he'd escaped his jailers after the American agent left him at Scotland Yard.

The constables had been shifting him from the magistrate's hearing, across the city, to a cell. The entire time he'd been in their custody that day, he'd played the beaten, humbled prisoner. The lingering purple and green bruises on his face and torn-up knuckles from his scuffle with Battenberg helped. His slumped posture, silence, and attitude of misery gave him a docile appearance. When one of his two guards went off for a piss, Gregory slammed his cuffed fists onto the bridge of the other man's nose, stunning the copper just long enough for Gregory to hobble off and lose himself in Whitehall's labyrinth of gritty warrens.

He stole clothes to replace those that marked him as a prisoner. Ridding himself of the leg and wrist shackles had been more of a challenge. Pick a few pockets; bribe a smithy to saw them off. Foraging for food and money as he went, he made his way across the English Channel to Germany. To the one place he felt safe. The one place he could always count on for shelter. With Wilhelm.

"Well, now you look more presentable," the Crown Prince said cheerfully when Gregory had stripped off his traveling clothes, washed away the grime and changed into trousers and shirt leant to him by one of the prince's retainers.

"It wasn't a pleasant journey, let me tell you." Gregory said with a tired sigh. "I think I'll sleep for a week." He took a seat at the mammoth banquet table, at the end of which Wilhelm sat. It was bare except for the single place setting in front of Wilhelm. The food, whatever it was, smelled delicious. *Sauerbraten* perhaps. His mouth watered. "Thank you for the clothes. And for letting me come here."

Wilhelm used his good arm to gesture expansively while cradling the deformed appendage against his chest. "What else could I do?"

"Well, turn me away for one." Gregory gave a tight laugh. "After all, I failed to accomplish our mission. But—" he added hastily in his own defense, "—I don't expect any man capable of melting that bitch's heart."

"Dear Aunt Beatrice? Yes, I expect she was a challenge. Except...Henry Battenberg seems to have found a way."

Gregory grunted. "He'll be sorry when he discovers nothing but a cold fish in his bed!"

Wilhelm nodded but was uncharacteristically silent. The prince had dismissed his butler and servants, he explained, so that they could speak in private. He poured wine into a second chalice and held it out to Gregory. "You must be thirsty. Such a long, difficult trip."

Gregory smiled, relieved. He'd worried, apparently unnecessarily, that the prince would be furious with him. Gregory drank deeply, standing up to circle the room while taking in the paintings on the walls—a Rembrandt, a van Dyck, a magnificent Richter landscape. He felt the prince studying him, as if considering what errand he might next assign his old school chum. But Gregory had already decided there would be no more schemes for him. He'd find a rich widow to marry. Settle down. Live the life of a gentleman. Not as grandly as he'd imagined with Beatrice, but he would have enough to be comfortable. He smiled. *If she is rich enough.*

When Gregory had drunk down half of the wine, Wilhelm roused himself from his private thoughts. "The thing is—I said to myself, Gregory MacAlister is a cherished old friend. We've been through a lot together. We know each other's minds so well. And he understands the importance of power, of control…and the critical nature of my political goals."

"I do." Gregory toasted the prince and took another mouthful of the very fine wine, as rich and dark red as congealing blood, with a slightly unusual, but pleasant, nuttiness to the grapes. He'd have to ask the prince for a few bottles to take to his room. He'd undoubtedly be staying in the castle until he worked out other accommodations.

Wilhelm was still speaking in a tutorial tone, as if he were one of their professors from the old days. "…and so you will comprehend that, although I do appreciate your efforts on my behalf, I cannot condone your methods. The aggressiveness with which you pursued my aunt—" He shook his head in disapproval.

Gregory turned his back on the Richter's lush trees and stared at his benefactor. "But when I wrote to you and reported that a certain amount of force might be required—"

"I assumed you would be far more subtle in your seduction."

"Subtle? *With that cow?* You said yourself, that the ends justified the means and I should do whatever I thought was—"

"Within reason, dear friend. Within reason." When the prince's eyes lifted from his cup to focus on Gregory's face, they were flint, conveying no more emotion than that rock. "Things got out of hand. Didn't they?"

"There were unexpected obstacles."

Wilhelm put down his cup and rubbed his withered arm with his good hand. "You murdered two women to get to my aunt. Then you would have raped her in the woods, had you not been stopped by my cousin, Battenberg."

Gregory narrowed his eyes at his friend. He had told the prince nothing about his mistress's death nor about the lady-in-waiting's plunge, and as little as possible about what had happened at Osborne House. "How did you know about—"

Wilhelm held up a hand. "A letter arrived two days before you dragged yourself into my father's palace. From Beatrice.

It's my guess she heard of your escape from someone in London and, having learned that you and I were involved in past adventures, projected your coming here to hide out from British authorities."

Gregory laughed. "Well, so what? How can it matter whether or not the bitch knows where I am?"

"It matters." The prince settled a gaze over him that felt like a sheet of ice.

Gregory gulped down another half of the remaining wine from his cup. His hand shaking, he refilled it from the carafe on the table.

The prince continued. "That you are *here* at all is an indication of our former friendship." *Former?* Gregory thought. "The worst of it is—someone might discover you were sent by me, and assume I ordered you to attack my aunt. God forbid my grandmother should believe I had anything to do with your outrageous behavior."

"But y-y-you—" Gregory stammered to silence. What the hell was Willy saying? Would he cast him out of Germany? Fine, then he'd return to Scotland and disappear into the Highlands, assume a new name, start a new life. "I don't see how anyone can find out or, even less likely, prove you were involved. I'll certainly never tell."

"No, of course not. Unless you are drunk or bragging to one of your whores, or—"

"Never!" Gregory shook his head violently. This was wrong, all wrong. He'd had to be creative. How could the prince possibly fault him for carrying out his orders?

Wilhelm stared thoughtfully into his wine. "The problem is—even if *you* never talk about our plan, even if neither of us ever breathes a word of it, someone still might discover my involvement. That American my Aunt Louise runs with, he's very clever. And then there's Bea herself—surprisingly savvy, as it turns out. Her letter was most troubling. I almost think she knows all of it. How? What connection can she have theorized between the death of those two women, herself, a Scottish stable

313

hand…*and me?*" The prince blinked at him with an impossibly innocent expression. "What did you let slip, friend?"

"I said *nothing* to her! Oh, my God, Willy—I said nothing to implicate you!" The sound of his own voice, unnaturally high-pitched, echoed back to him off the castle's stone walls. He sounded like a stranger, taunting him with his own words. And the wine—*the goddamn wine!*—was making him thirstier rather than soothing his parched throat. He looked around for ale, water, anything liquid. Nothing. In desperation, he poured himself more wine and gulped it down between hasty words.

"Stupid pig," he muttered. "Foolish, ignorant old maid. What does she know?"

Wilhelm observed him over the rim of his cup. "Careful, my friend. Bea is, after all, family. I may hate Victoria and find all things English disgusting. But Beatrice is blood. She's always been kind to me. And in her letter, she has asked a favor of me that I feel curiously to my benefit."

"Really," Gregory scoffed, stumbling toward the prince, one hand on the table's edge to steady himself. "What does she want? Your appearance at her wedding—if it ever takes place?" He laughed.

"She asked that if you showed up here, I might administer fair punishment for your crimes."

Gregory stared at him, stunned speechless. So it was Beatrice who had revealed all to Willy. Willy the Emperor-to-be. Willy, whose appetite for power had yet to be satisfied and—if Gregory's sense of the man was accurate—would stop at nothing to get what he wanted.

"It seems," Wilhelm said, "Bea was most grievously hurt by the loss of her lady-in-waiting. She never met your mistress but feels remorse for what you did to the woman. Blames herself, I expect, since it was your need to divest yourself of your lover in order to get to her, the queen's daughter. And, if I interpret the tone of her letter correctly, she was rather offended by your fumbling attempts to deflower her." Wilhelm gave him a smug smile.

314

Gregory closed his eyes. Opened them again. He felt so very dizzy. His stomach tumbled and twisted. *The wine. Red wine. Bloody German wine. More potent than I'm used to. Drank it too fast.* It had gone to his head.

"Punish-sh-sh-ment?" he slurred. "I should be *rewarded* for what…for what I went through for you." He thumped his chest with a fist. "My own wo-woman. Sacrificed her for your stupid plot. I raked horse shit, for God's sake! I suffered the disdain of those royal snobs and—" "But you failed. Didn't you?"

"No one could have, could have—" Gregory waved a fist in the air, grasping for words that wouldn't come to him. Why did he drink so fast? He needed his wits about him now, and they were floating far above his head.

Wilhelm said, "Let me finish. There isn't much time now."

Time for what? Gregory thought.

"My grandmother is already wary of me. If Victoria ever came to believe that I put you up to molesting her precious Baby, there would be hell to pay. She would stop at nothing to thwart my every venture. I cannot afford to have Beatrice whispering in her ear, suggesting she suspects me of sending my agents to do harm to her and her Court."

Gregory pressed his free hand to his head. "Sit," he mumbled. "Got…to…sit." The room spun and spun—a living kaleidoscope of images and hues—tapestries, dark oak furniture, paintings, coats-of-arms, Willy's frowning face.

Then his fingers went numb. He heard breaking glass, felt cool wine splatter his ankle. Suddenly, he was down on the floor, on hands and knees. The pain in his gut—horrible. Panting for breath that didn't reach his lungs.

"Poi-son?" he snarled. "You…you fucking poisoned me!"

Silence.

When Gregory managed to lift the leaden weight of his head, Wilhelm hadn't moved from his chair. The prince shrugged. "My dear friend, I no longer can afford you."

"But—"

"My crown. I must protect it."

48

"Courage, my dear," Henry whispered in Beatrice's ear as he took her hand and led her into the ivory-and-gold drawing room that overlooked the gardens at Osborne House.

Beatrice looked up at him and dared a tremulous smile. Never had Henry looked more dashing. In his regimental colors, medals ablaze on his chest, epaulets of gold fringe and polished black leather boots, he was the image of a nobleman of valor and distinction.

They had chosen to wait two weeks after his arrival at the Isle of Wight, and Gregory's ignominious departure, before approaching Victoria again in the hope she might bless their union. The longer Henry remained in the household, a source of pleasant male companionship and security, the more comfortable the queen would become with him. Perhaps she'd even, in her advanced years and selective memory, forget that she'd kicked him out of England? In fact, neither she nor anyone else had mentioned his banishment.

Beatrice turned to Henry and dug in her heels to stop their progress across the room, toward where her mother sat. "What if she still won't—"

"Hush, my darling. Let's not think the worst until it happens."

"Happens *again*. Like before. What if she still won't give her blessing, after all you've done to win her over, after saving me from that monster of a man?"

"You did a fairly impressive job of saving yourself before I arrived." He laughed, his vivid blue eyes alive. "I'll never forget the sight of you galloping across that meadow like a steeplechase jockey. What a magnificent sight!" He touched his lips to hers, sweetly. "We must be strong now, my love. Just as strong as you were then."

Beatrice's stomach clenched. Her heart stuttered like a steam engine out of fuel as she considered facing her mother.

This time, they had asked for a formal audience. "No surprises," Henry had said. But Beatrice feared this might put them to a disadvantage. Victoria would know why they were coming to her. She would have had time to prepare her objections, arguments, denials, and perhaps even a royal declaration that Henry leave Osborne, and perhaps all of England. Forever. There would then be nothing they could do to convince her— and Beatrice would be forced to choose between the two people she loved best in all the world.

It didn't seem fair. Not at all.

Beatrice closed her eyes, drew a shaky breath, then stepped forward when she felt Henry fold her hand over his arm and lead her across the room to face the queen.

Victoria sat between two of her ladies, all three of them intent upon their needlework. The two attendants looked up briefly, then at each other when they saw Beatrice. No smiles. No greetings, except for a simple murmured, "Your Highness." Then the ladies swept up their muslin, hoops, needles and colored threads, and drifted silently from the room.

Leaving Beatrice and Henry alone.

With the queen.

Henry looked at Beatrice. His eyes said, "Go ahead."

Beatrice took a deep breath. But the words—the heartfelt, beautiful words she's rehearsed to win her mother's approval— she swallowed them down, unable to force a syllable past her lips. Instead, a familiar standby exploded from her lips, "Are you well, Mama?"

Victoria's gaze remained lowered to her stitchery, her head

of white hair a cloud hovering over her. "As well as I ever am, plagued by age and gout."

Beatrice wet her lips. "May we join you for a while before dinner?"

"Of course." Still not so much as a glance their way. Beatrice exchanged worried looks with Henry, wondering if her mother was even aware that he was in the room.

Henry settled Beatrice on the divan across from her mother, then perched beside her, putting a respectable space between them. Even so, she could feel the heat of his body radiating toward her, reminding her that *this* is what she wanted. *Him. I want him!*

They sat, all three, in silence. The only sound was the heavy tick-tock-tock of the Austrian clock on the marble mantle and the ka-chunk from the fireplace as a log fell into the embers, sending up a roar of sparks.

Beatrice reached out and clasped Henry's hand so tightly his fingers turned white. She loosened her grip and cleared her throat. "Mama, I, that is *we* would like—"

"Herr Battenberg," the queen interrupted, "I presume it is your doing that this audience has been requested?"

Beatrice rolled her eyes. *Oh, no, this doesn't sound good.*

"It is, Your Majesty." Henry's voice sounded strong, determined. Beatrice smiled. *Dear man.*

"Then say your piece, sir."

Henry released Beatrice's hand and shot to his feet. Then, changing his mind, sat again, as though deciding he shouldn't put himself above the little queen.

"Your Royal Majesty, I come seeking your grace and approval. I have acted on behalf of your daughter to protect her, more than once. I will continue to make her safety and happiness my priority." He cleared his throat then continued. "I remind Your Majesty of my attempt, albeit futile, to rescue General Gordon from the Sudan. I am at your service still, as I've ever been and ever will be. I feel I deserve your trust."

Beatrice sighed. So far nothing at all about a wedding. What did Henry think he was doing? Perhaps he had decided to avoid the word *marriage* entirely, since it always sent her mother into paroxysms of fury? But how could he ask for her hand without mentioning taking her as his bride? She suddenly felt ill.

Victoria laid down her needlework on the cushion beside her and looked across at Henry, her sharp eyes as black as the tiny jet buttons up the front of her dress. "Come here, my boy." She patted the seat on her other side.

Looking as confused as Beatrice felt, Henry stood and strode across the six feet between the two divans and sat gingerly on the edge of a cushion beside the queen, careful not to touch even as much as a single ruffle of her black silk mourning dress.

"Now, that's better," Victoria said. "I can see your face. And your eyes. The mirror of the soul, or so they say." She gave him a coy smile. "What have you in mind, sir?"

Oh lord, Beatrice thought. She wished she could run from the room and not have to watch as her mother crushed their hopes.

"I, well," Henry began again, "I suppose you have already guessed my intent. It has not changed since I first proposed to engage myself to your beautiful daughter. I love her and wish to be a good husband to her. To Beatrice."

"I see."

"And although Your Majesty and I may not have connected cheerfully on my first mention of this intent, I hope that my actions since then have softened your heart toward me and won your trust."

"So, in your rambling way, you are asking for my Baby's hand in marriage. Is that so?"

"I, well, yes I am, Your Majesty."

"Because you think you deserve her, is that it?"

Beatrice saw a flash of panic cross Henry's vivid blue eyes. He too must sense a trap. "No, ma'am. Because I believe I can be a good and proper husband to her. I don't suppose I shall ever truly deserve such a wonderful woman."

The queen observed him, her head tipped to one side, eyes narrowed as though to better peer into those cerulean mirrors of his soul. Then she turned to Beatrice. Without smiling.

Beatrice recognized the wily glimmer in her mother's eyes. She knew that look only too well, having seen it from across a card table, time and again. It warned that the queen was about to play a game-winning card.

Beatrice swallowed over the jagged lump in her throat. "Mama, please, I beg you not to—"

"Hush, Beatrice. I shall have my say." The queen turned back to Henry and settled her plump figure more firmly into the brocade cushions. "I have developed a fond and admiring opinion of you, young sir. I will allow my consent for you to marry my girl, but only on two conditions."

Beatrice struggled to breathe. *Ohmygod-ohmygod!* Was her mother actually saying 'yes'? But her next thought was— *Conditions? What conditions?* Perhaps Victoria was only toying with them, demanding impossible concessions from Henry. If he refused, all would be lost. If he accepted, he might resent his surrender and, for the rest of his life, blame Beatrice.

Beatrice was certain she would die right here and now in this room.

Henry retained his equanimity. "And they are, ma'am?"

"First, you must renounce your German citizenship. Secondly, if you become my son-in-law, you and my daughter will live wherever I live and travel with me whenever I travel, until I am no longer of this world."

Too much, too much! a voice screamed in Beatrice's head. How could her mother expect Henry to forfeit his country, his family and friends, his commission in the Prussian military, everything he held dear—for her?

"Agreed," he said, standing to attention before the queen.

Beatrice stared up at him in shock, certain she hadn't heard him right. Her imagination must have supplied that precious, hoped-for word.

But he turned to look steadily down at her, his eyes fixing on hers. "Agreed," he repeated. "There is nothing I wouldn't do for my Beatrice. *Nothing.*"

Suddenly, she couldn't breathe. She reached out for his hand, pulled herself to her feet then clutched his arm for support as she took two steps to stand beside him. She didn't know what to say. Dared not open her mouth for fear she'd start crying. She was so very, very happy.

Victoria reached for her needlework. "Would you please send my ladies back to me? I'm sure the two of you have much to discuss, plans to make. You'll let me know when you've carried out my requests, Henry?"

"Yes, Your Majesty. Of course." He bowed from the waist then, tucking a supportive arm around her waist, swept Beatrice along with him and out of the room.

~

Henry glanced at Beatrice as they walked, arm in arm, along hall leading away from the public rooms at Osborne. "That's a most mysterious smile, my dear," he said. "I hope it means you're as happy as I am."

"I am." But she couldn't help laughing. "Henry, do you not realize what has just happened?"

"We've been given the queen's blessing." He winced, as if he'd felt a sudden twinge of doubt. "Haven't we?"

Through her joyful delirium, Beatrice had understood the deeper meaning behind her mother's acceptance of their union.

She looked around, aware of servants and ladies of the Court moving past them. Here wasn't the place to discuss anything that might fuel gossip. "Come, Henry. I'll explain, in a more private place."

She led him back through the high-ceilinged passageways, through corridors lined with portraits and landscapes by the masters, until he squeezed her hand and pulled her to a stop. "Dearest, do you think this is wise? This is the way to your room, is it not?"

"Yes," she said.

"There must be other places of privacy to talk."

"None that will do as well," she said, feeling excited to be so close to him. She wanted to feel his arms around her, longed for his kisses, and for more. So much more.

"As you wish," he said with an amused laugh.

Her maids must have heard her coming, for they had the door open by the time she and Henry reached it. She gave each of the girls a look then drew a line with her eyes toward the doorway. They ducked out immediately, closing the door after them. She thought she heard the titter of a laugh from the hallway.

Then all was silent. And she was alone with Henry Battenberg. Her prince. Her love.

He looked around the room, a bit uneasily she thought. "Well? What did I miss during that auspicious audience?"

Beatrice moved to stand in front of him, took his hand and guided his arm around her. She snuggled her head to his chest in utter contentment. "The queen, my mother, is a gifted negotiator."

"Yes, I expect so." But his tone remained puzzled.

"Having foreseen our determination to wed, she first tried sending you away. When that didn't work, she waited us out. And when we still refused to be dissuaded, she cut herself the best possible deal."

Henry leaned back and looked down at her. "The consummate politician?"

"Oh yes," Beatrice assured him. "Now, not only has she succeeded in even more firmly tying her youngest daughter to her side, she has captured a new male for her family and Court. She fully expects you to provide her with companionship and security through her waning years."

"Ah," he said, light dawning in his beautiful eyes. He grinned. "So now I'm a prisoner as well?"

Beatrice took a deep breath. "Are you having second thoughts? Are you still willing to make the sacrifice? You won't hold it against me, will you, Henry?"

He wrapped his long arms around her. "I'll say it again, no sacrifice is too great if it means we will be together, my love."

She couldn't contain her smile, couldn't hold all of the happiness in. It was spilling out of her, lighting the room, brightening her world. She moved even closer into his embrace and felt him react to their bodies' closeness.

He moved back from her, taking her hands in his and kissing them, then setting her away by three paces. "I must go, before I...before we..." He was blushing, his eyes alive with passion.

"No," she said.

"No?" He laughed. "Bea, if I stay alone with you in this room one minute longer, I'll...well, not to be indelicate, but I'll ruin a perfectly good pair of trousers in my excitement."

She smiled at him, feeling just wicked enough to be pleased with herself. "So remove them," she said.

"Take off my trousers?" He coughed, then choked. "You're asking me to take them off, woman?"

"I am. And your jacket. And waistcoat. I'm not at all sure what else may be under there, but they'd best come off too. Don't you think?"

He stared at her, blinked, shook his head, mussing his hair and making her want to comb her fingers through it. "If I strip off my clothes I absolutely won't be able to contain my ardor for—"

"I know."

"Are you sure?"

"I am. I want you, Henry. I want you *now*."

He still hesitated.

"Consider it a royal command." She fought the smile that tugged at her lips, but failed to keep a straight face. She couldn't resist the ecstasy she anticipated in his arms. In her bed. Shared with him. "Make love to me Henry. I'm twenty-seven years old, and I've waited long enough."

He opened his arms to her. "My darling, it will be an honor."

ACKNOWLEDGMENTS

This is a novel meant solely for entertainment. It was never intended as a historical rendering of true events. Although some of the characters were inspired by the lives of real people, the story itself is an invention of the author's imagination.

However, an author needs more than imagination to create a book. I can't begin to thank all of those who have invested their time, talents, and energy to help this novel be born. But here's a start...

Thanks to the amazing team at *Diversion Books*, particularly Mary Cummings and Sarah Masterson Hally, for their vision, their professionalism and enthusiastic support.

Kudos, as always, to my brilliant literary agent, Kevan Lyon at Marsal Lyon Literary Agency, who always exceeds my expectations.

My gratitude to members of the Columbia Critique Group, for their on-target solutions to fiction's thornier problems. And to my soon-to-be-famous students at *The Writer's Center* in Bethesda, Maryland. They teach me far more than I teach them.

And finally, my loving appreciation to Tempest, who purrs and cuddles and tries to climb up onto my keyboard whenever possible. (I think she has the soul of a writer in a cat body.) And to Miranda, whose job as a dedicated calico it is to make me stand up at least once every hour to stretch...and let her out onto or in from the porch.

CPSIA information can be obtained at www.ICGtesting.com
Printed in the USA
LVOW12s1205020214

371965LV00006B/778/P